A DEAD PLACE

Time ticked by and he did not reappear. "Something's wrong," I said, my voice almost a whisper. "He's in trouble. Do we split up or stay together?"

"We split up," Jack said.

We divided up the areas of the hospital and began looking. "There's always the morgue," a guard suggested. "It's a dead place this time of night . . . if you'll pardon the pun."

I walked toward the morgue. He unlocked the door and we stepped into a room where the temperature was at least forty degrees colder. The air was heavy with the smell of chemicals.

Only one body was in the room. "Nothing here," said the guard after looking around.

I was at the door when something caused me to turn and stare at the one occupied gurney. One arm of the corpse dangled down. Surely that was unusual? Surely whoever brought the body in had enough respect to tuck all the limbs under the sheet. I closed my eyes and said a small prayer for the deceased, whoever he was.

And when I opened my eyes, I saw those fingers twitch . . .

PINNACLE BOOKS HAS SOMETHING FOR EVERYONE—

MAGICIANS, EXPLORERS, WITCHES AND CATS

THE HANDYMAN (377-3, $3.95/$4.95)
He is a magician who likes hands. He likes their comfortable shape and weight and size. He likes the portability of the hands once they are severed from the rest of the ponderous body. Detective Lanark must discover who The Handyman is before more handless bodies appear.

PASSAGE TO EDEN (538-5, $4.95/$5.95)
Set in a world of prehistoric beauty, here is the epic story of a courageous seafarer whose wanderings lead him to the ends of the old world—and to the discovery of a new world in the rugged, untamed wilderness of northwestern America.

BLACK BODY (505-9, $5.95/$6.95)
An extraordinary chronicle, this is the diary of a witch, a journal of the secrets of her race kept in return for not being burned for her "sin." It is the story of Alba, that rarest of creatures, a white witch: beautiful and able to walk in the human world undetected.

THE WHITE PUMA (532-6, $4.95/NCR)
The white puma has recognized the men who deprived him of his family. Now, like other predators before him, he has become a man-hater. This story is a fitting tribute to this magnificent animal that stands for all living creatures that have become, through man's carelessness, close to disappearing forever from the face of the earth.

Available wherever paperbacks are sold, or order direct from the Publisher. Send cover price plus 50¢ per copy for mailing and handling to Pinnacle Books, Dept. 681, 475 Park Avenue South, New York, N.Y. 10016. Residents of New York and Tennessee must include sales tax. DO NOT SEND CASH. For a free Zebra/Pinnacle catalog please write to the above address.

DEADLY MEDICINE

Charlotte White

PINNACLE BOOKS
WINDSOR PUBLISHING CORP.

To Kelly, with love

PINNACLE BOOKS

are published by

Windsor Publishing Corp.
475 Park Avenue South
New York, NY 10016

Copyright © 1993 by Charlotte White

All rights reserved. No part of this book bay be reproduced in any form or by any means without the prior written consent of the publisher, excepting brief quotes used in reviews.

Pinnacle and the P logo are trademarks of Windsor Publishing Corp.

If you purchased this book without a cover you should be aware that this book is stolen property. It was reported as "unsold and destroyed" to the Publisher and neither the Author nor the Publisher has received any payment for this "stripped book."

First printing: January, 1993

Printed in the United States of America

Chapter One

What should have been a great day in my life wasn't. *Should have, would have, could have, ought to have, if only* . . . all of those useless words came flying up to smack me in the face as I drove at a very low speed through the streets of Dalton, Mississippi, for the first time in fifteen years.

Funny the tricks that memory plays on one. In my mind's eye, I had seen Dalton quite clearly all these years. Now I realize those memories were faulty ones, images and impressions formed as a child. *Then* I was a child, *now* I am not . . . and therein lies the difference. The place that had once seemed so big, bright, and wonder-filled shows up as an ordinary southern town, a town too small to be classified as a city, yet too large to have the lazy, rural charm of a typical Small Town U.S.A.

Although I was not ready, not quite yet, to stop at the Albert B. Creighton Medical Center and claim my place, I found myself steering the car in the direction that would take me past the three-story building of rose-colored brick. I took a bit of comfort in the familiarness of the hospital. *This* looked right; the place where I had often tagged along with my father when he made his rounds. The place where one of his colleagues had removed my tonsils and adenoids. There were some changes, sure . . . signs that Albert B. Creighton—ABC Hospital, as it was known to the townspeople—was growing, keeping pace with the times. Still, the additions had been made so skillfully and artfully that the building retained its original design.

For the majority of the coming year I would be within those walls. As Devin Hollister, I had applied to ABC to take my internship. As Devin Hollister, I had been accepted. To those who reviewed my application and approved it, the first eleven years of my life had no importance. Would that time, little more than a decade, when I was known as Katie Clark have made a difference to anyone here today? It made a difference to me, too much of a one.

"Why on earth, Devin, are you going to bury yourself in such a little place?" asked virtually everyone who knew me. To them, it made no sense for one who graduated *summa cum laude* from the University of Massachusetts Medical School at Worcester to take an internship at a 350 bed hospital in a southern community.

"Because I have to," was my answer to all of those who asked, and to myself. I might have said it was really no one else's business, which it wasn't, but I found their concern touching. "I'll come back East," I would explain. "It's only for a year. I can decide there if I want to undertake a surgical residency or not. Albert B. Creighton isn't world famous, but it does have an excellent reputation for a facility of its size. As I said, it's only for a year, and it's just something I have to do. I spent the first part of my life in Mississippi, you know."

Most of them had smiled at that and said something like, "No kidding?" Through the years, I have absorbed the eastern speech patterns into my way of talking, but the underlying southern drawl still betrays me at times. My mother worked hard at correcting my accent, yet traces remain to this day. On some level of consciousness, I am certain I resisted the efforts to change my way of speaking. It is a part of my heritage. Something my mother, with good reason, wants to forget. But the fact remains that those years did exist.

"Devin is the only one in our crowd who can make two syllables out of 'nine'," had teased one of my good high school friends. It had been good-natured teasing and I had never minded, had even taken a sort of pride in my "difference." Now I had to be careful and watch those betraying "nines." Knowing I couldn't always, I had my story prepared: "My grandmother was from Biloxi. I always loved the way she talked. I guess I picked it up from her."

I wasn't yet ready to ask them if anyone remembered Dr. James Stuyvesant Clark and his Katie. I didn't worry that anyone would recognize me as the chubby, flaxen-haired child who had so often trudged along beside her father. As it so often does, adolescence had darkened pale blond hair to a light brown and a sudden spurt of growth had taken me to five feet, eight inches in height, with no trace of the former chubbiness remaining.

"You're how old now, Katie?" Dad asked.

I smiled, knowing that he was teasing me. He was too good a father to his only child to forget her age.

"Eleven," *I replied gravely, choosing to play his game.*

"I see. Quite an advanced age. Almost grown, really."

I waited impatiently while he pretended to think something through ... but I knew it was pretense. I could tell he had something on his mind, and that something was to be a surprise for me.

"Like to see some surgery today?"

"Real surgery?" *I asked, eyes widening. I had been after him for over a year to let me observe in surgery.* "Not yet. You're too young," *had always been his steadfast reply. The sitiching up of an occasional laceration in the emergency room was the most I had been allowed to witness.*

"Real surgery," *he had answered.* "I just had a call and have to go to the hospital. It sounds as if I'll have to do an emergency appendectomy. You can watch, but you have to promise ..."

I was so excited I felt like dancing, but the need to appear mature kept me anchored to one spot on the carpeted floor of our living room.

"I know, Dad. I really do. If I begin to feel sick or dizzy at all, I'll move quietly out of the way at the first signs. I promise."

"Jimmy, do you know what you're doing?" Mom asked.

She was the only person in the world I knew who called my father "Jimmy," and also the only person who dared to ask if he knew what he was doing. But he never seemed to mind. After all, she knew him as no one else did. She had known him as Jimmy Clark, that pesky kid who shinned up the neighbor's peach trees and, hidden from view, pelted stolen green peaches down on her and her friends as they passed through the orchard. Most people saw Dr. James Stuyvesant Clark as an eminent surgeon and respected member of the community. Mother was never intimidated. I suspect that was one of the things that kept their marriage strong, for there were times, I am sure, when he needed to let his guard down and be that pesky boy again.

"Trust me, Laney. If Katie is to be a doctor, she can't learn the ropes too young."

"It just could be 'Katie' might not be a doctor."

Aghast, I wheeled about to face her. "Not be a doctor? Come on, Mom. You know I'm going to be a doctor."

She let out an almost weary sounding sigh. "If that is what you want, Devin. Just remember it doesn't have to be that way."

Devin? She scarcely ever called me that anymore. My father, as always, had been the stronger force and his name for me had triumphed. Because my mother liked fanciful names, I had been christened Devin Miranda, Devin meaning "poet." Perhaps what she had wanted was a daughter with a romantic, poetic nature. Perhaps she had just liked the sound of the names she chose. I had been told that, when I was born, my father said to my mother, "Why, she looks just like your mother . . . a proper little Katie." From that day forth, that was what he called me, persisting until everyone, sometimes even myself, had to stop and think what my name really was. How characteristic of my father, that he would not argue with my mother over the name I was to be given. He just let her have her way, then ignored that way.

As my father and I hurriedly walked those two and a half blocks to Albert B. Creighton, he asked, "Know the incision most commonly used for an appendectomy?"

"Of course," I answered promptly. "It's most likely to be a McBurney's."

"*And?*"

Now it was my turn to give a weary sigh. The testing seldom stopped. "*In typical appendicitis, the point of maximum tenderness is at McBurney's point and the incision is made there. Half the incision is above the point, half below. You cut along from the anterior iliac spine to the umbilicus.*"

"*Paralleling the fibers of . . . ?*" he prompted.

"*The external oblique muscle.*"

"*Fantastic!*"

Fantastic? Was that the word for it? There had to be a word for an eleven-year-old girl who had more anatomy posters on her wall than posters of Rod Stewart, Billy Joel, and Kiss. My friends frequently supplied a word: weird.

I never minded their teasing. I liked my friends and they liked me. In a way, I think they were envious that I had already chosen my career.

It was exciting to scrub for the first time and to dress in surgical greens, even the smallest size swallowing me. Skeptical looks were cast in my direction, yet no one said a word. As I had already noted, no one questioned my father, no one but my mother.

When the appropriate level of anesthesia was reached, the anesthetist nodded to my father. All that told me that the gowned, capped, and masked figure before me was my father was the keen hazel eyes, eyes like my own, the only physical feature I had inherited from him. I suspect my eyes were shining with excitement over my own mask as he began to make the incision.

A leery nurse looked in my direction when the blood began to flow.

"*Better start the suction,*" I heard my father say calmly. "*It's just seepage. The appendix is inflamed, but it hasn't ruptured. We've caught it just in time.*"

Fascinated, I watched as his skilled hands suctioned away the blood.

"*Look at the kid,*" the watchful nurse said. "*Her eyes are shining! Under that mask, I bet she's grinning.*"

I was. And proud of it.

All in all, it was an uneventful operation, a simple one, a good starter for me. On the way home, he talked me through it, with his narrative re-creating the surgery for me.

"You were great, Dad."

"Great? Nah. Just adequate. That one was a breeze."

"Can I watch you do a hard one someday soon? I mean, I didn't get sick or cause trouble or anything."

"True. You were a real pro in there. We'll see. Trouble is, I don't always know which cases are going to be difficult. Katie?"

"Yeah?"

"You really do like medicine, don't you? All of this isn't just to please me. You mother says I force it on you. I don't want it to be that way."

"It's not that way, Dad. Truly, it's not. I can't think of anything in the world I'd rather be than a doctor. I can't imagine ever changing my mind about that."

"Then I'm glad. But if you change your mind, it's okay."

"I won't," I said firmly. "I guess it's just in my blood."

He laughed. As much as I adored him, that hurt my feelings a bit, for the laughter had a patronizing ring . . . the sound adults make when a child has been unduly precious. It was in my blood. Sometimes when I had trouble settling down to sleep at night, I would soothe myself by saying some of the glorious sounding words I had memorized from the posters: Latissimus dorsi, Sternocleidomastoid, Cricoarytenoideum posterius, Abductor pollicus brevis, Chorda tympani. I couldn't identify them all yet . . . so many of them: muscles, ligaments, nerves, and so on. Miles and miles of things in the human body and they all had names, names and functions.

"You'll see," I said in the face of that laughter. "You'll see."

"I know I will," he said, his tone apologizing for that rare moment of condescension. "We'll be a team, you and I. That is if you want to be a surgeon."

"I haven't decided. But even if I go into another field, we'll still be a team. I can refer my patients who need surgery to you."

"Not a bad idea. Still, if you change your mind . . ."

"Daddy, why do you keep saying that? I tell you, I won't change my mind."

"You know, I believe that. You'll be a doctor. I can see it in my mind's eye as clearly as if it already happened."

"What is it you see, Dad?"

"I see you walking across the stage to get your diploma, such a tall, straight, proud young woman."

"Am I pretty?"

"Of course. Really quite gorgeous."

"Hmmm. I like the things you imagine. Tell me, what else do you see?"

"A sign on a door that says: James S. Clark, M.D., Devin M. Clark, M.D."

Laughing, I said. "That's the first time I've ever heard you say my real name."

He smiled slightly. "Well, Devin does sound more professional than Katie. I'm not sure I'd go to a doctor who called herself Katie. But you'll always be Katie to me. When I'm an old-old man and you're middle-aged and oh-so-very proper, I'm sure I'll still think of you as my Katie. But let's not rush things. Let's take each day as it comes. We have days and days ahead of us before we have to decide what to put on the door. Come on, Katie I'll race you the rest of the way home."

Driving more slowly than was probably even legal, I eased my deep red Mustang convertible, a gift from my stepfather on my graduation from medical school, down the two and one-half blocks of 1406 Macon Street. It was an eerie feeling, as if I had suddenly moved back in time, to be once again where I had learned to ride a bike; where I had first tried out roller skates; where my friends and I had played, giggled, and argued, and where I had explored all the ditches and far corners of this section of earth with little Jackson Lee Fraser. My eyes sought out familiar landmarks.

The two-story cobblestone house was still there. Until I saw it, I hadn't realized how afraid I had been of its possible loss, but it had not changed a lot. The woodwork and awnings that had been forest green when I had lived there had been changed to burgundy red by someone else. I imagined children living there, for as a child I had found it a wondrous place to live with so many "secret" corners and crannies. With a sigh I noted the silver-haired lady working in the flower bed in front. Chances are, there were no kids in "my" house.

Passing the house, I went the rest of the way down the block, turned the corner, and parked. I then walked back, on the opposite side of the street. I wanted to recapture the flavor of Macon Street, yet I didn't want to alarm the present resident of the house. If it hadn't been important to me to keep my identity a secret for a while, I could have gone up to the lady and explained that I used to live there and would like to see inside the house for old times' sake. But did I really want to? Because of that one awful moment, now frozen in time in my mind, my memories could never again be happy ones. It had all been taken from me. Those first eleven years of my life had been allocated to a special place, a place that had nothing to do with who and what I was now . . . nothing and everything.

After Dad and I had returned from Albert B. Creighton that day, he had retired to his den, saying he had some medical journal reading to catch up on. Mom had laughed and teased him by saying they both knew he was going to take a nap. Then she and I went out shopping to find me some new tennis shoes. That mission was quickly accomplished. However, Mom ran into a good friend and they wanted to get coffee and talk awhile. It was only a fifteen-minute walk back to the house, so I told Mom I was going on home.

"Dad, I'm back!"

When there was no answer, I tiptoed into the den. The shades were drawn and it was quite dark in there, especially to my eyes since I had just been out in the sunlight, so I didn't see him at first. Disappointed, thinking I had missed him, I was about to leave the room when something caused me to turn and take another look. He was lying on the floor, face down, arms at his side. As soon as I saw the pistol just beyond the fingers of his right hand, I screamed. Even as I moved to turn him, I knew . . . knew that he was beyond my help. There was a hole neatly placed in his brow. I dialed the emergency number, then ran for my closest neighbor's house.

It seemed that within seconds our house was filled with people, most of them strangers. Over and over again, I heard the word "suicide" spoken.

"My father didn't kill himself," I said to each and every person I encountered. They gave me pitying looks and soothing words. No one really listened.

"He didn't kill himself, Mom. He couldn't have."

She sat in a chair like a wooden figure, her face as pale and smooth as porcelain, her eyes deep pools of hurt.

"I suppose there are things we aren't meant to understand, Devin."

Devin. And so it was. Never again, from that moment on, did my mother call me Katie. Within three months, she had sold the house and we moved to Boston, Massachusetts, where her sister and her family lived. Soon after moving to Boston, Mom was introduced to Charles Hollister, a business associate of Uncle Matt's. They were married before my father had been dead a year. Oddly enough, I never did resent Charlie. In his own way, he let me know he was my friend and was on my side, that he wasn't out to take my father's place in my life. As the years went by, I became closer to him in many ways than I was to Mom.

She changed after Dad's death. So did I. How could we not have changed? It wasn't something we asked for, yet it happened. When she and Charlie suggested things might be simpler if I legally took Charlie's name, I agreed. I felt no disloyalty. It was as if, on that terrible day in May, Katie Clark had died along with James Clark.

"Darling, let the past be the past," Mom had pleaded with me when I finally had to inform her of my intention to intern in Mississippi.

"Before I can do that, I have to look it in the face. We ran away, Mom."

Closing her eyes for a moment, she said, "You still can't accept the fact that he committed suicide, can you?"

"I didn't think so then. I don't think so now. But people don't listen to eleven-year-old kids. Kids have no choices. Not unless adults allow them to have. But I'm not eleven anymore."

"It's been fifteen years, Devin. What can you do after all that time has passed. And how can you be so sure?"

"I just know I have to go back for a while, okay? Don't worry."

She worried, of course, but I came to Dalton anyway. Now I shivered despite the warmth of the day. Macon Street was not a friendly place now. From across the street, the silver-haired lady looked my way, noting that I had lingered.

"Are you looking for something, miss? Perhaps I can help you."

Managing a smile, I said, "Oh, I'm just out for a stroll. I really like your house. I grew up in one a lot like it."

"We like it too," she replied, obviously pleased. "Too large for us, really, but we enjoy the older style houses, so much more character than in the cracker boxes thrown up today."

When the pleasantries had ended, I headed back for my car. Maybe Mom and Charlie were right, maybe it was best to let things go.

In my belief that my father had not committed suicide, I only had two things to go on. The first was the way he had been with me earlier in the day, so filled with good spirits and plans for the future. The second was the lack of blood. I ought to know. I had found him, I had turned him over, and I had been the first to stare at the gaping hole in his brow. Shouldn't he have bled from that? Of course he should have. If he had pulled the trigger. But if he had *already* been dead, and someone else had pulled the trigger, then that would explain the lack of blood.

But no one listens to children. Perhaps no one will listen now. It had been fifteen years. Any and all trails are cold.

I shut my eyes tightly to push back tears. No time for that I told myself. I drove back to Albert B. Creighton where I presented myself to the administrator's office.

"Devin Hollister, Intern, reporting for duty," I said to the secretary, giving her my most charming smile.

For the next few weeks, I must smile and smile and smile until I have the confidence of those around me . . . and then I can ask some questions, look for some answers.

Chapter Two

We were a self-conscious lot, the four of us, as we faced Jane Goldstein the administrator, and Dr. Paul Linden, the current chief-of-staff, of Albert B. Creighton Hospital. I remembered them both quite well and, as we interns stood in a row facing the two of them in the administrator's spacious office, I felt my heart skip a beat or two. What if they recognized me? Maybe I hadn't changed as much as I thought I had. But as the interview proceeded amiably, and without any signs of recognition on the faces of either of them, I relaxed somewhat and played the role in which I had cast myself: Devin Hollister, Intern . . . a role that was the truth but, as so often is true of life, only part of the truth. It was not that a lie had been told, just that some of the facts had been withheld.

Funny how time and age are such relative matters. When I had known these two people before, I had felt them to be quite old, especially Jane Goldstein. Facing them now, I suddenly realized they hadn't been old then at all. Even though her hair was totally silver, Jane's face was smooth and unlined save for the wrinkles at the corners of her eyes. How she and my father had fought at times! "Jane the Inane," he had taken to calling her when he was on one of his tirades about some policy she was enacting that went against his grain . . . and this had often been the case. For twenty-five years now, she had held the reins of ABC Hospital. And in all that time, the facility had grown and flourished. Had it happened because of her or in spite of her? In contrast to the scorn my father had expressed for the administrator, he had always heaped praise on Dr. Paul Linden. He had only been at the hospital a short while, no more than a year or so, when my father had died. So great had been Dad's admiration for the young surgeon, and so tall and handsome had Dr. Linden been, that I had viewed him in total awe. He had been like some mythical god. The young doctor, and he *had* been very young fifteen years ago—thirty or less, I would guess—had only to smile at that long-ago version of me to render me red-faced and speechless. Not that it had happened often. He hadn't been the sort to notice kids. Paul Linden had to be in his early-to-mid forties now, but he looked at least a decade younger. Quite a nice looking man, I thought.

As if he could read my thoughts, Dr. Linden caught my eye and smiled, the corner of his mouth twitched as if he were already to break into laughter, as if he were a joke we shared. In response, to my dismay and outright chagrin, I felt myself blush. Perhaps I only *thought* I was grown-up and mature if all this almost-stranger had to do to reduce me back to pre-adolescence was smile.

"And I'm sure," Jane Goldstein droned on, "you will all enjoy your time here at Albert B. Creighton."

Enjoy? I glanced at the three other interns, all men who were to share the duties of this coming year with me. We exchanged looks and corners of our mouths twitched lightly, for we did truly share a joke. From the horror stories we had heard, we scarcely expected enjoyment.

Long days and longer nights. Thirty-two hour shifts without sleep. Eating on the run. Working our fingers to the bone, doing all the things the "real" doctors didn't want to do. And all for a stipend of a salary. An internship, we had been told, was not a pleasurable experience, just a necessary one. Before we could hang out a shingle as a G.P., or before we could go on to whatever residency we chose, we each had to survive an internship.

"You seem a good crew," she continued. "I fancy you

will be one of the better groups we've had in here since we started the internship program. I'm looking forward to getting to know each of you better."

Inane Jane. I smiled to myself. How on earth could she, on such short inspection, know we would be one of the better groups? I suspect she said the same words each year. As the odds would have it, she would be right part of the time, wouldn't she? Some of the interns had to be the better ones. I looked them over again and decided it might as well be us.

Intern David Francis was a nerd, a dweeb . . . it stood out all over him, from the plastered-down hair to the horn-rimmed glasses to the intent look on his face; the stiff posture of his spine that said medicine was a serious business, one in which levity had no place—I sized him up as a pain-in-the-posterior, but definitely a man one could rely upon in a pinch. Intern Chris Palmer already had a head start on the God complex that so often attacks members of our profession; I predicted that he would often be cocky, rude, even ruthless . . . and yet would so often be right, for both hauteur and intelligence flashed from his eyes. And the guy on the end was Intern Anthony Toretta, Mr. Nice Guy . . . just as sharp as the other two, but secure enough that he didn't see any point in advertising it; his dark good looks would have told of his Italian heritage even if he had called himself John Smith. Mentally, I compared them all to my fellow students back in Massachusetts, and decided that, most likely, there was not a bumbler in the bunch. These guys would be on their toes . . . and I would have to be on mine or suffer by comparison.

Suddenly, I wanted Goldstein to be right. And I went her one better. I didn't want our group to be one of the better ones. I wanted ours to be the best, the most memorable, the one to which future groups of interns could only hope to aspire.

"And don't *you* think that is right, Dr. Hollister?"

Blinking, I looked at Jane Goldstein. While I had been woolgathering, apparently she had made a statement that she now wished me to corroborate. Smiling slightly, I said, "Undoubtedly," and felt as inane as my father had accused *her* of being. In relief, I noticed there were no exchanged glances or stifled laughs. I had lucked out . . . this time. I silently vowed to pay closer attention during the remainder of the interview.

"You're from the East, Dr. Hollister. From Boston, I believe. What made you come to a little place like this?"

So there it was, for the first time, but undoubtedly not the last. "I used to visit my grandmother in Mississippi when I was a little girl. I always loved it here. After she died, we never came back. The ties were broken, I guess. But I decided I wanted to try it for at least a year. Everyone has told me I'll miss the city. We'll see. If I do, I can always go back, right?"

"Right," she said, smiling at me. "And, you know, I think you picked up a little accent on those visits of yours long ago. You don't sound like any true Bostonian I've ever met, Dr. Hollister."

In due time, we were excused from the administrator's office. "Dr. Hollister, you start on my service first," Dr. Linden said as I filed by with the others. "I'm looking forward to it."

"So am I," I managed to say. What luck, I thought, as I caught my lower lip between my teeth to keep my smile from growing inappropriately wide. Once in the corridor, I looked at the schedule I had been given. Sure enough, my first assignment was to Surgery service, Dr. Linden. My time with him would be a month . . . surely long enough for me to find a way to introduce the subject of Dr. Clark.

Apparently I had quit biting my lip and allowed the grin to have its way because I noticed Anthony Toretta standing across the hall, looking at me.

"Wish I were that excited about my assignment," he said, "but my lot is on the obstetrical unit. Oh, well, I might as well get broken in right, don't you think?"

"Sure. At least you'll get it out of the way first. I was just pleased at the luck of the draw in my case. I haven't fully decided yet if I want to do a surgical residency, and I have to make up my mind right away and get some applications out if that's my future. I've heard Linden is one of the best. A month of assisting him ought to make an impression on me one way or another."

"Surgery, huh? I've thought of it, of course, but . . . say, would you like to go get a Coke or cup of coffee or something? As I understand it, the day is ours. Tomorrow, well, that's a different story."

Glancing around, I saw that the other two had already drifted off. With a shrug, I said, "Why not?" Intuition told me that if I were to have an ally among my peers, that ally would be Toretta. The other two were too competitive, too self-absorbed for friendship at this point.

We spent a pleasant thirty minutes in the cafeteria dawdling over coffee neither of us really wanted. In that time, we learned a lot about each other . . . surface things, of course. Where we were from, what we had in mind for our future, where our respective apartments were, why we had decided on the ABC Hospital for an internship. But I learned other things too, the things of which we do not speak. Anthony was a gentle young man, a strong and kind one. He would, in my opinion, make the best sort of physician, brilliant and decisive without being hard. Doctors have to have a degree of objectivity for the protection of both themselves and their patients, but in so many that objectivity takes the form of aloofness. As I watched and listened to Anthony Toretta, I could not imagine him ever becoming that way.

Another thing I learned was that I would have to be cautious. His eyes were warm when he looked at me, too warm for such a short acquaintanceship. At this juncture I needed a friend, not a lover.

"I suppose I'd better go get settled into my apartment. I haven't even really unpacked yet," I told him, "and the grind starts tomorrow."

"Same here. You wouldn't by any chance be interested in going for a pizza this evening? As you said, the grind starts tomorrow. No telling when we'll get a chance again. We'll probably be like ships that pass in the night from now on."

I hesitated just a bit too long for politeness, I suppose, for I saw the uncertainty in his dark eyes.

"Look, Devin, I don't mean to be giving you the rush. I like you, and God knows you're pretty enough for a guy to rush, but pizza is all I have in mind."

Laughing, I said, "I didn't think otherwise. And it sounds fine. It really does, Tony."

He winced. "Not Tony, please. It isn't that I hate the name. If my last name were something different, I could handle it. But Tony Toretta? No way I can handle that."

"Suit yourself. Anthony it is. I have some errands to run after I get settled, so I'll meet you at the Pizza Palace at seven o'clock, okay?"

"I'm looking forward to it."

Caution, I told myself again, for I knew the danger lay not in Anthony, but in my own errant, involuntary responses. How I wished at least one of the other interns could have been a woman. Perhaps then the friendship I needed would have been available without complications.

The apartment I rented was nice, though quite small and not in a very fashionable part of town. Both Mother and Charlie had uttered many words of protest when they had learned of my plans. We are affluent people. They can easily give me anything I want, within reason . . . in addition to which I have a private income from my father's estate.

"I'm not going there to show off, to flaunt my money," I had argued. "I have the nice car you gave me. That's enough. Most medical students have no money. They're receiving scholarships or grants or going through on loans and part-time jobs. Having too much could make me resented. I don't want that. As far as anyone there is concerned, I'm just another intern."

For just a moment, Mother's warm blue eyes had grown cold and hard. "If no one is to know your father was Dr. James Clark, then how can you talk to anyone about his death? I swear sometimes I just don't understand you, Devin. You have a brilliant mind, no question about that. But when it comes to practical matters, well . . ." Her voice trailed off and she let her upturned palms say the rest of it for her.

"I don't know anything yet, Mother. But it's not as hare-brained as it sounds. I know Dad's death happened a long time ago. And I'm 90% sure no one is left there who would remember enough about it to be of any help to me. But it's that 10% that bothers me. I want to go back. I think I *have* to go back. In some ways, I don't think I ever came to terms with losing him. As I've said before, I have to face the ghosts before I can get on with the rest of my life."

She had shaken her head at that. "Charlie's tried to be a good father to you, Devin."

"But this has nothing to do with Charlie. You know I love him. Not only has he tried to be a good father, he has succeeded. You've both given me a good home and a good life. But there is something wrong. I think it has to do with the past. Please try to understand."

"I am trying, but . . ."

"Mother, did you really love him?"

She grimaced slightly. "I suppose I expected that. I expected it long ago when I married Charlie so quickly after Jim died. We were golden together, Devin. I don't know how exactly to explain it to you because there hasn't been anyone like that in your life. We were neighbors. We grew up together. But even as children, I think we were very much aware that we weren't like brother and sister, that some day we would be lovers. And I think everyone in both families expected that too. It was almost like one of those old-fashioned arranged matches where the children are betrothed while still in their cradles. But better than that because it was also what we wanted. In time, we married and we had you. We had wanted a large family because we each had been only children and regretted that. As it turned out, you were an only child also. Funny how unreal it all sometimes seems. That was my life, then suddenly it was over. I had never known life without Jimmy Clark in it. In a way, I lost myself when I lost him. I suddenly had to be someone different. It was hard. You never said anything. Not in all these years. But I always expected it."

"Never said anything about what?" I asked, genuinely puzzled.

"What you just asked . . . if I really loved your father. Because I married Charlie so soon, I expected you to ask it."

"It wasn't a criticism. I'm just trying to put it all together. Sure, I wondered. But I couldn't help adoring Charlie myself. And I think I was really so numb at that point that nothing mattered much one way or the other."

Mother nodded. "It was hard. So very hard. And, God, how I hated being alone! I suppose if I hadn't met up with Charlie Hollister it would have been someone else. I got lucky there. He's been better than any woman could hope for."

With a nod of my head, I agreed with her. She had not approved of my quest when I had first brought it up. She did not approve of it at the time that conversation took place. She did not approve even as she helped carry bags and boxes to my shiny new Mustang. And she was not approving when I called to let her know I had arrived in Mississippi safe and sound. Initially, I had thought she might change her mind. Now, I don't think that will ever happen. My mother is an accepter. As hard as it had been, she had accepted the fact of my father's suicide and had come to terms with it. She did not want the boat rocked or old wounds torn open. I could understand that, even sympathize with it. What I could not do was give in to it.

In my unpacking, I took two framed photographs from a box and placed them on the bureau in the bedroom. There was a black and white one of my father showing him caught forever at the age of thirty-five. The other was a recent color portrait of Mother and Charlie. Sometimes people said I looked like her. I've never been able to see that. I had inherited her Nordic coloring, but she had always worked at retaining her childhood blondness while I had never cared that much. At fifty, my mother was still more beautiful than I will ever be. Most of the time I don't mind. Yet once in a great while, caught off guard, I catch flashes of resentment in myself. We go out in public together and it is she who turns heads, who catches the attention of strangers. It's a strange feeling to introduce your boyfriends to your mother and watch them turn to mush in her presence. Just as my father had adored her, so did Charlie. Even in the photograph, you could see that in the way he was looking at her. I moved my gaze from that picture to the other one. Except for the eyes, I wasn't like *him* either. When I was younger, I had thought my darkening hair would make me look more like him. It hadn't. His hair had been dark from the day he was born and his features were set in a different mold.

Enough. Impatiently, I shoved the picture to the back of the bureau top and went back to the task of finding places for the rest of my things.

At a quarter after six, I carried the last load of cartons out to the trash bin in back of the apartment house. Then I hurried back in to shower and change so that I could meet Anthony as we had arranged. Just as I stepped out of the shower, the telephone rang. I was more than halfway expecting it to be Anthony cancelling our pizza date. Holding the towel around me, I picked up the receiver.

"If you know what's good for you," the raspy, unidentifiable voice said, "you'll mind your own business and not ask any questions."

Suddenly any warmth from the hot shower was gone and my blood ran cold.

"Who is this?" I managed to say. "What is it you want?"

"You heard me, *Katie*. Now heed."

With that, the connection was severed. I was to have no answer to my questions. I stood there shivering. *Katie*. The caller had used the name no one had used for fifteen years. And yet that couldn't be. No one in Dalton knew I was Katie. Or did they? Besides, the call might not have been a local one. I had no way of knowing. The call sapped my energy. More than anything, I wanted to telephone Anthony and cancel our date. But a glance at the clock showed me that there was no time left to do that. I was going to be late as it was. Of course, I could always call the restaurant and leave a message there. I decided that was what I would do.

The telephone rang again and I nearly jumped out of my skin. The covering towel fell to the floor at my feet. My hands were trembling visibly as I reached for the receiver.

"Is Harold there?" said the voice.

"Pardon?"

"Harold . . . let me talk to Harold."

The voice was querulous, old, but scarcely menacing. The trembling stopped and I breathed a sigh of relief. "You must have the wrong number," I said gently.

"Oh, dear. I'm sorry."

"That's quite all right."

That did it. I was not going to sit here all evening listening for the phone to bring me another obscure and frightening message. In record time, I had put on clean jeans, shirt, and shoes, rushing out to jump in the car, my hair still damp from the shower.

"You're late," he said, more as an observation than an accusation.

"Things took longer than I thought. Consider yourself lucky, Intern Toretta, that I showed up at all. I'm bushed."

"But you're also hungry, I'll bet."

I hadn't thought of it. After the call, butterflies had taken over my stomach. I looked at Anthony and smiled. There was something very soothing about his presence. "You know, now that you mention it, I'm ravenous. I didn't take time for lunch. Let's go in and order lots and lots of lovely pizza."

He pretended to groan. "Just my luck. Why do I always offer to buy pizza for ravenous maidens? Why can't I ever meet one of these picky eaters I'm always hearing about?"

"You partial to dieters?"

"Only when it's my turn to pay," he said with a grin.

"Then ease up. I'll pay."

24

"We could go dutch."

"Look, Toretta, I said I'd pay."

He sighed. "Now I know you really don't trust me. You think if I buy your pizza, or even my own, I'll try to demand my just rewards at the end of the evening."

A giggle escaped me. "You know my mind so well already. Fancy that."

He pulled his face into a caricature of primness. "I know it better than you think, my dear. Enough to make me wonder at your motives. You pay . . . then what do I owe *you* at the end of the evening? I have my standards, too, you know. I haven't worked this long and this hard to prove myself just for women to treat me casually, to regard me as a mere sex object."

I felt another giggle form in my throat, then move upward to make itself heard. Despite the warning I had been giving myself, another part of me said this guy was good for me. Almost, just almost, he could make me forget the things that had drove me to Dalton. Or perhaps forget is the wrong word because I can never forget. But being with him takes the edge off of it. Sometimes that is respite enough.

"Let's order. I'm hungry. We can haggle over the rest later."

Not that the haggling ceased. Seated, we had a serious debate over the merits of thin, crispy crust over thick, chewy crust . . . and it didn't end there for serious decisions were still left to be made about the pizza toppings. Lucky for us, and for her, the waitress was good-humored, for it was only on her third trip back that we were able to place a coherent order.

For the most part, conversation flowed easily. Even at the moments when words did not surface, we were not uneasy with the silence. Odd how that happens. There are people one can know a lifetime and never be able to be with in this kind of free and effortless way. It just can't be explained how friends click, look at each other and instantly know, though the words are never spoken, that there is a bond that time and space can not eradicate.

"I think they want us to go, Devin."

I looked around and saw the restaurant was now empty of customers save ourselves. It wasn't quite official closing time, but the employees looked restless and fatigued.

Nodding, I said, "We've been selfish. Or *I* have. I hadn't even noticed the time."

We settled the bill and walked out into the moonlight. "Such a lot of moonlight," I observed. "It never looked quite this way in Boston."

"Too much there to obscure the skyline, I suspect. I wouldn't know for sure. Until I started college, I had spent little time in any city."

"And it's to a small town that you want to return to practice?"

"That much I'm sure about." He nodded adamantly. "I may even opt for a rural area. I know there are disadvantages, distance from specialists and diagnostic equipment and such. But I like the open spaces, the atmosphere. When I have time off, I want to tromp the woods, to scale the cliffs, to swim in the river . . . that sort of thing. What I don't want to do is put on a pair of green shorts and a polo shirt and go hang out at the local country club, buying rounds of drinks between golf games. But I suppose it's hard for you to identify with my feelings since you've lived in a large city."

I did not correct him, did not tell of those first eleven years of my life, and, in that omission I felt as if I had lied. By my silence, I concurred with what he said. But head won over heart and I maintained that small deception. What I did do was trot out the story of my grandmother again.

"I remember now that you told Mrs. Goldstein about that this morning."

"It was a memorable time in my life, a good time. I have never quite gotten it out of my system. So, before I settle down to the serious business of working, I want to give myself some time in a setting like this."

"Far away from home."

"Not in reality, Anthony. Just a few hours by car. But the way my parents carried on, you would have thought it was China. They wanted to see me intern someplace more prestigious."

"And?"

I shrugged. "It's pretty obvious they don't always get what they want."

We stood there beside our cars, faces and forms bathed in moonlight.

"It's late," he said softly.

It was the second time he had had to tell me that. And still I was not ready to go home. He had handed me the opening. It was time for me to make leaving noises, to say it had been great and that tomorrow was going to be a big day so we needed rest. But I said nothing. Instead, I gazed at the moon.

"Devin, what's wrong?"

I drew in a breath, held it too long for comfort, then let it back out.

"Nothing really," I hedged. "I know I should go home and rest. I guess I'm just excited thinking about tomorrow."

He wasn't buying it. "It's more than that. You've been fun. It's been great. But it's been like spun glass, very brittle. Your mood is strange. Like it could break at any time. I know you've handled a lot of pressure in school, and suspect you sailed through it relatively unstrained, so I doubt that interning at ABC is that big a worry on you."

"You're very observant," I said. "It's a strange mood. I just don't want to go home. But I have to. Thanks for the evening, Anthony."

His smile was regretful but accepting. "Ill never pry. But if you ever want to talk about it, hunt me up. My shoulders are broader than they look. But no thanks needed for the evening. You paid, remember?"

"But it was all your idea."

"Then next time let it be your idea and I'll pay. Same deal as now. No strings attached."

That was that. Within seconds, he was opening the door to his somewhat battered-looking car. The comparison between his car and mine was enough to make me flinch, to feel that familiar stab of guilt. Until college, the people with whom I had come into daily contact had all been from the same world I inhabited. Reality hit when my first college roommate was a scholarship student with virtually no spending money, few clothes, and no transportation. I had felt like a pig . . . a feeling her open resentment had only intensified. And there were many like my old roommate Gloria. It had been quite an eye-opener for this "spoiled brat."

"See you around soon," I said.

Now there was nothing for me to do but to go home.

There was silence in the new apartment. Not a comfortable silence. I threw open the blinds to let in the moonlight. Better that than the ominous shadows it cast when filtered through the blinds. The telephone did not ring that night. But the fact that I expected it to made for a restless sleep for me. So much so that morning came none too soon.

Chapter Three

The next morning, I saw Dr. Paul Linden before he saw me. He was seated at the nurses' station on the surgical floor with his head bent over a chart. For a while, he deliberated over the page, then began to write his progress note and new orders.

He was a distinguished-looking man, I thought, his healthy tan making a nice contrast to his light eyes. The strands of silver through his medium brown hair added to his overall impression of calm authority. He was, I knew, a man such as my father had been . . . the sort of doctor to whom others listened, and for whom they clear the path and clean up the act. Remembering how much my father had praised the young surgeon, I now saw why. In Paul Linden, he had recognized a kindred spirit.

Seeming to sense my presence, he looked up and smiled my way, saying, "Hi there." Although I suspected he was always courteous to a fault, kind, seldom purposely harsh or rude, still I noted that the smile did not extend to his eyes. Not that I believed he could help it. Some people are just made like that, never really letting go, so reserved that there is always a portion of them in check. But how could I criticize that trait in this man when I so often recognized it in myself?

For a moment, as he regarded me so watchfully, I was an awestruck eleven-year-old again. It is always said we can't go back, can't go home again. And that's true in the sense that time and circumstances do change things, enough so that it's impossible to return to a former state of being. On the other hand, in some ways we can go home all too easily when faced with the places and people of our formative years, we tend to regress, to be malleable children once again.

Squaring my shoulders, I mentally shook off as many remnants of Katie Clark as I could, looked into those cool eyes, and said, "Intern Hollister reporting to duty, sir," with a lot more vivacity and confidence than I felt at the moment.

"So I see. Been in on much surgery?"

"The normal amount, I guess. I'm 90% sure it's what I want to specialize in. I'm hoping this month with you will give me that other 10%."

"Why surgery?"

It was not a casual question. Somehow I knew that Dr. Linden was not just making conversation. The answer I gave could well be an indicator of what our relationship was to be this next month . . . indeed, this next *year*. Albert B. Creighton was small enough that our paths would cross frequently over the months to come. On a professional basis, I would need a strong letter of recommendation from him. On a personal basis, I would need information about my father.

"Why not?" were the words that issued from my lips as my gaze never wavered from his face.

Again, I saw his mouth curve into a half smile—the same smile I had seen the previous morning, and one I would come to know well.

"Fair enough. Why not, indeed? But it wasn't a sexist question. I wasn't trying to say, 'Why would a pretty little thing like you want to be something like a surgeon?' I ask all doctors headed toward a surgical residency the same thing."

"I don't doubt that. I suspect if I had been a man my answer would have been the same."

"Fine. Some of the interns are prickly about various things. I just wanted us to get off on the right foot."

"I see no reason why our feet shouldn't be in the right place. Seriously, the interest in surgery is not a whim.

Nor is it a recent interest. It runs in the family, I guess. My father . . ."

Quite on purpose, I did not complete the sentence, hoping he would draw his own conclusions, albeit erroneous ones.

"A surgeon? That's great. I like to see traditions carried on, but so often that is not the case. My own two sons show no interest whatsoever in medicine. They think it's a drag. John Paul wants to be a space scientist and Zachary wants to be—and for his age *is*—a computer whiz."

"How old are they?" I asked, knowing they had to be quite young since he had not been married when I first knew him.

"Twelve and eight," he said, his expression and voice both softening somewhat. "They're great kids. Life is hard, but I predict they'll both survive it in fine shape. Since I'm sure you'll hear it on the ABC grapevine anyway, I'll tell you, since we got off onto the subject, that their mother and I recently separated. We both hoped—at least *I* did—that the separation would make us want to go back. Unfortunately for the kids, and for us, it doesn't seem to be working that way."

"I guess things like that just happen sometimes," I said lamely. As I had observed earlier, he wasn't a man who confided or gave himself easily, so his crisp and accepting manner, though possibly a cover-up, made it hard to respond with great sympathy. He did not, I am sure, want my pity.

"More often than not, it would seem. Ah, well, enough of that. Barring an emergency, we won't be operating today. We'll go make rounds on the postsurgical patients and I'll familiarize you with the particulars of their cases. Tomorrow is quite a different story. Five cases scheduled. Very busy day. Think you're ready for that?"

"More than ready. I can hardly wait. I'm looking forward to doing more than hemostasis and closing."

"The itch to feel the draw of the blade across the skin?"

"Something like that."

He smiled again and *this* time the smile almost, but not quite, touched those frosty eyes. "Then tomorrow we shall see. Till then, come with me. Let's go to room 131 first. Interesting case. Mrs. Bantry. One of the worst lots of adhesions I'd ever seen. The word 'massive' would not even begin to describe. Pity it couldn't have happened a few days later. It would have been a learning experience for you. Hell, it was a learning experience for *me!* Ever not be able to see the forest for the trees?"

"Not in person. But I know what the expression means."

"Anyway, I'm not sure it's exactly the same thing, but the saying did pop into mind when I laid open the incision and tried to peer into the abdomenal cavity. Nothing . . . and I do mean absolutely *nothing* . . . was visible. Not a single organ was clearly identifiable. Operating time, of course, was prolonged. It took forever and a day. Luckily, our Mrs. Bantry is a plucky lady. As you shall see, she came through it like a trooper."

He was right about that part. Geneva Bantry was a bright-eyed woman in her sixties who, now that most of the pain was behind her, seemed to be delighting in reliving her experience.

Leaning close to me in confidence, she said, "Dr. Linden said it was like a ball of yarn had gone wild in my stomach and wrapped itself around everything in there. Did he tell you that?"

"Indeed he did. Strange how some people develop no adhesions and others have them form so rapidly."

"And so many!" she said, seeming quite pleased. "I am a lucky woman to have had such a good surgeon." Leaning closer once more, she whispered, "And such a good-looking one, too, don't you think?"

"Very much so," I replied with a slight smile, aware that the patient's whispers were not quite soft enough to escape the "good-looking" one's ears. He pretended to be engrossed in her chart, but I did detect that betraying twitch at the corner of his mouth.

One by one, we saw Dr. Linden's patients, most of them postsurgical. In most cases, those to have surgery the next day did not come in until in the afternoon or, in some cases, early on the morning of the day the surgery was to be done. When we were done with rounds, he took me to a dictating booth where, instead of dictating, he began to lecture to me on what we had just seen. He talked enthusiastically, almost lovingly, about each of the surgeries, why they had had to be done, what techniques he had employed in each procedure, what instruments he had used, how he had closed, and so on. On a pad he took from the pocket of his snow white coat, he drew diagrams for me. I did not have to feign interest. To me, *this* was what it was all about. I did not marvel that a surgeon of so much experience was still in love with his work. That was the way it should be, the way it had been with my father, and the way it would be with me.

Before he had quite finished, there was a rap on the glass. Looking up, I saw another familiar face, one that had not changed greatly from the way I remembered it.

Dr. Linden lifted his hand in greeting and motioned that the older man should join us.

"Dr. George McCracken, meet Dr. Devin Hollister, intern."

The old gentleman looked at me from beneath very shaggy eyebrows Did he still practice? I wondered. He seemed so elderly, but I supposed he must have been still active. Why else the white coat and stethoscope?

"Prettiest intern they've sent us in a while," he said in his raspy voice. "At the risk of being misunderstood and taken for a dirty old man, I *do* think I've seen you somewhere before."

At that, Linden laughed out loud. McCracken sent him a look of mock disapproval.

"She doesn't look familiar to you?"

"Well, to tell the truth," he replied, "it had crossed my mind that there is something familiar about Devin. But I suppose she just reminds me of someone else I know, though I can't think who. The lady isn't from these parts, George. She's an easterner. By way of Maine. Her father's a surgeon there."

"Massachusetts," I said softly, letting my corrections

stand at that. Let them think poor Charlie was a surgeon. If he knew, he would only think it funny.

"Don't know him, of course," McCracken barked, "but, then, I've never been to Maine."

"Massachusetts," I said again.

"Right. There either. Expensive place, I hear."

"Quite, but one gets used to it."

The moment passed. The two doctors were soon deep in conversation, sounding off on medical staff politics. It was as if I had ceased to exist. But I didn't mind. I looked at the diagrams Dr. Linden had drawn for me and tried to remember everything he had said. "Then tomorrow we shall see," he had said to me. I shivered slightly just thinking about it. Did those words mean he was considering letting me do more than observe and assist? Surely not, with no more than he knew about me. It was just wishful thinking on my part.

I was glad they had forgotten me. It had felt awfully claustrophobic in the booth when they had both said I looked familiar to them. For a moment, I tried to imagine what I would have said and done if one of them had said something like, "By jove, it's young Katie Clark, Jim's girl, only all grown up." But they hadn't. And I did not think they would. It had been too long ago and I had been such a minor character in their lives . . . the tag-along child, the nuisance. They had loomed big in my life, the near-heros of Albert B. Creighton Medical Center, but I had been of no importance to them.

Soon their conversation was interrupted by another rap on the glass. It was getting a bit crowded in the little booth. Glancing up, I found myself eye-to-eye with Elizabeth Carey, R.N. She was still quite a pretty woman, though by no means young.

"Dr. McCracken, you said to remind you about Mr. Rogers, to tell you when he was back. He's back in his room now. The tests are done."

"Thanks, Lizzie, I'll be along in a second."

Elizabeth Carey had been a nurse at ABC in my father's time, and apparently still was. Perhaps my mother was going to be very wrong after all. From the time she had learned of my plans, she had steadfastly maintained that very few would be left at the hospital who would have any memory of my father. It was only my second day inside the facility, and I had already encountered several figures from the past. In time, I would talk to each of them about James Clark. In time. But not yet.

Dr. McCracken directed a final brief flow of conversation at Dr. Linden. The words had nothing to do with me and he made no attempt to include me in the discussion. I sat there as an onlooker, totally ignored, perhaps quite forgotten. After that, McCracken turned back and caught sight of me. I saw then that he had, indeed, forgotten my presence. "I hope this is only the first of many meetings for us, Dr. Hollister. We knew you came highly recommended. Your beauty is a bonus we shall all enjoy in the months to come."

I blushed and, again, I hated myself for it. His words had no meaning and I knew that. He was a pompous windbag and employed gross flattery as a way of life. His charm, when on, was a wondrous thing, but he could activate the off switch suddenly and mercilessly and I had no patience with his charm, no liking for him as a person. So why the blush at his blarney? Because, I assumed, Paul Linden was there to witness.

Somehow knowing the twinkle was back in Linden's eyes, I avoided direct contact with his face. When McCracken was gone, I busied myself with some papers I had in my hand.

"What do you think of our Dr. McCracken?"

I shrugged, still not looking up. "Quite old, isn't he? I would have thought he retired years ago."

As soon as the words were out, I literally bit my tongue.

"Retire? George? Not likely. Oh, I suppose it will happen someday. Unless he dies first. But I doubt that he goes out willingly. Medicine is his life. Not just medicine ... medicine at *this* hospital in *this* town. He was here when the hospital was built, you know. He's strictly an old-line doctor. Not many of them are left."

"May I ask what you mean by an 'old-line doctor?'"

35

"Don't you know? I'm sure you do, that you just haven't heard it referred to by that term. They're everywhere, I think. I'm sure you've encountered some in hospitals where you studied. They became doctors when it was still part of the training of an RN to stand up when a doctor entered the room. They were around when ether was the only anesthetic used and when penicillin and sulfa were the only viable drugs for fighting infection. They made do without laser beams and without scope procedures and without ultrasounds and other sophisticated testing procedures. George resents a lot of the new ways. He has refused to flow with the times. Not that he doesn't avail himself to the testing and drugs at times. By in large, though, he still treats patients according to the old ways. And the old ways weren't always wrong, something the rest of us need to be reminded of occasionally. We tend to prescribe the latest and most expensive wonder drug in cases where a simple course of penicillin would be just as effective. They used to diagnose pneumonia with only a stethoscope, now we do serial X rays to document its existence and evolution. These older doctors, I think they sometimes think we aren't 'real' doctors, just jigglers of technology. But we do what we can. Just as they did . . . *do*. And there are always cases when nothing we do is enough. People die, Dr. Hollister. You are aware of that?"

Swallowing hard, I said, "Very much so. One of my last student assignments was on the oncology ward at the university hospital. Yes, I am aware that patients die, and that the dying is often a long and difficult process, a painful thing for the patient and for those who care about them."

"And if you could find a way to save them all, would you?"

I found that a curious question. I looked around at the walls of the small dictating room, then, at long last, looked at his face. In his eyes, I saw the pain of all the patients he had lost as well as the pain of not being able to do enough to prolong their lives, to ease their final suffering.

"I would, I suppose," I answered slowly, "and yet I see where your question leads. If we saved them all, if no one were permitted to die, then we would soon be suffering from massive overpopulation. In turn, people would suffer from *that*, lack of space, lack of food. Sometimes in life there are things to which there is no happy solution. In policy, I am against euthanasia. I, for one, do not want the responsibility of selecting which people are to die and which people are to live."

"And, yet, in becoming a physician, it is inevitable that you will have to, in certain cases, decide whether to prolong life or to let it end. Sometimes surgery, I think, is the worst for that. To weigh the risks against the benefits, to effect a 'cure' when there is no assurance of any quality of life to follow that cure."

I nodded. "I grew up seeing my father tangle with such choices. It didn't always make him easy to live with, but even as a child I think I understood. We can't do it all. But we can help some. We have to work at making that be enough. Otherwise, we'll get bitter and eaten up inside until we are of no use to anyone, even ourselves."

He gave a short laugh. "I don't often get like this. Especially with people I barely know. You seem to bring it out in me. We barely say 'hello' and I'm telling you my marital problems. Now I'm baring my soul as a surgeon. You figure it out."

"I wouldn't even dare try. But I doubt it has anything to do with me. I've just happened to wander along on an introspective day for you."

"You think that?"

I met his gaze. "What else could it be?"

"Fate has thrown us into this surgery rotation, and our lives are bound together, can't you feel that?"

His tone and eyes were mocking, his mood now completely changed from before.

"Can't say I felt any such thing. You use that line on all your interns?"

"Of course not. Only the female ones."

"And I would guess not limited to interns. Tell me, Dr. Linden, do the RNs still stand up when you enter the

37

room? I know it's no longer required, but . . ."

His eyes held mine. "It's neither required nor expected, but a fair number have ways of showing their respect."

Laughing to break the tension, I said, "No wonder that marriage of yours is in trouble."

"Methinks thou dost judge me too quickly and too harshly. A flirtatious manner doth not a cad or layabout make."

"Shakespeare said that?"

"Him or St. Paul or Ben Franklin. Surely *someone* did."

I shook my head. "I think we have rounds to make. And, back to the subject that started it all . . . yes, I have encountered the peers of Dr. McCracken. I know exactly what you mean. I enjoy them. If my career has a normal span, then I shall see the end of the breed. That is regrettable."

"Ah, yes, but something else shall happen . . ."

"And that is?"

"You will turn into the 'old breed.' You will be the old-line. Just as I am now fast becoming that."

I gritted my teeth in mock consternation. "Surely not."

"No? Ah, but, yes. For instance, only very recently here at ABC have we gotten the equipment and the trained personnel to do the extensive laser surgery. Yet the new doctors, the ones such as yourself, I am sure witnessed laser surgery in the teaching hospitals. You have yet to pass your boards, but in some ways your experience and knowledge exceed mine."

"Perhaps," I said, feeling both wary and skeptical, "but, as any old-liner will tell you, there is no substitute for experience. I have observed the masters, but have rarely been allowed, as you put it, to feel the scalpel across the skin."

He opened the door and we were ready to enter the corridor, go back to seeing the pre- and postsurgical patients.

"You handled that quite nicely," he commented.

A nurse walked up to join him as we made rounds and there was no opportunity to ask what exactly it was that he meant. What had I handled nicely? What had impressed him? The response of the philosophies? The sidestepping of what could have been the beginning of a verbal pass? The balance of holding my own without being disrespectful? Perhaps I would never know. Paul Linden was a man of many moods, several of which I had already seen. His reserve had returned and I wasn't tempted to shatter it. There was safety in that reserve for both of us.

I spent the morning with Dr. Linden and the afternoon on the floor. Nursing personnel on the surgical floor were helpful and tried to make things easy for me. It was a good experience and I learned from it. But even as I learned, I yearned for tomorrow, for the participation in surgery I had been promised.

Before going home to catch a few hours' sleep, I stopped by the doctors' library to check in the little cubbyhole, that had my name below it in the rack on the wall. Here, I had been told, was where I would receive paperwork or any messages addressed to my attention.

Anthony was there, managing to look both tired and flushed with excitement. I could identify with that look, imagining it akin to my own. This was the first time I had seen him all day. His first assignment was to the obstetrical unit, a totally different floor of the hospital.

"How's OB?"

"Great so far. Not much action yet. But they tell me it's bound to happen soon. Seems that they come in spurts. The pull of the moon or something. And Surgery?"

"Routine follow-ups today. The real thing tomorrow."

"I don't need to ask if you're excited about it. All those little golden thingamabobbies in your eyes are fairly dancing. You impressed with Linden?"

"Ask me after I've seen him operate."

"I meant otherwise. I've heard he has quite a way with the ladies."

I had no way of knowing what emotion prompted his

comment. Perhaps he was jealous of the older, more smooth man. Perhaps he was merely protective and warning me of what he had heard or observed. Perhaps, for some reason, he disliked Paul Linden. Whatever had brought it on, he had caught me off guard and I had no idea how to respond. After several seconds of awkward silence, he treated me to a wry grin.

"I suppose that sounded a bit out of place."

"It's neither required nor expected, but a fair number have ways of showing their respect."

No, not so very out of place.

Smiling, I reached out and touched his hand for a moment. "No offense taken. I appreciate your concern. But I can handle Dr. Linden. At least, I think I can. If I can't, you'll hear from me. I've no interest in becoming a statistic to any Lothario. Not at this point."

"At what point might you be?"

The question, and the comment that had brought it on, was so ridiculous that we both broke out laughing. With a shake of my head, I looked at the three items I had withdrawn from my box. One was notification of a meeting, one was instructions on how to use the hospital's dictating equipment, and the third was a small white envelope with my name neatly centered and typed on the front. The message inside was also typed.

"It was a mistake to come here, Katie. Get out while you can. Things are never as they seem and some things just aren't meant to be known. It is said that the truth will set you free, but that isn't always the case. Sometimes the truth is a killer."

I felt weak and knew the color had drained from my face.

"Devin? Devin, are you okay?"

"I will be," I said shakily.

"Something in the mailbox, I assume."

With an attempt at smiling reassuringly, I said, "Just a note from an old friend. I didn't even know they knew I was here. It was quite a surprise."

"More like a shock, I'd say," he observed.

"Not really," came the lie. "I guess I'm just excited and on edge. Thanks for everything, Anthony. I'll see you around soon."

"You're sure you don't want to talk about it?" His nod was toward the white envelope and small sheet of paper I still held in a death-grip.

"I'm sure. Truly, it's nothing."

His dark eyes said he did not believe me. His dark eyes also said that he was hurt . . . partly by my unwillingness to confide, partly by his belief that the note was from a lover, past or present. I felt a pang of guilt, then angrily pushed it aside. I had not asked him to care, had I? We barely knew each other. He had no business being vulnerable to anything I said or did. No business at all.

And so it was on that note that we parted. I kept hold of the message and its envelope. At the apartment, I put them in a drawer in the bedroom. Maybe it was in the back of my mind that the messages, if they became persistent or threatening, could be traced. But I preferred to believe that this would be the last . . . preferred it, but could not convince myself of it.

Chapter Four

I had seen her yesterday, this Annie Overlease. Then, she had been a friendly, chatty woman of seventy years. Of course she had been fearful of losing her leg, but the news that amputation was inevitable had not been a surprise. For the majority of her adult life, she had been a diabetic patient . . . and, I gather, a diabetic patient who had not been particularly compliant with her diet and medications. The diabetes had been, as the years went by, joined by peripheral vascular disease. For quite some time, she had been plagued by diabetic/vascular ulcerations of the legs that would not heal. It had gone far enough that she now had gangrene of the right foot, a condition that would spread if not quickly halted. Yesterday, when I had seen her, she had been tearful but accepting.

Now, under the anonymity of surgical conditions, she was a patient. Her name and personality were immaterial. She was a flaccid, unresponsive form. On this form, Dr. Linden took a marking pen and marked the lines on which the incisions would be made. I watched in total fascination as the skin, then the tissue, was incised, the muscle layers subsequently divided. Throughout it all, there was not as much blood as I had anticipated. I watched, and fancied I learned from, the deft way Linden handled the operation. This was his arena and he stayed constantly in command of it.

"Drains?" asked a nurse.

He shook his head and said, "None required. I can see the area well enough. There's adequate blood supply to the skin, wouldn't you say, Dr. Hollister?"

I was startled out of my awe. He was asking *my* opinion? Looking down, I observed and found myself in full agreement, though I wondered what I would have done if I had felt otherwise, because there was no evidence at all of duskiness or cyanosis.

"Yes, sir," I managed to say. "Color's good."

When he had finished the procedure, he was handed the stapler. I watched closely as it was fired, doing its job of closure. There was so much to learn.

"I'm ready for the saw," he said. No sooner were the words out of his mouth than he held the instrument in his hand, which he employed to amputate the leg.

"You saw what I did?" he asked me directly when the procedure was terminated and the care of the patient was left to the nurses and anesthesia personnel.

"Of course."

The corner of his mouth twitched. "I guess what I meant to say was did you know why I did what I did."

"I suppose I will when you tell me," I said dryly. "This was a new one for me. I've never seen a leg amputation before."

"What I did was to divide the femur well proximal to the skin flaps. That way, we avoided the end of the femur jutting through the staple suture line. I had that happen once. And let me tell you, once was enough. It wasn't an experience I care to ever repeat."

I mumbled something to the effect that I could imagine that it had not been. "What's next?" I then wanted to know.

"Bloodthirsty, aren't you?"

"Somewhat, I guess. If you want to look at it that way."

"Is there another way? But never mind. Let's go sit and talk until they have the next case ready."

"That's what I asked . . . what's next."

And he proceeded to tell me. The next surgery was to be a colostomy on a patient with cancer of the colon. He

43

told me all about the patient, the progression of the disease, the stage it was in at the time of diagnosis, the alternatives to this particular type of surgery, and the likely fate of the patient without the surgery. "People don't like the idea of colostomies. It offends their sensibilities, I think. But, given the alternatives . . ."

"Exactly," I said. "Just as with poor Mrs. Overlease. I'm sure she would have preferred to finish life with both of her legs intact."

"The threat of amputation was always there in her case. Neither that nor the threat of blindness, kidney failure, or any of the other possible effects of diabetes run rampant were enough to keep her from eating apple pie and such."

"And thus she deserved what she got?"

"I didn't say that."

"Not in so may words. But what you did say, and the manner in which you said it, did imply as much, now didn't it?"

He smiled slightly. "You started out being so nice. I should have known it wouldn't last. Good-looking women are so seldom meek. Actually, I like Annie Overlease very much. To say I love her would be an exaggeration because, you see, we surgeons, except in a few rare cases, have limited patient contact. As opposed to, say, your general practitioners and internal medicine people. *They* are the ones who have the same people under their care for years. As a rule, the surgeon sees them a visit or two preoperative, does the surgery, and then a postoperative exam or two. Once the staples or stitches are out and there is no infection or pain, the patient goes back to the other doctors. No, I wasn't being judgmental. It wasn't *my* advice Annie ignored. I got her when it was far too late for dietary advice. If anything, my words were simply a commentary on what we do to ourselves. Some people are determined to self-destruct. They can know something is killing them and keep right on doing it. Tell me, Devin, are you so fond of anything . . . cigarettes, Twinkies, grease-soaked french fries . . . that you could *not* give it up if told plainly how you would suffer if you did not?"

Laughing, I said, "Since I'm not fond of any of the examples you gave, I'd have no trouble forgoing them. But I know what you mean. Like anyone else, I do have a few foods that are my favorites. But if they were killing me? To save my life, even a leg, I could do without hot fudge quite nicely."

"Precisely. Just as when I discovered my cholesterol and triglycerides to be at appallingly high levels, I found I could eat chicken and fish baked and broiled instead of deep-fried. But some people won't do this. And I'm really quite convinced it isn't the fondness of the addicting substance that drives this stubbornness, but the need to die."

"The death wish?"

"Precisely. Known cases of suicide rank statistically as eighth in leading causes of death. I believe that it is much, much higher. Tell a person gasping for air, 'Quit smoking or you'll die,' and yet the smoking persists. Why? *Because that person wants to die.* This way, he or she can commit suicide without being accused of it. Even if they believe suicide's a sin, they're still off the hook. Because, you see, no one calls it that: it's nicotine addiction. You understand where I'm coming from?"

I nodded and tried to think of something to say, something to keep this conversation going.

The house was still. He did not answer when I called to him. He lay there on the carpet in his den. So very still, so quiet. Now that I am an adult I am ready to admit that there were things I did not know about him. I am ready to admit that he could have had troubles I didn't know about, troubles Mother didn't even know about. Even so, I reject the idea of suicide. Yet I still cannot find it comprehensible. He had talked about how it would be when I was a doctor, when I could hang out a shingle beside his. The man I was with that day was not a man who was living his last few hours on earth. He had Mother, he had me, he had his home, career, and place in the community. The question I asked myself was: if you are so very sure he did not kill himself, then why can't you listen to the arguments that he did; if you are to know the truth, you have to listen to the other side.

"How prevalent," I asked, "do you believe this death wish, this subconscious form of suicide, to be?"

"I don't know. I'm a surgeon, not a psychiatrist, so I'm more of a casual observer to the syndrome than a studier of it. From where I sit, I'd say it's present in us all from time-to-time. That's only natural. In deep despair, we long to die, to remove ourselves from the necessity of thinking, of bearing pain. But with most of us, it passes. Well, maybe not most. Hell, I'd even venture to say that at least a third of the people walking around today in affluent America would choose death if they dared."

I shuddered involuntarily.

"Grizzly subject, isn't it? Forgive me, Devin. My moods are most strange lately."

"Don't go blaming *that* on me again."

"I shan't," he said with an attempt at laughter. "And please, don't let me depress you."

"You aren't. At least not for the reasons you think. There was a suicide in our circle not long ago. An associate of my parents. He seemed to have everything to live for, and then he killed himself one day. I didn't really know him well, but I've thought about it a lot. It greatly affected my parents, so I can only imagine the way it must have devastated his immediate family. He left no note. The last I heard, no cause for his action had been uncovered. No affairs or disclosures unearthed. No hidden financial problems. No blemishes on his career. So odd. He seemed to have it all, then . . ."

"Richard Cory," he said softly,"

"Yes, we all thought of that at the time. It seemed so apt. God, this *is* a grizzly conversation. But while we're on the subject, did you ever know anyone who committed suicide? Not the kind you're talking about, not the overeaters and chain-smokers, but overt suicide."

He paused for a moment. "I've known two. Not a lot, perhaps, for as long as I've lived. But, in my opinion, too many. The first was a fellow I knew in college. He fried his brain with drugs, was in danger of flunking out of med school, got caught stealing to feed his drug habit. Rather than face his family and the disgrace of it all, he killed himself in the frat house. Not neatly by OD'ing, but by hanging himself at the top of the stairwell."

Even now, his voice cracked at the memory.

"And the other?" I dared to ask, my voice slightly too breathless to seem casual, but perhaps he was distraught enough by the painful memories to not pay close attention to me.

"A colleague, a doctor—another surgeon, actually—who was here when I first came to ABC. A brilliant man in every way. The most gifted surgeon I've ever watched operate. Too good, actually, for a small town like this. I can't claim we were close. But we might have gotten there. I hadn't been here too long when it happened. Jim Clark wasn't like poor Scott in med school. He seemingly had it all. No one had a clue. Like your parents' friend, a regular Richard Cory. Come to think of it, very like Richard Cory. Jim shot himself in the head."

"Note?"

"Not that I ever heard mentioned. If there was one, the family kept it to themselves. The wife and child left right after it happened and, as far as I know, were never seen or heard from again. It was a very tragic thing. *Very.*"

"I can imagine. Tell me, was there . . ."

The blue capped nurse popped her head in the door. "Next patient is ready, Dr. Linden. Operating Room 2. Scrub as soon as you're ready."

Getting up, he said, "Duty calls, Dr. Hollister. Say, I hope you don't think I'm being selfish or that I don't trust you. I'll give you a chance at the hands-on part of a surgery soon. It's always been my policy to start out on the slow side with you interns. Let you see how I operate—literally—and let me see how you react to the general atmosphere. That way, we both know what to expect."

"No problem," I said quickly. "I know I'm just an intern, not a surgical resident. I don't expect too much too soon. When you're ready, just say when and I'll give it my best, but I won't nag you."

47

He smiled. "I like that, the way you say without hesitation, 'I'll give it my best.' You don't know much fear, do you?"

"When it comes to medicine, no. I don't mean I'm cocksure or that I don't have butterflies in my stomach when I have to do something new. But the truth is, I always figure, given time, I can do about anything any other doctor can do."

"No argument there. But enough talk. The colon awaits us."

There was nothing to do but follow him. As eager I was to observe the colon surgery, I truly wished it could have been delayed just a few minutes more. It had been quite a stroke of luck, a break I had not expected this soon, to hear my father's supposed suicide discussed by someone who had known him, had been around at the time of his death. By a fluke, the subject had arisen and I had put out feelers. But something told me there was not going to be an easy way for me to reopen the subject without seeming unduly interested. Paul Linden's mind, as I was rapidly discovering, was like quicksilver. He had a keen interest in everything around him and his conversations flitted here and there to include whatever touched him at the moment. But at least I had had this moment, this much. "He seemingly had it all, a regular Richard Cory." That had been the surgeon's assessment of my father.

He was wrong, of course. My father had not been like Richard Cory, not at all. He had not killed himself. As daft as it seems when I try to explain my certainty (even to myself at times), I never have any doubts. I was only eleven at the time, a fact my mother is always ready to point out to me. But I do not need to be reminded. That day is engraved on my heart and mind forever. I have no proof. Not then, and not now. There was, of course, the lack of blood. No one else saw the importance of that then. Without other evidence, perhaps I cannot get anyone to see it as significant now.

Jim Clark was not subject to melancholia. He had dark moments, moments such as we all have, that were hard for him. When he lost a patient, or a case did not go as he expected, he would go to his den and start pulling books off the shelves in an effort to find what went wrong. Sad, yes, but never truly despondent. Even in his hurt, he would always be looking toward the future, trying to find a way to keep the same thing from occurring again with another patient. My father was a man who looked forward, not back.

That day had gone well, that bright and glorious summer day. A spring had been in his step, a lilt in his voice. His mood had been light. In looking back, I could not even recall a bad mood that had occurred at any recent time before his death. Nothing, *nothing at all*, could have happened so distressing that he would have decided to shoot himself in the space of that hour or so from the time I left him living to the time I found him dead.

He did not kill himself. HE DID NOT!

"Devin, you going to scrub or not?"

I came back to the present with a start. My face flushed scarlet. My thoughts had been so intense that I wondered if I had spoken the last words aloud. However, no one asked me about it, just waited for me to snap out of the trance and catch-up.

"Sorry," I said lamely. "My mind won't wander in the OR, you'll see."

"No problem," joked one of the nurses. "Dr. Linden daydreams in Surgery all the time."

"Not all the time," he said, going along with the good-natured ribbing. "Personally, I think it's the mark of a master to be able to do that. The hands are such highly skilled instruments that they can do their stuff while the mind is on a loftier plane."

"Loftier plane is about right," retorted the same nurse. "Have you made a decision on buying a new one yet?"

"I think I will. Just as soon as things settle down a bit on the home front. With my wife in her present frame of mind, I don't need something else to be considered joint property of the marriage."

"You two won't split, not for long."

"What makes you think that?" he asked, seeming mildly amused.

"I know Drusilla better than I know you, Doc. She doesn't let go easily."

His scrubbing routine completed, Linden smiled again, but this time the smile seemed ever-so-slightly forced. "You may be right. Dru doesn't look like her father—thank God—but she does have something of his tenacity."

"Tenacity is a nice word to use on a McCracken. I can think of a few other ways to put it: downright stubborn, hard-headed, mulish . . . the list could go on and on."

I finished my own scrub and backed away from the stainless steel sink.

"You married Dru McCracken?" I blurted out. "I didn't know that."

Paul Linden's gray eyes were grave as he regarded me. "Can't think of any reason why you should know it."

Ouch! I flinched inwardly (and I hoped *only* inwardly) at the error I had just made. Laughing, I said, "Well, as you said yourself, I *am* here to learn. I guess, just having met Dr. McCracken yesterday, it just . . . well, when you introduced us, you didn't say a thing about him being your father-in-law."

The nurse wisecracked, "That's probably because he's not sure how long that state of affairs will exist. Right, hey, Doc?"

"Whatever you say," Paul said. "Let's just say that the goal at this time is for no one to get hurt."

"Lofty goal," the other nurse said softly, "but not exactly a realistic one."

Paul nodded without speaking. His eyes wore a far-away look and I wondered if he were thinking of those two boys he had spoken of so fondly. Even if the parents parted amicably, it was inevitable that the children's lives would be altered.

"Married, Dr. Hollister? You aren't, are you?"

"Not yet," I replied to the nurse. "And, to tell the truth, I sometimes wonder if I ever will be. You see, when I marry, I want it to be forever. I won't marry until I can be sure of that."

"Happy spinsterhood," mumbled Paul.

Work awaited us and the conversation ended abruptly at that point as we approached the operating arena. I breathed a sigh of relief that my *faux pas* had been so easily covered over, and subsequently vowed to be more careful before I opened my mouth in the future. The news had surprised me, but I knew I had to keep such reactions to myself. I cannot say I knew Drusilla McCracken since I doubt that we ever even spoke to each other. When I was a child, Dru was one of the favorite topics of conversation in Dalton. Wealthy, personable, beautiful, and willful, Dru had dominated the local high school, and then had gone on to triumph in a similar fashion at an exclusive private college. I think it is safe to say that Dru has been the only person in the history of Dalton High School to wear a Paris original to the prom. "I pity the guy who marries Daddy's spoiled little darling," was often said about town. And that guy had turned out to be Paul Linden. Funny, I wouldn't have thought he, of all men . . .

"Ready?"

"Ready."

With that, my reverie ended. Business was at hand. Paul deftly opened the abdomen, then motioned me forward for a closer look. No need to hunt for the malignancy. It was there waiting, making its virulent way through the intestines. In this case, the pathology report would be a mere formality. This was cancer, no doubt about it.

"Can you get it all?" I asked, my voice barely above a whisper.

"Too soon to tell. We can only try."

And try they did. An hour and twenty minutes later, sweat streaming down his forehead, he completed the closure. He had done all he could. What was left behind in the patient looked clean. Only time would tell if that were really the case or if enough malignant cells still lurked in there to recur, or to move to another site. Whatever the case, he had been brilliant. Not that I was any expert judge, but one does not have to be an expert to recognize the skill Linden possessed. I found myself thinking how pleased my father would be to know he had been right about this surgeon. He had seen the promise, and Paul now had fulfilled that promise.

We had started at seven o'clock in the morning with the first case, poor Annie Overlease, and it was slightly after seven in the evening when we were done. I felt limp and drained. It maddened me to see that Paul still looked as fresh and dapper as he had in the early hours. He was bound to be dead on his feet, but his fatigue did not show as most people's would.

"Okay?" he asked me softly when he had broken scrub for the last time.

"Okay, but worn out ... and I only watched. It doesn't show, but you must be exhausted."

His smile was slow and easy. As always, the smile erased years from his face. "Exhausted? Not really. Call me perverted, but I find operating exhilarating. I always have. When it stops being that way for me, I imagine it will be time for me to quit. Still, I admit I could have done without that emergency appy we had to squeeze into the schedule. Ever see an appendectomy on an emergency basis before?"

"Is there another way?" I hedged. "People don't exactly make routine appointments to have appendectomies."

"True, Ms. Wiseacre. But in some cases, they sneak up more on you than in others."

"I know. And I've seen others. Not many, of course. But a few. As a matter of fact, an emergency appy was the first major surgery I saw performed."

And that was when I was only eleven years old . . . and right here in the surgical suites of ABC.

"Katie, know the incision most commonly used for an appendectomy?"

"It's most likely to be a McBurney's."

"Oh? And how would you say my technique compared to these other surgeons you've observed?"

"He's looking for a compliment," shot one of the

surgery personnel in passing.

"And 'he' damned well better get one," Paul retorted.

"Well, you see, Dr. Linden," I deadpanned, "the first time is always the most impressive, the most memorable. The fact that the guy got all that stuff out of the abdomen and back in made him an idol in my book. Now I'm more blasé. It takes a lot more to impress me these days. I've had time and opportunity to study the techniques of numerous surgeons. I'm learning."

"And?" he urged, obviously impatient for his compliment.

I offered him the sweetest smile I had in stock. Keeping my face straight, I said, "You're quite good."

His eyebrows lifted and he waited. Obviously my compliment had not been extravagant enough.

"And?"

"More than quite good, actually. The adjective briliant comes to mind."

He beamed at that. "It's an adjective I always liked. That is, when it's applied to myself, of course. You really like the way I ligate?"

"Doctor, you can tie me in knots anytime."

Chuckling, he said, "I'll have to think that one over. Give me a few seconds."

"Can't. Have to get out of here and grab a bite."

"You aren't on all night duty?"

"Not tonight. But I do have a few hours to cover . . . just till three in the morning."

"That's not enough sleep."

"No matter. You don't operate tomorrow. By the time you operate again, I'll be fresh as a daisy."

"There ought to be a law . . ."

"So I say. I keep reading stuff about making regulations to shorten the hours of interns, but it never seems to happen. Maybe someday. But not soon enough for me. This is, I think, my first *and* last stint as an intern. See you around tomorrow."

"Sure enough. Take care, now."

For just a second, our eyes met. It was a second I could have done without . . . and I fancy he felt the same way.

In that flash of time, he had been unguarded, something I sensed he rarely was. His eyes had been filled with mixed emotions, one emotion being longing. There was no time and place for that. Not between *us*. Not now. And probably not ever.

Or maybe I was imagining it all. Exhaustion makes a person imagine all sorts of things. Maybe I was even getting delusional. Here I had barely set foot on Dalton soil and was fancying I had two men interested in me—or, at least, attracted to me. To make matters worse, I was interested in both of them—or, at least, attracted to them. A complication to one who, deep down in her heart, chose to believe *one* man existed somewhere for her . . . and would be recognized when he presented himself. I smiled at my own silly, tired self and dragged myself to my car.

My heart leaped when I drew close enough to the Mustang in the parking lot to see the piece of paper behind the windshield wiper on the driver's side. Had someone hit my car? My eyes scanned the gleaming sides and saw no defects. Moving closer, I still saw no signs of damage. I took the note from the window, unfolded it, and read. "There are those who know how to fix a car so it blows to bits when the key is turned in the ignition. Give it up, Katie."

My immediate reaction was anger. I quickly tore the note to little pieces. In the next breath, I regretted that hasty action. I had not saved either note. If any action were to take place against me in the future, it would be good if I saved the notes for evidence. The anger was soon replaced by sadness . . . and by fear. I felt nauseated and also weak about the knees. I felt as if crying might help, yet no tears were forthcoming.

I looked the car over and saw no signs that it had been tampered with. A few people were coming and going across the parking lot, but I could not imagine—especially since I had destroyed the menacing note—going up to anyone and asking if they knew how to check my car for explosive devices.

"Trouble, miss?" one man asked in passing.

"Not really," I said, not knowing what else to say and yet curiously reluctant to let possible help escape me. "It's been slow in starting. Someone said maybe I had a loose battery cable."

"That'll just take a minute to check."

In an instant, he had the hood up on the car. I hadn't the foggiest notion how to do that. Neither Charlie nor my mother was mechanically inclined, thus even the slightest problems in our automobiles were turned over to service people.

"Looks fine to me," he pronounced, drawing his head back up from the depths.

"Er . . . by the way, did you see anything else in there that might be loose?"

"Such as?" he asked, his face wearing that superior, smug smile people have when confronted with an obviously ignorant specimen of the human race.

"Oh, stray wires that shouldn't be there. Something like that. Maybe something leading to the ignition. As I said, it *has* been slow."

He was nice enough to look again, so I forgave him for the smugness. Shaking his head, he said, "Can't see a thing out of line. New car, isn't it?"

"Very new."

"Then it's your friendly Ford dealer's headache. A car like this doesn't start right, they should straighten it out for you, miss."

"You're right, of course. If it keeps it up, I'll check into that. Thanks ever so much for your help. You've been most kind."

"No problem. My pleasure."

He wandered off and I was left staring at the car. The man seemed sure there was nothing wrong under the hood. And *I* was sure no one could have gotten inside the car since I had locked it . . . probably not a habit necessary in Dalton, Mississippi, but a very necessary one in Boston, Massachusetts. I felt that there was nothing left to do but to try and start it. No one was going to blow me to bits . . . not yet. They wanted me to leave, or at least to forget about delving into James Clark's death, but so far they were only trying to scare me, not physically harm me. When I had myself fully psyched up that this was the case, I gingerly unlocked the car, got inside, placed my key in the ignition, then turned it. I had told myself there was nothing to fear. But I knew I hadn't believed myself. The engine started up, just as smooth and quiet as ever. There was no other sound, nothing at all. I felt limp as a rag and sick to my stomach.

As soon as I had completed the short drive home, I made a mad dash to my apartment and headed straight to the bathroom. I emerged a short time later feeling weak and utterly dejected.

I had started this. And I had to finish it. Never in my life had I been more sure that my father had been murdered. Nothing else made sense. If he had committed suicide, why would someone want to scare me off? No, I could not back away.

Like Scarlett O'Hara, I decided to think about that another day. I had to be back at ABC in forty-five minutes . . . not much time to shower, change, and eat, so I had no time to brood and plot just now.

Later. Yes, later. I will *not* stop.

Chapter Five

Anthony and I were having spaghetti in my apartment. It was one of the rare occasions when we had a few hours off-duty at the same time. The rain was coming down at a steady pace, making it seem all the nicer not to have to be out. Since the skies had been dark and dreary all day, we scarcely knew when the grayness deepened to nighttime.

I had provided the ingredients for our supper. Anthony had provided the wine—and the know-how for putting the ingredients together. It was an equitable arrangement—and a warm and cozy evening. In no time at all, so it seemed, the newness had worn off our relationship and it was as if we had always known each other. To me, he was already as familiar and as comfortable as some of the boys I had grown up with.

Two weeks had passed since the ominous note had been placed on my windshield. I regarded it as a plus that no other threatening incidents had occurred. Conversely, I felt it was a minus that my so-called investigation was going nowhere. I tried not to be discouraged, telling myself it was part of the plan to go slowly at first until I had established myself in Dalton, in ABC in particular, and was more sure of those around me before I starting probing in earnest.

"We didn't have dessert," Anthony pointed out.

"Glutton! How can you think of more to eat after all we've just stuffed down?"

"Because I have a sweet tooth and no matter how

much I eat otherwise, I know I'll remain dissatisfied until I have at least a little bit of something. Don't you have any sweets, maybe some ice cream?"

"Nothing, Anthony. I'm here so little that I just don't keep a stock of groceries. It isn't worth it for just me. Much simpler to eat out when I'm not at the hospital." He looked so sad that I laughed and said, "But feel free to rummage in the cabinets and the fridge. There could be a loose candy bar lurking in the corners somewhere. While you look, I'll clear away this mess. Then you can tell me all about OB."

"What's to tell?"

"Anthony, don't be maddening. I want to hear about the babies, the procedures, how you now feel about natural childbirth versus all the epidurals and whatever else is being used. I want you to give me your honest opinion on how many Caesareans are truly indicated and how many are done as a prophylaxis against lawsuits. I want to know . . ."

"Good grief, girl! I've only been there three weeks."

"I know, but you're a person with strong opinions."

"Maybe. But why does it matter anyway? I thought you wanted to be a general surgeon."

"Probably. But it isn't set in concrete yet. I . . ."

The telephone rang and I went to answer it, leaving my friend still looking for something to satisfy his sweet tooth.

"Devin, darlin', it's me . . . your mother."

As if she had to announce that! Who else talked in that lilting, sing-song way; her accent a curiously attractive mixture of south and east?

"How good to hear from you," I said. "I got your letter only yesterday, but it has been a while since we talked."

"No fault of mine. It seems to me I try to call daily and you're never there. Tell me, Devin, do they really work you that hard or are you in the midst a wild social whirl?"

"Guess."

Her sigh was deep and filled with near-regret. Although she would never, ever actually say so, I think something inside my mother longed for a daughter who was more of a younger version of herself. Instead, she had me.

"Face it, Mother," I said cheerfully. "I'm a grind."

"I wouldn't say that," she protested very quickly.

"Of course you wouldn't. You're much too nice. But I have a feeling you've thought it many, many times. But enough of that. How are you and Charlie?"

With that simple quesion, she was off on a running commentary to keep me up-to-date on life in our corner of Boston. All I had to do was listen and utter an occasional "really" or "hmmm." I turned to find Anthony watching me from the doorway. He pulled his mobile features into a caricature of lewdness and waved a nearly full bag of miniature candy bars at me. He had found my private stock, chocolate bars I kept squirreled away against a bad day that only calories could make bearable. Still wearing that awful look, he popped an entire bar into his mouth at once. An involuntary giggle escaped me . . . and went straight from my lips into the telephone receiver.

"What was so funny about that?" came my mother's puzzled voice. "Poor Edith was mortified, not to say heartsick."

"I'm sorry, Mother. I wasn't laughing at you. A friend is here, one of the other interns, and is clowning around— that's why I laughed. Not at what you said about Edith and Mark. I *am* truly sorry to hear the marriage is on the rocks. It really seems a shame after all this time, But, still, if he won't leave the young girls alone, well . . . one can't expect her to sit still for that."

"Exactly," she said, and was off and running with the remainder of that tale, then spinning off into another one. While she talked on and on, I saw the supply of candy bars dwindling. How could he eat so much and stay so thin?

When at long last, she ran down, I found myself asking, "Mother, did you tell anyone at all in Dalton that I was coming here?"

"Not a soul, darlin'. Why do you ask? I didn't know it was a secret, but there isn't anyone left there with whom

I keep in touch, you know."

"I didn't think so."

"Is there a problem, Devin? You sound a little strange."

No problem. Just three threatening incidents, two of them bearing a name I hadn't used for fifteen years.

"It's nothing, really. Just a feeling I had that perhaps someone here knew. Undoubtedly just paranoia on my part."

"You aren't being imprudent, are you, dear? You don't know how I wish you'd let the past be, just let it go."

"I don't think I have much of a choice. I have so little time. And, as we've known all along, it all happened a long, long time ago. Another lifetime, really."

She seemed relieved at that. Again, I felt as if I had lied. I knew I had given the impression I wasn't actively pursuing my quest, had given that impression quite deliberately. After all, there was no need for her to be worried. And the fib wasn't such a dark one as there had truly been little opportunity for me to learn anything more about the past.

"Give my love to Charlie," I said firmly when she gave a slight sign she might be running down.

Either she took the hint or was ready to close anyway and the connection between us was severed quickly after that.

Anthony looked at the telephone and at the clock. "Forty-five minutes," he said. "During which you said about as many words."

"My mother," I explained. "She almost always has a lot to say."

"I wouldn't know about always. But she certainly did seem to have a lot to say this time."

"You're a great one to sneer at excesses. Look at you! You've eaten nearly all my candy. And after all of that spaghetti and bread."

"There are two left," he offered, "and a bit of wine. Tell me, does red wine go okay with chocolate or should I go out for white?"

"If I told you to go for white, would you?"

"In this rain? Not on your life."

"That's what I thought."

We settled on the couch. He "generously" divided the two remaining candy bars between us.

"What's your mother like, Devin?"

I swallowed the bite of delicious chocolate and said, "Why do you ask?"

"I don't know. Just because she called, I guess. I found myself wondering if she was much like you. And decided she wasn't because you don't 'chat' that much."

"My mother is a beautiful woman—tall, blond, thin. She looks very much like a model or actress and not at all like a mother. She's talkative and outgoing. Her career is her family, her home, her friends, her social circle. She has never worked and never regretted it. She is what she wants to be. That's to be envied. It isn't what I want for me, but it suits her. She is very content. How many people can claim that?"

"Not many. So, how did you end up so quiet and serious-minded?"

I smiled slightly. "You make me sound dull."

"Do I? It wasn't meant that way. I like the way you are. Surely you know that."

There was too much warmth in his voice and I had to back away from that, pretend I hadn't noticed.

"Maybe it's just unconscious rebellion that shaped me. I could never equal *her*, so I've stayed out of the arena entirely and entered my own. But come on . . . you haven't told me about the time you've spent on OB."

If he noticed that I was trying to divert him away from my personal life, he made no comment and let himself be diverted. Most likely, he preferred it that way. Like me, he was in love with medicine and there was nothing else more fascinating to discuss.

We talked and talked, then I committed the social offense of yawning.

Laughing, Anthony said, "Me, too. As much as I hate to end this wonderfully pleasant time, I know duty awaits me early in the A.M."

He bent to kiss me then. I was not surprised. Neither would I have been surprised if he had walked away without it. All in all, I would have preferred that he do that. The embrace was warm, comforting, pleasurable, but it brought with it a complication I did not need, that I was not ready for.

Before I had a chance to break away, the telephone rang again.

"Oh," I said, "how are you this evening?" My voice sounded slightly breathless even to myself . . . perhaps due to Anthony's sweet kisses, or my confusion over them . . . or perhaps due to the fact that my caller had identified himself as "Paul." Not Paul Linden or Dr. Linden, just, "Devin, this is Paul."

"I'm fine. I just received word, however, that there's a youngster at the hospital who isn't quite so fine. He was thrown from a horse. A bad injury, I gather. The doctor on ER duty seems to think there's an intra-abdominal injury, possibly to the spleen. Chances are, there's going to be at least an exploratory laparotomy. Want to come watch?"

"What time?"

"Oh, I'd say you have an hour anyway. He has some bad signs and symptoms, but doesn't seem to be critical at this point. On the other hand, it seems foolhardy, and an unnecessary risk, to wait until morning. Can I count on seeing you there?"

"Of course. You knew I'd want to be, didn't you? Thanks for letting me know. I'll be there soon."

Anthony was watching me intently. I sensed he was not pleased.

"That was Paul Linden," I began to explain.

"I surmised as much. By the lilt in your voice, the sparkle in your eye, and the fact that your tendency to yawn has ceased. He brings you to bloom, doesn't he?"

I opened my mouth to protest, then closed it immediately before saying a word, furious at Anthony for his comments and at myself for almost catering to his gall by trying to explain.

"Sorry," he said softly. "That was out of line."

"Yes. Yes, it was. The call wasn't a personal one. And I don't owe you an explanation, but I want this very clear. He called to tell me about an emergency case over at the hospital. They're going to do an exploratory laparotomy on an injured boy very soon. He gave me the chance to be there. That's all."

Possibly he did not believe me. I wasn't altogether convincing even to myself. Yes, the chance to participate in emergency surgery was exciting, yet the fact that the call had come from Paul made a difference . . . a difference I was not ready to openly acknowledge.

Anthony's farewell smile was mocking, but not unkindly so. He was a realist, accepting, nothing more.

"See you around."

"Sure, Anthony. Thanks for everything."

"Everything?" Again, those dark eyes mocked me, reminding me of kisses I needed to forget.

"Everything," I answered softly. "One can't always regret just because, logically, one should."

"Then you aren't shutting the door entirely?"

"Let's just say it's ajar. That has to be the status quo. I can't open it either. It isn't a cat-and-mouse game. Mostly, it's a matter of timing."

He nodded, accepting that. The timing wasn't right for him either. We have both heard the married students and interns talk. The guilt and pressure they feel from being able to contribute so little to a relationship. It is not at all enviable.

Anthony left then and I found myself unable to settle, and thus decided to go on ahead to ABC. Catching sight of myself in the mirror as I quickly combed my short hair, I saw that my friend had been more right than I wanted to admit. Gone were all signs of sleepiness. I looked bright, alert, almost sparkling. Dismayed at my betraying emotions, I mocked myself aloud, "Amazing what news of an emergency procedure will do for a girl's looks."

Paul. I wasn't sure I liked him. There were times that I most certainly did not. Yet I was never bored by him, and the fact that I was going to see him now did put a spring in my step.

At the hospital, it was all business. Any personal fantasies were pushed to the back. Both parents of the injured boy were fearful. The mother was crying and the father was acting with irrational anger, probably in an effort to keep from breaking down himself. They blamed themselves, they blamed each other, they blamed God. So hard in such moments just to say that these things happen all the time and that fate would have it that it was their turn now.

"He's only ten. He had no business out on a horse alone. Especially not in this kind of weather."

"I know that, Alan. But, for God's sake, he wasn't out with *my* permission. Sure, I said he could go to Derek's house, but I didn't say he could ride Star. He knew he wasn't supposed to. I suppose it was an adventure, a game. Something he did on a dare. He and Derek are like that with each other. You know that. They egg each other on, make dares."

"But didn't you wonder, Sue, when he didn't want you to drive him there?"

"Not after he said they were picking him up. He *lied* to me. You'll have to accept that. I suppose you never lied to your parents when you were a boy Simon's age?"

The boy's father was tight-lipped and unresponsive to that. I watched them with great interest, able to sympathize with all of their conflicting emotions, although I wished they had been able to use their emotions to comfort each other. In the experiences of my hospital stints while a student, especially in emergency settings, I had noted the strange way people seem to create trouble for themselves even when they aleady have a surplus of it.

"It's okay," I said gently, surprising myself by stepping into the fray. "Things like this happen. Most often, they aren't anyone's fault. I've been taught that kids who never get hurt are usually overprotected and watched too carefully. They have to learn and grow on their own some. Dr. Linden is here. Simon will be getting the best of care. He'll be back home with you—even back on that horse—sooner than you think possible right now."

"You really think so?" the woman asked. She seemed ready to crumple. "I feel so guilty. I should have realized, knowing that boy, that he was up to something."

"But we can't always know. And we can't always do something about it even when we do know."

I was able to lead them out and get them talking. It was easier with the woman, but the man eventually relaxed and talked with his wife and me without the earlier belligerence. I observed that, deep down inside, each felt guilty and, I suppose, by blaming the other hoped to share some of the guilt.

Out of the corner of my eye, I noticed that Paul Linden had reentered the main part of the emergency room and was watching me with what looked suspiciously like amusement.

"You came early," he said when he saw that I recognized his presence.

"I didn't want to miss anything."

"You haven't."

He then stepped forward and gave all of his attention to the injured boy's parents.

"Your boy is going to be okay. They're preparing him for surgery right now. The nurse is getting the necessary forms ready for you to sign. Before you sign them, I need to explain to you what this is all about. From a cursory exam, we're fairly sure Simon has a fractured spleen. We need to open up the abdomen and take a look, make sure nothing else is amiss. If the spleen is, indeed, as injured as we think it is, we'll remove it. It's a relatively simple procedure, barring, of course, too much trauma to other organs. Luckily, the spleen is one of those body parts we can do nicely without. He can lead a normal life and never miss that particular organ."

He then proceeded to explain, frankly but gently, the complications that could occur from the surgery and the use of anesthetic agents, including the omnipresent demons of hemorrhage and postoperative infection. It was all so scary sounding to those who did not understand that it was merely a matter of routine, that complications were quite rare, but this day of free and easy lawsuits made all this explanation necessary.

The mother shuddered. "It sounds so dreadful, like there's no hope at all."

"It isn't that way, Mrs. McCaulla. Not at all. As I said in the beginning, I truly believe your boy is going to come out of this fine. We *have* to make you aware of the possibilities, but please understand how rarely these complications occur. Your child is young, healthy, and has a strong will to live. He is not at high risk. Truth is, he is at higher risk when you take him on a car ride."

Both of them nodded.

"We'll sign," the father said. "After all, we really don't have a choice. If he has something wrong like you said, it needs to be fixed."

"Right."

I noted that Paul touched them frequently during the interview, just the pressure of his hand on their shoulders. He was good with them, gentle and kind. I don't think it was an act, this bedside manner of his. The warmth in his voice was genuine. I imagine having two boys of his own he especially identified with their distress.

In due time, the papers were signed, the results of the STAT lab work were on the chart, and there was no reason for further delay.

Paul indicated I was to be his first assistant, a fact that both pleased and terrified me. He opened the abdomen and we immediately were confronted with a great deal of old blood. I suctioned it away so that we could have a better view of the inner structures.

"Look there," he said. "The primary vascular tree is affected, is very much involved in the trauma. If it hadn't been, I might have tried to preserve the spleen, but, considering this, I don't dare. Out it comes."

"The colon looks traumatized. Isn't that a bad sign?"

"Not good. But not as bad as you're thinking. Look, the blood supply is intact. As I guessed, we'll just have to remove the spleen."

"Now?"

"Now."

I sweated, but the removal was easy. I then stepped back while Paul mobilized the spleen. In no time at all, the spleen was no longer part of Simon, was merely a specimen being handed off for pathologic examination.

"Are you going to put a drain in the splenic bed, doctor?"

"What do you think, *doctor?*"

I surveyed the situation, swallowed, and said, "There doesn't appear any real need, does there?"

He nodded his approval. "Not that I can see. We can take the suction off him, too. There's no more sign of bleeding. He's nice and dry. A piece of cake, right?"

"Right," I agreed, suddenly feeling wan and tired. Apparently, the boost of adrenaline the news of the emergency had given me was wearing off fast.

After cleaning up, we sought out the anxious parents in the surgical waiting room. Again, I was struck by the deft way Paul explained to them the details of the surgery using terms they could understand, but not once coming across as condescending.

"I should have let you talk to them," he said in an aside as we walked away from them."

"Why me? You're the surgeon."

"True, but you're the one with a knack for dealing with people."

"How do you figure that?"

"I saw the way you got them soothed down earlier, just stepped right in and took over. I admire the ability to do that. I can talk to people about the surgery, both pre- and postoperative, but I'm no good when they're hotheaded. And I can't just jump in like you did. Dealing with the public isn't my strongest point."

I shook my head. "From what I've seen, I wouldn't say that. Your bedside manner is very impressive."

"Not always. You caught me at a good time. And, as I said, you had them soothed down before I had to deal with them. Maybe you've missed your calling."

"Meaning?"

"As I told you earlier, Devin, we surgeons don't often get involved with people in-depth. You're so good with people, perhaps you should be an internist."

"Or a dermatologist?" I said dryly. "No thanks. Actually, I didn't think I did half-bad as a surgeon in there."

He laughed. "Nothing small about your ego."

"Well, isn't it true?"

"Yes, Devin, it was very much true. I was only kidding you earlier. Not that I wasn't sincere about admiring your knack with people. I can already tell you also have a knack for surgery—a cool head, and a steady hand. I think, even no better than I know you, I'd be sorely disappointed to hear that you'd decided against going ahead with a surgical residency."

I smiled. "Then there's little chance you'll be disappointed. The more I do, the more fascinated I am."

"Great. Now let's go change and I'll treat you to a snack before you go back home."

"No home tonight. In exactly forty-two minutes I go on duty."

"All the more reason for a bit of fortification first. Meet you in the surgeon's lounge."

I finished washing and changing before Paul did and wandered into the newly furnished lounge I had never seen before. Looking up, I turned pale to see my father staring down at me from a photograph in a massive-looking frame. A gold plaque was below the picture and I stepped forward to read it.

"This room is dedicated to the memory of James Stuyvesant Clark, M.D., F.A.S.C." Beneath that, the dates of his birth and death were listed.

"Something wrong? You look as if you've seen a ghost."

Until he spoke, I had not been aware that Paul Linden had entered the room.

"I . . . well, I hope not. This is the surgeon you mentioned to me a while back, isn't it? The one who supposedly killed himself?"

"Supposedly?" he asked, raising one eyebrow slightly. "it was a shock to all of us who knew him, but, as far as

I know, there was no doubt that it was suicide. Tragic. So tragic. But why so pale and wide-eyed? It was all before your time."

I braced myself and forced a smile. "Pale and wide-eyed? Not a very flattering description. Just the strain of my big assist-job back there, I guess."

How I longed to go on talking with Paul about my father's death, but I dared not! I could think of no way to keep the subject open without making him wonder why I was so interested in a man who had died fifteen years before I even came to town. I settled for saying lamely, "This is a nice room."

"Recently redone. The medical staff of ABC, at the time Jim Clark died, kicked in for the original renovation in his memory. As times goes by, there are less and less of us here who worked with him. The cost of the new redecorating came out of general expenses, I guess, but the vote was that the dedication remain intact."

"That's nice," I said softly. "I'm sure he would be pleased if he knew."

"Maybe he does. Ever think about the hereafter?"

And off he went. We walked companionably down the hall to the snack bar where we sat and talked until I had to report to the duty station. That is, Paul talked and I listened. I didn't mind. He had a lot of fascinating ideas and philosophies. As I had observed before, his mind was like quicksilver . . . and it did not light on the subject of my father again.

Don't be impatient, Devin, I warned myself, but the warning fell on deaf ears. I felt as if there were a time bomb ticking away inside myself. Before I could give myself wholeheartedly to medicine—and most certainly before I could give my love to any man—I needed my questions resolved. My father's death haunted me to the point of obsession. My heart remembered all too well what my father was like and, what the heart remembers, the mind cannot forget. He was *not* suicidal. There was no way my still-aching heart could ever accept what the rest of the world believed to be a cut-and-dried fact, a dead and buried part of history. I have a feeling young Simon's body will heal long before my heart gives up its fight. There are some things to which I cannot yield and still be me.

Soon I was on duty and it was a hectic tour of duty—not so much in terms of large numbers of patients or of crisis situations, but just a series of things that went wrong. IV's wouldn't drip properly and some, worse yet, infiltrated. A patient fell out of bed somehow despite rails. One of the nurses gave a patient the wrong medication, two of the nurses got in a heated fight, a patient in the end-stage of alcoholic cirrhosis was threatening to walk out, and so on. The flurry of activity and confusion was a mixed blessing. It kept me from brooding, but the other side of the coin was that it also kept me from doing any further research.

By the end of the shift, when I felt I surely must be dead and just didn't have sense enough to lie down, I had made the resolution to become more active in my "detecting." That is, as active as time and prudence allowed. When I had ten minutes to grab a cup of coffee, I scribbled some ideas down on a piece of paper and stuck it in the pocket of my blue lab coat:

1. Go to the library or newspaper office and see if I can find the papers of the week my father died—maybe the month before—to see if there were things going on in town that might have had to do with him. Check out his obituary, find the names of all those who served as pallbearers.
2. Find office and hospital records from that time period. Perhaps there will be a clue in the patients that he saw those last few days and weeks.

"Dr. Hollister," called one of the aides. "Mrs. Bacon wants to see you."

"Again?" The poor lady had what is known in medical lingo as multiple co-morbidities . . . which really means that she has so many bad illnesses that there is no way she can get well. Death will be her fate in the very near future. She knows that and, always having been a demanding person, is determined to see that she gets all the attention she feels is her due. She is one of those patients who regard a hospital as a sort of resort hotel where the staff should be at her beck and call.

"Again," the aide replied with a chuckle, obviously enjoying the fact that I had been chosen by Mrs. Bacon as her personal slave of the evening.

I turned wearily to see what I could do to pacify the patient and, in my tiredness, nearly ran into a portly figure rounding the corner.

"Dr. Hollister, isn't it?"

I did my best to smile at Dr. George McCracken. "Yes, sir. What are you doing out at such an hour?"

"Edna Bacon. She thinks she's dying."

"Isn't she?"

He lifted his shaggy gray eyebrows, then wiggled them quite comically. "Well, of course. But from what the nurse on the phone told me, it probably isn't going to be tonight. The poor old thing is just having an anxiety attack. My wife and I had been out this evening and had just gotten in when I received the call. Since I was up, I decided to come put her mind at ease before I put myself to bed."

"I was just heading that way. The aide said she'd asked for me. I've been in there with her several times tonight. As they must have already told you, she's clinically stable right now. She just needs reassurance."

"And maybe an extra dose of sleeping medication?"

"It couldn't hurt. Well, I don't suppose she'll need me now."

"Nonsense. Come along. You know something? You remind me of someone. Did I tell you that when we met before?"

"Yes, come to think of it, you did. Ever think of who it was?"

I had to challenge him. His steely eyes peered deeply into mine. "Not yet. But I will. Never fear. Just give me time."

It was nothing. I told myself that. There was nothing marked about my resemblance to either parent, so anything that reminded him of me had to be so minor... just a mannerism or attitude... that he would never be able to pinpoint it, not after all these years.

"Well, when you think of it, let me know."

"I will. Never fear. My memory used to be phenomenal. But I admit it isn't what it used to be, however, it's still a damned sight better than most people's."

"Yes, sir. I'm sure it is."

I wished him no bad luck but, in this case, I was hoping his bad memory would prevail. As I recall, he had paid me little mind in all the times I had been around him. He'd never connect it... never.

I willed myself to believe that, but a slight uneasiness remained. I pushed it aside and trailed along with George McCracken to get yet another lesson in bedside manners.

Chapter Six

"It's a lovely idea, Anthony. Really, it is. Maybe the next time we have a day off together . . . if the offer still holds then. But I can't this time. I just can't."

"It's just what I said it was, Devin. Exploring the countryside. The weather is supposed to be great. We could take along a picnic lunch, maybe even roast some hot dogs. I'm talking hiking in the daylight. No passes. I promise."

Remembering my reaction to Anthony's kisses . . . well, *both* of my reactions . . . I felt my neck and face grow hot. How I wish I could stop this awful blushing habit, but I am beginning to think it is something I'll never outgrow. When I am even slightly agitated, be it in anger, guilt, embarrassment, or confusion, the emotion always triggers the same response, and I get this humiliating rose-colored blush across my face.

"You read me wrong," I said calmly after the worst of the flush had subsided. "I'd *love* to go on the outing with you on Wednesday. But there are all these things I've kept putting off and they can't be done on a weekend. If I don't do them Wednesday, God only knows when I'll get another chance like this."

"Fine then, do what you have to do. I'll go alone."

He sounded petulant enough that a sharp retort was on the tip of my tongue when I turned slightly to look more fully at him. There was a childlike aspect to him that melted me. Beneath the petulance was real hurt. And I liked Anthony. In him, I recognized all the makings of a good friend, and, thus, I let the sharpness die before it had expressed itself.

"Can't you accept that I have other plans? Nothing more complicated than that. After four in the afternoon, I'll be free. I have no plans from then until I have to report to the hospital early Thursday morning. If you're free between four and when I have to crash, then . . ."

Now it was his turn to be embarrassed. Although he did not have my problem with blushing, the other betraying signs were there . . . the fidgeting and shifting of the eyes and the obvious searching for something *right* to say.

"I'm sorry, I've always hated this behavior when I saw it in other guys, always swore I'd never act that way. Sometimes I have things I have to do on my own too, and I'd like to think I'm smart enough to recognize that the people I like do also. If a girl isn't free for me, it isn't always personal, right?"

"In your case, I'd wager it seldom is personal. You can't tell me a guy like you gets many rejections."

"I don't know," he muttered, embarrassment obviously on the uprise. "I haven't kept records. Anyway . . . I'll accept you on *both* provisions. I'll take a rain check for the outing. And if I call right away, I can get us reservations for this restaurant I've heard about."

"Not the Dalton Diner?" I asked quickly.

He laughed. "No, but that does sound a likely place, doesn't it? This is an old antebellum mansion that's been turned into an inn. The food is supposed to be excellent, but the seating is limited and you do have to have reservations. The Fraser Inn, I think it's called."

I blinked, recognizing one of the oldest names in the town. "I didn't know . . . is this on Magnolia Street?"

"Yes, I think so. You've heard of it, too?"

"Must have," I mumbled, realizing I had been all too ready to again betray my prior knowledge of Dalton history. "It's a shame, isn't it, that these old houses can't stay in the family? I guess it's better to see them turned into public places than to see them torn down, but, still . . ."

"A symbol of a dying era?"

"Dying?" I made a grimace. "Long dead, I suppose. We just tend to romanticize the glorious old south, I guess. Some families die out. Others have descendents that move elsewhere—or just aren't interested in the old traditions. And I suppose there are many that cannot afford to maintain an old mansion."

"You don't want to go? Is it going to depress you?"

"Nonsense! I'd love it. Just make the reservation early enough that I won't fall asleep in the soup. I'm not much of a live wire these days."

"Given our grueling hours, who among us is?"

And so it was settled. Anthony went to his duties and I went to mine. I did not do so, however, before I gave thought to the Fraser clan and what had become of them. During my early years in Dalton, I had been in school with Jackson Lee Fraser. He had been a lonely little boy, one who was often the butt of jokes, given the combination of his short stature, thick glasses, and overly serious manner. Jack, I recalled, was being reared in the Fraser house on Magnolia Street by two maiden aunts. Something mysterious, or at least not fit for the ears of children, had transpired with his parents and had left him to be raised by the well-meaning, but inept, fading southern belles. His father, also Jackson Lee Fraser, had been the baby brother of Miss Emmaline and Miss Dorothea.

"Woolgathering?" asked a nurse in passing. "You look a thousand miles away."

"Not so much miles as years," I said softly, then pulled myself together. Why, I wondered, had my mind been so taken up with the Fraser mansion's fate? And after all these years of him not entering my mind, why was I suddenly able to see Jack Fraser's little face so clearly? Just one of those things, I decided, then picked up Mrs. Jurgenson's chart. The nurses had informed me she was demanding something for her constipation. A long time laxative abuser, there was no way *I* was going to change her mind, not at 79 years of age, so I reviewed her other medications and then wrote out an order for Doxidan.

* * *

In due course, Wednesday arrived. I left behind scrub suits and lab coats in favor of jeans and a T-shirt—and left ABC behind in favor of the office of *The Dalton Journal*.

"How far back do you keep your old newspapers?" I asked the girl at the desk.

"We have *every* issue since December of 1949," she announced with pride. "Before that, it's kind of patchy. There was a fire in November of that year and everything burned. People have brought in old papers from pre-1949 that they had for one reason or another and we have been able to make a file of sorts, but copies of some issues were never found. What issue do you need?"

"Not *that* far back," I answered with a smile. "I'd like to start with 1979. If I can't find anything of interest, I may need to take a look back through '78."

She showed me back to the storage room where volume after volume of *The Journal* was bound. The area evidently was seldom used, for it had a barn-like dusty and musty atmosphere.

I thanked the clerk and asked her if I should find anything of interest, if there was a way I could get a photocopy of the article.

"Sure. No problem. But I'd have to charge 35¢ a page. I know that's higher than a lot of places—the office supply store does copies for a dime apiece—but the owner here figures it takes so much time and effort. Those books are heavy and not easy to take apart and get back together."

Looking at them, I said, "I can see that. There probably won't be anything I need. If there is, I think the price is very reasonable. I brought a writing pad so that if need be, I can jot down facts."

"School paper or something?"

Why not? It was as good an explanation as any. Careful not to say yes or no, I created the impression of a yes by saying, "Special project. A pain, but it has to be done."

"Don't I know it! I'm glad that's behind me now. My

76

folks wanted me to go to college, but I don't think it's for everyone. I liked the social stuff at school, but not the work. Mr. Ames is good to work for. I started here parttime when I was still in high school. I like it here and he's training me to do some extra stuff so I won't have to be a clerk all the time. You're new here, aren't you?"

Nodding, anxious to be about my business, but not wanting to seem rude, I said, "I've only been here a month or two. I work at the hospital. My name is Devin Hollister."

"Devin? Such a pretty name. One of the soaps I watch has a character by that name."

"And yours is . . . ?" I asked, feeling duty bound now to do so.

"Diane Miller . . . see, such a plain name. No class at all."

"But at least not an awful name like Ima Hogg."

She giggled at that. "No, at least not like that."

"I haven't met any Millers since I've been in Dalton . . . that is, until now."

"You ever stop at Lesevier's Market?"

Not lately, but the old-fashioned style store with its open bins of wares had been a favorite place of mine as a small child. "I know where you mean," I hedged.

"Well, my father owns that store. It's been in my mother's family for years. When grandpa retired and Daddy took over running the store, he didn't change the name. It's *always* been Lesevier's, he said."

"I'll pop in sometime," I told her, then turned toward the many files facing me.

Lesevier. Another old Dalton name. I had no memory of this Diane, a girl I estimated to be nineteen, certainly no more than twenty-one. There had been a boy in my class called Butch Miller . . . probably an older brother. It was a common name, but, as I recalled, his features were set in the same mold, his head crowned with the same sort of frizzy hair. And, as I further recalled, Mrs. George McCracken—Helene to her friends and family—had been a Lesevier, probably making this girl a niece, as well as being a cousin to Drusilla Linden. I had forgotten what a small town was like, where everyone you met was in some way connected to someone else you had met, where it was not at all prudent to utter a hasty comment about anyone else since it might well offend a relative, a neighbor, or a friend.

I leafed through the large sheets of newsprint and found myself taken back in time. For me, it was no longer the 1990s, it was the 1970s. The energy crisis was in full swing and there was talk of gasoline rationing. In the nearby state of North Carolina, an outbreak of violence between Ku Klux Klan members and some anti-Klan demonstrators resulted in numerous deaths and injuries. The stageplay "Grease" was setting records. The art world was rejoicing over the discovery of two long-lost paintings—one by da Vinci and one by Frederic Edwin Church. Moshe Dayan resigned. The president of South Korea was assassinated. Iranian militants seized the U.S. Embassy. There was no lack of violence throughout the decade, ending with the Soviets invasion of Afghanistan in the last days of December.

Those were among the front-page headlines. In the back pages, I found the local news. Dru McCracken was queen of everything at the college she was attending. Her father was chief-of-staff at Albert B. Creighton. The new movie theater had opened. Dr. and Mrs. James Clark hosted a party at their home for their daughter Katie's eleventh birthday. Early in the year, the high school basketball team made it to the state tournament for the first time in Dalton history. Interestingly, a final judgment had been made in an ongoing battle between ABC Hospital and the City of Dalton over property lines. The hospital's campaign had been led by Jane Goldstein and the judgment had been in favor of the hospital. The hospital was then able to go ahead with its expansion program without paying the exorbitant fees the city claimed were its due. All of this helping to make poor Jane one of the most loathed people by the city government. Fortunately for Jane, the city administrators had all changed since then, while she had remained in her original post. There was the usual measure of birth announcements, marriage announcements, and obituaries. My father's obituary was there. On my pad, I wrote down the names of the pallbearers listed. Even reading as carefully as I could, nothing of significance popped out at me. There was no other hospital news of any import. No names on the obituaries prior to my father's that connected with anyone he had known well, or cared for professionally. In October of that year, long after Mother and I were settled in Boston, Jackson Lee Fraser had died in St. Louis, Missouri. A wife was not listed among the survivors. If anyone had ever told me Jack's father died not too many months after mine did, I had forgotten it. Funny, the second time in just a few days that I had been reminded of poor Jack.

Seeing the obituary of the older Jack, I had a vivid flashback to a time when the younger Jack was being particularly persecuted. Frustrated, hurt, and angry, he had given in to tears . . . and the tears had only earned him further harassment.

"Just wait," he had cried out. *"My father is going to come get me soon and he'll make you all sorry for what you've said and done. He'll get you all, and then he'll take me away with him in his big red Cadillac. He's busy now making lots and lots of money so we can live it up right, then he's going to come get me."*

"Yeah, sure, Jackie-baby. And what about that mother of yours? She coming to get you, too? My folks say ain't neither of them wanted you. Can't see as how I blame them. Nope, can't blame 'em at all for leavin' you behind."

"It isn't so," he screamed at his tormenter. *"That isn't the way it is at all. They do so want me, but my mother is sick and my dad has to work all the time and travel. But now he's almost rich enough to quit working and we can be together."*

The tears had run down his rounded little cheeks and, when he had taken off his thick glasses to wipe them off, his dark eyes had looked sad and vulnerable. I could not remember how long they had kept tormenting him or what event had broken it up, but I do remember that part quite clearly.

I bent my head down and pressed my forehead against

the sections of newspapers in front of me. Another memory was coming to the surface and I sensed I'd rather it didn't.

"You could come to my house, I guess, Katie. My aunts won't care. They like me to have 'little friends' over, but I don't have many of those. They'll give us fancy cookies and tarts to eat and milk to drink—or hot tea if you don't like milk. After, we can play in the yard. You'll like it there. I have a tree house. A real tree house. Aunt Emmaline and Aunt Dorrie had it built for me for my last birthday. Sometimes I just sit up there and look down on the world. It's peaceful up there.

Jack had been right. I had liked everything about his house and yard. Despite their marked eccentricities, I liked the Fraser sisters . . . and I *adored* the wonderful pastries and cookies they concocted. But most of all, I had liked the tree house.

The summer I was nine, Jack and I had met up by accident. Our houses were only a few blocks apart and our separate treks, sometimes on foot, sometimes on bicycle, had caused our paths to cross. I had seen him at school, but we had never been in the same class. For that one summer, we were friends. I no longer thought of him as odd or funny looking. Beneath that overly serious surface, there was a kid with a sense of humor bigger than he was. Sometimes we laughed until we were gasping for air.

Up in the tree house, our tummies stuffed with homemade cookies and jugs of milk or Kool-Aid, we would solve the problems of the world, particularly Dalton's corner of it.

When school started that fall, Jack and I were in the same class. My school friends, the members of the popular crowd, and I met up again and went about business as usual.

One day during the first week of school, Jackson Lee Fraser came up to me on the playground. And I saw him again as all the other's saw him, not as the person I knew he really was. He was dressed, not like the other kids, but like the old ladies thought a well-bred little boy should dress, with pleated trousers, polished shoes, shirt buttoned all the way up to the top, and wheat-colored hair cut off so pitifully short that, from enough distance, he looked quite bald.

"*Katie, you think you can come over Saturday? Aunt Dorrie cleaned out the closets and she's given us some new things for the tree house. I haven't started fixing it up yet because I thought you'd like to help. What do you think?*"

I felt the betraying scarlet blush as it stained my neck and face in ugly blotches.

"*I'm not sure. I'll have to let you know.*"

Looking slightly puzzled, he backed away. He was only a few feet away from us when my friends burst into giggles. I joined them in their laughter, then found myself explaining—apologizing, really—about Jack Fraser's invitation. I looked across the playground and saw him looking back at us. The thick glasses hid whatever emotion his eyes might have shown, but his shoulders sagged and I could swear—though how could I know from such a distance—that his lower lip trembled slightly before he shrugged and went back to the corner of the playground where he loitered alone a portion of each and every day.

I did not go to the Fraser house that Saturday, nor any day, and, needless to say, another invitation was never forthcoming.

When another summer came, I took my walks and bike rides in other directions. In time, I almost—*almost*—forgot the summer Jackson Lee Fraser had been my friend. I had wanted to forget. Even now, I felt the shame as deeply as if it had happened only yesterday. That was the first time I had ever openly and consciously snubbed and betrayed someone. I hope it is the last. The memory of my betrayal still hurts. It was one of the few things I never shared with either of my parents. No wonder I had felt such a pang when Anthony had mentioned the Fraser house, for the mentioning had brought back memories I had pushed aside long ago.

Reluctantly, I closed the newspaper files and left the office of *The Dalton Journal*. I hadn't gained any information pertinent to my father's death. If something came to mind later, I could always go back and look again. As I drove the short stretch from the newspaper office to the public library, I wondered how much of my childhood I had pushed out of my mind. Until prompted unexpectedly, I hadn't let Jack enter my conscious mind for years. How much else was I keeping back? If all else fails, perhaps I could find someone I trusted to hypnotize me and bring forth things about that summer I may have pushed aside, maybe something that could prove helpful.

But that would have to be later. Right now, there was no one I was willing to trust. Not just yet.

The library yielded me little more than the newspaper office had. Looking through the high school annuals was amusing, but not greatly edifying. There were collections of scrapbooks put together by different civic clubs, then donated to the library for storage and/or information. However, there was little there that I had not already gleaned from the newspaper files.

"You seem perplexed," said the kindly, silver-haired librarian in attendance. "Is there something I can help you with?"

"Probably not," I said with a shake of my head, "since I'm not completely sure what I want. I've been trying to do some research. History of Dalton—even the county—but not the *original* history. I assume that history would be easy to come by. What I need is information on culture and socioeconomic changes in the past two decades."

"I see. Well, the type of records you've just looked at is about the best we can offer in that regard. Through the newspaper clippings and high school annuals, one gets an overview of the changes in clothing and hairstyles, grocery prices, that sort of thing. How one would get actual statistics on changes in attitudes and habits . . . well I just don't know how it could be ascertained with any accuracy."

"It's hard to explain what I do need, but I'm not doing an exposé. It's just a fun type of human interest article, rather than a deadly serious one."

My, how easily the lies came, once I put my mind to it!

They rolled out, one after the other. Suddenly, I recalled something I had once been told: A liar needs a very good memory. Now those vague words had meaning. It would be all too easy to forget what story I had told whom.

She looked at me very keenly and I do believe her somewhat faded blue eyes were dancing. "I'll make you a list."

"A list?"

"Why, yes, of people you might interview. There are people here who have made this town's happenings their lives, one might almost say. They are good chroniclers and I don't doubt that they could provide you with valuable information of any type you might need—scandalous or harmless, either one."

"Are you one of those people?"

"Me? Heavens, no! I've only lived in Dalton fourteen years. One has to be born here, and preferably at least a third or fourth generation product, to qualify as a real Daltonian. I'm still regarded with great suspicion, a virtual newcomer."

Laughing, I said, "You're wonderful."

"Scarcely. By the way, I'm Lucinda Platt."

"Pleased to meet you. I'm Devin Hollister . . . and newer here than you. Less than two months, in fact. I'm interning at the hospital."

"How nice! It's so wonderful to see the opportunities girls have now. But I thought . . ."

"The research? A hobby. It has nothing to do with my work or medical studies."

We chatted pleasantly for a while, then Lucinda Platt went to her ancient oak desk to make the list for me. No wonder she had not looked familiar to me. I had searched her face from time to time ever since I had entered the library, but her features had brought nothing to mind. However, the name Platt . . . that was something else. My dentist had been named Platt. A distinguished, white-haired gentleman who had seemed quite ancient to me. His wife had had a stroke and died suddenly about a year before I had left Dalton. It seemed likely Miss Lucinda was a second wife he had brought to town from parts unknown. I wondered how I could find out without betraying that I knew her husband, then decided I simply could not. If she did not offer information that made it clear, undoubtedly some other time I could find out from another source without arousing too much suspicion. Probably there was a way to easily bring up the subject now, but a way I was still too unskilled at this game to know. For the first time in my life, I gave appreciative thoughts in the direction of detectives and spies and such. Being devious and clever and always on one's toes is hard work.

Lucinda Platt handed me a list of three names, addresses, and telephone numbers on a piece of lined tablet paper. Her writing was very clear and meticulous.

"You used to be a schoolteacher?" I ventured.

Now it was her turn to laugh out loud. "Am I that transparent?"

"Not you, just your handwriting. A teacher for sure, and an elementary teacher, no doubt. You had to keep your penmanship clear as an example to those you taught, right?"

"Right, my dear. And now that I no longer teach, I find I simply *cannot* write carelessly. Old habits are hard to break, that sort of thing."

"I know. You've been most kind. I really appreciate these names and will be getting in touch with them soon. Thanks again for your time and help."

She waved her hand in a sign of dismissal. "No problem at all. Breaks a dull day. When you get this article published, just see that we get a copy here."

"Fine, I'll do that," I said, feeling like a louse. To clear my conscience, I could see that I might have to do an article of some sort and present it to Miss Lucinda for approval. I would hate for her to know that I'm such a liar. I liked her tremendously.

Outside in the sunlight, I studied the list the librarian had given me. Lucien Stuart. Mathilda Clairmont. And Virginia McVeigh. All names and faces well-known to me. Of all of them, I knew Stuart the least well, and felt there was little chance he would recognize me. He was Dalton's artist-in-residence. His crude, yet curiously lifelike, drawings of the town and its residents of the town and its residents were prized statewide. Having been away, I wasn't sure if his fame had ever spread much beyond the state borders. Why, he must be at least eighty... another factor in my favor if he still had all of his faculties. Mathilda Clairmont was also a possibility. Her claim to fame was not her artwork, but her tongue and her memory, both razor sharp. Never having worked outside the home a day in her life, Mrs. Clairmont's work, she felt, was knowing everyone else's business. I had always hated it as a child when she had stopped me on the street or in a store and began prying for information about my parents. Happily our encounters had been few and brief, but memorable... still, I doubted that she would recognize me. The third name on this list... Miss McVeigh, there was no way I could go to unless I was ready to "confess" and take her into my confidence. Like Lucinda Platt, she had been a teacher most of her adult life. Most particularly, she had been a third grade teacher... and specifically my third grade teacher. I fancied the amount of years and change of name would make no difference to Miss McVeigh's odd greenish eyes. She had always been able to penetrate through to my innermost thoughts. One look at me and I had no doubt she'd see Katie Clark... that is, unless senility had claimed her, and surely Mrs. Platt would not have listed her if that were the case.

With a sigh, I folded the list and put it in a special compartment in my handbag. When I had the opportunity, I just might contact some of Mrs. Platt's people. Mostly, it was a matter of timing. As distasteful as I found gossips like Mathilda Clairmont, I had to admit that someone like her could be invaluable. In a small town like Dalton, tongues must have wagged themselves frantically with speculations when one of the town's most solid and leading citizens shot himself.

Despite my growing frustration and dejection, I recognized that the day was a glorious one... so glorious that I could almost have kicked myself for not going trail exploring with Anthony Toretta. After a stop at a convenience store, I drove to the city park and sat for a while on a bench, sipping cola and munching a candy bar, and feeling slightly sorry for myself.

Sitting there, a slight wind ruffling my hair, a breeze that was pure and clean, a completely different quality from the air I knew in Boston, I tried delving into my mind. I felt I needed to know my own motives. Why could I not let this matter rest? It had happened a decade and a half ago. If, by some miracle—and it was beginning to look as if it might take a miracle—I unearthed enough information to prove that my father had not killed himself, well . . . what did I think would change? Dad wasn't coming back to me. He never could, not after that day. Whether his death had been by accident or design, his life had been cut short. Nothing would change that. And if I found his life had been taken from him, what then? That was the scary part. There was no statute of limitations on murder. But how far was I prepared to go to discover the truth? I was obviously the only one who cared. Dad had been an only child. His parents were both dead. Close friends and other relatives, well . . . as I kept telling myself, it *had* been a long time. New information would attract some attention for a while, but others connected with him years ago had made their way without him. I certainly expected no thanks from Mother for anything I might find out. Mother is not a confrontational person. She had, at least on the surface, been able to put the past aside. She seemed content in her life with Charlie. And I am not sure that there is a place now for the truth in her life.

My mullings brought me no great insight into myself. It was just something I had to do, that's all. No matter how harsh or cruel, or even dangerous, the truth might prove to be, I had to try to elicit it.

"Tell me, what else do you see?"

I had asked Dad that as we walked along, me almost having to run to match my stride to his. My hair, still as pale as wheat, was in a single braid down my back, but my bangs were due for a trim and blew in the wind, whipping into my eyes, and I had to keep pushing them back. Dad wore jeans and a forest green polo shirt that I had picked out for his last birthday. He was, at that point, the most important person in my life. Of course I loved my mother, but it was my father to whom I listened . . . and to my father that I was mostly likely to pour out my heart or share my confidences. And so it was that I waited impatiently for his answer. It was just an idle conversation, a game almost that we made up as we walked. Even so, it was significant to me, as all things involving him were.

"A sign on the door that says: James S. Clark, M.D., and Devin M. Clark, M.D."

And I can remember him, that last afternoon, challenging me to a race home from the hospital. Fair to a fault, he hadn't immediately bolted, but waited for me to get in gear. He had let me take the lead initially, but then passed me easily, leaving me to gaze ahead at that shirt, a shirt the color of four-leaf clovers—but evidently not as lucky.

I did not even realize that I was crying until the tears dripped down onto my hands. I looked at them in surprise, thinking the blue sky had somehow betrayed me.

"You all right, honey?" a kind stranger asked in passing.

"Sure," I said, doing my best to smile. "Just being silly, I guess."

"Silly? I wouldn't say so. Tears have their place and purpose."

Nodding, I smiled and then dug into my handbag for a tissue. In a flash, I knew why I had to complete this quest. If my father had gone in that house right after that conversation, knowingly put a gun to his head, and pulled the trigger, then my whole childhood was a lie, my memories of him were lies . . . and *he* was a lie. I had cherished him in life and I have cherished his memory all these years, but if he left me willingly, I have cherished a lie. The anger wants to break through whenever I permit myself to even consider that this might have been the case. I cannot bring him back, but I feel I have to know my memories are not lies. *"We have days and days ahead of us,"* he had said. But we hadn't had. Time had run out. We just didn't know it.

After blowing my nose in a vigorous and decidedly undignified fashion, I deposited my trash in the barrel provided for that purpose, buckled myself into the Mustang, and headed toward ABC.

"You look different . . . and comfortable," said Marian Dibbler, the director of Medical Records, smiling at my casual, maybe even sloppy, attire.

"How far back are records kept?" I asked, although I think I already knew the answer.

"Why, forever. From the time the doors were open, I suppose. It's all on microfilm, of course. The actual records aren't kept over two years these days. As we become more and more crowded, the life span of the actual paper record itself is very, very limited. What kind of old records did you need, Dr. Hollister?"

"Records covering the year of 1979, maybe 1978," I told her, as I had explained to both Diane and Lucinda earlier in the day.

"Not ancient," she said, heaving a sigh of relief. "I shudder when they come in wanting full records from the forties and fifties. Those are in what we call the crypt . . . very hard to get to. Can you work the microfiche machine?"

"Yes, ma'am."

"Then come with me to the storage room and you can look to your heart's content."

She led me to the basement. The door she unlocked was for a huge and strictly utilitarian room at what had to be one of the most far-reaching areas of the entire hospital. At one point, to get there, we actually had to exit the main building, cross through a physicians' parking garage, and reenter the building. The linoleum was stained and brown with age. We were below ground level so there were no windows. The light switch turned on bare light bulbs uncovered by decorative fixtures to break their glare.

When she saw me taking in my surroundings, she smiled and patted me on the shoulder. "This job has its drawbacks. But we don't complain when we have to come here . . . believe me, the crypt is much, much worse."

"I don't expect to be here long in any event. Thanks for everything."

"We'll all be leaving soon from our department. A key isn't needed to get out. I just ask that you make sure the door is locked as you leave."

She proceeded to show me how to assure that the old-fashioned door was locked. I agreed to exercise the utmost care. She then left me to my own devices, the heavy metal door closing behind her. I turned to the task at hand with a reluctant sigh. It is so hard to look for pertinent findings when you have no idea what is pertinent and what is not.

Through it all, I worked with such a feeling of pressure, like being under a weight so great that it threatened to crush me. At this point in time, my primary goal is—as it must be—to become a doctor. Although I would have hated to admit it aloud to Mother and Charlie, I was having more and more moments when I doubted the wisdom of combining my internship with this other quest. The internship allowed me so little time, and thus I had to make each moment count that I did have off. In my mind's eye, I kept seeing the hurt on Anthony's face—and somehow that hurt became my own. I had allowed myself no time for friends, no time for fun, no time for relaxation. With a sigh, I pushed aside the feelings of self-pity that threatened to engulf me. The decision had been mine. Quite possibly, it was the right decision. I could not have it all. My first priority was the internship. My second priority was to find out more about my father's death. The rest could wait. A year is not forever. With that in mind, I put my mind to the task at hand, and soon I was so engrossed in my work that all else was forgotten.

Chapter Seven

Since there was no one to see me and accuse me of boredom in their presence, I made no attempt to hide my yawns, just let them have their way. I glanced at my watch and saw that I had stayed later than I had intended to. It was going to mean rushing to get home and changed before Anthony arrived. On the microfiche machine, I had made copies of some of the old records. My choosings had been somewhat random. I had made copies of cases in which my father had been involved during the six months or so prior to his death. I selected unusual cases, cases in which the patients did not survive, and a few uneventful cases because I had heard him mention the names. What I had was probably nothing, but I had to start somewhere. I kept reminding myself that I had the majority of a year left. In that length of time, more pieces of the puzzle would appear and I could, as time went by, fit them together and try to make some sense of them. "Patience is a virtue," we are always told. I won't argue with that, but it *isn't* a virtue easily developed.

I put on my jacket, folded the small stack of papers, put them inside the jacket, and then zipped the jacket up. Although it was not unusual to see interns or medical students leaving the hospital with papers in their hands, I did not want to risk some sharp-eyed person noticing what I had and asked questions.

I tried the door. Nothing happened. The knob did not turn. Unbelieving, I tried again. And again and again. No matter what twisting and turning maneuvers I employed, the knob did not move. I felt rather foolish at my own helplessness. Nevertheless, after a few more futile attempts, I had to admit that I was, indeed, helpless. I pounded on the heavy door, but there was no response to my pounding. I looked around for a telephone with which to call someone to come and open the door from outside. But there was no telephone, nor was there any type of communicating device.

Time after time, I pounded on the door and hollered at the top of my lungs and, time after time, there was no response to my efforts. I knew there were surely people moving around out there, at least occasionally. Medical Records was one of the very few areas in the hospital that did not have to staff around the clock. However, it did not matter if there were people there if I could not make them hear me and thus turn them into my rescuers.

When the skin of one knuckle cracked open and began to bleed, I had sense enough to stop my vigorous pounding. It was obvious that the heavy fire door was keeping the sounds on my side, and a surgeon, even a mere budding one, did not need damaged hands. There had to be another way. I took a deep breath, then perched myself back on the stool used at the microfiche machine. I looked all around, surveyed my options . . . that is, lack of options. Unless there was something I was overlooking, and I didn't see how there could be, I had to face the fact that I was stuck here until I was missed and a hospital-wide search was undertaken or until someone needed to use this room again . . . whichever came first.

I looked at my watch again and saw it was now just fifteen minutes until Anthony Toretta would appear at my apartment and find me not there. I tried to guess what his reaction would be. Would he shrug, turn away, and decide that wishy-washy Devin had merely not shown up on purpose . . . or would he say to himself, "Nah, Devin wouldn't do that, I'd better go look for her?" It struck me how little I knew of his character. Or of my own, for that matter. If the shoe had been on the other foot, if I had been able to be ready and waiting and he did not appear, would I try to locate him, or would I retreat into hurt and/or anger? Uncomfortably, I rather imagined my own decision would be the latter. My only hope at getting out of here before the night was over was that Anthony was more trusting and less pigheaded than I was . . . or more in love.

Time ticked on. At one point, I cried. The frustration was such that the tears could no longer be held back . . . and why try? There was no one present to witness my moment of weakness. When the tears were spent, I withdrew the packet from my light jacket and rescanned the material. Since nothing there held any clues, I went back to looking through the old files . . . futile, I supposed, but at least it passed the time.

It was fifteen minutes past eight when I turned off the machine. I had found very little else worth copying and I was tired, bored, and angry. Just a few seconds after I had restored the packet of papers to my jacket, I heard something and whirled around to face the metal door. Sure enough, it was opening. For a moment, I knew fear. I *had* been threatened and that fact put my imagination in high gear.

"It seems unlikely . . ." said a male voice I did not know.

"I know," said a familiar voice, "but we've tried about everyplace else, and she has to be here. Her car is in the parking lot."

"Anthony," I screamed and ran straight for his arms.

Laughing softly, he smoothed my hair, and said, "If I'd known it would get this kind of reaction, I would have locked you up long ago."

"It's been awful," I said, my voice catching in a near-sob although I had commanded it to be calm. "It's such a dismal room and I was so bored and cold and beginning to wonder if I'd be here all night long."

"You're okay, Dr. Hollister?" asked the burly maintenance man, the one who hadn't thought there was any point in looking here for me.

"I'm fine," I said, giving him my best try at a smile. "I have no idea how it happened."

The man shrugged. "I guess whoever let you in here accidentally locked you in."

Stepping away from the circle of Anthony's arms, I reinspected the latching apparatus of the door. I shook my head and said, "Marian Dibbler did not lock me in here. I'd swear to that. She showed me how the door worked, then left. It was in this open position when she left."

"You're sure?"

"I'm positive. And so was Marian. She wasn't about to leave until she was sure I knew how to work it properly."

"That sounds right. Marian is . . . uh . . ."

"Meticulous?"

He grinned. "I guess so. I was going to say picky, but your word sounds better. Well, I'm just glad you're okay. I'll go along now. Just make sure the lights are out and the door relocked when you're ready to leave."

"I'm ready now," I said quickly, then stepped outside the door and reached back in to switch off the lights. Together, the three of us ascertained that the door was locked. Jangling his keys, the hospital employee went on his way, and Anthony and I were left staring at each other in the physicians' parking garage . . . mostly desolate now, since most of the "real" doctors don't have to work at night and had taken their Porsches and BMWs and gone home.

"Your face is dirty," he said gently.

"And we've missed our reservation at Fraser's." I realized with a pang that I was sorry, that on some level of consciousness I had been looking forward to the experience.

"I called and cancelled. When I went to pick you up and you weren't there, I didn't know what to think, so I went back home. I called a couple of times and, when there was no answer, I called the restaurant and gave them our regrets."

"When did you decide to look for me?"

"Oh, not until an hour or so ago," he said, looking and sounding as if he felt foolish. "I was hurt and angry that you had stood me up, so I just went home and pouted. But that wasn't a lot of fun and I was restless. Having nothing else to do, I drove by here. I saw your car in the parking lot. I came in to have it out with you, see maybe if you'd been called in on an emergency or something before I blew a gasket. But no one said they'd called you in, and no one had seen you. So I started looking. I almost didn't. I thought maybe I was making a fool of myself, that you'd parked your car and gone off with someone else."

I looked directly at him and we did not say a word, no name was mentioned, but the presence of Paul Linden hovered in the air.

"Well, obviously, I didn't."

He touched the tip of my nose with a fingertip and smiled, "No, you didn't. What did happen, Devin?"

"I'll tell you what I know about it. But first I need to find a bathroom. And then would it be asking too much to find a place to eat? I'm famished. I had no real lunch, just candy and a Coke in the park."

"But the reservation is gone," he deadpanned.

"You've eaten?"

"Nope. First, I pouted. Next, I searched. No time for luxuries like eating."

"Then it's your turn to provide dinner. The way I look, a hamburger from a drive-in will do nicely. Please?"

Minutes later, my face washed and my hair combed, I felt presentable, if not glamorous. We located a fast-food restaurant and settled into a corner booth with burgers, fries, and colas.

"No gourmet food we could have gotten at Fraser's for twenty bucks a plate would have tasted better," I admitted. "My mother always did say I was a plebian when it came to food. She is still waiting for the day I quit smothering everything in catsup."

"She may wait the rest of her life."

I looked down at the golden brown french fries topped generously with catsup and said, "She probably will."

"And?"

From the look in his eye, I knew he was ready to hear why and how I had ended up in the records room.

"There were some old records I wanted to look up," I

said, glossing over the whys of the situation. "It was about 3:30 or so in the afternoon. I figured it would take me thirty minutes or so, they I'd buzz home and get ready for our date. They all leave in Records by 4:30, so Marian showed me how to let myself out. She closed the door and left. It was only a quarter after four when I discovered I was locked in. They weren't due to be gone yet in Records, but they had no reason to check on me. That stupid, dismal room has no phone, no window, and no connection with the intercom. Look what I did trying to pound on that fire door for attention . . . for all the good it did me."

Anthony solemnly lifted my hand to his lips and kissed the cut knuckle.

"Oddly enough, it *does* feel better."

"Nothing odd about it. It's an old family secret. We Torettas have magic power in our kisses, healing powers. Certain members of us, that is. We just try to keep it as secret as possible."

"You don't want to share your powers with the world?"

He wrinkled his nose at me. "Only under certain conditions. Maybe it's little of us, Devin, but when I was very young, I was forewarned to use my strange gift with caution."

"And why is that?" I questioned, knowing full well I was being teased.

His answer was grave quiet, and very solemn. "The magic only works with direct touch of the lips to the injured part."

I burst out laughing. "So you're going to be selective about your healing? What about the Hippocratic oath?"

"With the conventional healing techniques that I learned in school, I'll do my best to uphold that noble creed. But when it comes to old Italian family secrets, well, I feel that is up to *my* discretion."

"I see. And do you think you'll incorporate this into your medical practice in some way? If so, the word might get around that Dr. Toretta heals boo-boos *so* quickly."

He shrugged. "That remains to be seen. I'll use it

some, most assuredly."

"Does it work on major injuries or just little things?"

"No injury is so great, unless mortal, of course, that it will not yield to the touch of a blessed Toretta's lips. No need for stitches and splints and such."

"Can you explain the principle?"

"Only when you explain laser surgery to me. I'm a practitioner in both areas, Devin. Not a scientist. One cannot see the lasers, but one learns to utilize them. The same is true of the Toretta touch."

"You win. I give up."

"Great. I like to win. Ice cream?"

"Why not? For just this one time, calories be hanged! I'm still famished. I think my imagination worked overtime and I have myself psyched up to believe I was locked up for days, instead of a very few hours. But, believe me, my hips will know the difference."

Anthony's brown eyes regarded me quizzically. "You don't have a tendency toward anorexia, do you?"

"New to me if I do. Why the question?"

"You sounded so sincerely concerned over the calories and you're thin as a rail."

Smiling, I said, "I know. Carry-over, I guess. I haven't had a problem for a long time, but I *was* a bit of a chunk for a while as a child. It worried my mother a lot and she did a lot of fussing over me and trying to keep me on a diet. Being a perverse child, I resented it instead of being grateful for her care and concern and all that. When she wasn't looking, I ate everything in sight. Most of my allowance went for junk food. Not that I liked being fat . . . but I don't know. It might be interesting to hear what an analyst would have to say on the subject. As I told you before—I did, didn't I—Mother was always so svelte and beautiful. I suffered in comparison. Knowing I could never be like that, I didn't try . . . I just pigged out constantly."

"And? Tell me the rest of this saga. You somewhere down the road developed a full-blown case of bulimia?"

"Not exactly," I said, laughing. "Fortunately, things never got to that point. What happened was a burst of adolescent growth. Between the ages of eleven and fourteen, I outgrew a complete wardrobe every six months. For a while, I was truly worried I was going to be a giant ... I think my folks even wondered if I might be right in my worry, but, bless their hearts, they never let on. I just shot up through all the fat and flab and, thus far, it's never caught up with me again. And here's hoping it never will. Such a boring story. But you *did* ask. Inside me, there's this fat little girl who feels a burst of guilt at even looking at a marshmallow sundae."

"You're talking more than usual," he said with a grin.

Looking into his expressive brown eyes, I felt a strange sensation come over me. "It's because I'm nervous and scared," I admitted in a voice not quite my own.

"It was just an accident, Devin."

"Was it? I'm not so sure."

"Talk about paranoia," he began, then looking at me closely, he let the joke fade away. "You're serious, aren't you?"

I had to tell someone. I had to trust someone. Anthony was from another state and there was no way he could have connections with *my* past. He had such lovely eyes and eyes like that could not lie.

Between spoonfuls of ice cream, I told him the whole story. He listened gravely and intently, occasionally asking a question for his own clarification to keep the tale straight in his mind.

"And you didn't keep these notes?"

"A real airhead, aren't I? To be honest, the thought didn't even strike me until after I had destroyed the last one. I was angry and frustrated, and I totally demolished it. As it scattered in the wind while I stood there in the ABC parking lot wondering if I dared get in my car and turn on the engine or not, it struck me that I had destroyed my proof that I was being threatened."

He shrugged. "We all do things like that. It goes with hindsight being better than foresight and all that, I guess. And you truly have no idea who might be here in Dalton that knows who you really are?"

I shook my head, but also managed a laugh. "'Who I

really am.' That makes me sound so mysterious. I *am* really Devin Hollister. That's the name I've used for fourteen years. It's legally mine. Little Katie Clark is a lifetime away."

"Is she?"

Tears formed in my eyes at the gentleness of his voice. "No. No, that isn't true. She isn't a lifetime away. She's still me, a part of me. The little girl I was will always have something to do with who I am now, or who I become in the future."

"It isn't that I doubt what you say, Devin, because I don't. But I'm still having a hard time understanding today. You told *no* one what you were doing, you say?"

"No one at all . . . including you. When I was at the newspaper office, I mentioned going to the library next. And I did tell the women at both places that I worked at the hospital, but I most certainly did not tell them I was headed that way to do more research. No one could have known *why* I went to the records room. People use it a lot to look up really old records on patients for one reason or another. Since I hadn't *told* anyone what I was doing, someone just guessed or . . ."

"Yes?" he prodded when my silence went on too long.

"Maybe it didn't matter *what* I was doing there. Someone saw me go in . . . someone connected with the prior notes and call . . . and decided it was time for another scare, and thus took the opportunity to lock me in."

"You could be right. But there was no overt warning. Wouldn't they have definitely wanted you to know what was behind locking you in? It would be so easy to regard it all as a mistake . . . Marian thinking you were gone and locking it or something."

"I plan on asking her tomorrow, but I think I know the answer to that one. And I don't know that I haven't been sent an 'overt' warning. I haven't been to my car. I haven't been home. I may well have another note, or get another call. It's getting to me, Anthony. It's giving me the willies."

An involuntary shudder shook my body . . . a small

and short-lasting tremor, but a very unpleasant one.

"I can see that," he said kindly. "Bottoms up. Let's go check this out. I'll go with you to your car. Then I'll follow you home and help you check that. I can even wait for a while, if there's been nothing else, and see if there's a call."

"Nice thought, and I'll accept your invitation to go with me to the car and the apartment. But there isn't a whole lot of point in sitting around with me and waiting for the phone to ring. If I'm really being watched closely, it probably wouldn't ring until you were gone."

"Hey, I could stick around there indefinitely. I don't have to go home tonight at all. Say the word and I'm yours for the night."

"I threw what was meant to be a withering look his way and said, "I assume that was a joke. I'm going to treat it as such."

"Far be it from me," he said airily, "to stand in the way of your sense of humor. Make of it what you will. My aching heart can bear the pain."

"It wasn't a joke?"

He grinned. "Yeah, sure. But, on the other hand, what is it that's always said . . . many a true word is spoken in jest, or something like that. Ready to go scout this out?"

Pushing aside the empty ice cream dish, I sighed, then slid out the booth. In truth, I did not want to go. I wanted to sit in the homey little restaurant with Anthony, making corny jokes, and stuffing my face with food I really didn't even want. Whatever was out there, I didn't want to think about it.

Anthony accompanied me to my car in the parking lot and a scanning of both of us failed to reveal any evidence of messages or tampering. With that, I breathed a sigh of relief. Maybe—just maybe—being locked up in the out-of-the-way records room had been an accident of some sort. Finding that out might make me feel a bit foolish, but, considering the alternative, I'd rather feel foolish than afraid.

I led the way to my apartment in my car and Anthony followed in his. By the time we reached there, I had quite convinced myself that today's happening was an accident and that I had let my nerves and imagination run amok. I was so convinced that I was almost back to being lighthearted.

Together we crossed the lawn, walked up the steps, and I turned my key in the door. "And what shall we find inside?" I asked, my voice mockingly low and solemn. "Will it be that the phantom has struck again?"

I pushed open the door. It took a while for things to register. "I'd say he has definitely struck," Anthony said. There was nothing mocking about his voice or manner.

"Oh, my God, no!"

"Hang on, Devin. Don't fall apart on me. I think it's not as bad as it looks. Come on in and look it over, but just stay calm."

Everything was where it shouldn't be . . . furniture out of place, throw pillows on the floor, lamp shades knocked askew, the drawers from the study desk in the front room.

As soon as the light had been turned on and the door pushed open, I had been horror-struck. But the longer I looked, the more I understood what Anthony meant. It looked a mess, but no real harm seemed to have been done. On cursory exam, nothing was missing and nothing was really broken. In reality, it didn't even look as if much of a search had been conducted. Even though the drawers had been pulled out, the contents of the drawers were undisturbed.

"It's another warning, isn't it? They haven't really hurt anything. They're just saying, 'See what we did . . . and next time it might be more.' You think?"

"Exactly. Devin, how important is it to you to keep up the search for information about your father?"

"How can I back down? What can I do? Anthony, I haven't done any real snooping. From the beginning, my plan was to get to know people first, to keep my ties with Dalton and Dr. Clark hidden. Whoever is doing this wants me out of Dalton, out of Albert B. Creighton. How can I do that? I have no place now to transfer to intern this year. If I leave now, just take off, it might be this time next year before I can get accepted somewhere else. You're in the same position I am. Would you want to be scared off and lose a year? I came here to intern. I have to stay for that. Can't you see that?"

"Most definitely. I understand what you're saying. If you don't stick it out here until August, you've probably lost the whole year. And you're right . . . medical school is too long and too hard for you, or any of us, to start having delays at this point."

"So what can I do? Take an ad out in *The Dalton Journal* classifieds that makes a public statement that I promise not to make inquiries into the death of Dr. James Clark?"

"When you put it that way, there doesn't seem to be much you can do."

"Right. So I'm going to put this place back together, take a hot bath, go to bed with a good book, and try to forget this day ever happened."

"What about the police?"

"Forget it," I said shortly. "No real harm was done. We'd sound like idiots. There's nothing but my 'imagination' to connect this with the other incidents . . . and there's no note, no hard evidence."

Nodding, he then began helping straighten up my apartment. When we were done, he said, "I was kidding before. But I'm not now. Let me stay. Nothing romantic. But you can't feel good about being here alone."

"Truth is, I *don't* feel good about it. But I'd better get used to it. You're sweet to offer and I appreciate it. But, after tonight, what then? We won't often have time off at the same time. I'll have lots of hours I need to spend here when you have to be at the hospital. As badly as we may want to, we can't stick together."

"Maybe not physically. But we *can* stick together emotionally." Leaning forward, he kissed me lightly on the forehead. "I'll go now. Sleep well, kid. Call if you need anything."

"Thanks for everything," I said. Funny how I felt that the kiss on the forehead wasn't enough. I needed his arms around me. But since I was in no way sure if the desire had to do with emerging feelings for Anthony or the basic need for security, I did not give in to my weakness. I did not want to hurt him. Nor did I want to be hurt. That meant I'd have to stand on my own, forgoing the luxury of embraces at this point.

"You don't have an answering machine, do you?"

"No, why?"

"Get one. Whoever this is might call. You get it on tape, you got some proof. And some clues. Okay?"

"Good idea. I'll find the time to pick one up tomorrow. Again, thanks for everything."

"Hey, no thanks required. No sweat. See you around."

And so I was alone. It was an eerie feeling, considering everything. A fine mess I had landed myself in. If Mother only knew . . . well, Mother would enjoy saying, "I told you so." But Mother doesn't know, and I was going to keep it that way.

Chapter Eight

Very tentatively, as had become my habit, I reached my hand into the "box" designated as mine in the doctors' library.

"There isn't a snake in there, is there, Hollister?" asked Chris Palmer, one of my fellow interns.

Feeling myself flush, I struggled to act with composure even though I felt quite foolish. Taking care had become a habit, one I hadn't meant to adopt. Never knowing what I might find anywhere, I had become most tentative quite involuntarily.

"Would you believe tarantulas?" I remarked lightly. "Once you've been the victim of a practical joke, you watch where you put your hand."

"Someone put a tarantula in your mailbox as a joke?"

"No, of course not. Let's just say it was something about as unpleasant, even if not quite so dangerous."

"I gather from that you're not going to tell me what . . . or whom."

"As for the 'what,' there are still some things, in this day and age even, that are best left unmentioned in mixed company of short acquaintance. And, as to the 'whom,' I'm still searching. But when I find out . . ."

"You'll let me know?"

"Just check the front page of the local paper . . . murder makes news in a small town like this."

And so the moment passed without further questioning. There was, of course, nothing amiss in the box.

There had only been the one note there, nothing since. I sat down for a moment on one of the leather sofas and began looking through the reports and messages. Chris Palmer was doing the same. His blond head was bent toward the papers. From time to time, I caught the glimmer of a smile on his face. Someday this would be old hat, this thrill of seeing your name as having dictated a history on a patient, of seeing your name listed as first assistant on a surgery. But for now Chris was glorying in it, and I could identify with that. Even with all I had on my mind, I still felt a slight thrill at the realization that I was almost a doctor, almost the real thing, just a small step away from being a student to being an M.D., *Dr. Hollister.*

Maybe I had been wrong to change my name legally. Charlie would have understood if I had said I wanted to keep my father's name. In an effort to put the past behind me, and also out of a deep numbness in that period of my life, I had *wanted* change. Out of the changes, my mother had apparently achieved some level of forgetfulness. I had not. Now I could never be Dr. Clark. But, no, that wasn't true either. No name was permanent unless you wanted it to be. It was a matter of where my loyalty lay.

"Hey, Hollister?" said Chris Palmer in an effort to get my attention.

Hollister . . . yes, Hollister I shall remain. Unless, perhaps, something happens to Charlie before I set up practice—and God forbid that that should occur. Not knowing what the afterlife is like, I have no idea if changing my name back would please my father or not, or if he was hurt or understanding when I had first changed it. That was all rhetorical, all guesswork, all imagination. Charlie was on this earth with me and I *knew* he would be very hurt if I changed my name back to Clark. He would be kind, supportive, and understanding . . . and, beneath it all, hurt. I could not do that to him. As long as I was alive, my first loyalty had to be to the living.

"You overly tired or something, huh? I've said your name three times now."

"Sorry," I said with a smile. "Not so much tired

as . . . I don't know . . . spring fever, I guess."

"This is the end of September."

"And so it is. But I've never heard of autumn fever."

"So, maybe you're suffering from dog days fever."

"Dog days? Is that a genuine syndrome, or what?"

"A syndrome, Hollister? I don't think so. I think—but I'm not positive—that dog days are when it's especially hot—and terribly humid along with it—for days and days on end. It makes people lethargic. Nothing official like a 'syndrome,' just folklore or something."

"Okay, Palmer. Maybe I do have dog-dayitis, but you *do* have my attention now, so what was it you wanted to say to me?"

"These reports we get . . . you ever see any mistakes on them?"

Laughing, I said, "Oh, some. Typing what we say can't be an easy job. I try not to be too picky. I just like to look at my name there, so official-like. Warms the cockles of the heart, doesn't it?"

"Name the exact anatomic location of the cockles," he challenged.

"Adjacent to the posterior cusp of the right atrioventricular valve."

"I'll be damned. No lie?"

"No lie," I said solemnly.

With anyone else, especially with Anthony, the conversation would probably have gotten sillier and sillier. With Chris, it stopped right there . . . and it probably wouldn't have gotten even *that* funny with the fourth one of us, David Francis. Closer acquaintance with them had merely proven my initial character assessment to be accurate. Nice guys, both of them, highly intelligent, higly motivated, and undoubtedly destined to be credits to the field of medicine . . . and both so totally self-absorbed that they could forget in the blink of an eye that anyone else existed.

Chris glanced at the copy of the operation report on the top of my stack.

"I'm on Linden's service next."

"I know," I said, not ready for the pangs of regret I

felt. I wasn't ready to give up being on surgery, and with Paul Linden; however, as I had known from the beginning, I would work on several different services while at Creighton, and my few weeks with Paul were nearly over . . . just a few more days and I would move on to Emergency Department services for a month or so.

"What's he like?"

"A brilliant surgeon."

"I know that," he said, giving me a withering glance. "I meant, what is he like to work for?"

"Exacting but fair."

"You like him?"

"Dr. Palmer," came a voice from the doorway, "quit putting your cohort on the spot. Whether she likes me or not is neither here nor there. She spoke the truth . . . I'm exacting but fair. You'll find out everything else you need to know in October."

"Yes, sir," Palmer said, obviously quite discomfited.

"Lighten up, Palmer."

"Yes, sir. I'll try sir."

With that, he beat a hasty retreat out of the library.

"Does he think this is the military?"

Smiling, I said, "I doubt it. As you said, he just needs to lighten up. Who was it that said, 'Life is too important to be taken seriously?'"

"I have no idea. Probably Shakespeare, Ben Franklin, or Abraham Lincoln. Among them they had all the good sayings."

"Actually, I think maybe it was Oscar Wilde."

"Could be. Come to think of it, he had a lot to say, too."

"Definitely. And then there's always Andy Warhol."

Paul laughed. "You only have a few more days on my service. I think I'm going to miss you."

"You only 'think' so? Well, do let me know when you know for sure." I kept my voice arch and light, not an easy feat when you stopped to consider the way my pulse had taken off. It was beating so rapidly that I was glad no one was likely to take my vital signs. Surely my blood pressure was in an abnormal state also. "Seriously, I'm sure the other three interns are very competent. I've been favorably impressed by them all. Each very different from the other, but top-of-the-list caliber."

"Oh, I agree, Dr. Hollister, quite," he said, his tone telling me I wasn't the only one who could be controlled, be so purposely lighthearted. "I've heard nothing but good reports on all the young men. But I've been wondering if they'll have your repartee."

I considered that for a moment. Anthony would come the closest. The other two were far, far too serious, and too uptight, to spar with a physician of Linden's experience and reputation. "Possibly not. I always was a smart aleck. It didn't come with the degree. But I didn't know repartee was a qualification."

"Oh, it isn't. Just a very nice side benefit. Like long legs and a dazzling smile."

"You're making me blush," I said in protest.

"Dr. Hollister, *everything* makes you blush. You think I haven't noticed that?"

His comments served to intensify my already crimson face. "Please, stop."

"You really want me to?"

That *was* a pertinent question, and one to which the answer did not come easily.

"I'm not good at this sort of game, Dr. Linden. As a doctor, I'm very sure of myself—while still realizing my limitations. But when it comes to this sort of thing, I guess I've got a lot to learn. I never know what's teasing and what's not."

"We men do that. Then if you women tell us to buzz off, we can always say, 'Didn't you know I was just putting you on?' Handy technique, isn't it?"

"Possibly."

"Devin, I don't know if what I'm about to do breaks any rules or not. And I really don't care. I enjoy your company. After the end of the week, we won't see each other professionally nearly as much. That means that, if I want to keep seeing you, I have to make other arrangements. I know you work long hours. So do I. But I'd still like to take you out to dinner, or even to lunch, soon. Fraser's Inn is nice. Have you been there?"

Swallowing hard, I felt a struggle going on inside me. I wanted this too much, but my own sense of excitement was warning enough to me in and of itself.

"A friend and I almost went," I said slowly, "then something happened and we had to cancel the reservation. I'd like to go there. And I think you realize I like being with you. But . . ."

His voice was barely audible. "But I'm married, right?"

"There is that," I said, and knew I was trying to make his forthrightness more of a virtue than it probably was.

"I doubt that I will be much longer. I think Dru probably feels the same way. When we separated, I believe we expected to miss each other more than we do. I told you that, I think. It's bad for us. Worse for our kids. But it can't be helped. People change. Whatever your answer, Devin, I'll understand. I'm sure I'm quite old enough to be your father, a fact that would exist even if the marriage did not."

I looked directly into his eyes, then had to look away very quickly. They were blue and clear and seemed to shoot fire the way a truly excellent diamond does.

"Your age isn't a factor. And you *aren't* old enough to be my father . . . not unless you would have started at a very, very early age. It's just that you caught me by surprise. I hope I didn't act ungracious . . ."

His eyebrow shot up at that. "Ungracious? Unusual word for someone of your generation to use."

"*My* generation? Goodness, you are hung up on the age issue. I tell you again, it isn't that. I just . . ."

"I know what you mean. It's bad form. You can't believe how I've agonized on how to handle this. I had decided it was best not to make a request for a date, just to hang around and run into you here and there. But I knew all along that was junior high stuff. You and I aren't likely to run into each other outside of this place. I didn't know what I was going to do until I walked in here and it immediately hit me that, if I didn't place my bid, someone like young Palmer is likely to walk off with the prize while

I'm still sitting on the sidelines mourning about what could have been."

"Somehow, I never thought of myself as a prize," I muttered.

"And, for that bit of modesty, you are additionally prized. Devin?"

It was flattering, immensely flattering.

"I really . . ."

"If you can't, or just don't want to, for any reason at all, I'll understand, and I most certainly won't make a pest of myself. I'm strangely drawn to you and would like to get to know you better, but if you don't see it that way, I'll not bother you again in this way. And you can be assured it won't affect our working relationship. What this is not is sexual harassment. It's just an invitation. Believe me?"

I did believe him. He wasn't smooth. He acted every bit the nervous and frustrated swain. If this were a performance, then Paul was second in acting ability only to Sir Laurence Olivier.

"This is an odd experience for me. I wish . . ."

"There, I've gone and made you feel awkward. I *knew* I should have left well enough alone."

The corners of my lips trembled as I struggled to hold back my laughter. "Dr. Linden, how can you hope to ever get to know me better if you won't let me finish a sentence?"

He smiled, abashed. "I *have* been interrupting you, haven't I? Probably because I'm afraid of what you're going to say."

"What I am going to say is that, yes, I'd love to have dinner with you some evening. While I agree that this might not be wise, both for professional and other reasons, I find I *want* to go very much. One dinner. What can it hurt?"

"Exactly. When are you free?"

I sighed. "That's always a problem." Turning to the wall behind me, I checked the interns' rotation schedule. I was off on Wednesday evening of the next week. Feeling like a rat, I sneaked a look at Anthony's schedule.

He had to work that night. In fact, it didn't look as if Anthony and I had the same day off again until way into October. Anthony had wanted to take me to Fraser's Inn and I felt a stab of guilt that I had made arrangements to go there with someone else, and most especially with Paul Linden. I knew Anthony, probably sensing my feelings for Paul, was jealous of him already. That could not be helped, I decided. I had made Anthony no promises. And, at this point, neither had I made any to Paul other than to agree to one dinner.

"Then a week from Wednesday it shall be," he said gravely, almost bashfully. "I'll call and make the reservations right away. Thank you, Devin."

"No thanks required, Dr. Linden. It's I who should thank you. It's very flattering to have you take an interest in me."

"And an interest I do seem to have taken. Given all that, do you think you could bring yourself to use my first name?"

Again that dreaded blush flooded my cheeks. "Out of here, possibly. While in ABC, I'd best stick to the protocol."

He seemed to think it over, then nodded in agreement, after which he walked out of the library without another word or a backward glance.

Over the next few days, my last on his service, it was as if the strange conversation in the library had never taken place, as if the invitation had never been offered.

We made rounds together on his surgical patients. Practically elbow to elbow, we worked in Surgery, he allowing me to do more and more and me glorying in the experience.

On Friday, his work completed, Paul was preparing to leave ABC. He was not on call for the weekend and had mentioned that he was going to take advantage of the time to see his sons, to perhaps take them into Biloxi for a sporting event or something. I, on the other hand, was scheduled to be at the hospital practically all weekend. No free time for this rookie.

"Well, Dr. Hollister, it's been great. I'll have my

secretary type up that letter of recommendation you requested early next week and get it back to you."

"No hurry. And thanks again for everything. You've taught me a lot."

Laughing, he said, "Listen to us. We sound as if we're parting."

"In a way, we are, aren't we? Unless an emergency arises now and then, I won't be the one assisting you."

"True. We won't work together again that closely on a regular basis. But emergencies do occur. That is why we have hospitals. Incidentally, you do understand how lucky we were today in surgery, don't you?"

"I probably—well, most *surely*—don't appreciate the gravity the same way you do. But I know what you mean. You were only an inch away from having to remove her gallbladder with a lot of other important organs."

From the faraway look in his eye, I could tell, or thought I could, that he was reliving every moment of that tricky operation.

Clinically, and according to the patient's history and all of her preoperative studies, she was a perfect candidate for the less-invasive surgical procedure. Nothing had prepared us to expect the extensive internal damage had nearly prevented the gallbladder from being reached.

"The patient is so young, and no surgical history at all. You ever encounter this before?"

"Not like this. Of course, I've seen more damage than this. And so, I am sure, have you."

"Sure. Like Mrs. Bantry. Well, I didn't *see* them, but you and she detailed them for me most graphically. But she was quite old and had had an extensive surgical history, whereas Barbara Harris . . ."

"Exactly. Ah, well, nothing ventured, nothing gained. She came through it fine. Poor woman wanted to avoid abdominal surgery so badly . . . I had to tell her it would be inevitable at some point in the future, that the damage would become symptomatic."

At that point, my page number was announced over the intercom.

"Duty calls."

"For me, too. And, as fascinating as gallbladders are, we can always discuss them later. Unfortunately, problems will always be around. Gardeners have weeds. We surgeons have diseases."

We surgeons? The recognition, even if gross flattery, sent a glow of pleasure through me. "And damaged tissue. There's that to contend with."

"Yes. When we're extremely lucky, we have both."

Standing there, looking at each other, each reluctant to turn and leave, I felt strangely out of time and out of place. This moment was a life in itself, an experience that was not in the least intertwined with anything else going on . . . and I was not alone in this moment. Paul and I were together, caught out of time, in an intimacy so intense it defied any explanation.

The page sounded again, breaking the mood.

"We're still on for Wednesday evening?" he asked, his voice quite gruff and unnatural, like the voice of someone coming out of a dream.

"Yes. Yes, of course we're still on." My own voice came out breathless, excited. Too aware of what I had betrayed, I turned and walked away without looking back again.

He is what I want. There is no rationale. My head tells me all the reasons this should not be: He is older. He is married. Two children are involved. He is moody and often remote. This is not a point in my life when I should become heavily involved with anyone. There were other more minor reasons, but my heart turned away from my head. I knew how I *felt* and that was all that seemed to matter. I had never thought of myself as naive and inexperienced. Life had toughened me, I thought, I had lived for many years in a busy city, a sophisticated environment. In the brash way of youth, I *knew* what I knew and was unshakable in my beliefs. I had scorned people caught up in the throes of love or lust—or the combination thereof. In that fleeting moment, I had experienced a taste of being out of control, of being so caught up with another person that sanity had nothing

to do with anything.
   It's time to run, I told myself. I have had the warning. My head knows the best course of action. But even as I talked to myself, I gave no serious consideration to breaking the dinner date.
   "We're still on?" he had asked.
   And the answer had been—and was—my breathless, "Yes, yes, yes, and yes."

Chapter Nine

I searched my meager wardrobe, but nothing I had was "sophisticated" enough. Not anticipating much of a social life, I had brought little in the way of dress-up clothes with me. I had a basic black dress and I had this turquoise sateen number with a balloon-type skirt. Looking at it, I laughed out loud despite the fact that I was very much alone. I wondered what sort of trance I had been in when I had decided to bring it along. It wasn't exactly my sort of dress, not even in Boston, and it was hard to imagine an occasion here in my Dalton life where it would be appropriate. And then I remembered.

"*Isn't this lovely, darling? I was shopping and couldn't resist getting it for you.*"

"*I appreciate the thought, Mother, but what am I to do with it?*"

"*Why, Devin, surely there will be parties . . . young people having dances. Perhaps a reception at some point for you interns. Take my word for it, you'll need something like this.*"

In my haste to get packed and ready for my new experience, I had not argued. She had placed the dress, still on its padden silken hanger and encased in tissue paper, in one of my suitcases, and I had not given it another thought, other than an initial stab of resentment that I could have used the space for another pair of boots or jeans. I had anticipated no use for turquoise sateen at that point, and did not anticipate a use for it now.

Oddly enough, the dress would have suited Mother, even given her age and the frivolous, youthful cut of the frock. It was *not* my sort of dress. My decision, perhaps partly based on resentment, was firm. That left me with no other choice than the black. At the hospital, when not wearing scrubs, I wore tailored skirts or slacks under my white "doctor's coats." Off duty, I wore, depending on the weather, shorts, jeans, or sweats. There had been no need for anything else . . . until now.

With a sigh, almost detesting myself for caring so much how I looked, I pulled the black dress off the hanger. Another of Mother's decisions. For several years now, I had had so little time and interest in clothing that she had felt compelled to do such shopping for me. Slipping the dress on, I stood before the mirror and had to admit Mother hadn't *always* been wrong. I didn't know what the dress had cost, but I could guess the general price range. It showed. On the hanger, the dress had looked limp, a real nothing. However, its cut and fabric were such that it came into its own on the human form. It looked . . . *right*. I recall Mother had once said, quoting from some source I did not know, that the proper clothes showed enough to let it be known you were a woman and hid enough to make it clear you were also a lady. This little number achieved that.

Feeling smug and satisfied with the black, I turned to my hair. Not much that could be done there. My haircut was, quite purposely, such that there was only one way it could be. No problem . . . with eye makeup, something I scarcely ever wore, and oversized earrings in the place of the tiny ones I preferred . . . I felt I looked quite formal enough.

"You look lovely," he said when I opened the door to him.

And I knew I did, maybe just for this night, but I did believe I shone. It was a mistake. Even as I made it, I recognized the mistake. At a point when I should keep one hand on the emergency brake, I was, instead, concentrating on acceleration.

The first part of the evening went well. Dalton is a

relatively small town and I felt that people looked at us... and, of course, they did look. But rather than increasing any discomfort I felt at being out with a married man, the attention served to relax me. I felt somehow comfortably defiant. Paul hadn't asked me to sneak around. He hadn't suggested dinner in an out-of-town restaurant. Obviously, he felt in the right, clear in his decision to go through with a divorce and make public his sincerity of intentions toward me. Given that, I *basked* in the craning necks and, perhaps sensing our lack of embarrassment, the other diners went on about their business.

Fraser's was delightful. Not exactly the Fraser home that I remembered, but very delightful. It had been very tastefully restored and redecorated. And it was obvious that no item had been chosen in haste. Nothing was out of sync with the period and the mood. When one walked across the white-pillared veranda, through the double doors, and into the marble-accented foyer, one entered the old South at its most gracious.

The waiters and waitresses moved unobtrusively, their uniforms in keeping with the theme without being gaudy or corny. It all came together nicely, something that had not happened by accident. The training of the personnel had been undertaken, as the decorating had been, with great meticulousness.

"Do you come here a lot?" I asked, eyes shining.

"Some. There aren't many really nice places around here. Even without the atmosphere, the food is superb. Like it?"

Nodding, I started to reply, then changed my answer. My original answer would have been a comparison to the Fraser home as I had known it as a child, something I was not yet ready to betray to Paul. Instead, I said, "I've never seen anything quite like it. It's wonderful."

"Then, as I said, wait until you've eaten the food."

The menus came and I smiled to myself at the prices. This might be little Dalton, Mississippi, but someone obviously had seen menus from Boston and New York. No wonder it didn't matter too greatly that the seating capacity was so limited. A working person could not often afford a dinner here. I wondered if Anthony had realized tht dinner for the two of us here could easily have cost him $50.00. Given the shape of his automobile and shoe leather, I did not think that such dinners were a part of his normal routine.

While we waited for the food, I looked about and took in more details of the inn. Once again, I thought about little Jackson Lee Fraser and wondered what he would think of what had been done to his childhood home. I wondered too if his maiden aunts would be appalled or delighted in the changes that had been wrought.

The food was, as Paul had said, outstanding. It was quite a change from the hospital food to which I had become accustomed. I was savoring every delicious mouthful when I was aware of someone standing behind me.

"Is everything okay here? Is the food prepared to your liking?"

"Wonderful," Paul said. "As usual, of course."

"Do let us know, Dr. Linden, if there is anything else at all that you need."

I knew that voice. It had changed, of course, in timbre, in depth, but the basic elements were there. Even before I was aware of Paul saying, "Jack, this is Dr. Devin Hollister. She's interning with us this year at Creighton," I was well aware of who I had to turn and face.

"Devin," Paul continued with his introduction, "this is Jack Fraser. He owns this place. In fact, it's his old family home. As I understand it, the house was erected by Frasers and has never left Fraser ownership."

Feeling miserable and scared, I turned and faced the childhood friend I had betrayed. As much as he had, oddly enough, occupied my thoughts lately, I had never dreamed of this.

The near-white hair of childhood had not darkened much in his case. However, it was now expertly cut and lay in smooth wings against his head. His eyesight was such that glasses could never be replaced with contacts, but the glasses now somehow suited him. His clothes, navy blazer and khaki pants, were impeccably groomed and fitted.

I saw the flash of recognition, then the immediate narrowing of the eyes and puzzlement at the announcing of my name. As much as I could, without alerting Paul, I gave him a signal for silence. "Please," I whispered when Paul's attention was away from us momentarily, "I'll catch a chance to explain."

We then went through the customary civilities with Jack not once letting on that he had ever previously laid eyes on me.

"Something wrong?" Paul asked.

"Not a thing. I'm just not used to eating this much at one time. You know how it is at the hospital. You tend to grab snacks and sandwiches when you can, rather than sit down to a full meal."

"Does this mean you don't want the dessert we've already ordered?"

Laughing, I said, "That isn't the case at all. I have to *try* the apple pan dowdy even if I can't conquer all of it. But, if you'll excuse me, I think I'll go to the ladies' room before that."

I didn't need to go to the ladies' room. I needed to see Jackson Lee Fraser. Noting that Paul wasn't really watching me from across the table, I circled back and went toward the kitchen doors.

"May I help you?" asked one of the well-trained, white-coated waiters.

"I'd like to see Mr. Fraser for just a minute. No problem. It's a personal request. I'm Dr. Hollister."

In a moment, Jack appeared at the door, gave me one long look and then escorted me into the impressive kitchen, gleaming white and very modern, equipped with every gadget possible . . . not exactly the homey kitchen in which we had shared milk and Miss Emmie's tarts.

I knew I could not stay away long without arousing Paul's curiosity. But Jack apparently did not intend to make anything easy for me. If I had expected a moment of privacy, I was a fool. Amid the hustle and bustle of the Fraser's Inn employees I would have to find a way to say what I had to say.

"You know me, don't you?"

No use pretending. His eyes mocked me. I could fool most of the adults who had known me as a child, but I couldn't fool a child I had known well. No more than Jack could have fooled me. He had changed . . . oh, yes, he had changed, and for the better physically . . . and yet he was, unmistakably and irrevokably, Jackson Lee Fraser.

"I thought I did. The name threw me until I recalled that Katie was only a nickname. But I'm willing to admit I was mistaken. You aren't Katie?"

"Would you believe it if I said I wasn't?"

He shrugged. "I'm willing to act as if I believe it. Is that what you want?"

"I'm not trying to fool you, Jack. I just didn't expect to see you, that's all. Devin Hollister *is* my name. After we moved from here, Mother remarried. I legally took my stepfather's name. Considering everything, I know you're the last person I should ask a favor from. But I do have to ask, if you can see it that way at all, that you not tell anyone who I am or that I used to live here."

"Nothing to me either way," he said, his voice cold and hard—that easy Southern voice that could be so lazy, so kind, now held no trace of charm and warmth. "I don't know what you mean by 'considering everything,' *Dr. Hollister*, but, as I said, it's nothing to me. You want to be anonymous, fine."

As Paul had observed once, I blushed at *everything*. At this point, my neck and face were on fire. This was not a blush. It went beyond that.

"I owe you an apology," I said slowly. "What I did back in school was cruel and snobbish. Whether you believe me or not, that was the first time I had ever betrayed anyone like that, and the last time. I've always . . ."

Cutting me off, he said, "How nice that you singled me out for such an isolated event in your life. Now, if you'll excuse me, I have to get back to work. If you and your charming dinner companion need anything at all, do let me know. I'm here to serve. Things really haven't changed at all, have they?"

I itched to say something else, but the place was bustling with activity. It was obvious Jack was not interested in accepting an apology or explanation. There was nothing to do but return to my table and hope that Jack would not betray me, this despite the fact that he owed me nothing—except, perhaps, spite.

"I said I was sorry and I meant it."

And that was that.

"Sorry," I said to Paul, reseating myself across from him. "I ran into Jack Fraser and we talked a bit."

"Great fellow, isn't he? Oh, here comes the dessert. You didn't miss a thing."

"And neither do you, Paul, do you?"

The words were etched in acid. With a sense of dread, I raised my eyes and looked into the face of Drusilla McCracken Linden. Two women of her own general age-group stood behind her, dressed to the nines and looking awfully worried.

Now it was Paul's turn to blush . . . the first time I had ever witnessed that particular phenomenon. After a moment of watching him, I realized he wasn't embarrassed or guilty, just angry.

Rising, he said, "Dru, how nice to see you." Nodding to her dinner companions, he added, "Peg, Carol, you're both looking good. Families okay?"

They muttered replies. I doubt that he heard. They looked as if they wished they were anywhere but here.

"Dru," said the heavy one—Carol, I believe—, "let's go to our table. I'm starved."

"Go on ahead," she said heavily. "I'll join you in just a moment. White wine for me if the waiter wants to bring drinks right away. I see you're having water as usual, Paul. How dreary."

The deep flush had faded, but the set of his chin was hard, unyielding. "I don't think, Dru, as you well know, that drinking is a habit a person in my profession needs to take up."

"Such a virtuous man," she said mockingly. Turning to me she remarked, "He does have *so* many sterling virtues. Why, my own parents think he is the white

120

knight straight out of the fairy tales. He is *so* strong, *so* stoic. Not even separation and impending divorce can make him reveal his emotions. Then, again, maybe he doesn't have any to reveal. He's quite good in bed though, as I recall. It's been a while, but . . . but, *silly me*, you know *that*, don't you? Paul, you haven't introduced me to your latest playmate."

"Excuse me," Paul said to me.

Taking his wife by the elbow, he led her across the room toward the table where her friends sat waiting, their faces stressed and anxious.

When he returned to me, he said, "I'm sorry. You don't know how sorry I am."

All eyes might not have been on us, but all ears most certainly were.

"I think I'm ready to leave," I said softly.

I looked down at my expertly prepared dessert, a treat I had barely tasted. I could not have eaten it now if a gun had been held to my head with a command to do so.

The evening had gone completely sour. I could foresee no way in which it could be salvaged.

"Of course."

He left enough cash on the table to cover the meal and a generous tip, and we exited without a backward glance.

"Devin, I'm sorry," he said again once we were in the car, his voice too controlled to be healthy. I sensed he was filled with anger, and about ready to erupt.

Choosing my words carefully, I said, "You have nothing to apologize for, Paul. It wasn't your fault. I don't know what the story is with you two, but, obviously, she is the one who behaved badly tonight. Everyone there saw that."

"I had so wanted this evening to be *right*."

So had I. But first there had been Jackson Lee Fraser, surfacing like a ghost from the past, and then there had been the unfortunate meeting with Paul's wife.

In her own way, Dru was still attractive, but she had changed so much I doubt that I would have recognized her if I hadn't been told who she was. When I had left Dalton, she had been no more than twenty or twenty-one, a pretty brunette with fair skin and rosy cheeks. Now, it looked like a beautician kept her hair streaked, creating an effect of blondness, and, by contrast, I guessed that a tanning bed kept her skin brown ... brown but quite leathery in texture. She was too thin, too wrinkled for her still-young years, too brittle of speech. Not a happy woman, Dru Linden.

Before I could say again that it was all right, Paul again burst into speech, talking as I had never heard him talk, the words coming in quick little bunches, all scrunched up as if with anger too long held in check.

"She was drunk, you know. Hell, why am I telling you that? I'm sure you could tell it as well as I could. That's the problem. One of the biggest anyway. I've never said anything. To talk about it seems so ... so *ungallant* ... and disloyal and ungentlemanly. My wife has had everything, literally *everything*, handed to her on a silver platter. And that everything has never been enough. So she took up drinking. Maybe it makes it easier for her to stand herself. I don't know. I confess I've not been tolerant about this. When it comes to patients, I can look at them and say, and mean, this person's alcoholism or drug addiction is an illness and they need support and help. But I've never been a drinker and never liked being around those who drink. When it came down to my home, my wife, well ... it didn't seem so much like a sickness. I seemed like a choice she had made, a choice she could reverse at any given time. Maybe I could still buy into the illness spiel if she'd admit there is a problem and go for help. But Dru has never in her life admitted she was wrong about anything, and she isn't going to start now.

"I haven't handled it well. When she is drunk, even just tipsy, I find myself revolted. Maybe when she needs me the most, I turn away in anger and hurt. I can't make love to a drunken woman. It makes me sick at my stomach to even think about it. Now, she says she drinks too much because I'm cold and won't touch her. But, as God is my witness, the drinking came first.

"It ... all badly affected our sons, John Paul and Zach. It comes out in them in ways a stranger wouldn't notice, but I can tell. If I fight her and take them away from her entirely, what have I then done to her . . . and will it really be a favor to them? But if they stay with her, what kind of influence is it? They might take up her habits, her ways. I've always prided myself on being in control, on handling everything that came up. Well, I'm not handling this well at all. I thought once I had the world by the tail. Now . . ."

"Do you love her, Paul?" I asked, stepping into territory that had been made my business by his uncharacteristic emotional outburst.

He was driving in the same manner in which he talked, abruptly and jerkily. Sometimes too fast, sometimes too slow, and I feared that we might be stopped, an event that would do nothing to soothe his overwrought state.

"No," he said without hesitation. "And therein lies my guilt, doesn't it? If I had loved her, perhaps she wouldn't have felt the need to drink. I am guilty of many things, Devin. I've always been an ambitious man. I was thirty or so. No one had come along I was really serious about. Then George finds a way to ask me to the house. Nothing too subtle about the way he pushed Dru at me. She had said she was interested in me, so he was doing his part, as he always had, to see his daughter got what she wanted. He pushed and I received. Why not? She was beautiful, rich, educated, and, I thought, used to the grueling routine a doctor has to keep. Love? Even then I didn't kid myself. She was a spoiled kid. Still is. To not get her way about something, no matter how small, turns her inside out. It was okay at first. The sex was great. I've heard being in love enhances sex. I can believe that. But I also know you can have great sex without being in love. Dru wasn't without experience. Not that I altogether hold that against her. But maybe I'm old-fashioned. Seems to me there's a difference between a few love affairs and legions."

"Legions?"

"When drunk, she liked to tell me about her past experiences . . . in graphic detail. But I'll say for her that she did hold marriage to be of some importance. I know of no affairs since our marriage, and I'd be very surprised to learn that there had been any. At any rate, in the early days of our marriage, she passed on a case of gonorrhea. Undergoing treatment was a humiliating experience. Perhaps the distaste began at that point . . . even before John Paul was conceived. But there is no love between us. There never was. I was something she wanted and, like everything else, it meant nothing after that point. So she thought up things to want, lots of other things. I want out, Devin. I've tried to *want* the marriage because of the face of things, because of my sons, but the fact is that I don't want *her*."

I could think of nothing to say. He pulled up in front of my apartment building and stopped his car at the curb. "I've disgusted you, haven't I? Ranting like a madman. I must seem so cold and calculating to you."

Admittedly, he had come across like that. That is, if one listened only to the words, but I sensed a deep underlying hurt. This wasn't all being dismissed as easily as he tried to let on the surface.

"Were you never in love at all, Paul?"

"In love? Once. I was a medical student and she was a nurse at one of the hospitals where I studied. She was a petite little redhead, just as cute as a button. And she held me off at arm's length, as young and horny as I was, until she had the engagement ring on her finger. She then, very solemnly, told me she thought it would be all right since we were engaged, that probably God would regard us as already married even if the state didn't. I thought our lovemaking was out of this world. My experience wasn't vast and I'd never been truly serious about the other little flings. She'd met my parents. The date was set.

"One day at the hospital I walked up to a nurses' station and wasn't seen. I overheard a conversation about Stephanie's—that was her name, Stephanie—her affair with a very prominent doctor on staff . . . a married doctor, of course. At first, I thought it was just vicious gossip. I mentioned it to her, not in the way of questioning, but almost a joke. She acted a little funny, but agreed it was just gossip. A month later, just three weeks before our wedding was to take place, she gave me the ring back. The whole thing had been a ploy on her part, to try to force her married paramour to give up his wife and kids for her. Confronted with the actual proof of her upcoming marriage to me, he caved in. She got what she wanted and I was out in the cold. That's why marrying Dru without love didn't seem such a bad thing. It didn't seem likely I'd love anyone else. I couldn't let myself get that close, not after the fool I'd been for Stephanie. And Dru wasn't the lovable sort, so I told myself it wasn't as if I were depriving her of anything. So that's the whole ugly story. Sorry to have spilled my guts like this. It isn't usually like me."

"I know it isn't. And it's okay that you talked. You have to let it out sometimes."

"Yeah? Maybe. You know what Stephanie told me when she broke the engagement? She *did* love me. It hadn't been pretense. She loved me a lot more than she did Richard. He wasn't even good in the sack, she said. But he had old money and new money and all kinds of power and prestige and I was just getting started and, as she put it, 'It's the smartest move for me at this point.'"

"Paul, do you want to come in and talk some more? You're welcome to do so. I can't really do anything, but I can listen."

He got out of the car, went around and opened the door on my side. When I got out, he took my arm. "I'm walking you to the door. But I'm not coming in. I'm going to go home and try to forget this god-awful night ever happened."

We were at my door now.

"Are you sure you don't want to come in?"

"I'm not sure in the least. There's nothing I'd like better. What I said is that I'm not coming in."

"But why . . ."

His arms were around me and his mouth silenced mine. How long we stood like that there I do not know. Time had no meaning as we drowned in each other. In those moments, I felt not only the force of his passion, but the warmth of his tenderness. When we broke away, I looked into his eyes and understood.

"Goodnight," I said, feeling myself tremble from all

the conflicting emotions warring within. "Are you sure you'll be okay?"

Smiling, he was suddenly the Paul I had known before. "Devin, I'll always be okay. Don't you believe that?"

Nodding, I said, "I know."

With that, we parted. Nothing was said about another "date." Too much was unsettled and *this* one was such a shambles.

Inside, I stripped off my finery and donned my favorite nightshirt. Oh, yes, I did understand what he meant. He *would* be okay. And so would I. We were both survivors. He could stand alone. And so could I. We were luxuries to each other, a sweet desire, a fantasy, but not a necessity. Falling in love is sweeter that way, when it is a gift, not something arising out of need. Or at least should have been sweet.

The evening, such as it had been, was over. It was now, both the good and the bad aspects, merely memory. Knowing I had long hours coming up, I willed myself to relax, to try to sleep. But that was not to be.

The phone rang. Somehow I knew, even as I picked it up, that this was not a wrong number or the hospital wanting me to come in.

"Katie, get the hell out of Dalton. If you don't, you're going to be a dead bitch as well as a stupid one."

"Who are you?" I screamed into the plastic receiver. "Don't be such a coward. Tell me who you are and what you want of me."

There was, of course, no reply to my outburst. The connection was severed at the other end, and probably had been before I had even spoken. I had to fight against the tears of frustration that wanted to flow. It was such an empty and helpless feeling to be threatened by this faceless person and to have no time or means to find a way to fight back. As important as it was, I had to put it on the back burner. Tomorrow I had to function as a doctor. In order to do that, I had to get some rest tonight. The part of me that is playing Nancy Drew . . . well, that's a secondary role. Dr. Hollister is, as must be, front and center stage.

Chapter Ten

"He's shocky, unresponsive," said the burly male R.N. "He moans and groans, but we can't get him to answer a question at all. I don't think he can."

While listening to him, I looked down at the patient on the emergency room cart. There could be no doubt in anyone's mind, looking at the poor fellow, that he was extremely ill.

"Who's his regular physician?" asked Dr. Rick Sinclair, the ER physician on duty.

"I don't know. Like I said, he can't talk."

"Look how ashen he is," I commented, "and his breathing is labored."

"Very much so. But with no history, it's hard to know where to begin." Dr. Sinclair turned toward Dan Whiting, the R.N. "No relatives with him?"

"Ambulance crew said the wife is on her way. She wanted to have the car here so she could go home or whatever when she needs. Should be here any second, I'd say."

"Guesses, Dr. Hollister?" asked Sinclair.

"Too soon to tell, with no more information than I have. He looks somewhat jaundiced. If you force me to guess, I'll say hepatitis or pancreatitis."

Sinclair gave the patient another once-over. "I wouldn't bet against you. But, whatever the problem, he needs help."

Rapid fire, he began to give orders to start fluid

resuscitation on the patient, as well as getting him on oxygen. "And STAT I want a CBC, liver enzymes, ABGs, chest and abdomen X rays. And before we add any antibiotics to the IV, get what cultures you can."

"Excuse me, Dr. Sinclair," said Dan, "but the wife is here now."

"Go interview her, Dr. Hollister. And take good notes. We need the best history we can get. I'd better stay here and watch him right now. He's not looking good."

I was reluctant to leave the critical patient, admittedly out of curiosity because I knew he was in good hands with Dr. Sinclair and the efficient emergency room staff, but I realized getting what history we could was also crucial at this point.

I was met in the doorway of the emergency room by an attractive young woman with strawberry-blond hair falling in disarray across her shoulders and back. Obviously anxious, she reached up and pushed some of the hair out of her way only to have it fall right back where it had started.

"I'm Pete Delancy's wife, Louisa," she said hesitantly. "How is he doing?"

"Ill. He's in good hands, though. They're doing what they can. Since he isn't able to talk to us, we need to find out what we can about his illness from you. I'm Dr. Hollister. Come on back here. We have a cubbyhole where we can talk more privately. Would you like a cup of coffee or something?"

"No, thanks. I'm fine for now," she said, obediently following me back to the little room.

Within just a few minutes, we had filled out the top of the report.

"You say he's thirty-four?"

She nodded her head in agreement. "He was thirty-four this past August. So was I. Our birthdays are only two weeks apart. He's always kidded me about being older than he is because mine is first."

Funny. I would have guessed her at close to a decade younger than that . . . and I would have guessed the patient at least two decades older.

"It started two days ago," she related when we had the preliminaries out of the way. "I tried to get him to come before, but he wouldn't do it. 'They'll just tell me to quit drinking,' he said. I *know* he drinks too much. He has for years. But it's more than that. He's really sick."

"How much does he drink, Louisa? And *what* does he drink?"

"Just beer. Never anything else. We've known each other all our lives, almost. We went all through school together and married right out of high school. He started drinking beer when he was a freshmen or sophomore, and that's all it's ever been. He never drinks whiskey and he doesn't use drugs. Neither do I. We never have. Not even marijuana. But he's always said beer was harmless, that you couldn't be addicted to beer."

"Do you believe that?"

Solemnly, she shook her head. "Maybe once. I don't believe it now. I don't think he can quit. He drinks three six-packs a day. Sometimes a few more than that, especially on weekends when he isn't working."

"That's quite an intake. He's never said anything about undergoing a treatment program, trying to stop?"

"He always says he's not an alcoholic. That it's just beer and he can stop when he really wants. He's had some stomach trouble. He had X rays and some other kind of a test where they run a tube down to the stomach, and he's had ulcers. That's when he got it in for doctors. He just wanted something to heal the ulcers, not lectures on stopping the drinking."

"Okay. Now go on with how this present episode started."

"First—and, like I said, this was two days ago—he had pain in the left shoulder. He got sick to his stomach with it. I worried that he was having a heart attack, but he said it wasn't really in the chest. But the pain must have been pretty bad. He was up all night with it taking Tylenol every few hours. He was still sick all the next day, but I don't think the pain was quite as bad. His color's been awful. But when he started rasping like he couldn't get his breath, well . . . I freaked out. I said he *had* to come here. He must have been scared, too, because he let me call the ambulance. By the time they got there, he was . . . well, like he is now, I guess. He'd cry out and groan, but he wouldn't answer me or them."

We went through some more history, getting the background on Peter J. Delancy, ascertaining that he had no known medical allergies, that his only past surgery had been a childhood tonsillectomy, that his family history was essentially noncontributory to his present illness. As soon as I had gotten all of the pertinent information, I showed Mrs. Delancy to the ER waiting room where she could stay until her husband was stabilized (if, indeed, he could be stabilized) and taken to the Intensive Care Unit where she could be with him for a while. Before going to relay the information to Dr. Sinclair, I made an in-house call to locate the patient's old medical records. Even though his gastrointestinal work-up had been done as an outpatient, we probably would find the test reports of some benefit in assisting with diagnosis and treatment.

That done, I gave Dr. Sinclair and the rest of the staff working with the patient a capsulized version of the history I had obtained from the wife.

"He's an alcoholic," I said softly.

"I guessed as much. How bad?"

"He's only 34, and he's been drinking beer heavily since he was fourteen or fifteen. For quite some time, he's been up to a minimum of 16 beers a day. He's never been an inpatient here. In fact, he's never been hospitalized anywhere since he had a tonsillectomy as a kid. But he did have a gastrointestinal workup here a couple of years ago. Our files confirmed a gastric ulcer and significant duodenitis. He was put on Zantac and Carafate. Dr. Kamali did the endoscopy, but McCracken is the attending physician—or was back then. Chances are, he was lost to follow-up. Maybe we can get hold of Dr. McCracken and find out. Want me to place a call to him?"

Sinclair shrugged. "You can if you'd like. Right now, it doesn't matter. We have to get him stabilized. And that isn't going to be an easy task. The tube is in. I think we'll have to put him in the ventilator once he's in ICU. The breathing isn't good at all."

"Is it cirrhosis or pancreatitis?"

"Possibly both. Right now, I'd say pancreatitis would be the main problem we're dealing with. He's also malnourished. The wife sensible?"

"Very much so."

"Then take over here for me. Go to ICU with him as soon as the nurses are done with him here. I'll be down shortly, but have them get him going on the ventilator . . . another reason I need to talk to the wife."

With a nod, I obeyed. I was, to tell the truth, glad he hadn't asked me to go with him while he talked to Louisa Delancy. From what I had learned, and from what I had seen, the prognosis for Pete Delancy wasn't good. Therefore, Rick Sinclair had the job of relating that information to her and of finding out their wishes in regard to life support systems.

I counted on my fingers, an old habit of childhood I reverted back to at anxious moments, and confirmed what I already knew . . . this poor guy near death was only eight years older than I am. Only thirty-four and death was around the corner if he wasn't awfully lucky. Come to think of it, I might be as near death. Only I couldn't think of that now. If I started dwelling on the death threat I had received, I would not be able to concentrate on the business at hand.

For the next six weeks, my field of duty was to be the emergency room, a place that requires the utmost concentration. It is quite different from surgery, but as demanding in its own way.

"Get a lab workup of the abdomen ordered. I didn't get that one written down," Sinclair called to my retreated back.

"Will do," I said, nearly shouting to be heard over the clatter and confusion of multiple people and equipment.

"Poor old guy," said one of the nurses as she helped prepare him for transport to the ICU.

"He's thirty-four," I told her, that fact still fascinating me.

She shook her head in disbelief. "I called him an old guy and he's twelve years younger than I am. God, do I look that bad?"

"No, Delphine," cracked one of her coworkers, "but your pancreas isn't rotting and falling apart on you."

"No? You're probably right. But sadly enough, I can think of a few other body parts that are sagging."

Within moments, Peter Delancy was out of my hands. I was assisting in the ER, not the ICU. For a few minutes, I aided, passed on the information and instructions from Dr. Sinclair, and then it was out of my hands—and his. The patient's family doctor and the internist on call had been telephoned and were on the way to the hospital. I had touched the lives of the Delancys, and they mine, and now we no longer, for all practical purposes, had anything to do with each other. So it has always been for ER doctors, and so it will undoubtedly always be. I thought of what Paul had said to me when I accused him, ever so lightly, of being judgmental about the diabetic who would not adhere to her diet. A surgeon, he had said, does not become involved in the warp and woof of a patient's life. Maybe he was right. And maybe not. To touch is to become involved, even if that touch is destined to be fleeting.

As soon as I was back in the emergency room, Rick Sinclair gave me a questioning look. Without a word spoken between us, he asked if I was handling this okay and I affirmed that I was.

He left me to manipulate a fishhook out of an elderly man's hand while Rick screened a young woman who had just come in three days pospartum, crying with an unrelenting headache. My task was an easy one to complete. The hook came out intact with only minimal damage to the hand. I dressed the wound and ordered antibiotic and a tetanus shot. The patient was chatty and grateful, no problems there.

Walking over to me, Sinclair said of the crying patient, "It's spinal headache, the result of the epidural she had during labor and delivery. Best thing to do for that is a mild surgical procedure to correct the injury. Her obstetrician is on the way in, not happy but coming all the same. Only four or five doctors on staff are qualified to do epidurals, and he's one of them."

"I've heard of it, of course, but I've never seen it done."

"Perez will let you watch, I'm sure. Which is fine with me. He'll need an assistant anyway. So plan on it unless we're covered up with something dire by then."

Luckily, we weren't. By the time Dr. Jaime Perez had arrived, the nurses had the patient set up and ready in a treatment room.

Perez took one look at the pale and haggard young woman and said, "Dry your tears, little one. The pain is about to come to an end."

With the ease of a master, which he was, he quickly performed the procedure.

"Turn her on her back. Watch her for fifteen minutes. If all is okay, she can go home. If all isn't okay, call me again."

With that, he was gone. When the fifteen minutes had passed, the patient not only had no complications, but had no pain. She still felt tired and "washed out," as she put it, from bearing the intense pain for so long, but the pain itself had abated.

"How on earth does that work, what's the principle?" I asked Sinclair. "I was going to ask Perez, but he didn't give me a chance."

"Yeah, he's like that. And, to tell the truth, I have no idea *why* the procedure works, I just know it does. It's not my field. Maybe Perez could have given you an explanation. But as you saw for yourself, he's not one to stand around and chat."

"But he's good at what he does. And kind to his patients, even if brief."

"That sums it up. You're a quick study, know it?"

"I try," I said, lowering my head in mock modesty.

"To be a good doctor, it isn't necessary to be able to assess human nature astutely, but I've always found it to be an excellent asset, not to say a great diagnostic tool."

"You really like ER work? Most doctors seem to hate it."

Shrugging, he said, "If we were alike, we wouldn't be different, right? It's a challenge. It's something that needs to be done. I'm what's known as a people person. Here, that helps. We get a lot of fruitcakes. That drives some physicians nuts. And we get a lot of varied critical cases. That makes some physicians worried about their malpractice insurance. Me, I don't worry. I do the best I can. So far, so good. No lawsuits. Not to say it won't happen, but I don't intend to live my life in fear of what might be around the corner . . . and what might not be."

"I like your philosophy, Dr. Sinclair. In fact, I like it so much I'm going to try to adopt it for my own."

"I knew you had a good head on your shoulders."

The nurses called to let us know that the next ER patient was ready to be seen, so end of conversation. I liked Rick Sinclair. I was finding a lot of people in Dalton I liked. If, I told myself, I didn't have such a load on my mind, I could have really enjoyed my time here. However, that goes in a circle. If it hadn't been for my so-called mission, I undoubtedly would have elected to intern at somewhere more prestigious and advantageous than Albert B. Creighton Hospital.

When the long and busy night finally ended and I was free to go to my apartment for a few hours, I found myself putting off my departure. Most of the time, I cherished the free hours when I could take a leisurely bath, then fall into bed without it being on my mind that I was on-call and my sleep could be interrupted at any moment. At the hospital, sleeping rooms are provided for us on some of the floors. In those rooms, we catch catnaps. Just because we are assigned to be at the hospital for long stretches does not mean that we have to be on our feet and at attention for that long. That would be, for time after time, physically and mentally impossible. We just had to be there in case we were needed. The naps varied in length from just a few minutes to, on rare occasions, several blissful hours.

In thinking of those sleeping rooms, I had the impulse to volunteer to stay on. But, steeling myself, I signed out and turned toward the door. I had to face the world outside ABC sometime. Besides, there was no guarantee that I was safe within its rosy brick walls. When I mulled it over, it seemed frighteningly more logical that the person or persons threatening me were connected with the hospital. It almost *had* to be that way unless the threats had nothing to do with my search for clues into my father's death. And that was too farfetched even for my fertile imagination. There was no other reason on earth why anyone in Dalton would want to shut me up, or run me out.

I walked across the parking lot, grateful for the good lighting provided there. At the far end of the lot, I saw a uniformed security guard making his rounds. That sight, too, was a comfort. Deep in thought, I approached my Mustang, then reached down with my key to unlock the door.

"Devin, I . . ."

At the sound of the male voice, so close to me and so unexpected, every nerve in my body stood on end. A strange sound escaped me, a sound somehow both choked and shrill.

"I'm sorry," he said softly. "Considering everything, I should have known better than to walk up on you like that."

Now that I was paying attention, the voice was easily recognizable as Anthony's. I made a half turn and saw his faded and dented car parked next to me . . . something I had been too deep in troubled thoughts to notice before.

"It's okay. I guess I'm just tired and jumpy. It was a hectic night in the ER. You coming on duty?"

Making a funny face, he nodded. "Strange time to start work, huh?"

"It's all strange around here."

"You do look strained, kid. Any more problems?"

Talking quickly, knowing he had to be on duty very soon, I told him about the call, managing to omit that I had been out with Paul Linden prior to receiving the call. There was no connection between the two events and I found myself, once face-to-face with Anthony, unprepared to hurt his feelings. I was unsure of either man. More than that, I was unsure of myself. Sometimes I can't stand my feelings of indecision where these two are concerned, but then I excuse myself by saying that indecision isn't always weakness. Sometimes it takes a while to reach a decision, to gather facts, to gain insight, and maybe even to gain maturity.

"I really think the police should know about this."

"When I have something concrete, I may have to do that. Right now, face it, anything I have to say would sound like the loose ramblings of a lunatic. They'd chalk it up to the imaginings of a hysterical female scared at living by herself."

"Still . . ."

"Admit it, Anthony. You know they wouldn't take me seriously."

He admitted it with a shrug and a sigh. He then looked at me in the way a person looks when he really wants to talk. With another shrug and sigh, he said, "See you around. I'll call you when I get a chance. If you need anything before then, you know where I'll be."

"I know . . . same place I'll be most of the time."

Although I was admittedly anxious, maybe even shaky, I got the car parked and into my apartment with no further incidences. The inside of the apartment was intact. There were no weird messages on the answering machine. So-far-so-good. Maybe I could manage to relax . . . to have that leisurely bath and uninterrupted hours of sleep.

Just as I allowed myself to think in that direction, there was a knock at the door. I regarded the door with great trepidation. There were no windows, no peepholes through which I could look. This was Dalton, Mississippi, not the wicked big city, no need—or so most people thought—for the cautions considered standard there.

"Who is it?" I called, hating my voice for sounding so small, tremulous, female, and young—not at all the brave, strong and independent image that I wanted to convey.

"Jack Fraser. Sorry to bother you, but there's something I want to talk to you about."

Surprised, but no longer frightened, I opened the door. He was dressed very casually in jeans and a cotton shirt, not as dapper as in the restaurant, but still a far cry from the disheveled way he had always appeared as a child.

Without a word, I stepped to the side and, with a nod, invited him in. I had the feeling that this was going to be a very interesting end to a busy, busy day.

Chapter Eleven

"Have a seat, Jackson." Noticing his hesitation, I added, "Anywhere you want. I don't have a chance to be here enough to have a favorite spot. And, if I did, I'd offer that spot to you. Just like I'm going to ask right now if you'd like some tea or a Coke or something. So, do you?"

He smiled slightly. "Southern hospitality, huh?"

"Something like that. Not even fifteen years on the east coast can eradicate eleven years of training. Besides, Boston, at least in some circles, is also known for doing what is proper and gracious."

"So I've heard. I'll sit, but I'll skip on the refreshments."

We sat and looked at each other from facing chairs. The years were between us and yet they weren't. It was a most peculiar sensation. On the outside, we looked very different. I was no longer fat and flaxen-haired and Jack was no longer pitiful looking, a child who had always given off the appearance of being dressed from a missionary barrel. But inside? Well, inside ourselves, where I suppose the things that really count go on, I'm not so sure we were very much changed.

"I was rude in the restaurant," he said by way of opening the conversation.

"Rude? I wouldn't say that. No reason why you should want to be friends with me."

Again, that slight smile. "Still, there's a difference between friendship and ordinary civility . . . that plain ol' southern graciousness we just mentioned. As much as anything, I suppose I was embarrassed."

"Embarrassed? Why on earth would you be embarrassed?"

"The restaurant itself, I guess . . . that the only way I could think of to keep the house in the family was to turn it into a public place. There are those here in Dalton, and plenty of them, who feel sorry for me, I think. Sorry, and also somewhat derisive, that I'm such a loser I could not afford the house just as a house."

I uttered a rude word at that and he looked at me with surprise . . . and also, I believe, a measure of delight.

"You're twenty-six, Jack—the same as me. I have no idea what went on in your life after I left here at the age of eleven. But I know you didn't have an easy life up to that point and I suspect it wasn't easy after. At less than thirty, people aren't expected to have their fortunes made. Personally, I think the inn is great. I think it's admirable that you want to keep the house. And I suspect more people think that way than you give them credit for."

"Perhaps," he said, not sounding entirely convinced.

"Count on it," I replied firmly. "Jack, what has gone on with you the past fifteen years?"

Laughing, he said, "You want me to condense fifteen years into a few sentences? It's a challenge, I guess. My father died. It shouldn't have been a wrench because I had hardly ever seen the man. But I had this childhood fantasy, something I needed to believe, that he was working toward the time that he and I could be together. So that was the end of the fantasy. I loved my aunts. They were very good to me. They didn't understand children, especially little boys born to this era. But that didn't keep them from loving me and doing their best. It was their duty to see to me, I know, and we southerners are almost as big on duty as we are on being gracious. But with them it wasn't a joyless and grudging duty. I think they truly liked to have me with them. But, you see, to a small boy, that wasn't a 'normal' way to live. Just about everyone else I knew lived with one or both parents. I needed to believe there was a 'normal' life in store for me also. My father had come along very late in life to my grandparents. Aunt Dorothea and Aunt Emmaline were his older sisters, but they were both old enough to be his mother. Some told me, once I was grown and they were gone, that one reason they never married was because they doted on him and couldn't bear to leave him to establish their own homes. So, when they ended up with me, it was like he had come back to them. But they never confused the two of us. When he died, I guess they felt it more greatly even than I did, certainly more greatly than they wanted me to know, but they were never quite the same after that. By the time I was eighteen, they were both gone. Funny feeling, to walk across the platform at high school graduation and there's not a single person there for you. The house was mine. My impulse at that time was to sell it and get the hell out of Dalton, Mississippi. But the lawyers said, even though there was no question the house was mine, I couldn't sell it until I was twenty-one—just a technicality, a bit of red tape.

"I packed up my few clothes and left. There wasn't a whole lot of money. About enough to see me through college if I was careful and worked a little now and then. So that's what I did. I went the summer semesters also and graduated in three years. In those three years, I didn't once come back. Matt Yelton, the guy at the bank who had always taken care of things for Aunt Em and Aunt Dottie, saw to the house for me. I'd send him a check every six months and he paid someone for me to do whatever had to be done to keep it from falling into decay.

"At twenty-one, I came back, complete with a B.S. in business administration, all ready to see to putting that damned house on the market. Matt had done a bang-up job. There set the house, so beautiful, so well-maintained, so empty. I knew then I couldn't sell it, not yet anyway. I went to the bank and had a long talk with Matt. He agreed to continue as caretaker for me a while longer until I made up my mind for sure.

"I went to Biloxi and went to work for the local branch

of a large corporation. I quickly found out that I hated the corporate life. But in spite of my distaste, I did fairly well. After eighteen months, they wanted me to transfer to the home office in Chicago. I went. And I hated it even more there. I lived simply, except for what I had to spend for necessities, I saved. Three and a half years ago, I quit my job. I spent a few months learning what I could about the restaurant business. Then I came back here, sunk my savings into remodeling the house, and opened it as an inn. I've only been open a few months. It's doing great. I can only hope it's not a novelty, that people will continue to come after the new wears off. If not, I guess I can always go back to work for big business."

I was struck by the coldness of his brief narrative. He spoke in almost a monotone with little sign of emotion, not even when he spoke of the passing of his father and aunts. I suspected this was due to too much hurt rather than lack of feeling. Jack, I imagined, had been reared to suppress his emotions. "A gentleman does not let it show."

"No personal details?" I dared to ask. "No falling in love? No engagements or marriages?"

"None of those things," he answered, no elaboration forthcoming. "And yourself?"

I shrugged. "I was always my father's daughter. My whole life centered around becoming a doctor. There's been little room for anything else. Not that I haven't had a social life and friends, but there's been nothing I allowed to get in the way of my education and training process. No serious dating. No engagements. No illicit affairs. And, of course, no children."

"And for the future?"

Again, I shrugged. "What will be will be. If I'm to be a surgeon, then I have a few more years before I can allow myself to make those decisions."

"It must be nice."

"What must be nice?"

"To have a timetable and be able to stick to it. To say you will fall in love and marry after your career is established, not before."

I hadn't thought of it that way. Closing my eyes, I then opened my mind to new concepts. In my mind's eye, I saw the faces of both Anthony and Paul, two men who, through no fault of their own, had caused me considerable inner confusion. On some level, I had been trying to decide which one of them I was falling in love with and what, exactly, I should do about it. Jack's words made me look at the situation in a different way. Both Anthony and Paul were compelling human beings, each appealing to me in a different way. But I wasn't in love with either of them . . . at least not yet.

"Yoo-hoo," Jack said teasingly. "You still in there?"

Opening my eyes, I blinked, then smiled at him. "Very much in there. You know, Jack, one thing doesn't have anything to do with the other. I just haven't really fallen in love yet. That's been circumstances, chance, not a decision. I may be a businesslike and sensible person, but I'm not immune to the 'normal' emotions of other human beings. I'm not saying I would have given up being a doctor because I fell in love. But I could well have been one of the many I see struggling to balance a marriage, even children, with going to school and all that. Funny, the pair of us, sitting here at our advanced ages and saying we've never been in love."

An awkward silence fell between us.

"Jack," I said when the silence had grown too great to be borne, "what I did when we were children . . . it wasn't right. It always hurt my conscience. The only defense I have is that I was a child. It isn't enough of a defense, I know because even then I knew what I did was shabby. I'm not even sure why I did it. Funny thing is, the best times I had back then were with you. You were my friend in a way no one else has ever been."

He leaned toward me slightly and his voice was not much more than a harsh whisper, "Katie, I understand. Not that it didn't hurt, not that I didn't feel betrayed, and not that I didn't in my childish prayers wish you in hell a hundred times. But I did understand. You see, I would have given anything—literally anything—in those days to have 'belonged' in school the way you did. But I didn't, couldn't. It wasn't meant to be for me. Never did I believe you'd give it up for me. I guess one of my wilder fancies was that you'd befriend me openly and bring me into that crowd. But that was like pretending I was a horse or Superman or Billy-the-Kid or some of the other things we pretended at play. More realistically, I guess I hoped you'd opt for both. That they would be first, of course, but that you'd still allow some time for me. But that wasn't realistic either."

To my dismay, tears were rolling down my face.

"Hush now," he said, his voice dropping even another octave. "It's too far away and long ago for tears. We were just kids."

"Logically, I know that. It's my heart that isn't so sure. Just like when my father died and they were all saying it was suicide. And I knew the truth was so different. It's like yesterday, Jackson Lee. Sometimes worse than that. Not like yesterday, but like right this minute."

"I think I understand that, too."

Somehow I believed him. People say things like that and most of the times it's just words. Other people can't know how you feel. But I believed that Jack Fraser did. *Does.* It had always been that way between us. "Always" being the space of those few months in childhood when we'd grown so close.

Very slowly, choosing my words carefully, I said, "We talked of falling in love. Maybe the main reason I haven't is because I'm expecting something like my parents had. Not long ago, Mother told me that she and my dad were 'golden together.' To me, their marriage was what a marriage ought to be. I'm looking for that, I think—for someone I can bond to in that special way."

I stopped talking when I saw the perplexed look on his face, the obvious puzzlement that furrowed his brow. "What did I say that was wrong?"

"Nothing," he said, instantly smoothing his face out until it was bland and unbetraying.

"You lie."

"Some things don't change. You always did know when I lied, no matter how minor the lie."

"And . . ."

He turned his hands palm upward. "Katie, there are things . . . well, I don't know you that well anymore. And if I did, I still couldn't. Not if . . ."

I got out of my chair and edged closer to stand right in front of him.

"The reason I am interning in Dalton is not love of the place. It's to find out the truth about my father's death. If you know something I need to know, please tell me. I came here prepared to be hurt. If he didn't kill himself, then someone else did it, and possibly others covered it up. There's hurt in that. I know that the biggest hurt of all would be to find out he did commit suicide. But I'm even prepared to face that. What I am not going to take is another set of lies, of closing my eyes to the truth."

He seemed ready to say something when the telephone rang.

"Darling, I'm here!" said the voice I knew so well.

"Mother, what do you mean you're 'here'?"

"Well, to be more exact, I'm at the airport in Biloxi. I just got in a few minutes ago. I'm in the process of renting a car, then I'll be on the way to see you. Charlie had an unscheduled business trip come up, so I thought this would be a good time to go and see my girl. I'll be there in a few hours. This isn't a bad time, is it?"

Swallowing, I said, "You know I'll be glad to see you. Just as long as you understand that my schedule at the hospital doesn't allow me a whole lot of free time."

"Why, of course I understand that. And I can stay at a hotel if you'd like."

"Don't be silly. Of course there's no need for that. The apartment is scarcely used as it is and there's a small extra room, so come right on. You have the address and Dalton isn't large enough that you'll have trouble finding it. Luck has it that I'm off this evening, so come on over when you get in town. I'll be here."

We said the usual things, then the connection between us was broken.

"My mother," I explained. "She's come for a visit." Even as I spoke, I knew I was not glad, though I was not sure why I felt that way.

"So I gathered. Look, Katie, I'll go now. I have an appointment in a few minutes, and I'm sure you have things you need to do."

"But I thought you were going to tell me . . ."

Then the doorbell rang. Our eyes met, the frustration mutual. With an accepting sigh, I moved to open the door. Before I could say a word, Drusilla Linden pushed herself into the room. Even though I maintained a distance of a few feet between us, I could tell that she reeked of alcohol. Her frosted hair was disheveled, her manner overwrought. Her once pretty face, at close range, showed the signs that dissipation leaves in its wake.

"Bitch," she said, looking directly at me. Jack cleared his throat at that point and she turned sharply in the direction of the sound.

"And so," she said, emitting a loud and high-pitched giggle, "my husband and the cute Italian intern aren't enough for you . . . now you're collecting the locals. There's a word for women like you . . . one that I can't bring myself to use, not even to the likes of you."

"Dru," I said, feeling helpless—and feeling sorry for the woman despite her vile accusations, "please have a seat and try to calm down. I'm not having an affair with any of these men. Your separation from Paul had nothing to do with me. I didn't even know either of you when you decided that. Please, just . . ."

"Lies. All of it. Just black lies. But I must say you're good at it. Butter wouldn't melt in your mouth. You remind me of someone else. I think it's that married bitch that had her claws in Paul years ago. Yes, that's what it is. You have the same way about you. So sweet and innocent until one knows."

"Dru . . ."

But reasoning was to no avail. She attacked me physically, hitting away at my face and shoulders with her handbag, quick random stabs that caught me so much by surprise that I really did not feel them.

"Stop it, Mrs. Linden, you don't know what you're

doing," I heard Jack saying. He grabbed her from behind by the arms and pulled her bodily away from me. "Come on," he continued, his voice taking on a soothing quality, "I'll see that you get home. I'll take you where you can rest and think it over. You're not yourself, that's plain to see."

She broke out in sobs then, wrenching sounds that hurt me more than the blows had done. The fight was out of her and she allowed Jack to lead her out the door, his hand only a light touch at one elbow.

"I'll be in touch," he mouthed to me as they left.

Until that time, if, indeed, it ever transpired, I was not to know what he was going to say to me. I had meant to again ask him if he could keep my secret, and had not even had time or opportunity for that.

Dru thought I was having an affair with her husband. That much was clear. And my conscience was such that it pained me for the fantasies about Paul Linden that I had indulged in, and for kisses from him that I had taken, to which I had no right. Looking in the mirror, I saw the marks the handbag had left on my face and neck. I unbuttoned my blouse and saw the red marks on my shoulders, places that would turn into ugly black and blue bruises within a few hours. Bitch, I thought dully, wondering if the ugly appellation was not correct. He was her husband and I had willingly been drawn into his arms. No matter what the extenuating circumstances, that fact remained.

By the time I had showered and composed myself somewhat, Mother was there, arriving as she always did like a gentler form of a cyclone, the scent of roses in her wake. She had brought more luggage with her, for a stay of what was I assumed only a few days, than I had brought for the entire year.

"You sounded a bit strange on the phone, Devin," she said, gently reproachful. "I almost thought you weren't glad I was here."

"It isn't that, Mother. You should know I've missed you a lot and am always glad to see you. But we'd never discussed this. I thought you knew I'd come to Dalton without anyone knowing I'd lived here before, and then . . ."

"Here I come?" She laughed gaily. "Why, no one will remember little ol' me. It's been too long. And it's only for three days, then I'm off again. But I promise to lie low and not draw attention to myself."

She seemed sincere. Undoubtedly, she meant every word that she said. I looked at her, her slender frame encased in a designer suit that cost the earth, tiny feet displayed in Italian shoes, ash blond hair artfully cut and arranged, and looking at least a full decade younger than her years. Not call attention to herself? She was not the sort of woman to go unnoticed anywhere, let alone in a small town like Dalton. I sighed. Sometimes we just have to accept people for what they are. Trying to change them only makes us frustrated and unhappy. And I did love my mother.

"I *am* glad to see you," I said, moving to enfold her in a warm embrace.

For a long time, we talked. As always, she did most of the talking, assuming with the innocent ego of a child that I was as interested n her social world as she was, when, in truth, I had never been interested, and was less so now than ever before. It was another world, another life, that Boston social whirl.

When I yawned several times in a row, she quickly became the concerned mother, never once suspecting that the yawns stemmed from boredom as much as from the need for sleep.

"I'm tired and sleepy, too," she maintained. I did not protest and was glad when we retreated to our beds, me to the room I always used and her to the cubbyhole the landlord had the nerve to call a second bedroom. A dresser and a twin bed made it looked cramped, but, for once, she made no comments. As she had said herself, her stay was to be a short one.

Chapter Twelve

The banging on the door rudely awakened me from the deep sleep in which I had found a brief respite from my problems. Throwing on my robe, I stumbled from my room in the direction of the door. I was vaguely aware of Mother standing in the doorway of the tiny spare room, rubbing her eyes with her fists like a sleepy child. Even in my half-awake stupor, I was aware of the peach silk peignoir that put my oversized T-shirt and worn terry robe to shame.

"You're Devin Hollister?" asked the blue-uniformed policeman when I had opened the door. Another man, a younger one also in uniform, stood behind him. I had the impression that the question was just a formality, that they knew quite well where they were, and who I was.

"That's right. Could I ask what the problem is?"

I looked at the clock on the table across the room. It was 4:30 A.M. Even to someone with my helter-skelter schedule, it seemed an ungodly hour for a visit.

"May we come in? I'm Officer Hodlitt. And this is Officer Daniels."

There was no flashing of IDs like one sees in the movies. This was Dalton, not the big city. I'm sure most people in town knew Hodlitt and Daniels, even if I did not.

"I ... well, yes ... please do. And, yes, I'm Devin Hollister. Have a seat if you'd like. But I would like to know what this is all about."

Then I saw two pairs of eyes drawn to the other end of the room as if by magnets. Without looking that way, I knew what had attracted their attention.

"My mother," I explained. "Her name is Elaine Hollister. She just got in last night from Boston to visit me for a few days. Now, please . . ."

Hodlitt tore his gaze away from the picture she made, tousled fair hair, breasts barely concealed.

"We have something to talk to you about, miss. Do you know a woman named Drusilla Linden?"

Puzzled, I nodded. "Slightly. I've worked with her husband at the hospital. I'm an intern there. I'm aware that she's also Dr. McCracken's daughter."

"Was," he corrected.

"Pardon?"

Speaking for the first time, the one named Daniels said, "What Walt is trying to tell you is that Mrs. Linden was found dead just a couple of hours ago."

"Dead? Dru? I don't understand. Why are you here? How did it happen?"

"We got a call at the police station around midnight that someone had seen what looked like a body lying by the curb in the street that runs behind here. This is a small town, miss. Most calls we get like that are, thank God, crank calls. We thought this one was because the caller refused to give a name. But, like always, we had to check it out.

"Sure enough, there was a body up against the curb. Her purse with full ID was right beside her, but we recognized her anyway. Quite a bit of cash and credit cards—watch and rings and such on that must have cost a pretty penny. Pretty well rules out robbery."

"Maybe she was hit by a car," I suggested.

"Good guess. But not one that goes with the bruises and scratches we found on her—and especially not with the bullet hole in her chest."

A disapproving glance from Hodlitt told the younger policeman that he had divulged too much information, it also served to inform me that this visit was not a casual one, that to some degree, I was a suspect.

"Oh, my God," I said, my knees weakening to the extent that I had to wobble to a chair and sit down. "She was here, earlier in the evening. I suppose that's why you're questioning me. She was drunk when she came in, as she was when she left, but she was very much alive. And I saw no marks on her."

"Maybe you just didn't notice, not if you had no reason to look."

"Possible. Probably not, though. I'm a doctor. I'm trained to look for injuries."

"I see. May we ask *why* she was here. And, also, if you could give us the time of her visit we'd appreciate it."

I turned to face mother, an instinct springing from old habit, I suppose. She was instantly by my side, face strained and pale.

"It was right after you called me, Mother. Do you recall exactly what time that was?"

"It was 7:23 P.M.," she replied promptly.

"How can you be so sure?" asked one of the policemen.

"Because that's what is stamped on the papers for the rental car. I have to have it turned back in by that time three days from now."

"I see."

"Mrs. Linden, *Dru,* was here only a few minutes. Five at the most, I'd say. As I said before, she was intoxicated and upset."

"What you haven't said is why she was here at your apartment in the first place."

I turned scarlet, something I could not help. I hoped they did not mistake the blush as a symbol of guilt, but there was nothing I could do to call it back.

"As I said, I work with her husband at the hospital. Quite recently, I completed a month of surgical study under his direction. He and his wife, he told me, had separated before I came to Dalton. Last week he asked me to dinner. We had never been out together before. There was no romance, nothing to hide. If there had been, we wouldn't have gone to such a public place."

"What place is that?"

"The Fraser Inn. Dru was there with two women friends. She created a scene. Not bad, just enough to spoil the evening. Dr. Linden and I left the restaurant soon after that. She was still there with her friends when we left. He brought me home." I looked into the officer's eyes and answered the unasked question. "He did not come in. This was last night. I hadn't seen either of the Lindens again until she burst in here tonight. I went to work early this morning... I guess now that was *yesterday* morning. I don't know if Dr. Linden was at the hospital during the hours I was on duty or not. I was in the emergency room and did not see him. I got off duty at six in the evening and came straight here. I hadn't been home long when Jack came over... Jackson Fraser, that is. We were talking when Mother called. Then Dru came. He had been ready to leave anyway, he said he had an appointment. He escorted her out, indicating he'd see her safely home. When Mother arrived later on, I didn't mention any of this to her, I didn't want to upset her."

"But you still haven't said," Hodlitt said slowly, his manner an insinuation in itself, "*why* Mrs. Linden was here."

I looked him right in the eye, my cheeks burning now from indignation rather than shame, though it was doubtful he could tell the difference.

"She accused me, though she didn't use these exact words, of sleeping with her husband. She also indicated that I had the same sort of relationship with two other men. The truth is that I have no such connection to any of them. But she was obviously hurt, angry, and drunk, and, I suppose, looking for someone besides herself to blame for the break up of her marriage."

"And you did not engage in physical battle with Mrs. Linden?"

Three pair of eyes shot to the telltale bruises on my face and neck. Undoubtedly, while I had slept, time had changed the red welts to blue-black marks.

As evenly as I could manage, I replied, "A battle has to have two sides. Mrs. Linden attacked me, hitting me over and over with her handbag. I did *not* hit her back or retaliate in any way. Any marks you found on her did not come from me. I'm sure Jack will back me up on that."

"I assume Jack would be the Jack Fraser that owns Fraser Inn?"

"Correct."

"And you say Mrs. Linden left with him?"

I swallowed, wondering what the repercussions would be. There was no way, considering the gravity of the situation, that I could *not* have involved Jack, and by mentioning his name I had already done so. After the initial stab of guilt, I told myself that his "involvement" was such that it had to be mentioned, and that to avoid doing so would merely have suggested that there was something to hide.

"Yes. Yes, that is true. He told her he'd take her home where she could rest and think things over. When he left, he told me he'd be in touch. I didn't hear any more from him tonight . . . not that I expected to."

"Then Jack Fraser was one of the last people to see Mrs. Linden alive? Perhaps even the last person?"

It only took a second for the implication of the policeman's statement to sink in. My rebuttal was quick and, even to me, surprisingly strong. "Don't talk like that. Jack could never hurt anyone. Not in a thousand years."

Eyebrows raised and looks were exchanged. I bit my lower lip, wondering how I was going to explain *this* away.

The question that followed was slowly paced and carefully phrased . . . very cool and gentle, but deadly nonetheless. "You seem to have been very busy this evening, Miss . . . or is it Doctor?"

"Doctor in all but the most technical of terms, but I won't insist on the title. What is it you were going to ask?"

"Why Mr. Fraser was here. For someone new in town, you seem to have become well-acquainted with the locals." Now there were more looks exchanged, this time between mother and me. With a deep sigh, I settled back in my chair and, not for the first time, longed for clothing. It was enough of a chore to have such a narrative to relate, let alone having to do it in rumpled nightclothes. However, as with many things, the opportunity had chosen me rather than the other way around.

"I'm not really new to Dalton," I began slowly. "Neither is my mother. However, it has been many, many years since either of us has been here. I moved away from here after the death of my father, when I was eleven years old. Once we moved, there was no reason to come back. It was too painful. But years later, I was grown-up, I felt I had to face the past before I could get on with my life, make important decisions. My name *is* legally Devin Hollister. When I was about twelve, my name was changed to that of my stepfather. Before that, I was Devin Clark . . . but most people around here called me Katie, a nickname my father had given me. My father was Dr. James Clark. Fifteen years ago . . ."

And so it went. They did not interrupt me until I had given my history, my reason for being in Dalton, Mississippi. At the conclusion of the tale, the older of the men let out a long, low whistle.

As I had talked, Mother had cried some. I had been aware of it, although the awareness had not made me stop and see to her. My mother cries prettily, and carefully. Never for her the bleary-eyed and red-nosed look that makes a ruin of a face.

The young policeman, taking advantage of a lull in the questioning, said, "Could I get something for you, Mrs. Hollister? A glass of water maybe?"

"How kind of you! But, no. I'm fine. When my daughter was talking, it brought it all back. The horror, the pain, the loss."

"We each have to deal with grief in our own way, ma'am," was the polite reply.

"I'm afraid, Dr. Hollister," the younger one said softly, "that we'll have to ask you some more questions. Please don't be frightened, it's only a technicality, but we do have to advise you of your rights . . . and that you have the right to have an attorney present before you say anything."

I almost laughed. Mother let out an outraged cry,

somehow more convincing to me than the soft patter of her tears had been.

"Do you mean to tell me I'm under suspicion?"

"I'm not saying that. I'm just saying we *have* to ask further questions. We're talking murder here. It's important to talk to the people who saw the lady last, and to those who knew her best. You do understand that?"

Reluctantly, I nodded. I fell into the former category, but not the latter. To me, Drusilla McCracken Linden had always been a peripheral figure in my life. She was just a person in town, a prominent person with whom I had vague ties because of the medical profession that had united her father and mine.

"Devin, don't say another word," Mother announced firmly. "I'm going to call Charlie and have him . . ."

"Mother, Charlie isn't in Boston. That's why you're here, remember? If I have to have a lawyer, it's best I find one locally. But I don't think we're at that point yet. I understand my rights, gentlemen. I have nothing to hide. Whatever you need to know, ask."

Mother was disapproving. With an impatient air, I brushed away her cautionings. "I didn't kill that poor woman, Mother. Neither did Jack Fraser. We have to help the authorities find the person who did."

With a meaningful look toward the policemen, I gave them permission to ask their questions. I guess my last words had given them fuel for the first of the barrage of questions I had invited, if not welcomed.

"How can you be so sure, miss, that Jack Fraser didn't kill Mrs. Linden?"

That was a hard one. How can you explain feelings in the heart? I knew my answer would sound foolish, even juvenile, to two practical and somewhat hardened men, but it was the only answer I had.

"I guess I don't *know*—not in the sense that we were together and I can provide him with an alibi. But I knew him before we moved away. We were children together. He couldn't kill someone."

Even to my own ears, it sounded lame. How much more so it must have sounded to them. I didn't even want to think about how great their derision would have been had they delved into the depths of my relationship with Jackson Lee Fraser. A decade and a half ago, for the space of one hot summer, we had been friends. That is all.

There was no way I could ever explain to strangers the Jack I had known. He was the only little boy I had known who took care to avoid stepping on bugs, who refused to catch fireflies and put them in a jar or punch out their lights to make a glowing ring for the finger. Together, we had ministered to motherless bunnies, baby birds fallen from the nest, wounded grasshoppers, and, once, a half-starved kitten with a sore leg. Like a sponge absorbing all around me, I had taken in, without realizing it at the time, the way he had taken care to please his aunts, to not worry them. He had not protested his awful clothes and haircuts because he had not wanted to hurt their feelings rather than because he lacked the courage to protest. Even as a child, Jack was strong. Not in the way most boys are strong, but in his will, his control, his endurance, if not daring, the childhood curse of being different. Only now, as I sat and thought, did I truly see that Jack's very passivity had been courage itself, the willingness to patiently endure.

"Jackson Lee, what are we going to do with you?" Miss Dorothea scolded. *"Take that kitten back where you found it and leave it there. No tellin' what disease it might have.*

"You hear me now, get rid of it."

"No, ma'am."

"What did you say, boy?"

"I said that I can't do that, Aunt Dorrie. He's hurt and sick and he needs me and Katie. No one else cares, you see. If we put him out, he'd die. He's not strong enough to find food and he can't run on that leg. It's up to us. But we'll be careful."

"Hmmmmpf. Well, see that you are careful. And, for goodness sakes, wash with hot water and plenty of soap after you've handled that cat."

And so it had been. He had submitted to the haircuts, worn the clothes, not asked for the material treasures other boys had coveted. But where it mattered to him, he had not submitted. Spotty, as we had called the rather ugly multicolored cat, had, within weeks, become a solid part of the Fraser household, even allowed inside status. But most of our patients hadn't been so lucky, some escaping to unknown fates, others dying first, to be given elaborately staged funerals by us with much tears and piety.

"You do know that we'll have to talk to Mr. Fraser. I'm sure he'll appreciate your opinions, but . . ."

"Exactly," I said, snapping out of my reverie. "I'm sure, but I appreciate your position. An opinion is not a fact to be presented in a court of law."

They agreed to that with solemn nods. I answered all the questions that they asked. And after what seemed like hours longer than the clock would verify, they left. Although they did not say so, I assumed they were going to seek out Jack.

Moving to the telephone table, I looked up Jack's number in the directory and called him. His sleepy voice told me I had awakened him and, given the circumstances, that he did not know of Dru's death or he could not have slept so soundly.

"Sorry to get you out of bed. This is Devin. I just thought I should tell you the police just left here. A few hours ago, Dru Linden was found dead. They said she'd been shot. I had to tell them you'd been here and that she had left with you. I imagine they'll be contacting you right away. Understandably, they want to talk to those who saw her last."

"I hope they don't think I did it," he said.

He sounded half-amused at the idea. The gravity of the situation had not yet really registered.

"Murder investigations aren't exactly the norm in Dalton, I gather. They aren't yet sure what they think. But I gather I'm not in the clear. I don't suppose you are either. I got read my rights."

"You're serious!"

He was more alert now, more awake.

"Yeah. Well, let me know how it goes. For the next few hours, I'll be at home. After that, I'll be at the hospital a straight thirty-two hours. You can call there and have me paged . . . or come by. That is, if you want to talk about it."

There was a brief silence, then he said, "I might *need* to talk about it, Ka . . . uh, Devin."

I gave a short laugh. "Call me whatever comes naturally. Before you left here, I meant to ask you to keep my identity a secret for a while, then Dru showed up. Now it's out anyway. I had to tell the police . . . tell them everything. About the break-ins, the threats, all of it."

The audible sharp intake of breath reminded me he knew nothing of those things.

"I don't . . ."

"I know. And there isn't time now. As I said, maybe we can talk later."

While Mother watched with disapproving eyes, I severed the connection, hunted up another number, and found myself talking to Paul Linden. No sleepiness there. Long before I had been awakened, he had been disturbed from sleep, officially notified of his estranged wife's death.

"Paul, this is Devin. I know about Dru. I just wanted to say I'm sorry, that I know what a shock it is. If there is anything I can do . . ."

At such times, there is little else to say. Not adequate, but, then, nothing is.

"The hard part is yet to come," he said woodenly. "The boys don't know. Her parents don't know. They're all together. Since Dru was out on the town with friends, she had dropped them off at the McCracken's. I've put it off, not wanting to rob them of sleep. But soon it will be morning. Then I'll have to go."

"I'm sorry," I said again, sounding as ineffective as I felt. I did not know Zach and John Paul. I had not yet even been shown photographs of them. Still, I had a picture in my mind of them, of how I thought they might be. I shut my eyes in borrowed pain. They had lost a parent just as I had, at very close to the same age. I did not know them, yet I hurt for them, I think, more than I did for Paul. Not that I underestimated his grief, realizing it might be made worse by his guilt for not loving her enough, for the part he had in the separation. But the child who lost her father is, perhaps, still the strongest force inside me, and it is with those unseen children that I most identified.

"Devin, we need to talk," Mother said when I, at last, turned away from the telephone.

"Can we do it later? I have to go on duty very soon. If I had known you were coming, I might have traded with someone. But unfortunately, I didn't know. And I feel like I need to lie down and rest for a bit before I go."

"Honey, you can't go to work. Not after an ordeal like this."

Smiling slightly, I have her a brief hug and an almost perfunctory peck on the cheek. "It's an unpleasant experience, Mother, but not deeply personal enough that I can get out of work because of it. I scarcely knew the woman. It isn't as if I had a deep and personal loss. I'm sorry she's dead, especially in such a horrid way. And I'm selfish enough to admit I'm nervous at being somehow involved in this. But that's all."

"It's enough to unnerve most people. You don't have to be stoic."

"I'm okay, Mother. Really."

She sighed deeply and ran her fingers through her sleep-tousled hair. Automatically, I touched my own hair, knowing it to be a mess rather than prettily disarranged.

"I don't mean to complain, Devin, and I know you don't mean to come off the way you seem at times, but I feel *dreadfully* unwelcome. If changing my flight wasn't such a hassle, I'd be tempted to do just that."

She looked so hurt that I melted as I always did in the face of another being's pain, no matter how slight.

"I'm sorry," I said, and meaning it. "It's just your visit was so unexpected and I've been feeling worried and guilty that I'm scheduled to work during so much of it, not that I can do anything about it. If you had called, maybe we could have made better plans, had more time to spend together. Then, all of *this* came up. And I *still* have to go to work in a couple of hours. All in all, I guess my mood isn't the best in the world. But you know I'm always pleased to see you."

Rising from the couch, she bent to give me a quick hug. "Oh, I understand. And I'm sure I'd be much growlier than you if I had to maintain your schedule. Truth is, I felt guilty about coming. Because I knew you were trying to keep your past a secret and there was the chance we might run into someone who would recognize me. I had truly, darling, intended to keep a very low profile. All I wanted was to see you."

"I know, I know. And it's really no longer a problem. The secret seems to be out now. Look, I am going to go lie down for a bit of a nap. You do the same. When I catch a lull at the hospital, I'll give you a call. You can come over and we'll have lunch—the finest the ABC cafeteria has to offer."

She brightened at that. "You're sure you don't mind?"

Actually, I wasn't sure at all. Awash with guilt, I frequently find myself making gestures that aren't wise or practical. However, I carried through with what I had started and assured Mother that lunch at the hospital would present no problems.

I'd choose a table in a dark corner. I'd keep the lunch brief . . . inventing, if necessary, an emergency I had to see to. But even as I planned, I know that my mother going unnoticed was a long shot, if not an impossibility. Still, perhaps it didn't matter. With things as they were, it could not be long until everyone in town who cared to know, and some who didn't, would be aware that Elaine and Katie Clark had hit Dalton again.

Chapter Thirteen

The day was terrible . . . it started out that way and did not improve.

In some ways, a hospital the size of ABC is a big place . . . the capacity for 350 patients, 800 employees, 80-some physicians. In other ways, it is very small. For instance, hot gossip spreads like wildfire at ABC, as I suppose it does in any similar organization. The people inside the walls of ABC compose their own neighborhood. Because like it or not, everyone is united by a common bond. We move about in the same habitat and are, thus, oddly related to each other.

After the first couple of hours, my system had had enough and my violent blushing finally shutdown. I became, if not oblivious, at least somewhat immune to the stares, snickers, and barbed comments. Perhaps even worse was the sympathy I saw in the eyes of a few.

While a medical student some of my professors may have called me brilliant and gifted. But there are plenty of times that I doubt those adjectives apply to me. Incredibly naive on this occasion, I had not anticipated what the general reaction would be to me. Despite the white coat I so proudly wore, I had apparently become known as a scarlet woman. I had expected Paul Linden and Dr. McCracken to be absent . . . just as I had expected all to know of Dru's death. What I had not expected that my minor (at least thus far) relationship with Paul and the early morning visit by the police to become widely known, and so very rapidly.

"How is he in bed?" Darlene, one of the nurses on the third floor had asked boldly. She was known throughout the ABC network for her bawdy conversation, raunchy jokes, and eye for the men... a reputation she endeavored to maintain and enhance.

"Pardon?" I asked, not sure I had heard right.

With a grin and a wink, she had explained herself. "Dr. Linden—perfect Paul—how is he in bed? I've often wondered. Those skillful hands moving all over.... Well, one can't help lusting. So?"

I then found myself mumbling something like, "I'm sure I wouldn't know."

Later, when I had time to compose myself, I was more furious at myself than at Darlene. Too late, I could think of a dozen caustic and effective retorts I could have made instead of blushing and stuttering like a schoolgirl who had been caught necking in a corner.

The hardest moment came when I met Anthony in passing and he did not speak. In fact, he avoided all eye contact. At that moment, I was stuck on the third floor and he was serving duty on the second, but I was determined to have it out with him before going home.

When a respite finally came and I was able to take a break, I was torn between calling Mother as I had promised and seeking out Anthony. A study of the clock made my decision. It was only 10:30 A.M. too early for lunch. My tentative date with my mother could wait for the next break—although I knew full well that could easily sentence us to a very late lunch.

I found him at the nurses' station, dark head bent over a chart. In that position, a familiar one, he looked vulnerable and boyish—and very tired. The slump of his posture in the chair betrayed a fatigue that while working long hours we tried hard to ignore.

"Anthony, talk to me."

"Surely you can see that I'm busy. After I finish reviewing the lab work, I have to go see this patient."

"Fine. I have a few minutes. I'll go with you and perhaps we can talk after."

"Devin..."

His dark eyes said it all... hurt, anger, and betrayal.

"I'd like to explain things to you, apologize if need be. It isn't what you think."

Curious glances shot our way. I was sure even those too polite to be caught paying attention had ears strained to our direction.

"Please," I said very quietly. "Just a few minutes in the lounge. I'll buy you a Coke. And maybe a candy bar to go with it, since you have such a sweet tooth."

In the lounge, snacks of our choice in hand, we stared at each other in the wary way friends do when some event has suddenly made them feel like strangers. I hated that. The thing I had treasured most about Anthony Toretta was the easiness between us. I suppose I had had a hand in destroying that, although I preferred to sugarcoat it and not look at it that way.

"Anthony," I said, feeling awkward and having no appetite for the Milky Way I had purchased from the vending machine, "I know you're upset with me, and I have some idea why. But I'd appreciate it if you'd tell me what people are saying about me."

His gaze was cold upon my soul. "What do you think they're saying, Devin? They're saying you had a 'thing' going with Paul Linden and that his wife found out about it, that she confronted you and this somehow led to her death."

It was even worse than I had expected. Tears sprang to my eyes and I batted my lids furiously to fight them back.

"Surely they don't think I killed Drusilla Linden."

"I haven't heard anyone hint at that," he admitted, "although the bookies have the odds stacked against Linden himself."

"But why..."

"With her dead, he can have you, his kids, and all the money and holdings. With her alive, well... you figure it out."

My laughter was short and bitter, very unpleasant even to my own ears.

"Why is it I don't see myself as such a prize that a man

would kill for?"

He shrugged. "Beats me. Your seeming lack of vanity about your looks is part of your charm, I guess. You stand there with your flawless skin, your eyes like fine sherry, full lips that beg to be kissed, and a body that would make even St. Paul have impure thoughts, and you ask why a man would . . . hell, Devin, just forget it. You asked. I answered. Maybe it's my turn to ask a question."

"Please do. You may not like everything that I have to say, Anthony, but I'm not going to lie to you."

"No? I can think of a few lies. Or are omissions not considered lies in your book? Just rearrange the facts a little—no real big deal. Anyway, what I was going to ask is if you're in love with Paul Linden?"

I took a deep breath. I had expected, I think, for him to ask if I had slept with the man . . . and my answer to that could have been an honest no. This way, I wasn't as easily put in the clear.

"I don't know," I said at last. "I don't want to be. I admit he intrigues me. He always did. As a little girl, I was totally in awe of him. That's what you meant by my lying to you, wasn't it? I wanted to tell you the truth before I did. I felt rotten about holding back because I liked you, but I just couldn't bring myself to . . . well, what would you have done in my place?"

"I have to admit I don't know and that I too might have held back. So I guess I'm just going to have to say I understand at least part of the reasons, so all I ask is that you answer the original question squarely. In truth, you misunderstood anyway. All I meant by the 'omissions' was about your seeing Paul on the side, not telling me."

I had only thought my blush mechanism had worn-out, because I felt the crimson red steal across my cheeks. "As square as I can get about being in love with Paul is that I don't really know. I don't think so. Not yet. I admit I'm attracted to him and enjoy his company. I can say the same about you. Ironically, he's kissed me once, just as you have. I enjoyed both kisses. I don't know what to make of it. Maybe you have an explanation. But, first, I want to explain about the other. When he asked me to dinner, it was a spur-of-the-moment invitation, a real surprise to me. I even felt guilty when he said we were going to the inn because you had wanted to take me there. It was a dinner in public, not a clandestine affair. As I'm sure is all over town, we ran into Dru and a couple of her friends. She'd had too much to drink and made a scene. Paul was upset, understandably so, and uncharacteristically opened up to me on the way home. He kissed me at my door and didn't even come in to talk more. I haven't seen him since. Dru came to my place last night, again drunk, and accused me of all sorts of vile things. Incidentally, according to her, I'm sleeping with you as well as with Paul. Which makes me pretty busy for a woman who works the hours I do. Makes me wonder how I do it all. Superwoman, I guess."

Seeing my hurt, Anthony showed signs of melting. I had no intention of letting him off the hook that quickly.

"So," I continued, "add that as grist for the ABC gossip mill. Maybe you'll even feel flattered. Somehow, I don't. I always thought it would be fun to be a femme fatale. Now branded that, even erroneously, I find I feel dirty and cheap, not a good feeling at all."

There was no stopping him at that point. His arms surrounded me and I stayed there, relishing the comfort and support even if I was still angry at him.

"Anthony, please believe that the last thing I wanted was to hurt you. But I'm not even sure right now what it is I want or am looking for. Does that make any sense at all?"

"Too much," he admitted. "I've been a bonehead. I admit that. Even if you were having an affair with Linden, it's none of my business. There's no reason why you should confess or explain to me. As I said before, I find myself doing things I swore I'd never do. It's hard to love someone who doesn't love you back."

"But I do love you," I said gently.

"Yeah, sure. But not in the same way. That's not your fault, Devin . . . or Katie, or whatever your name is . . ."

"Devin," I said without hesitation. "Katie was long ago and far away. Still a part of me, but . . . please, just call me Devin as you always have."

"Sure. But if you fall in love with Paul Linden or with someone else who isn't me, well . . . hell, you can't help it. That's all I mean."

"I don't have an explanation. I'm too confused at this point to know my own mind. Since I'm not ready to admit I can manage to be genuinely in love with both of you, I don't know how to explain the feelings I have. Maybe the day will soon come when I'll know which of you I love. But some things can't be forced, they take time."

He nodded and smiled a sweet, but sad smile.

"The answer could be, sweet Devin, that you don't love either of us. As much as I hate to say it, that still could very well be the answer."

Then the page burst forth with Anthony's number. He made the call and received his in-house assignment. Duty called. Anything else we had to say would have to wait.

"Friends?" I asked as he made ready to make his departure.

"Sure. Why the hell not? Anger burns up too much energy."

"Anthony?"

He was already in the doorway and turned back to face me. I could tell, a doctor first and foremost, his mind was already on what lay ahead, what he could do in the way of healing.

"You really meant what you said . . . about my eyes being like sherry and everything?"

He burst out laughing, unable, it would seem, to help himself.

"You know me, kid . . . I'm grateful for a beer now and then. I wouldn't know fine sherry from bourbon from moonshine. I guess I read that line in a book or something. But it seemed to fit . . . and of course I meant it. Be easier if I didn't, wouldn't it?"

With that, he was gone. And it was past time for me to go back to my duty station. I felt better, though, having repaired our friendship.

Maybe we would become more than friends. Maybe not. Only time would tell. I was in no hurry for love.

It was a complication I did not need, although my hormones often raged and refused to agree with me. *But we would be friends.* I liked him too much to lose that. Not for the first time, I regretted the conflicting schedules that kept us apart.

I did have lunch with Mother, but not, as I had feared, until well past the customary hour. She did not seem to mind though. Within ten minutes of my call to her, she arrived at the hospital, magnificent in a broad-brimmed straw hat that hid her hair and a caftan-style dress.

Smiling, I said, "I've never seen you dressed quite like this before."

"Probably because I never have dressed this way before. As you can see, I came prepared to go incognito. Even though you say it isn't necessary now, I thought I'd try out the look. Besides, I didn't bring a lot with me."

I arched my eyebrow at that. It seemed to me that she had brought enough to see her through several major social seasons. But what did I know . . . I who lived in scrubs and tailored slacks?

"You look marvelous . . . as always," I said, proud and envious at the same time.

"I suppose," she said carefully some moments later as we toyed with the none-too-good tuna salad, "that Dr. Linden and Dr. McCracken haven't been around today. Is there much talk, do you think?"

"Mother, *really*. You grew up in Dalton. You know the least little thing causes talk. And this is big time news. You might be interested to know that I'm a veritable Jezebel. People seem to have forgotten that Paul and Dru were separated before I came to work here. Suddenly I'm the villain. At best, I broke up the marriage and drove her to drink. At worst, I killed her—or drove Paul to do it."

"Devin! They surely don't say those things to you."

"No? Maybe not directly. But I get the point."

"That does it. I'm staying with you for a while. There is no way I'm leaving with things the way they are here."

Alarms went off in my head. "No." I said with what I hoped was convincing firmness. "There is no way I can permit that. You'd be bored senseless. It's best to keep on with our regular plans. If something comes up, I know you'll come back."

"You're sure?"

"I'm positive." And I was, but the child in me was a bit crushed to see how relieved she looked.

On the day of Dru's funeral, Mother packed her bags and left. I was wrangling with myself over whether to make an appearance or not when ABC made the decision for me. David Francis was sick and I was needed to cover his duty station. The three other interns and I sent flowers. It didn't seem enough, but inside I was deeply relieved not to have to show up in person. It didn't seem to matter that I wasn't guilty. What mattered was that there were those who thought I was. When people looked at me accusingly, I burned inside and out as though perhaps they knew about an evil me I didn't even know myself.

I wasn't to get off that easily, however. Quite late that night, just as I was preparing to go home, I rounded a corner in the corridors and found myself face-to-face with George McCracken. His face was a storm, a storm that deepened when he comprehended who I was.

"Oh, so it's young Dr. Hollister," he said, scorn lapping like acid over the words.

Not willing to let it go, I planted myself in his path. "I'm so sorry about your daughter, Dr. McCracken."

"Are you? I should think otherwise."

"It disappoints and hurts me that you take stock in the rumors that apparently are floating around. Paul took me to the Fraser Inn to eat and we ran into Dru there. There was nothing clandestine about anything that happened. We aren't having an affair. Surely you know that Paul and Dru were having a considerable amount of difficulty before I came here."

His shoulders gave a strange heave, a motion I suspected was caused by a silent sob. Whatever Dru had or had not been, she was his daughter, his only child.

More gently, I said, "What are you doing here anyway? You should be home, be resting, be with your wife. Meeting people, being out in public . . . I'm sure it hurts too much now."

"Do you think it will ever stop? If so, you're even younger than you look. I have a patient who needs me. You see, I have to tell myself I'm needed. That's the only reason I could possibly have for going on."

Understanding that, I nodded. "Which patient did you want to see? I'll go with you."

"Young woman . . ."

"Please?"

He shrugged. Probably nothing made a lot of difference to him at this point.

"It's my knee, doctor," said Pearl Franklin when we were in her room. "I've asked and asked for help and it just hurts so much that I can't even think of falling asleep."

"I know, Pearlie. I know. You have been taking the tablets when they bring them?"

"Oh, yes. I do what they say. I try to cooperate. But it just don't help, nothing does."

"Then let me take a look."

He uncovered her mishapen legs with marked bulging, bluish veins. The right knee was swollen. He placed his hand on it and pronounced it hot. Looking my way, he said, "Go get us some acetaminophen and a fresh pad for her knee."

I did as I was told, then stood there as the gray-haired gentleman personally poured a tumbler of water and assisted Pearl in the taking of the two ordinary over-the-counter analgesics. That done, he placed the pad at the bend of her knee.

"You'll sleep. I guarantee it."

"I'm sure I will," she beamed.

Maybe it was my imagination, but I thought I heard the patient snore gently before we were even all the way into the hall.

"The healing touch."

"Some call if faith healing. Some call it hocus-pocus. Not to mention those who call it quackery."

"And what do you call it, Dr. McCracken?"

"Reassurance . . . one of the best tools we can use to

help other human beings in distress. The soothing voice, the laying on of hands . . . it goes a long way. I only wish . . ."

He did not have to finish. I knew what he wished . . . that someone could touch him, reassure him, and bring him peace.

"Are you ready to go home, doctor?"

He turned his palms upward and looked around him. Things were quiet. There wasn't anything else for him to do. I knew without asking that the nurses hadn't called him and told him Pearl was complaining of pain. *He* was the one who had called, had asked, and had insisted on coming. In this instance, the patient hadn't needed a doctor as much as the doctor had needed a patient.

"I'm leaving, too. I'll walk with you to the parking garage."

"I didn't park there. I'm just outside."

"So much the better. So am I. We interns aren't allowed the privilege of the parking garage, you know."

Outside, I was struck by the sweet smell in the air emanating from the nearby shrubs, whose foliage had not yet given in to the chill of the autumn nights.

"I love that smell," I said without thinking.

"Like the funeral home. I never saw so many damned flowers all at one time in my life."

"So many flowers, Katie, and all so beautiful. How people must have loved and respected your father."

I had hated them. They hadn't seemed beautiful to me at all. I had wanted to go home and that wasn't allowed.

"I know . . . oh, how I know," I said as much to myself as to him, my voice barely above a whisper.

Instead of attacking me, as I half expected him to do, he turned to me, eyes bleary and pain-filled. "You lost someone close to you?"

So that part wasn't out yet . . . Anthony hadn't known and it did not seem that Dr. McCracken did either.

I nodded, this moment seeming the same as the moments in those awful last days in Dalton. "My father. I was only eleven. But it still hurts. I still miss him."

"But you said your father was a surgeon in Maine."

"Massachusetts . . . I came here from Boston. But, no, I didn't say that. I told you my father was—had been—a surgeon. You knew I was from the east and added two and two to make five. My stepfather's name is Hollister. He's a financial wiz in the corporate world. Dr. McCracken, you knew my real father. In fact, you knew *me* once. I didn't want anyone to know about my Dalton background at first. I came back here to find some answers about the past, and felt I'd stand a better chance if people didn't know I had roots here."

He stared at me, looking as if he had seen a ghost. In a way, perhaps he had.

"Katie . . . my God, you're Katie."

I felt my own shoulders shake involuntarily from silent sobs, sobs never far from the surface these days.

"I said all along you looked familiar, didn't I? For a couple of days, it drove me crazy. Then I just forgot about it. It was the different name that threw me. You've grown-up, of course. But I can see, once I know. And you're very like your mother, too."

"Not really," I quickly denied.

"Oh, yes," he said, something almost like a smile on his lips. "And like him, too. The eyes, I think. Yes, you do have his eyes—not just the color, but the depth, the expression. Katie, child, why . . . ?"

Even knowing that this wasn't the appropriate time or place, I still was unable to restrain myself.

"The main reason I came here to intern was to find out about my father's last days. I know I'm the only one who thinks this, and I know I was just a child when it happened, but I've never believed he killed himself."

"I had some trouble with that, too. Still, it was years and years ago. Can it matter so much now?"

"It does to me. Maybe it's not what you need to hear right now. But some pain doesn't go away, you just get used to carrying it around. You see, if he did kill himself, then everything I knew of him, of the way he was with me—it's all a lie. Fiction of the worst sort. And I've never been able to accept that."

His eyes were intent on me and I broke off there.

"How rotten of me," I mumbled. "Please, perhaps we can talk later. Now you look dead on your feet. Can I drive you home? I can walk back here afterward to get my car. It isn't far."

"That's kind of you, but I'm fine. Don't worry. I'm going straight home. But Katie . . ."

"Yes, sir?"

"Let the past be the past."

"That's good advice. But if I could take it, I wouldn't be here."

"You think right now that you can never be more hurt than you were, that the truth would be kinder than being in the dark. That isn't true. Let it be. Get ahead with your life."

"But you will talk to me later?"

He shook his head in a manner that could have meant anything.

"Let it be," he said, then climbed inside the shining dark blue Eldorado.

Let it be. The words echoed through the darkness. They had a bitter sound to them, so bitter not even the sweetness of the flowering shrubs gave me pleasure now. George McCracken was right . . . the heavy, sweet scent was the same as in a funeral home.

Let it be. Let it be. Good advice to those who will take it.

When I got back to the apartment, I found I was relieved Mother had gone back to Boston. The last thing I needed was to deal with her superficial prattle. She had left the scent of roses in my small apartment and, oddly, I took comfort in that scent. I love my mother with all my heart. But there is a gulf between us, a gulf that time and effort will undoubtedly bridge, but it was with a stab of guilt that I realized the bridge will have to wait.

Let it be. Let it be. As I lay in the darkness striving for sleep, the words were like a mantra . . . a mantra in which there was no comfort, no peace. I would have traded it for another one if I only could have. I felt I was getting a first-hand taste of what being obsessive/compulsive was like.

Chapter Fourteen

Jackson Lee Fraser came to my apartment the next morning. Sleep hadn't come easily the night before, but I *had* finally slept and my body, once it gave in, had not been eager to awaken. By the time I showered and washed my hair, dressed in jeans and a red-striped shirt worn over a tank top, and combed my hair back carelessly to let it dry on its own, the clock told me it was disgracefully near noon. When I answered the summons of the doorbell and saw him standing there, I was as little surprised as if he had called ahead. He had said he would be in touch. When most people say that, it is a vague social statement, akin to, "Do come see us sometime." But what Jack said, he meant. A promise was a commitment, even a "promise" that light and vague.

I stepped aside and let him in without a word.

"Time?"

"Some."

"Great."

"Sit."

"Thanks."

I opened my mouth to bring forth another monosyllable and burst out laughing instead. "I hadn't thought of that game in years, Jack."

"Neither had I. Seeing you, the years just fell away. It seemed the natural thing to do. Incidentally, you just lost."

"You were always the best as I recall, I almost always

did. Some people think I'm on the quiet side, but compared to you I was a real conversationalist. Anyway . . . how did it go with the police?"

He grimaced. "I really got the third degree. For an hour or so there, I was really sweating. I thought those goons were going to haul me down to the station and book me."

"How ridiculous. On what charge? Why would you possibly have wanted to kill Dru Linden?"

"Don't ask me. Ask them. I never knew there were so many ways to ask the same questions."

"Probably they were just trying to trace her last steps, find out where you left her and in what condition. I can't see *you* as a likely suspect. You just happened to be in the wrong place at the wrong time. But the fact is that someone did kill her. Things like this don't happen every day in a little town like this. It's pretty serious business."

"Murder isn't serious business in Boston? My, things have gotten blasé in this modern world."

The droll comment, delivered in his slow, thick southern drawl, was too much for me. Again, I laughed.

"Not that blasé, Jack. But, face it, it *is* more commonplace in cities. I don't suppose you've heard if there are any real leads on Dru's killer yet?"

"If there's any real evidence, the authorities are keeping it to themselves. I think our boys in blue are mostly out of it and the majority of the investigation is being carried out through the sheriff's department. But I'm sure if there had actually been an arrest, we would have heard. Things like that don't stay shut up around here for long."

Recalling my experiences at ABC right after the murder, I winced.

"Something wrong?"

"No. Just thinking about something unpleasant."

"Then stop."

"I'll try . . . but, face it, a lot of unpleasantness is going on. Tell me the truth, have you heard any comments yet about my 'true identity?'"

"Not really, but, then, I haven't asked. And probably

most people don't know I knew you then. Or now, for that matter. Katie, have you run across anything at all yet that gave you any insight into your father's death?"

I shook my head. "Not a thing. There hasn't been a lot of time to look. And I've been so afraid of scaring someone off if they knew what I was really looking for. I hoped to ease into an investigation gradually. I'm beginning to think, for a supposedly smart girl, I've been incredibly dumb and naive about this. My mother kept telling me before I ever came that it's been fifteen years. The reality of that is just beginning to sink in. On some level, I think I imagined I'd come back to Dalton and find everything and everyone just as they had been back then. It isn't that way. People die, move, forget. What happened was bad, but I guess it didn't vitally touch a great many people on a personal basis. I've tried explaining over and over again why I *need* to know. The explanations came out hollow sounding. It's hard for me to put my feelings about this into words people can relate to."

"He led you to believe you were of great importance to him. If he could leave you voluntarily, and without a word of warning, then you must not have been important at all."

I sat there with a huge lump in my throat and tears spilling down my cheeks. Without a word, Jack left the room and returned carrying a handful of tissues.

"Thank you," I said simply when I was able. "Do you think I could be right?"

"Possibly. I wasn't around him a lot. He didn't seem to be suicidal to me. But we were children, Katie. Tell me what's on your mind."

"It's very, very important to me for you to realize I'll always love and accept you, no matter what you choose. But I do believe you'll be a doctor. I can see it in my mind's eye as clearly as if it already was."

And I could see *that* memory in my own mind's eye, see it just as clearly as if it happened today instead of fifteen years ago. He wore the hunter green shirt and the summer sunlight reflected in his hazel eyes to make them seem more green than amber. He had been in such a good mood.

In detail, I told what I remembered of that day to Jack and he listened intently just as others had done.

"Does this tell you anything?" I asked anxiously when he did not immediately make a comment at the end of my narrative.

"On the surface. But the human mind is a peculiar thing."

"What do you mean?"

He hesitated again.

"Go on, say it."

"I was just wondering if maybe he could have been at peace because he had made his decision."

I considered that. "I suppose that happens sometimes. But you have to consider that this wasn't an isolated good day, that he *wasn't* a morose person, that he was generally a very sunny-tempered man."

"He had that reputation. I recall that much. Most doctors, especially surgeons, are noted for being prima donnas. But Dr. Clark wasn't known for that. I don't know a lot about him. I'm not even sure where I heard that much. Probably from my aunts. He 'did' them both, you know, in the space of my childhood."

"'Did' them?"

"Yes. Aunt Dorrie's gallbladder and Aunt Em's appendix."

"I see. Jack, when you were here last, we were talking about marriage. You acted somewhat strangely and seemed ready to say something when I mentioned my parents' marriage."

"Did I?"

"Yes. Yes, you did. It wasn't all my imagination. And don't tell me it was."

"Okay, I won't tell you that. But first things first. There's something we haven't talked about. Somehow I don't think you've even considered it. Not that I'm putting you in the 'dumb and naive' class you mentioned. But I do think maybe you've been so single-minded, almost obsessed, that you've not considered all the angles."

"And the angle is . . ."

"Katie, if you manage to prove beyond a shadow of doubt, with the goal being only your satisfaction and peace of mind, that Jim Clark did not put a gun to his head and pull the trigger, then what?"

"What do you mean 'then what?'"

"Think about it."

"If he didn't kill himself, then someone else killed him. But you're wrong . . . I have thought of that."

"In terms that apply to the real world?"

Reverting to childhood, I stuck my tongue out at him.

"Seriously," he said, grimly unyielding. "Murder, Katie. You're talking about another murder. You've had threats. Doesn't that tell you something? Someone, at least one person, doesn't want the past dredged up. There is no statute of limitations on murder. The person who killed him, if such was the case, can still be punished just like it was yesterday. Your father and mother knew important people . . . the cream of society in this little town.

"Think about it."

"I am. I have. And it isn't that I haven't thought about it. It's just that I push it aside and say I'll deal with that *after* I know what I need to know. And he wasn't killed with that gun. There wasn't enough blood for that. Just a little on his temple. Mother didn't even have to have the carpet cleaned."

"I gather you're not about to stop in this investigation?"

"No way. In fact, now that my cover is blown, I'm going to devote more time to it. *Now*, are you going to tell me whatever it is that you're being so secretive about?"

My beeper went off then, making me jump out of my skin. I should be used to the sound by now, and generally am, but my thoughts had been in such a different world. Not often do I forget I'm a doctor, but on this occasion I had almost done just that.

Going to the telephone, I dialed the number of the hospital and reported in. "I have to go," I told him as I hung up the phone.

He grinned. "As I said, first things first. Mind if I tag along? Or is this going to be hours and hours?"

"I don't think so. They're intubating a patient in ER. Not only could they use some help, they think I'd like to be in on it. Mind?"

"On the contrary, I'm looking forward to it."

"We'll talk later? It shouldn't be long."

"As I said before, first things first."

The patient was a man in his seventies who apparently had suffered for many years from chronic lung disease and congestive heart failure. It had been a long time since breathing had come easily to him, but his family had noted that he was severely short of breath and had brought him to the emergency room. On arrival, he was found to have severely high blood pressure as well, in addition to having an elevated heart rate. By the time I was on the scene, he had been given medicines for the heart and blood pressure symptoms as well as being placed on an oxygen mask.

Rick Sinclair was playing the case with a slow hand. The internist on call had been notified, but was not yet on the scene. For the time being, the care of the patient was the ER physician's responsibility.

"Switch him to the nasal tube," he ordered to the nearby nurse.

I hadn't been sure he was aware I had arrived on the scene until he said, still without looking up at me, "That's because we had him on 100% non-rebreather mask. I switched him because I'm afraid of impending respiratory failure."

"I see," I said, stepping forward so that I could see and touch the patient. His breathing was labored. Although he was alert and sitting up, he was in anything but good shape. His color was ashen and he was coughing with nearly every breath and it was obvious he was using all his energy to breath.

The intubation procedure was to pass a tube fully through the right nostril to aid the patient's breathing. At the end of the procedure, I placed my stethoscope against the patient's chest, then announced, "Good breath sounds on both sides."

"Great," Dr. Sinclair said, pleased and relieved to know there was no sign that the tube hadn't been placed correctly.

"Next?" he asked me in a challenge.

"Morphine."

"Why morphine? You think his pain is that great?"

He knew . . . and I knew he knew and was just seeing if I could defend my decision. "To rest him and thereby assist him in breathing. It's taking all his strength just to breathe."

"And how are we going to administer this morphine?"

"In five milligram doses—a total of ten may be enough, no more than fifteen, I'd say."

He nodded and said, "Cut it in half for now. We don't want his blood pressure going too low. And you're right, as you already knew, about the morphine, so see that it's given STAT."

"Yes, sir."

"And next?"

It was like being with my father again, the countless questions, the goodnatured, though serious drilling.

"Get a portable X-ray unit in for a chest X ray. The chest sounds are clear for intubation, but we need to be certain."

"Great! You'll make a doctor yet."

"Gee thanks," I said drily. "When do I get my biscuit?"

The patient laughed at that. Despite what it was taking just to keep him breathing, he laughed at my little joke.

"Give that girl a biscuit, doc," he wheezed.

I patted him on the shoulder. "Thanks for sticking up for me, Mr. Kowalski, but please don't try to talk right now. Believe me, I'll see this character gives me that biscuit. Anyone who puts up with his lip deserves a whole box of biscuits, right?"

The man nodded, attempting a smile but not yielding to the impulse to communicate verbally. I am sure he found that those few words has cost him considerable effort. I turned away to give the morphine and slow the rate of the IV and found that I had to blink away the threat of tears so I could work unobscured. How I hate it when they are so damned brave! It tears me up, breaks my heart into little pieces. It's much easier on me if they whine and cry and complain. But a goodly number are like Kowalski here, joking in the face of what could be their last moments.

Within minutes, the chest X ray was before us and confirmed that the ET tube was in place. Sinclair came up behind me. Before he could even ask, I said, "No signs of displacement of the tube. Heart's on the large side. And there's pulmonary trouble—moderate-to-severe."

The attending internist arrived and the patient was taken off to the ICU where he would be monitored. As with the other admitted patients, he was then out of our hands.

I walked slowly to the door. With a smile, I acknowledged Jack's presence. He had waited for me in the ER, propped up against a wall, well out of the way and yet able to view what was going on from a distance.

"I'm surprised they didn't run you out of here."

"Don't be. I get to stay a lot of places I'm not really supposed to be. I think I'm unobtrusive."

"Yeah, and you blend well, too."

As we bantered, I felt myself coming back to the other world. I won't say the real world because both are real worlds. It is just that my role in each is different. When I am working, I am a physician first, a person second. In that other world, I am Devin Hollister, a person who just happens to be a physician.

"So that's what you do," he said, nodding toward the area where we had labored over Mr. Kowalski.

"That's it."

"I'm glad I got to see you in this habitat. It tells me a lot."

"Such as?"

"I don't know . . . it's hard to explain. You ready to go now?"

"Almost. I . . ."

"Hi, Devin. I thought you were off today."

I turned in the direction of the voice and faced Anthony. Face flaming for reasons I could not define, I mumblingly introduced the two men to each other while they sized each other up.

"I am off," I explained once the introduction was completed. "I just got called in on an emergency case. Not that they couldn't have done as well or better without me, but Rick Sinclair is beginning to know me well. We had to put the patient on a ventilator. I hadn't seen that before, the actual process. So awful."

"Yeah, I'm sure it is. Uh, look, I'll see you around. I'd better get back where I belong. Give me a call when you get a chance."

"I will. Thanks." Turning slightly to face Jack, I said, "I'm going to go check on a favorite patient, then wash up. I'll be right back and then, to answer your question, I'll be ready to go."

As I walked away, Anthony matched his step to mine and stayed beside me. Although I could not see, somehow I knew that Jack's eyes were intently upon us.

"You do attract them like honeysuckle does the bees, don't you, Devin? So much competition. It almost makes me feel like throwing in the towel . . . but only almost. For a while, I'll hang in."

"Come off it, Anthony. It isn't like that with Jack. It's more like we're brother and sister. I knew him when I was here before, when we were just children. Truth is, I didn't treat him well at all. It's surprising he'll even speak to me."

"Not surprising at all. You always underestimate yourself. Like I said before, I guess that's part of your charm."

Reaching the floor, I stopped at the corridor where I'd turn down to see Mrs. Nickerson. "I'll see you, Anthony. You've been great."

"I know . . . I'm a real pal. Which makes it my problem if I want more than that, right?"

"Anthony, this isn't the time or the place."

"I know." His dark eyes took in the now familiar

surroundings. "Trouble is, it never is. See you, Devin."

I spent a few minutes with lovely Mrs. Nickerson. Although my intent had been to cheer her up, I ended up believing she cheered me more. I was in an upbeat mood when I left her room to washup. Looking in the mirror, I laughed to see that I had never combed my hair since slicking it back when I was first out of the shower. "That's a decided improvement," I announced to myself when I had my hair restored to its proper waves. Maybe, I thought wryly, my carelessness with my appearance was also part of my "charm." Poor Anthony. I did not know how to handle his crush. Sadly enough, neither did he.

Once I was back in the emergency room I looked around for Jack, ready to tease him by saying I had combed my hair just for him. But he wasn't there. Shrugging, I decided he must have just gone to find a restroom or something. Ten minutes later, there was still no sign of him. I looked up and down the nearest corridors to no avail. Stepping back into ER, I picked up the telephone and paged, "Jack Fraser, return to the ER. Jack Fraser, return to the ER." To that, there was no response.

I made a trip to the parking lot and saw that my Mustang remained undisturbed where we had left it. Puzzled, I turned and went back inside the building. For a few moments, I went up and down the corridors asking if anyone had seen, "A blondish guy about my age, medium height, glasses, light blue cotton pants and a white Polo shirt." All of my inquiries were met with a negative except for one ER attendant who, with a vague and don't care air, said, "Seems like I saw the guy. Can't remember exactly when. I think I saw him talking to a taller, thinner guy who looked something like Dr. Linden. But he wasn't dressed in hospital clothes and I wasn't close and didn't pay a hell of a lot of attention." My attempt to question as to if this was before or after the respiratory patient had been transferred to ICU met with a blank stare and a "don't know—like I said, I wasn't really paying attention."

Going to the physicians' lounge, I called the numbers

listed for the inn and for Jack's living quarters in the house. There was no answer at Jack's personal number and no one at the restaurant had seen the owner in the last couple of hours, but if I did run into him would I please tell him they were about out of white cooking wine? Frustrated, I sat and waited for a few minutes, then decided waiting at the hospital was a futile act.

He was not back at my apartment when I arrived there and another call to his home confirmed he had not yet arrived back there or at the inn. Now what? I would feel a bit foolish combing the countryside for Jack if he had voluntarily taken a hike. On the other hand, I would feel even more foolish to sit on my duff and find out later that he had been in real trouble somewhere. And foolish was exactly what I felt when I called the local police station *and* sheriff's department to ask if they had seen Jack, perhaps asked him to come back in for questioning.

"You've lost Mr. Fraser?" one smart aleck officer asked, not even trying to hide his amusement.

"He's disappeared, that's all I know," I snapped, "and considering that there's already been one murder, you just might be sneering out of the other side of your mouth if there *is* something wrong."

With that, I slammed down the receiver, then plopped on the couch to ponder the siutation.

As unlikely as it seemed, Jack Fraser had disappeared into thin air, and for no accountable reason.

Chapter Fifteen

Beeper clipped to the belt of my jeans, I combed the streets of Dalton, going slowly up and down side streets and thoroughfares. I made several checks at the inn without locating him. Initially, the main concern was still that the supply of cooking spirits was low and the dinner hour was approaching.

"Can't someone else go buy the wine?" I asked, worry making the question come out more irritably than I had intended.

It appeared no one had thought of this. Mr. Fraser was always the one to see to supplies. The conclusion of the hurried conference among the inn employees was that this was, indeed, a crisis situation and they were certain he would want them to take some initiative rather than vary the recipes and shortchange the customers. One of them made a quick run after white cooking wine. When I checked back again an hour or so later, the concern was, I thought, in the right place.

One sober-faced member of the crew told me, "Mr. Fraser has never missed presiding over a dinner hour since the restaurant opened. We can't believe he'd miss today's without telling us ahead of time."

"Neither can I. That's what I've been trying to tell you. I *feel* that something is wrong. But I don't think I can get the police to do anything. He hasn't been missing long enough yet. I'm going to see if I can get some help somewhere."

They all offered to help. Another quick conference brought forth the opinion, with which I was in agreement, that Jack would want the restaurant business to go on as usual.

"And perhaps one of you could do what he does . . . go by the tables and check on the diners personally, maybe explain that he couldn't be there but sends his regards. Something like that. You know, that famous southern charm."

They nodded, knowing what I meant and agreeing. I left amidst assurances that they would help join the hunt after the dinner hour if Jack had not reappeared.

For what seemed like the hundredth time, I went back to ABC and was told again, of course, that there had been no sign of Jack Fraser there. I went to the library and checked the intern rotation schedule. Chris was to be in the building and David on call. Anthony, like me, was free . . . one of the rare times that had occurred lately.

Knowing he would be off duty and leaving soon, I went in search of him. I found him just finishing with a patient. He looked pale and haggard. I knew the extreme fatigue that went with that look and felt extremely bad at asking for his help, but desperation overrode compassion.

"Anthony, I know you're dead on your feet, but I don't know where else to turn. Jack—the guy you met in ER with me—has completely disappeared. Something is wrong. I just know it. The authorities are no help and I don't know anyone else I can ask."

"Let's get this straight . . . you've lost your boyfriend and you want me to help find him?"

Again, I snapped—something I was getting good at in the past few hours. "He isn't my boyfriend. And it isn't a laughing matter. Good grief, you sound just like that smart aleck policeman I talked to on the phone. If you don't want to help, fine."

A slow grin erased some of the tiredness from his face. His dark eyes were kind when he said, "Whoa, Devin, can't you take a joke? I admit my wit isn't at its sharpest, but I am trying. Come on, I'm out of here. Tell me what it's all about on the way to the parking lot."

I didn't know what it was all about. That was the problem. There wasn't a lot I could explain without sounding like a fool. Therefore, for just the moment, I chose not to mention that, until the past few days, I hadn't seen Jack since he and I were both eleven years of age.

"Jack Fraser is as solid as a rock. A regular living, breathing steadfast tin soldier. He would *not* leave unexplained like that. Not unless it was an emergency. And if it was an emergency he went to, why doesn't someone else know about it?" Then, as added argument to get Anthony involved in helping in the search, I gave him a melodramatic version of Jack disappearing into the night with an inebriated Dru Linden on his arm and his subsequent third degree by the authorities.

"Okay, kid, you've sold me. If nothing else, I'd believe no man who was with you would bolt voluntarily. But where do we start? It's a little town in some ways, but still . . ."

"I know," I said wearily. "I've cruised up and down the streets ever since I left here. Not a high likelihood, I know, that I'd run across him that way, but I felt like I was doing something. Know what I mean?"

"Sure, I know. It's the sitting and waiting that drives you crazy at a time like this. And speaking of crazy, I guess that's what I am to help you hunt for my rival . . . one of my rivals, I guess I should say . . . but I've been accused of mania before, so off we go. But we're going to have to at least make an emergency run through a drive-up window or something and get me a sack of hamburgers. I haven't eaten anything since my bowl of cold cereal at breakfast."

Come to think of it, neither had I. Despite my worry, the calorie and cholesterol laden sandwiches and fries were delicious, filling the empty pit of my stomach.

"Any ideas?" Anthony asked between bites. He was such a nice guy, his fine Italian eyes so filled with concern. Joke though he might, I felt he believed along with me that there was genuine cause for worry, especially after I explained how the inn employees felt when Jack hadn't shown up for dinner there.

"Only one idea. And you won't like it. I don't like it myself. But it's the only clue I have. One of the guys working ER thought it was possible he saw someone who fit the description I gave of Jack talking with someone who may or may not have been Paul Linden." I took care to explain to Anthony that there was no reliable time frame connected with the event . . . and that the event probably hadn't even happened.

Anthony frowned. "I didn't see Linden at the hospital anywhere today. Of course, I'm not on the surgical floor now, but . . ."

I knew exactly what he meant. It wasn't expected that Paul would be at the hospital. He had made arrangements for all of his surgical cases that were scheduled for the next few days to be either postponed or handled by one of the other surgeons. "I'll be back next Monday," he had told them, "I need some time with my boys to help them adjust to what's going on."

"I hate to bother him, but I don't know what else to do."

"I understand, Devin, but . . ."

Again, I knew what he meant. He didn't have to put it into words. Paul was chief of surgery, one of the main forces at ABC with which we interns had to reckon. The thought of irritating him by intruding at a time like this, well . . . it wasn't altogether pleasant.

"We have to. I don't think it's an exaggeration to say Jack's life may be at stake. For all I know, we're already too late. But we have to try."

With a deep sigh, Anthony then nodded his agreement. "In person or by telephone?"

"In person," I decided. "He'll be more understanding at our bothering him if he sees how distraught we are."

"You know where he lives? I sure as heck don't."

I kept my face averted from him, knowing one of my telltale blushes was sure to stain my face when I said, "I think it's over in that new subdivision across town—Oak Knoll Estates, it's officially called, but locally known as

Pill Hill. All of the houses are so big and fancy that only doctors can afford them." I hadn't been by there. I was clear of being *that* adolescent, but I *had* looked Paul's name up in the telephone book. Like it or not, my interest had been such that I wanted to know where he had lived with Dru, what his home was like. Only fear of being seen and thus embarrassed had kept me from driving by.

Anthony made no comment. Since I had turned the Mustang over to him temporarily, I gave him directions to Oak Knoll. He gave a low whistle of appreciation as we drove in through the wide entranceway that was flanked with brick posts and elaborate light fixtures. "Someday?" he asked, gaze sweeping over the beautifully landscaped new homes. At a rough guess, the least of them had a market value, even in Dalton, Mississippi, of a quarter of a million dollars.

"Which one?"

"I don't know what it looks like, But I think it's number twenty-seven. I'm not sure. Look for a silver Mercedes. That's what he drives. I don't know what Dru's car is like."

"Maybe she had a gold one," he muttered. "And, yes, that's sarcasm. I'm jealous as all get out, if you want to know the truth. You know what my car is like . . . and my apartment matches it. This is . . ."

"Sumptuous?"

"That'll do."

"It is. Even by Boston standards, this is nice. *Real* nice."

The house was number twenty-seven . . . something I had been more sure of than I had wanted Anthony to know. There was, however, no Mercedes in view. It and any other vehicles were neatly hidden away in the multiple car garage, doors discretely placed at the back of the house. Not for Oak Knoll was the gaping garage door at the front of the house, left open to reveal tools and toys and junk. We knew before we even looked for the house number because Paul and the boys were on the front lawn. Three heads were studiously bent over a bicycle. It was not hard for me to recognize Paul as his stance was the same one he used when bent over the operating table.

"I feel weird about this," Anthony hissed, nevertheless pulling my car to a halt in front of the huge Tudor-style home.

"It was my idea. I'll do the talking."

He was in agreement. "He'll probably take it better from you. You're prettier than I am. Not a lot, mind you, but some, especially from his point of view."

By the time I was out of the car, three pairs of eyes had turned in my direction. The boys were merely curious. Paul's eyes were veiled and unreadable. He took a few steps toward me.

"Be right back, guys. It's some people from the hospital, that's all.

"Devin," he said simply, inclining his head in a slight nod.

I had never seen him look more handsome. Wretched, but handsome. He evidently was one of those people to whom tragedy is becoming.

"I want to apologize for being here like this. First, since I am here, I want to say again how sorry I am. Maybe that sounds hypocritical coming from me, considering everything, but I *am* sorry."

Very gently, expression still veiled, he said, "I know you're sorry, my dear. Believe it or not, so am I. You don't live with someone for that many years, have children with them, and not feel something when they're gone. And in such terrible circumstances."

"You're okay?"

"I have to be. For John Paul and Zachary. They're trying to be brave and grown-up, too much so. Inside, they're little boys who lost their mother. Oh, how I wish . . ."

There was no way to finish the sentence. There was too much to wish for. To wish would have been to change the course of the past decade or so, something that was not possible, no matter who did the wishing or why.

"Anyway," he went on, "I assume, from your manner, there is another reason for this visit?"

Again, apologizing, I hastened to explain about Jack's

disappearance. Anthony need not have worried. Paul was instantly concerned . . . eager to be helpful even if he was not exactly warm. His detachment was understandable though, under the circumstances. As I too well knew, a surfeit of emotion will leave us at times feeling numb, leaving us to wonder if we have any feelings left at all.

"I doubt you were there, but you can see why we felt we had to ask."

He smiled. But the smile did not reach his eyes. Nor did the corner of his mouth twitch in the way I had come to like more than I wanted to. I suspected it might be some time before he could again display genuine amusement.

"As a matter of fact, even if he seemed sloppy, your attendant had a keen eye. I was there for a few moments, and I did exchange the time of day with Jack. I had left my favorite watch in my surgical locker and went to pick it up. I probably wasn't there ten minutes. On my way out, I saw Jack. He said he was sorry about Dru. I said I was sorry about the scene at his restaurant. He told me I was to think nothing of it, that I hadn't caused it. When I left, he was still there. I haven't seen him since, but if there's anything I can do, I will. If you need someone else to help look for him, I'll . . ."

"Dad, are you about done?" one of the boys called.

Over Paul's shoulders, I viewed his sons. Although they were turned in such a way that I could not see their faces, I observed that the bigger one had fair hair like Paul's must have been at that age and the other had nearly coal-black hair like Dru's had been in her pre-bleach days.

"You have your work cut out for you here. We'll do what we can."

"Do let me know. I like Jack. He's a fine young man, with a good head on his shoulders."

"One more thing," I said, half turning away from him, "do you remember what time you talked to Jack?"

"Not exactly. Shortly before noon, I suppose. I had promised the boys lunch at McDonald's and they were waiting in the car. That's as close as I can get. Why?"

"No real reason. Just trying to pinpoint the sequence of events. I was wondering if you talked to him before I went to wash or after. We sent the patient to ICU at 11:45 A.M. I talked to Jack, said I had another patient to check on, then I'd wash up and be with him. When I got back, well, I told you that . . . he was gone."

He shrugged to indicate his helplessness. "I'm sorry, Devin, but I can't be more precise. I didn't see you. I didn't know he was with you. All he said to me was that he was waiting on a friend. It could have been before 11:45, but more likely was a bit after. I just cannot tell you. The battery was dead in my watch and I had slipped it in my pocket, intending to go have another put in after McDonald's. Actually, I did just that."

Both of us stared at the expensive Rolex on his arm as if it could tell us something when, in reality, the watch didn't have anything to do with anything.

"Well, anyway," I said, "thanks. And, again, I'm so sorry."

For just a flash, his eyes registered pain, but he quickly regained control. As Anthony drove away, I did not look back at him. Even if I had been able to see his face, I knew it would have told me nothing.

On a few occasions, Paul had come out of his shell with me, had lost his reserve. Like the quirkly little smile, I fancied that would not happen again for a while. Guilt, grief, and all kinds of other emotions would hold him chained in for a while to come.

"Well?" Anthony asked as he, with an audible sigh of relief, drove the Mustang away from the Linden house and back out through the elegantly designed entrance/exit.

I explained what Paul had said. "So he was there and did talk to Jack, but it all tells us absolutely nothing."

"Which puts us back where we were, not knowing where the hell to look for this Jack character. Devin . . ."

"Hmmm?"

"You ever give any thought to the idea this might all be connected to you?"

I gave a short, mirthless laugh. "It's there in my mind,

all the time. How could it not be? I'm here in Dalton because of my father's death. I'm threatened and urged to leave. I don't see how in the world *Dru's* death can be connected to his. But I can't know that, can I, without knowing what happened to Daddy? And Jack . . . he was one of the last people to see Dru alive. *And* he was on the verge of telling me something about what happened back at the time of Daddy's death? We kept getting interrupted. We said we'd talk more after I got through in the ER."

"Who all knew about this, that he was going to tell you something?"

"That's just it, Anthony. That's part of the frustration. No one knew. Not as far as I knew. And I can't imagine Jack just announcing to someone that he's going to tell me about something from fifteen years or so ago. I mean, he's a very reserved and reticent person. He just wouldn't be inclined to run around and chat with this person and that person about what he was going to tell me."

Anthony shrugged. "You know the guy. I don't. But I'll take your word for it. With a few notable exceptions, I think you have good insight about people, so I'll buy what you say."

"Thanks," I said, deciding again that this wasn't the right moment to mention how fleeting my acquaintance with Jackson Lee Fraser really was.

"But it's still no help. Devin, we don't even know where to begin looking for him, do we?"

"I admit it . . . no, we don't. I don't think he has any close relatives left in town. Since I haven't been back long myself, I have no idea who he runs around with, if there is anyone he's close to. Maybe we should check back at Fraser Inn. People there will know more about his daily routine than I do."

It sounded good. After all, they could scarcely know less than I do. On the way back to the inn, I told Anthony, "I'm gaining a grudging respect for the police. Until you start to do it, you don't realize how hard it is to look for someone. Their jobs can't always be easy."

"I guess all jobs have their pluses and minuses. Even doctoring."

"Tell me about it."

We found nothing at Fraser Inn to hearten us. No one there had heard a thing from Jack. The strain was showing on their faces.

I explained to them that I hadn't been around Jack for a long time and didn't know anything about his day-to-day activities. "Think about it . . . and pass the word to the others . . . and tell us anything that you suspect could happen that would make him bolt like that. Who or what is important enough to Jack Fraser that he would take off without a word to me—and remember, he had no transportation at the hospital. We had gone there in my car and it was still there. It almost looks as if someone came by and he went off with them."

"I just don't know," said the waiter who seemed to be acting as the spokesman for the group. "He's a quiet sort, pretty closemouthed about his personal life. That is, if he has much of one. He puts in a lot of hours here. It's taken a lot to get this place off and going."

"He doesn't date anyone?"

The waiter shrugged. "Not that I know of. That is, he goes here and there with first one and then another woman. But I've seen no signs that anyone is a regular. But I'll ask around. This business . . . at this point, it's his life. Like I said, he works damned hard here. He's proud of this place. He was away for a few years. Who or what he has from back then I have no idea, but here he's kept his nose to the grindstone pretty much. Know what I mean?"

Anthony and I both nodded vigorously. We knew, having kept our own noses to the grindstone most of the time.

"What time do you close here?"

"On a weeknight like this, I imagine we'll have the doors closed by ten o'clock."

"We'll be back by then," I promised. "If we haven't found Jack by then, maybe we can form a search party."

Anthony and I trudged back to my car. One look at his

face told me he was as dispirited as I was . . . and probably a whole lot more tired since I'd had a few hours sleep that he hadn't had.

"It has to be the inn," I said when we were back in the car. "It's a long shot, but what else do we have? If someone came up to him at the hospital and told him the inn was on fire or had been held up—anything that would constitute a crisis—then he'd drop what he was doing and go, don't you think?"

"Sure. Most of us would when it comes to what we love—or what we're responsible for. I may be dense, but I still don't see why knowing that helps a whole lot."

"Maybe it doesn't. I'm just grasping at straws. But we know he left the hospital and we know he didn't have transportation there. That must mean he got in a car with someone on some pretext—probably the restaurant. If so, whoever abducted him . . ."

"Abducted?"

I glared at him. "Don't sneer. It isn't becoming. Anyway, whoever this was surely at least started out in the direction of the Fraser house. It probably isn't much over a mile from ABC to Fraser's, so if we get enough people together, we can really canvass that distance. Look, it may sound stupid, but do you have any better ideas?"

He heaved a deep sigh. "Unfortunately, no. But something struck me while you were talking. You're assuming Jack left the hospital. Maybe he did. But what if he didn't?"

I felt myself go pale—at least a change from incessantly turning red. Not so very long ago, I had been locked in the record archives room. I am sure there are areas in ABC more remote and much less likely to be discovered.

"What first, then, Anthony?" Before he had a chance to answer, I took a good look at him. He looked, to put it mildly, awful. My voice softened as I said, "I'm not being fair to expect you to just keep chugging along as tired as you are. Go home. Get a few hours sleep. If we haven't found him by morning, surely the police or sheriff will

193

kick in and help."

Leaning forward slightly, he kissed my cheek, just a light brush of the lips. "Thanks for being thoughtful. But I'm caught up in this, too. Not that I know the guy, but I certainly don't wish him any harm. And it's such a mystery. Things like this might be expected to happen to a troublemaker, but not to a dweeb."

"I didn't say he was a dweeb!" I replied indignantly.

"I know you didn't. I just drew my own conclusions."

"Well, then stop it. Jack isn't . . . well, maybe he is—just a little, but he's a *nice* dweeb."

"I'm sure he is. Okay, down to business. We'll go with your idea since I have an idea it'll be a lot simpler. We aren't going to find him just wandering the streets, that much is for certain. Do you remember enough about Dalton to know if there are any likely hiding places or dumping grounds in the area we're talking about?"

"Except for the couple of blocks nearest the hospital, it's mostly residential. But it's been fifteen years. I remember well what it was then, but I'm sure some things have changed." I closed my eyes and tried to remember what I knew of the region of ABC, my house, and Jack's house. "There is a place we played one summer. It was as close to halfway between where we lived and where I lived as we could agree on. It was just a big ditch, but to us kids it was a wonderful place. We liked to climb down in it and play. You could enter a culvert pipe and go from one side of the street to the other. For the size we were at that age—and I was a bit of a chunk—it wasn't even a tight squeeze, but it made us feel adventurous. We even found a snake in it once. Just a harmless little thing, but we made it into a big deal. I thought it ought to be killed, but I wanted Jack to do the killing. He wouldn't. We draped it over a stick and carried it off to someone else's lawn. And then . . ."

"Tell me on the way there," he said dryly. "It *is* such a fascinating story."

"You're sneering again."

"What can I say? Fatigue just doesn't bring out the best in me. But I'm here and willing. So don't pick on me."

"Yes, sir. And when this is all over. I'll do *you* a favor, honest I will."

"Marry me?"

"You call that a favor? It would be more of a favor if I never spoke to you again, considering the way I have of causing you trouble. Anthony, that's Dahlia Street up there. Turn left. The place I was talking about is about three or four blocks down."

Feeling like a fool, but beyond caring, I barreled out of the car as soon as Anthony came to a stop. Just as I had at the age of ten, I jumped down into the ditch. Kids must not play there much now. Maybe they're too busy with their Nintendo games. The weeds hadn't been recently cut and were up to my hips. I got down on my hands and knees, pushed an overgrowth of weeds out of the way, and peered into the open end of the culvert pipe.

"See anything?" Anthony called down.

"Not really. Too bad I didn't think of this before it got dark. And I don't even have a flashlight in the car."

"Maybe I can help."

With that, he jumped down into the ditch from the other side.

"See anything?" I echoed.

"You know I don't. It's too damn dark. Devin, this is stupid. Talk about a long shot!"

"I know that," I shot back. "I'm the first to admit it, but what else do we have? I keep asking that."

"I know, and I keep not answering. Well, since we're here, rational or not, let's do it right. I'll crawl in from this side over to your side."

"I should do it. It was my dumb idea."

"True, but allow me to be macho just this once."

There was an edge to our banter—an edge that wasn't sharp, but could become so at any given moment. We were quite a pair: Anthony weary to the bone from being on duty for hours on end without respite, and me scheduled for a stint of the same by early morning, the thought constantly nagging me that if we didn't find Jack soon I wouldn't be as awake as I needed to be. And in the profession I'd chosen, fatigue was a deadly enemy.

"Sometimes I wonder why I think I have to be a doctor."

Until Anthony laughed and said, "I guess we all wonder that from time to time." I hadn't realized I'd spoken aloud.

"There are only two possible reasons," he continued. "One is the desire to serve humanity. The other is ego."

"Which reason is yours?"

He turned to face me more directly. "Like most, a mixture. In my case, I'd say about a 50/50 ratio. What about yourself, Devin?"

I took in the dark smudges beneath his eyes, the tautness of his skin. He had been awake for too many hours and it showed. Softly, I said, "With you, I'd weight it more like 80% serving, 20% ego. With me, well . . . I'd be tempted to add another reason: perversity."

"Some other time you can explain that to me. Right now, I'm going through the tube."

Minutes later, he was at my side, a bit worse for wear. Weeds and dirt were clinging to his hair and clothes and his face was streaked with dirt.

"It doesn't smell so good in there, but I couldn't really see or feel anything out of the ordinary."

I felt unaccountably dejected. It wasn't that, rationally, I had expected Jack to be in there; irrationally, though, it sure would have been nice if he had been—maybe neatly tied up but otherwise unharmed. That way, our mystery would have been over.

"Then let's go," I said flatly. "I know of a couple of other spots we can check out, then we'll go back to the hospital and start searching. Maybe the security and maintenance people on duty will help us."

"We can but ask."

Anthony was all the way up out of the ditch and had bent to offer me an assist up when we heard a sound that turned my blood to ice water—and must have had an equally chilling effect on him. His fingers had been around my wrist and quite suddenly lost their grip.

"Devin?"

"I heard."

"It was probably just a cat or dog or something."

"Maybe even just the wind."

"The wind isn't blowing. At least not up here it isn't. I'm coming back down. And I'm going back in the pipe."

"And this time you're not going alone."

Again, I heard the sound.

"That's no dog," he said firmly.

I stuck my head into the pipe and called, "Jack? If you are in there, please make some noise. Jack, please? Is that you?"

"Devin, you're going to feel dumb when it turns out to be a possum."

"So what? By now, I'm used to feeling dumb. *Jack?* Jack, it's Devin—Katie, to you. *Please* find a way to answer us."

The moan was louder, and unmistakably more human sounding. I wasted no more time in going into the pipe, Anthony came in right after me.

Chapter Sixteen

Going through the pipe wasn't enough, not in this darkness. Under my breath I cursed my stupidity in not keeping a flashlight in my car. Charlie had cautioned me to always do that and, as usual, I had brushed his well-meaning advice aside. Slowly and painstakingly I crawled, reaching out each inch of the way until I felt the side of the pipe. I was taking the right side, Anthony the left. Just when I was telling myself that the moans had been nothing but ordinary night sounds, I reached out and touched flesh—cold flesh.

I let out a scream, of course. And my scream was answered by another low moan—and by a vigorously uttered curse from Anthony.

"He's here," I cried out. "Jack is here."

By that time, Anthony had reached around me to touch the cold bulk also.

"How can you be sure it's Jack, as dark as it is?"

"I can't. But who else would it be? No one else is missing that I know about it."

My hand moved from the fingers of the person to the wrist, and all the time I was praying as hard as I could pray. The slight pulsation against my seeking fingertips was, indeed, like the answer to those prayers.

"He's alive, Anthony. *Whoever* it is is alive. The pulse is weak and thready but it's there and that's what counts. Let's get him out of here."

"We have to be careful. He could be badly hurt."

"I know we have to be careful, but we still have to get him out of here."

"A better idea might be for you to stay here with him and me to go to the nearest phone and call a rescue crew."

"One of us will call an ambulance, but we're getting him out of here first, okay? We can at least get him out into the uncovered ditch, even if we don't think it's safe to hoist him up out of it."

"Fine. But it isn't going to be easy."

"Most things aren't." To the limp form at my side, I attempted to give reassurance by pressure of my hand on his. "Jack, if that's you—and even if it isn't you—we're here. We're going to get you out of here and to the hospital. Just hang in there. Don't fight us. Squeeze my hand back if you hear me and understand."

He did not respond to the pressure of my hand. In the total darkness, it was not possible for me to ascertain if he was not hearing or if he was aware and physically unable to respond. He did not moan again. Perhaps he had passed out—or worse. Or perhaps he no longer felt the need to use up the energy it took to exert himself.

"I'll get around and take hold of the shoulders and head, Devin. I think I can support him better than you can. Get the best hold on the lower part of his body that you can. We have to avoid making any sudden moves. If he has fractures or internal injuries, a wrong move can do a lot of harm."

"Okay. So let's do it. Just tell me when you're ready to start moving. You're going to have to crawl out backward?"

"I know of no other way."

After a few moments of silence, he said, "Okay, let's go. Slow and easy. Don't let his legs dangle anymore than you can help."

We crept by inches, handicapped by darkness, weeds, and the cumbersome weight of our burden. When we were clear of the culvert pipe, out in the ditch itself where there was a dim light borrowed from the streetlights above, we looked at each other and nodded.

In tacit agreement, we scaled the side of the ditch, then gently deposited our burden on the ground.

Looking down, I caught my breath at the sight of the pale hair, the familiar face now bare of the familiar glasses.

"It's him . . . it's Jack," I said, more than a little dazed by it all.

Anthony was panting audibly from both physical exertion and anxiety. Shaking his head, he gasped, "I don't believe this. I'm seeing it, but I still don't believe it. Devin, you hiding something from me?"

"Such as?"

"That maybe you're psychic or something. I mean, this was such a preposterous idea. I was only doing it to humor you."

"I know. It was just a hunch. A long shot born out of desperation. Anthony, what do you think?"

As we talked, we examined Jack's still form the best we could under such adverse conditions.

"He's alive—barely."

A sob caught in my throat. "You go call an ambulance. I'll stay here with him."

"Devin, we're a couple of blocks from the hospital. As much as we've moved him around now, putting him in the backseat is going to be the fastest and best way."

We loaded Jack in the backseat of the Mustang and I sat back there with him, cradling his head in my lap. At ABC, Anthony pulled the car right up in front of the doors to the emergency room, then got out of the car and went running for assistance. Within moments, we were surrounded by help. Jack was out of the car, onto a gurney, and through the door into the hospital.

For a moment, I stood in the ER feeling stunned and helpless as the EMTs and nurses labored over Jack, taking his vital signs, doing the preliminary screening. I looked over at Anthony and tried to smile. He started to walk toward me and stumbled slightly. I think I could have pushed him over with one finger.

Stepping forward to meet him, I gave him a quick hug. "Anthony, go home and get a shower and some sleep.

He's in good hands now. I couldn't have done it without you."

"I'd like to stay and see that the guy's okay, but have to admit I'm too done in to be of any real help. Even my coordination is out of whack. So I'll do what you say—and I'll check back in on Fraser after I've had some rest."

"You'd better let someone drive you home. You're beat."

"I have to get my car home so I can have it for when I have to come back tomorrow. But don't worry, sweet Devin. I can keep going that much longer."

When he was gone, I addressed the ER crew, "I'm going to go clean up, then I'll help. I know I'm filthy, so I'll hunt up some surgical scrubs to wear."

I did that in record time, my heart beating rapidly all the while. Dr. Sinclair was with Jack when I returned. I asked him the same thing I had asked Anthony, "What do you think?"

Under the bright lights of the ER, Jack looked awful . . . so awful that I found myself being glad we hadn't been able to see him well on Dahlia Street. They had stripped him of his clothing to better assess his injuries and he lay there so still and so pitifully bruised, wearing only his undershorts, and covered by a blue surgical sheet.

A deep sigh escaped Rick Sinclair. "I'm not easy with this," he said slowly. "There's some minor bruising pretty well over his whole body, probably from being dragged around. Some of it—maybe even most of it—may have happened when you and Toretta were getting him out of the ditch and into the car. And that's *not* a criticism. It had to be done. But I see no signs, on gross examination, of fracture or anything that would make me suspicious of organ injury. Basically, I think we're talking head trauma—and *bad* head trauma. Be a sport and see if you can hold of Robinson, tell him what we have going here. I'd like his opinion. If he can't come till morning, I guess we'll make it without it, but . . ."

I trotted off as I had been ordered. If there was a wile or trick I could perform to get the neurologist, Garth

Robinson, to the ER, then I was prepared to use it. As it turned out, there was no need. He knew Jack and was instantly full of concern. Perhaps he would have come for anyone, but Jack's being his personal acquaintance didn't hurt, I'm sure. Before going back to inform Sinclair and the ER staff to expect Robinson, I took a moment to call Fraser Inn to tell them that their employer had been found and was being seen to.

"There's a concussion," Rick said when I got back. "I'm sure of that—and probably quite a deep one. He's taken some bad blows to the head. I'm going to hold off on skull X rays or a brain scan, however, since Garth's coming. Maybe he'd prefer not to have him moved. At this point, there's certainly going to be no patient cooperation."

There really wasn't a lot we—or anyone—could do for Jack at this point. They cleaned him up and put antiseptic ointment on the cut areas. He was breathing on his own, so no oxygen was required. Luckily he wasn't becoming dehydrated yet so intravenous fluids were not required. Before the evening was over, he would be attached to IV fluids, of course, but that could be done on the floor after he was officially admitted. While we waited for the neurologist to arrive, we tested Jack from time-to-time. He did not respond to verbal stimuli, but would flinch involuntarily and appropriately to pinpricks at various parts of his body. Despite his unconscious state, his vital signs remained stable.

"While we're waiting for Dr. Robinson, we need to get information on the patient," the ER clerk told me. "Can you give the information on him?"

"Me? I . . . well, no, I don't suppose I can. I can give you his proper name, address, birth date, and I think his wallet was still on him so we can search that for social security number and maybe even information about his insurance. There really isn't anything else I can tell you."

"Then is there a relative or very close friend we can call?"

Feeling very frustrated, I threw up my hands. "I knew

Jack Fraser when we were children together. Until the past few days, I hadn't seen him since we were eleven. We can rough in the things I mentioned, but if he has any medical problems, if he's on medication, if he's allergic to anything—I have no way of knowing. And I don't know who to tell you that might know."

"Then just come sit down with me and we'll get what you know. If he's ever been here at all, maybe we'll have something in the old records that will help."

"Sure thing." I trotted along obediently, prattling away like an idiot out of anxiety. "Actually, he was born here at ABC. So was I, for that matter. But I don't suppose that helps much. When babies are born, you don't know yet if they're allergic to penicillin or not, do you?"

She gave me a strange look and mumbled. "No, I suppose not."

"Maybe we should look into the idea of doing full allergy testing on newborns. Save a lot of trial and error later in life."

"Dr. Hollister, are you okay?"

What could I say? Jack was in good hands and I knew that. My standing right by his side would not hasten the healing process. I suppose it was just all getting to me. And I found myself so very sorry for Jack. When it came right down to it, he had no one. That is, no one that I knew of. But, then, Jack had never had a lot that I had had. And yet despite what seemed to be marked disadvantages, he had done all right with his life. Until now. When I got around to it, I knew I was going to feel awfully guilty about what had happened to him. I had this gut feeling that what had happened to Dru, and now to Jack, was connected to my wanting to open up an ancient can of worms. Until Anthony had more or less forced me into talking about it, I hadn't wanted to openly acknowledge the problem.

Maybe we were wrong. But I doubted it.

The clerk's concerned stare finally got to me.

Trying my best to laugh, I said, "Sure, I'm okay. When I'm overly tired and/or worried, I get silly. Reflex action.

Now, where do we start?"

After we had filled in the form with all we could find about Jack, which was more than I had expected, the clerk located him on the computer. Slightly less than a year ago, he had been at the emergency room. A search was made for a copy of that emergency record and, within minutes, we learned he had received a tetanus injection at that visit for a nasty cut to the finger, that he had no medication allergies, and that, at that point, he denied major medical problems or taking regular medications.

By the time we had all that completed, Garth Robinson was on the scene. Dr. Robinson is a middle-aged man who somewhat resembles an owl. When he took a good look at Jack on the gurney, I fancied that his kind face took on a look of deep concern. Due to Jack's total inability to cooperate with any voluntary portions of a neurological screening exam, I realized a lot of Dr. Robinson's findings would be guesswork at this point—highly trained and experienced guesswork, however.

"Admit him. Start an IV and do a cursory neuro-check every two hours. If there are any changes, call me. At this point, I don't want to risk shipping him out. But right now there would be no advantage to it and the movements could actually be detrimental. If he seems stable tomorrow, we'll get X rays, CAT scan, EEG, all that good stuff. Right now, let's just get him stabilized and through the night. If he'd regain consciousness, that would help immensely."

It would help *me* also, I felt.

"Can you make any sort of statement about how serious he actually is?" I asked, feeling like a totally layman in doing so. At this moment, I was not objective. I was being a worried friend, not a doctor.

"He's young and healthy, Dr. Hollister. That's all very much on his side. He's taken quite a blow to the head. Unless I miss my guess, there's a bit of a skull fracture there as well as the concussion. He's very likely to have amnesia for the event when he does wake up. Watch him and monitor him, that's all we can do at this point. If there are any signs of serious intracranial bleeds on the tests in the morning, we'll be forced into transporting him to a bigger facility where neurosurgeons are on staff. He could arouse at any time. Or it could be hours, maybe even days. I feel we're tremendously lucky in that we—that is, you and young Toretta, as I understand it—caught him before he had lain around for too long, and also lucky in that the weather is mild. Extreme heat or cold, either one, especially the cold, of course, would have gone really hard on him with a head injury of this extent. You didn't observe any seizure activity, did you, when you first found him?"

I looked toward Jack's still, silent form and said, "No. None at all. He was just like he is now as far as we could tell."

"Then he might not seize. I'm opting not to give him any anticonvulsants. I don't think it'd ward off late seizures anyway."

"So, basically, we're just waiting?"

He smiled and nodded. "It isn't easy, but sometimes that's all that is left for us to do. Healing can't be rushed. It's only a few hours until morning. Let's let him rest. Hopefully, he'll have regained consciousness in the A.M., and that will help us—and him—in diagnosis and treatment. So go home and get some rest."

After exchanging a few pleasantries with me and the others around him, he was gone. I hoped I had expressed my thanks clearly enough. Although he had not performed any procedures or done any real tests, he had provided what I needed most—reassurance.

Seeing me still standing around, Rick Sinclair said, "You heard the great man, Hollister: Go home."

"I was ready to do just that, but . . ."

He lowered his eyebrows and gave me a mock glare, "But, what?"

Since Sinclair knew nothing of my dilemma, unless it was through the ABC grapevine, I really did not know how to go about explaining my feelings to him. Just as I was ready to make some sort of explanation, two men in blue uniforms walked in the wide doors of the ER. By coincidence, and also due to the fact that Dalton's force was probably on the small side, they were the same two that had come to my apartment after Dru's body had been found, Officers Hodlitt and Daniels.

"Fancy meeting you here," I said, doing my best to smile. Turning to Rick, I said, "Another reason why I won't be going home right away—I have to explain to these gentlemen what happened to Jack Fraser. That is, tell them the little that I know."

"You did find him, then?" one asked.

"Another intern and I together. He's gone home. If your questioning of him can wait till morning, I'm sure he'd appreciate it. He'd been up for twenty-some hours straight before I even got him involved in the hunt for Jack. Come on, I think the coffee shop is still open. I'll spring for coffee while we talk."

They were, when I had finished my tale, as incredulous as Anthony that I had thought of the ditch on Dahlia Street and that Jack had actually been there. An uneasiness took hold of me and I tried to push it aside, telling myself it was merely anxiety born of fatigue, both mental and physical.

"I don't suppose we can question Fraser himself?"

"Not possible. They're admitting him even as we sit here now. Unfortunately, he's still unconscious. Although he couldn't tell for sure until we have X rays and tests, the neurologist seemed fairly sure that he *will* arouse before too many hours have elapsed. Unfortunately, he also warned us that Jack is likely to have amnesia for the event and for the events directly surrounding it, both before and after. It's common."

They both flinched. It wasn't what they wanted to hear. The idea didn't do a whole lot for me either. Whatever was going on needed to be stopped. If Jack was able to identify who did this to him, then we would be getting a whole lot of answers.

"Does it come back to them after a while?"

"In some cases. Not in most. It doesn't affect anything else. They can remember everything else and can learn with the same capacity as before the injury, but that little space in time is generally unretrievable."

"Even with hypnosis?"

I shook my head. "Dr. Robinson is the expert. I'm sure he can answer your questions in the morning. But hypnotism is generally a helpful tool when there is a psychological reason for the mental blocking, an unconscious will *not* to remember. Here we're dealing with real physical trauma, something entirely different. The damaged areas may never give us back what we need. In the meantime . . ."

"Yes?"

"Are you going to put a guard on Jack?"

"Why on earth would we do that, lady? As far as we know, he hasn't done anything. He's the victim, not the criminal."

I mentally counted to ten, exasperated beyond measure with the denseness of the officers across from me. "That wasn't exactly what I meant. Dru Linden was killed. As you already know, I received several threats myself before that. Not that we really know if it's all connected, but I'm afraid it may be. Jack was one of the last people to see Dru alive. Now *he's* been kidnapped and left for dead. When whoever is doing this finds out Jack is still alive, don't you think it's entirely possible that he or she will sneak back to try and finish the job? For that I think there should be a guard outside his door at all times. No one should be allowed in there except hospital personnel—and even they should go in on the buddy system. We can't rule out hospital personnel, or someone connected with ABC in some way, as the one doing this. But for right now, it's imperative to watch him."

They exchanged looks. I could almost read them. It was a great idea, they were thinking; however, they resented me for suggesting it. To save face they were going to have to find a way to protect Jack and make it look like it was *their* idea.

"We'll have to check with the chief," one said slowly.

"How long will that take?"

"Oh, a couple of hours at the most. We'll have to go back to the station and file a preliminary report, get in touch with the chief at home, see what he wants to do, if anything..."

"What do you mean 'if anything?' We're talking attempted murder here, you know."

"Sure, sure, we'll do what we can. But we have to have permission. Someone has to be assigned. This stuff doesn't just happen. There has to be a protocol."

I put my head down on my hands and groaned.

"You all right?"

Looking up, I gave them both my best Bostonian icy glare. "As right as I can be in the face of this idiocy. Fine, go find your protocol. But I'd appreciate it if you could put it in high gear. Until you're back, I'll stay in the room with him. But since I'm to be on duty early in the morning, I'll need a little bit of sleep before the night is over. I'd appreciate some relief, okay?"

"You aren't going to work so soon after all this, are you? Surely they can find someone to fill in for you."

I gave an unpleasant, and unladylike snort that would have made my mother shudder. "Internship isn't like that," I said bluntly. "Toretta's dead on his feet. There are only two others, and they do their share. I have this year to prove I have the stamina and ability it takes to be a doctor. How could I prove that if I called in and said, 'Sorry, but I'm tired, get someone else.' Tell me, would you shirk your police duty just because something else came up?"

That put a grin on his face. "Depends on the something else," he deadpanned, "but I get your drift."

"Then you'll have someone else here?"

"We'll see what we can do," was the vague comeback, which was a long way from being a promise or commitment.

With all the imperiousness I could muster at the moment, I stated, "I'm quite sure Dr. McCracken and Dr. Linden will appreciate anything you can do. They have quite enough on their minds without another unfortunate incident occurring, especially within the confines of the hospital. And I'm sure Jane Goldstein, the administrator here, will be equally appreciative of your timely efforts in providing protection for one of Dalton's businessmen and for the hospital itself."

As they prepared to leave, they gave me undisguised dirty looks. My feelings weren't hurt at all. If my shameless display of namedropping worked, I would be even more glad I'd done it. I felt I owed the law enforcement authorities zilch. When I could have used their help in finding Jack, they had insisted on remaining idle, putting down my report as that of one of a reactionary female. Before this was over, they'd know exactly what a reactionary female really was. I hadn't lived around Elaine Hollister all of my life not to know a few ways to play people.

By the time I located Jack's room, he was settled for the night. All of the lights were off in the room except one small one over the lavatory and the small bright ones on the monitors connected to him.

"Would you like a cot?" the nurse asked when I informed her I was going to stay for a while.

"No, thank you. I don't intend to sleep. Any signs of him waking?"

"Not really, although I do think his eyelids fluttered a time or two. Poor boy, he looks so pathetic!"

When she was gone, I looked down at Jack and had to agree with her assessment. His skin color was a good match for the linens on which he lay, the pallor so great that the bruises from both the injuries and the needle punctures since being at the hospital stood out darkly. Between that and the IVs and monitors connected to him, he was, indeed, a pathetic-looking case.

I am not a hating person by nature, but I felt a deep hatred for the person who had done this. Jack could not be involved in this thing except on the fringes. Why had someone felt it necessary to try to kill him? Questions unanswered, I sank into the uncomfortable bedside chair and waited.

The room had an eerie glow, something I had never really noticed before. On this side, it is very different. When someone you know on a personal basis is involved, a hospital can be an intimidating place, a frightening place.

With little to do but listen to the near silence, the quiet hum of the monitors, I sat on the edge of the chair. I caught myself staring at the brain wave and pulse monitors as if they were fascinating when, in truth, they said nothing. He was alive and holding his own. It wasn't a lot, but it was all we had and I drew what comfort from it I could. Which wasn't a great deal.

Chapter Seventeen

"Katie? Katie, is it really you?"

Blinking, I startled awake, my immediate reaction that of anger at myself for falling asleep despite all my noble vows and good intentions. The second blink aroused me completely. By the third blink, my eyes were adjusted enough to the dim light in the room that I recognized the face and form in the doorway.

"Ms. Goldstein," I said softly. "Do come on in and talk to me. That is, if you have the time."

With a smile, she approached me. "Oh, I have the time. As you can see by the way I'm dressed, I'm not very official at the moment. Thinking I'd want to know, someone called me about Mr. Fraser here . . . and also let me know you're staying with him, *and* that you are, indeed, Jim Clark's daughter. Funny how I can be at the helm of this place and miss out on gossip going through ABC."

"Not just gossip in this case," I said, doing my best to return her smile. I was tired, worried, and not sure how Jane Goldstein would feel about me . . . or, more specifically, about my motives for returning to Dalton and interning at *her* hospital. In a navy and white jogging suit, she *did* present a different sort of image than the one I was used to seeing; however, each tinted hair was coiffed and sprayed in place, not daring to move. As she regarded me so carefully, I recalled with some uneasiness that she and my father had not exactly been the best of friends.

She slid into the chair across from me and, her eyes adjusting also, shook her head, her smile broadening and wonder-filled. "Katie Clark, it is. God, how could I have not recognized you? It makes me feel like such an unperceptive idiot. Why on earth didn't you tell me, child?"

"Don't be so hard on yourself, Ms. Goldstein. It's been many years since you saw me. I was a little girl then. And I think I've changed more since childhood than some people do, so don't criticize you faculties. My name is different, so there's no reason you should have connected me to a little kid you knew—and not really very well—fifteen years ago. I must say you've changed little. Less really than anyone else I've met. I think I would have known *you* anywhere. You've carried the years well, very well."

Laughing, she said, "Ah, Katie, you've something of Jim's golden tongue, haven't you? Most of the time, flattery will get you anywhere. But I'm well aware you've sidestepped my question. Come now, child, tell me *why* the big secret?"

I took a look at Jack's still form to reassure myself he was okay. So peaceful looking, so quiet, he reminded me now more than ever of the Jackson Lee Fraser I had known so long ago, bruises, plastered-down hair, and all.

"A good friend, I gather," she observed.

I shrugged. "Like so many things, it's hard to explain. He was a part of my childhood. In a way, a part I think I tried to forget. Until I came back and faced Dalton and him, I don't think I realized he was maybe one of the best parts of that childhood. I honestly don't know if we're the same two people we were then, or if we're two entirely different people. And there I go, avoiding your question again." While evermindful of Jack and the monitors to which he was connected, I again told my story. From time-to-time, she shook her head in acknowledgement, but made no comment until I was done.

"Katie," she began, "it was all so very long ago and . . ."

"And you're going to be just like all the others, aren't

you, Ms. Goldstein? My mother, my stepfather, Paul Linden, Dr. McCracken, poor Jack here, even Anthony Toretta . . . they all tell me to get on with my life and let the past be. Even if they don't say it, I can see the reproach in their eyes. Maybe I'm even ready to concede that they're right. I've been threatened. Jack's been hurt. Dr. Linden's wife was killed. And it isn't over yet. It won't be until we find who is doing this. It's like a terrible nightmare. Only worse because it's really happening, it isn't something I'm going to wake up from."

Jane glanced toward the hospital bed. "You really believe this is connected to the search for the facts about your father's death fifteen years ago?"

"I can't know it. But I strongly suspect it. As people keep reminding me, if Dad didn't commit suicide, then he was murdered. Unless the person who did it died in the interim, he or she is still walking around. Spooky thought, isn't it?"

She nodded her well-groomed head quite solemnly. "Very spooky. But I wasn't going to say what you thought I was. Not in the least. I try not to give advice I couldn't follow myself. Like you, Katie, I'm a bulldog. I don't let go easily. Frankly, I was never comfortable with the idea of suicide in Jim's case. It was so hard to accept. Such a gifted man. Not just as a surgeon, but as a person. In his own rather quiet way, he had a great deal of charisma, a warmth that communicated itself to those around him. I would have said he was one of the strongest people I knew, and then . . . well, it didn't make sense."

I stared at her, not quite daring to believe what I was hearing, that I actually might have an ally and supporter. I knew I flushed as I spoke, but the dim light hid that, "Forgive me for being blunt, but I remember, I think, that you and my father didn't like each other much. Was I wrong? I remember some battles, not the details, of course, but his comments. He called you . . ." I broke it off there. It didn't matter. It was too late for tact.

"Jane the Inane?" she asked, her smile breaking bright and clear and obviously unoffended.

"You knew?"

Laughing aloud, she said, "One of the things I valued most about your father, Katie, was his lack of deceit. He seldom said anything about someone that he would not say *to* that someone. You remember some of it correctly. Jim and I were often on opposite sides of the fence when it came to ABC policy. That was inevitable. I was in charge of seeing that we ran in the black. His concern was totally with the patient, cost be hanged, regulations be hanged. He was a crusader. I *had* to be practical. But there were times when we battled on the same side. We made a good team. There were times, yes, when we ranted and raved at each other and came perilously close to childish name-calling. But there were other times when he would hug me and say, 'Jane, you're terrific.'" She wiped away moisture that had gathered in her eyes, then stuffed the tissue back in the pocket of her sweat jacket in a hurried stab that seemed to say, "I didn't really cry— you *didn't* see that."

"Then where do I go, Ms. Goldstein? Who do I talk to in order to get the truth? Maybe I can start with you, now that I can't hide anymore. Do you know any reason why someone would have wanted him dead? Do you know the reasons told in rumors as to why people thought he might have killed himself?"

"He was a private man, Katie. I imagine he confided in few people. If there were marital problems, and I'm not saying there were, loyalty and pride would have kept him from talking to me about it. I still say he was strong. We talked philosophy, we talked the hypothetical, but what we did not do was cry on each other's shoulders about our private lives."

"But maybe it wasn't a private thing," I said, needing somehow to believe it hadn't been, wanting to keep my memory, even faulty, of that golden marriage intact. "If he were killed, perhaps it was a disgruntled patient—or the deranged parent or spouse of someone he lost on the operating table. I looked in the archives for things of that sort, but I didn't have any luck. You've a sharp memory. Was there anything at all of that sort back at that time?"

She shook her head. "I'm not saying he didn't lose

some. Even the most brilliant doctors do. In time, all people die. No matter how well-attended, patients do die. It is a sad part of what we do here, but there is no use in running from reality. If your father talked much about his work while at home, I am sure you realized even back then that the cliché often came true: The operation was a success, but the patient died."

"I know," I said softly. "It hurt him so much when it happened. But he never gave up. He always went back, determined to make the next one a success. There was no way he was a quitter and I . . ."

"Exactly. Jim Clark wasn't a quitter. As a professional adversary, and a private admirer, I agree with you there, my dear. But I have no answers to your questions. I don't know who to refer you to. Things change. It was so long ago. I'm *not* saying that you should let it go. Obviously, if you could have, you wouldn't be here. I'm just saying I don't have the answers for you."

"At the risk of being rude, I'm not sure I can believe that. Oh, I can believe my father did not confide in you about his personal problems. But I believe, considering the way he died, that rumors would have come to your ears. Several times, you have called me 'child.' I am not offended by that. You knew me as a child, I'm young enough to *be* your child, and that is fact. But it is also true that I'm an adult now. I'm a doctor. I can handle the truth. I don't have to be protected."

"And what if it isn't you I'm protecting, Katie? Give some thought to the fact that the innocent can be hurt in this as well as the guilty. I don't know who might have hated your father enough to kill him. I truly don't. He had enemies. Most powerful men do. He had good looks, the charisma I mentioned, talent, intelligence. There are jealous people in this world, Dr. Devin Hollister . . . there are people who hate for no other reason than they resent those who are what they can never be."

"And I don't suppose you are going to tell me the names of any of these so-called 'enemies?'"

She hesitated slightly, then parted her lips as if to answer. Before she could utter a word, Jack gave a low moan. Instantly, I was up off the chair and at his side. Jane arose also and watched from the end of the hospital bed. I turned on the light and, at the inquiry from the ward secretary, said, "I need a nurse in here. Mr. Fraser is beginning to wake up."

For a few minutes, Jane watched as the nurse and I worked with Jack, then she turned and left the room. I heard her say something that might have been, "I'll catch you later," but I wasn't sure. My full attention was on Jack.

"Jack, can you hear me?" I asked softly. "This is Katie. You've been hurt. You'll be okay." I slipped my hand from the wrist where I had measured his pulse into his palm. As I had said before in the culvert pipe, I asked, "If you can hear me, squeeze." To my surprise, I suddenly found my hand held in a vise-like grip.

"Hurt?" he asked.

"Damn it, yes!"

"You lost. That's three words."

"How can I lose when I didn't even know we were playing the game?"

"Easiest way to lose."

The nurse's smile was broad, but I fancy mine was even wider.

"Go notify the doctor on call," I told her. "I'll stay here with him."

He kept my hand, his grip loosening only slightly. The pressure hurt some, but I found I didn't mind, for the slight discomfort reassured me that Jack was alive, that Jack was going to be okay.

"What happened?" he asked me.

"We're all hoping you'll be able to tell that to us. You remember meeting Anthony Toretta?"

"Yep."

"He and I found you in the ditch on Dahlia Street where you and I used to play. That arbitrary spot halfway between our houses. How much *do* you remember, Jack? Don't force it. We've lots and lots of time, but . . ."

"Don't take it unless I have to?"

"Something like that."

"I gather I'm in ABC?"

"You're doing great in the orientation department. You know me, you know where you are; if you know the date, you pass the test."

He supplied me with the date (the correct one) *and* with a rude comment I hadn't asked for.

"Pithy, aren't we?" I asked archly. "Can you quit being a smart-mouth long enough to be pertinent?"

"I was about to be just that when I was so rudely interrupted. Talk about a smart-mouth! By the way, could I have a drink of water?"

"Yes. But you'll have to let go of my hand."

"I can have it back?"

Touched, I said, "Yessir," then quickly supplied a few sips of water, followed by the return of my hand to his.

"I came here to the hospital with you," he said slowly and painstakingly. "I watched you with the patient in the emergency room. You talked to me a minute after you were done and said you'd be right back. After that, I . . . Katie, the next thing I remember is waking up here."

"You don't remember talking to Paul Linden in the emergency room? Someone told me they saw you two talking. Later, I asked Paul. He said you did exchange a few words. He attempted to apologize for the way his wife had acted at the restaurant. He said you told him it was nothing, and not his fault anyway. You don't recall that?"

His head made negative motions against the pillow. "You said you'd be right back. I woke up and heard your voice. Right now, that's all there is. Not real helpful, huh? Only . . ."

"Yes?"

He shook his poor damaged head again. "Nothing, really. A smell. I remember a smell."

"The best I can recall, it didn't smell too great in that drainpipe."

"Not a bad smell. A good one. Sweet, but not unpleasantly so. Like an expensive cologne."

"A woman's perfume or a man's cologne or aftershave?"

"Good grief, Katie, considering everything, how can I tell you that? Maybe I'd recognize the scent if I smelled it again. But I can't lie here and tell you what brand it was, for pete's sake."

"I know. Don't get agitated. I was just hoping."

"Hey, kid, don't pay attention to me. I'm just feeling a bit abused."

"Possibly because you were."

"Katie, you look worn out. Go home and get some rest."

"Not until the Dalton authorities put a twenty-four hour guard on you . . . something they'd better do quick, or I'll be out after their hides."

"Why on earth do I need a twenty-four hour guard?"

"What happened to you wasn't an accident. Grown men don't end up where you were by choice. You were, I'm sure, left for dead."

"Not very nice of someone, eh?"

"Not very. And that not-so-nice person is still at large. We can't take chances."

"Think you can fight them off?"

"I'll die trying."

"You know, somehow I believe that. Great to know someone like you would come to the defense of a dweeb like me."

"You're not a dweeb."

"No? Don't lie to me, Katie. I know myself better than that. I've always known I was a nerd. I never minded all that much. Except, of course, on a few notable occasions."

"I think maybe you're talking too much. Want to rest?"

"Later. My head hurts. But don't go rushing after your precious painkillers. I don't want to pass back out just yet. Hey, kid, you know you can be in danger with this, too?"

"I've thought of that. Believe me, I've thought about it a lot. But it's too late to back out now, so it would seem.

Not that I'd be smart enough to do that anyway. Jack, what was it that you were going to tell me when . . ."

But destiny imposed still another delay when Dr. Bart Gentry, the internist on call, made his entrance and all but elbowed me out of the way. Even as I felt the stab of resentment, I knew I was being unreasonable. Jack was seriously injured. I was only an intern. The physician bearing the responsibility for the case would want to examine the patient firsthand, not stand back and watch me do it or take my word for what had been found.

Gentry moved with skill and ease to do the neurocheck and reaffirm the vital signs. I watched his face as he backed away from the bedside at last, taking one more check of the eye movement before doing so.

"Mr. Fraser, I do believe you're going to be all right."

"Great. Because I need to get up and go to the bathroom."

"Now, now, none of that just yet. The nurse here will help you or get an aide in here to do so. You're *not* to be up and about for any reason whatsoever until Garth Robinson has been in tomorrow morning . . ."

"Nice fellow," Jack commented, managing to sound a little inebriated. "Nice wife, too. Whole family comes to the restaurant pretty often. But why don't you call him? He's a nice man. I'm sure he'll say I can get up."

I took a few steps toward the bed and placed my hand on Jack's arm. "Nice has nothing to do with it," I said firmly. "This has to do with your physical well-being. I talked with Dr. Robinson after he checked you in the emergency room . . . and he definitely wants you to stay in bed until he sees you again. He wants to get some tests—some pictures of what is going on in your head mainly. After he sees you and some of the results are back, he'll probably let you try your wings. Till then . . . stay put."

"Well said," commented Gentry. "Look, I'm heading home. Anything you need before I leave. Something to make you sleep? Something for pain?"

Jack made the negative motions with his head again. "Really, I'm okay."

"Fine. Just don't be noble. If it hurts, ask for something. There's an order on the chart for a painkiller, okay?"

"Yessir. And I do appreciate you coming out at night like this to see to me. I hate to cause any inconvenience."

"Yeah, well, you southerners are like that. Which is probably why I stay here. Where I came from, hospitality was just a word in the dictionary. Anyway, see you in the morning."

He left then, but resumption of the conversation with Jack was not to be. Hodlitt and Daniels were temporarily out of the picture. Jack's case had moved up a notch in the world and I found myself face-to-face with Chief-of-Police Abernathy and Sheriff Lemmon. They were close together in age, fiftyish I'd guess, and similar in build—that is, very burly, neither of them overly tall but making up for it in sheer breadth and musculature. Where the chief was dark, the sheriff was ruddy, but their features could have been set in the same mold. Only the differences in their coloring and names kept me from assuming they were brothers. Well-turned out, both of them, despite the late evening hour, not a wrinkle or a stain on either the blue uniform or the brown.

"I'm not sure he should be questioned yet," I said, standing squarely between them and Jack's narrow bed.

"We just talked to his doctor right outside in the hall, ma'am. He said there'd be no harm as long as we keep it short and don't pressure him. Actually, when we're through here, we'd like to talk to you. And to Dr. Toretta. He, incidentally, will be here shortly. We called him at his apartment and he offered to meet us here."

I sighed deeply. "You guys have no hearts, do you? Poor Anthony has only been in bed a few hours. Before that, he was up for over twenty hours straight. He needs to rest. And in just a few hours, I'll be starting a thirty-two hour stretch, so *I* need rest. Above all, we *are* doctors, you know."

"What can we say, ma'am? We're just doing our job. We're talking major assault here, maybe even attempted murder. And the gentleman *did* volunteer. We said it could wait until a more reasonable hour."

It *was* like Anthony, I suppose, to put personal needs aside in order to cooperate.

The combination of Abernathy and Lemmon did not get a lot more out of Jack than I had. He did not remember leaving ABC. He had no idea how he got in the culvert pipe on Dahlia Street. He could not, of course, describe his attacker or attackers because he did not remember seeing them. As he had told me, his mind was a total blank from the time I last spoke to him inside the ER and when he came to in the hosptial room just a few minutes ago.

"I wish I could help you all more," he kept apologizing.

"That's all right," they kept saying, "you're doing fine."

They did think to ask him something that hadn't occurred to me yet, and it turned out that he did remember what he had in his pockets and in his wallet. A check with what he detailed against what was found on him pretty well ruled out robbery as a motive. His watch, while not an expensive Rolex like Paul's, was of good quality and fairly new. They had taken it off his arm in ER and placed it in the envelope with his other personal belongings. The "thirty dollars or so" in cash was also still present.

Anthony arrived then and the officers wanted to talk to us outside the room.

"I'm not leaving Jack alone," I said firmly. "Didn't those other two tell you how I felt about that?"

"Yes, ma'am, they did. And you are, in all likelihood, very right. In a case like this, better safe than sorry. So if you two will just step outside, we'll tell you what we have in mind."

"But in the meantime..."

The brown-suited man heaved a deep sigh that told of his impatience.

"Nurse, we'll only be a few feet away in the corridor. Are your duties such that you can remain here with Mr. Fraser until we return?"

"Yes sir, I'll stay where I am."

"Thank you. We appreciate it. And do remember, Nurse, this *is* an emergency, so don't go running off to take care of another one unless you leave someone here in your place, hear?"

"I understand very well."

She did . . . Amy was a good nurse, a bright young woman, and I could tell that it rankled her slightly that he was being so *specific* with her. I don't know what it is with these Dalton authority figures . . . the charm characteristic of the Mississippian seems to be lacking, to put it mildly.

While Amy stayed put, Anthony and I trekked into the hall with Abernathy and Lemmon. Like weird twins of a sort, they stood turning their hats round and round in their hands while they questioned us. Anthony told them how it all had come about. When they were through with him, I went over with them what I had already reported to the other two. Then they asked a few other questions, which even I had to admit were more pertinent than otherwise, about my "past," and even wanted a detailed description of the threats I had been receiving, including my being locked in the out-of-the-way records room.

"We'll get someone in here to guard your friend, never fear," Lemmon said, reaching out to pat my shoulder. I gritted my teeth and bore the patronizing tone, saving my scathing remarks for the time when he called me "little lady" or something of the sort.

"When?" I asked. "I can spend the rest of the night, I suppose. But the hospital does expect me to work. I can't stay in there forever without a break."

"You shouldn't have to," Abernathy said with what, for him, was exuberance. "In fact, you won't have to. But sheriff here and I have a suggestion to make, something we'll need the cooperation of the hospital and a few employees to do. You've already figured out that we're dealing with a heavy situation here. If Mr. Fraser regains his memory, he's going to point his finger at whoever did this to him. And I got this gut feeling there's some connection between what happened here and what happened to that poor lady the other night. We appreciate your interest and concern, ma'am, but we aren't so dumb we had to have it pointed out that someone just might be looking for a chance to put Jack Fraser the rest of the way out."

"Then where do we go from here?" I asked quickly. Maybe they weren't my favorite people, but trust had to start somewhere, given the gravity of the situation.

"First off, who can you trust to help. We need someone who will do exactly as told without letting it slip what's taking place."

Anthony and I exchanged looks. "That's a tall order," I said. "Frankly, I don't have much of a list. It's not that I believe everyone connected with the hospital is involved. It's just that I don't know which people are and which aren't. You can count on me, for obvious reasons. And I trust Dr. Toretta here. But that isn't the same as saying it's right to ask him to do more, especially if it's dangerous."

"You know I'll help, Devin."

"Thanks."

Lemmon squinted his eyes and looked the two of us over. "Nothing personal, Toretta, but what makes Dr. Hollister so sure about you?"

He smiled slightly. "I guess you'll have to ask her that. Wish I could say it was because she's hopelessly in love with me, but I just don't think that's the case."

"I trust Anthony, subjectively speaking, because he's proven his loyalty, fairness, and a willingness to do what is right even if it works against what he wants for himself. But since it could be that he's only been nice to worm his way into my confidence, I have the objective fact that he is not from this area, and that he was somewhere between ten and twelve years old when my father was killed, which makes him an unlikely candidate as a killer or an abettor. That much is true of Jack, too. I have to believe he's clear where my father is concerned because, like me, he was a child when it happened. But the doctors and nurses, even the administrator . . . well, I can't *know*, can I?"

They agreed on that.

In his slow southern drawl, Abernathy drew up a plan of sorts.

"What we want to do is move Mr. Fraser on the sly. Just to another room, someplace where he can receive the needed medical attention, and we'll keep an officer right inside with him. Two if need be. That depends on the location, okay? We'll put a volunteer in Fraser's present bed. Instead of posting guards outside, we'll hide a couple inside. What we want you to do in the next few minutes, Dr. Hollister, is go about the hospital and make unhappy noises to anyone who'll listen about how the dumb cops won't spare a guard for poor Jack Fraser and that you guess you'll have to stay with him, but aren't sure you can stay awake because you're dead tired. Can you do that?"

Without a word, I nodded. "Easy enough. My big concern is moving Jack. His head injury hasn't been fully assessed."

"He's going to have a CAT scan in the morning anyway," Anthony said. "There's a big waiting/recovery room in that area. Move him on the QT tonight. Keep a nurse and, as you said, a guard there at all times. He'll be as safe as he is now. By the way, you think this guard or guards could maybe pose as hospital employees? Blue and brown uniforms, especially with guns attached, tend to attract attention."

"Exactly. We'll tend to that. You're sure it will be okay to move Fraser?"

"We don't know yet the extent of his head injuries, so it's all iffy at this point. But considering the situation, taken all the way around, he's safer in a different location, don't you think? No nurse even needs to know. The fewer people in on this, the better. I'll stay with him . . . me and your plainclothes guy. The tricky part is . . . and I assume one of your guys will take Jack's place in the bed . . . is how many nurses will check him during the night and figure out he's not Fraser. Even if you have a small guy with light hair and we keep it dark in the room so they won't see the features clearly, well . . . there could be those who know him . . . and the vital signs will run different. You can almost bet on that."

The officers looked stymied. "I'll do what I can there," I said firmly. "Just get a near ringer for him. I know you probably won't be too close, with no more people than you have working and on this short of a notice, but come as close as you can. I'll get real obnoxious in there. I can play the snooty doctor well when the stakes are high enough. *I* personally will do the neuro-checks and monitor the patient. The nurse can stand a few feet away and write what I tell her to write. Can't promise it will work, but I'll do what I can."

"All set, then. We'll go to the station, gather our recruits and be back. Hospital clothes?"

"Stay put," Anthony said. "I'll gather up some scrubs since sizes don't matter a lot in them and I'll be right back."

"I'm going to see Jack for a few moments," I told them. "I'll be in the room there when you're ready to put this into action. And thanks for your help. I realize this is risky for you."

"For all of us, ma'am," was the grim reply. "But when we got into this business, we knew it wouldn't be all fun and games, that risk was part of it. Truth is, you're in more danger than we are. A real sitting duck if you stay in that room. They could be after you too, you know."

"Somehow, I don't think so. I've been warned so much, yet not a hair on my head was harmed. Dru and Jack, as far as we know, weren't warned at all. But I will be careful. And I *am* staying. I just thought I'd tell you that in case you were getting ready to tell me not to, just to announce I'm staying, then go home."

"It's prudent though."

"Forget it."

They were of two minds and I realized that. If I stayed, the trap would look more realistic. But I am sure they could also imagine the hew and cry if the bait (me) were to come to harm. It was a risk I had to take and, thus, so did they.

Chapter Eighteen

"It's too dangerous," Jack said. Despite his condition, his manner was urgent.

"It's not my idea," I countered. "I doubt they would listen to me saying it shouldn't be done . . . not that I'm about to say anything of the sort. Personally, I think it's an excellent idea."

"I won't allow it. And that's final."

I squeezed his hand and laughed softly.

"What's so funny?" was the irritated reply.

"The idea of you allowing or not allowing anything. Your head isn't working right, your skull is probably broken, and you're hooked up to IVs and monitors. What exactly are you going to do to 'not allow it'?"

"I have no idea. But I must say it isn't very sporting of you to remind me of my infirmities. It hurts my macho image of myself. You must know a guy likes to feel in control of the situation."

"I don't know that it's anything I ever discussed with anyone, but it's certainly something I've observed. Such as in how many men seem to emotionally freak-out in hospitals. Even when they aren't the patients, when they're with someone in the family or a friend who is ill. In a hospital, the fact hits you that you *aren't* in control. It's worrying to take-charge people."

"Very astute. But don't try to sidetrack me with philosophy, Katie. I know the authorities mean well. I know it's to save my life. But I can't let someone I don't even know hide in this bed and pretend to be me. I can't even imagine how rotten and responsible I'd feel if something happened to someone else, and you know as well as I do that it very easily could."

"I know that. I'm not trying to sugarcoat the situation. But look at it this way: It's *not* only to save your life, it's to protect whoever they might go after next, and that could even include me. Besides, you don't have a choice. They'll be in here momentarily to move you. Anthony will stay with you, okay?"

"I suppose. But I don't understand why he's doing all this for me. Or maybe I do. It's because he's in love with you, right? You don't have to answer that. And I'm certainly not going to ask if you're in love with him. You might answer and I don't think I'm ready to hear about it."

"Anthony's a good person, Jack. Quite possibly that's all there is to it. He was around when the situation came to a head and he isn't the sort to sit on the sidelines. I doubt that personalities come into it. Anthony Toretta is a doer, that's all."

He tried to nod and failed. "Well, let's just say I owe him. I'm not one to look a gift horse in the mouth, but you are sure we can trust *him?*"

"I'm not going on gut feelings here because I know those feelings can be wrong, especially if you *want* to like someone and believe in him. But I trust him, to be frank, for the same reason I trust you . . . which is exactly what I told the sheriff and the police chief. We all think this has been stirred up because I was going to start investigating into my father's death, so that leaves people our age out. Enough of that. They will be in here right away. Please quit stalling and tell me, just as bluntly as you have to, what it is you've been hinting at."

He moved a hand as if to cover my hand with it, then let it drop back. IVs are really prohibitory when it comes to such things.

"Katie, it threw me for a loop the first time we actually talked in your apartment the night Mrs. Linden was killed. You so casually said something like you weren't going to settle for marrying until you were sure it could be as good as your parents' marriage. You remember that?"

"Not the exact words, but the general theme. And that *is* the way I feel. Not very long ago, I asked Mother if she had really loved Dad, and she told me they had been 'golden' together, that even as children they had realized that their destiny was with each other. As corny as it sounds, it was like a fairy tale. Even if it did end more like a horror story. Is it so silly to want that for myself?"

"Not silly, sweet girl. Maybe not realistic, but certainly not silly. I'm not saying your mother lied to you. Maybe she wanted to remember it that way. And probably it *had* started out that way. Most people, when they fall in love and marry, think they can beat the odds against unhappy marriages. What I'm trying to say is that *you* don't need me to tell you the truth. The truth is there in your memory. You've just worked at submerging it. Your parents weren't happy. At least not that summer you and I were together so much. Before that, I wouldn't know. But you did know they fought a lot. Which is one reason you and I spent so much time together those long evenings, even out after dark catching lightning bugs and such."

"Chasing," I said wryly. "The way I recall it, you wouldn't allow them to be caught."

"Not true. I just wanted to set them free right away. I guess I learned at an earlier age than you did that you can't hold something that isn't meant to be held. One way or another, you kill it. Katie, don't you remember at all?"

I closed my eyes, not sure even then if I was trying to remember or to forget.

"People envied them," I said in a little voice. "They were both so good-looking, so intelligent, so personable, and they seemed to belong together. They both loved me very much and I loved them. I think they had both wanted a large family. Maybe that was a disappointment, but I don't suppose it was a tragedy. Jack . . ."

"You need to remember on your own, you know. Anything I can tell you, you can choose not to believe.

But I know nothing you don't know. Like I can't remember a few hours ago, you just can't remember some of the details."

I gave a weak smile. "Not quite the same. As I explained to the policemen before you came out of it, you *can't* remember. There may have been enough physical trauma there to actually wipe out a center permanently so that you *can't* ever get those happenings back. But what you're saying to me is that my memories are selective ones, that I've almost deliberately 'lost' the bad memories. Anthony had suggested I might want to undergo hypnosis to see if I could bring back a clue that might be helpful."

"It's not a bad idea," he said soberly. "After all, you and I weren't close anymore in those last few months before your father died. They fought a lot the previous summer. *That* much I know. But those last months, well ... anything that happened in that house was something I had no way of knowing about."

"Jack, you have to help me more. It may come back. I realize now, as hurtful as the process may be, that I have to face up to it. Can you prime me? With what little you know, can you tell me what they fought about? Anything you heard yourself when you were at the house. Anything I confided in you about them. If it was really bad, I'm sure I was miserable. Because I *know* it wasn't always that way, that it wasn't something I grew up with."

Jack hesitated as he searched my face as if it were a map in which he could find some clues. Finally, evidently deciding I was sincere in my desire to know, he said, "In many ways, your mother was more ambitious than your father. He had the reputation for being such a great surgeon. But being great in Dalton, Mississippi ... anyway, she wanted to move to a larger place. Her sister was on the east coast. I gather there was a good deal of rivalry there. Your mother was envious. She wanted the big social whirl, not the little stuff you find here in Dalton. Your father was content here. He had no desire to move. They fought over that. And they fought over you. As you said yourself, if there had been more children. . . . Anyway, they each wanted different things for you. Your father was winning. You liked his company more and you were determined to be a doctor. Your mother had always shared him with Medicine. She didn't want to lose you to it also. Because of his long hours, because of his refusal to leave Dalton, she accused him of affairs. He said that was the pot calling the kettle black." He paused and searched my face again. "You don't remember any of this?"

Bitterly, I said, "It's beginning to sound familiar, dammit. Too familiar."

Before we could continue, Anthony and the policemen arrived. A stocky one was dressed in surgical scrubs. A slightly built one with sandy hair, not a ringer for Jack, but similar from a safe distance, wore a hospital gown over jeans and tennis shoes.

"I don't like this," Jack protested. But it made no difference what he said. Together, Anthony and I transferred him from the bed to the gurney, and the burlier policeman then took one end of the cart and he and Anthony wheeled Jack away.

That left me with a stranger.

"Better take off your pants and shoes before you get in bed," I advised.

For a change, someone turned scarlet besides me.

"Hey," I said with a grin, "I'm not being frisky. But if you're trying to pass for a patient . . . well, nurses might be in and . . ."

"I was told you'd keep them at bay. From the chest up, I look like a patient. That'll have to do, ma'am. I need the pants because I'm armed and I need the shoes in case I have to take off in pursuit. Bare toes are too vulnerable, okay?"

I shrugged. "Suit yourself. But, look, keep this conversation quiet, will you? This is the first time I've ever asked a guy to undress when I wasn't going to examine him . . . and here you've refused. Not a pretty story, right?"

My clowning seemed to help put him at ease. He

laughed, hopped in bed, and was very obedient about lying still while I hooked up the monitors to him and taped IV tubing to his arm to make it look as if intravenous fluids were running. That done, all I had to do was sit and wait.

As much as I wanted it to be over, I really didn't want anything to happen. My thoughts told me that Jack had been right. There *were* things I had chosen not to remember.

Moving slowly, almost as if robotized, as if what I was doing had nothing to do with me, I reached for the telephone at the bedside. I punched the 9 for an outside line, then dialed the numbers that would connect me with Boston.

"Hi, Charlie," I said, feeling warm all over when I heard the familiar voice. "Boy, have I missed you!"

"Same here," he replied. "Only more so, I'm sure. How's it going there, pumpkin? You have a good visit with your mother?"

"Short," I said, "but it was good to see her. Just wish you had come, too."

He said we'd get together sometime soon when I had a few days off. We exchanged a few pleasantries, then I took the plunge. If anyone could help me fill in the gaps, it was my mother. She would try to evade, as she always did. But this time, I had to try to see that she did not get away with it. "Is Mother there now, Charlie? I'd like to talk to her for just a minute."

"Why, of course not," he said, sounding puzzled. "I'm picking her up at the airport tomorrow."

"But . . ."

"She was going to fly on up to New York City and see a friend, do some shopping. Didn't she tell you that?"

"Maybe," I said, recalling with a stab of guilt that I had fallen into the habit of not really listening to all of Mother's chatter. "I thought she was headed home, but I may have forgotten. No big deal. I'll call her back tomorrow if I don't have the answers by then."

"Answers? Answers to what, Devin?"

"I'm not sure, Charlie. I'm not sure about anything

anymore. Except that I love you."

"I love you, too, pumpkin. Car running okay?"

"It's a great car, Charlie. It suits me."

"I thought it would," he said, sounded very pleased with himself. "Your mother wanted me to look for a BMW, but I said, 'Devin's not like that, Elaine. She'll like the Mustang better, sporty but still modest, and being American-made and all.' And I was right, wasn't I?"

"You usually are about me. You see me for what I am. She sees for what she wants me to be."

"But she does love you," he said quickly, thinking perhaps he had betrayed her in some way.

"I know that. You've both been good to me. Thanks for everything, Charlie."

I replaced the receiver and lowered the one burning light. As I had noted before, the room was very eerie. Unaccountably, a shiver ran down my spine as I looked at the stranger in the bed.

"Mind telling me your name," I asked, "since destiny has it that we spend some time together?"

"Mike Faulkner," he said. Looking down at the plastic bracelet on his arm, he added, "Alias Jackson L. Fraser, I guess."

Talk about realism. I had no idea how Anthony had managed to obtain a duplicate bracelet. Maybe I didn't even want to know.

I said, "Well, good to meet you, Mike. Or Jack, as I guess I'd better call you for tonight. I'm Devin Hollister." After a pause, I added, "Alias Katie Clark."

"Yeah, I heard about that," he said, his voice lowered with a display of minor sympathy. "I didn't know you. But I knew your dad. He took my appendix out, as a matter of fact, when I was fifteen. Nice guy."

After a while, conversation dwindled. There is only so much chitchat you can make with a person you've just met. We discussed playing cards and decided that was impossible. To anyone who walked in, he had to *look* incapacitated. The relief from boredom wasn't worth taking a chance on.

Time ticked inexorably on. The monitors, to my trained eye, told of a boringly normal "patient." The lights from them glowed eerily. It was all so strange, so tedious, so tense. Although nothing was going on, I was too anxiety-ridden to become sleepy. And it occurred to me there was to be no relief for me, not in the immediate future. Suddenly that was okay. Adrenalin and determination would see me through my professional duties as they arose. I could no more have gone off somewhere and gone to sleep than I could have sprouted wings and flown. A doctor I might be, but the Nancy Drew in me was asserting itself. I could sleep for long, unbroken hours *after* my thirty-two hour stretch. This was *my* shining hour. How many chances would I have in life to be doctor, detective, and protector all at the same time? It also occurred to me that in the process I'd be absolving my guilt over the way I'd betrayed Jack fifteen years before. In my heart and mind, I owed him. Funny way to pay a debt, but it was what the roll of the dice had brought about.

I leaned back and let my mind dwell on what it had tried so hard, and so long, to resist.

"I'm Jackson Lee Fraser."

"I know who you are," I said crossly. *"I've seen you at school. You live on Magnolia Street with those two old ladies."*

He blinked, solemn as an owl behind those glasses that seemed too large for his face. Instead of wearing, as other ten-year-old boys did, jeans, T-shirt, and running shoes, he was dressed in neatly ironed starched short pants, cotton shirt buttoned all the way up, knee socks, and brown oxfords. His hair was cut painfully short and had been combed down with water until it was plastered-down tight against his scalp.

Here, I thought, was a human being my own age who had, quite obviously, endured more than I had. This was not a person with whom I had to pretend. With my other "friends" I had to do as my mother had taught me, 'Hold up your head, be proud. Keep your hurts and shames to yourself.'

"Well, I know who you are, too," he answered me. *"You're Katie Clark and you live on Macon Street in that*

rock house. I like those green things over the windows and doors."

"Awnings," I said.

"Yeah, them."

"They're forest green. That's my dad's favorite color."

"I know your dad, too. Well, sort of. He operated on Aunt Em and Aunt Dorrie."

"At the same time?" I asked sarcastically.

"Of course not, dummy," he replied, gaze still unblinking. "Anyway, what are you doing hanging out in the ditch?"

I shrugged. "Dunno. Guess I'm bored and don't have anything else to do."

"Sometimes I come here to be by myself."

"Do you mean you want me to leave, Jackson Lee Fraser?"

"No. I was just wondering if that was why you came, too. If it is, I thought maybe we could be alone together."

It sounded so silly that we both laughed.

"You're right," I admitted. "My folks were fighting. I wanted to get away. I hate it when they fight. They never used to, and now it's all the time. I don't like it there anymore when they're both home."

He regarded me owlishly. I tried to think of another friend I had to whom I would have said those words. There wasn't another one. With them, I always felt somehow compelled to let on that all was perfect in every way.

"You can always come to my house," he said. "It's not far from here. My aunts like me to have company. But I hardly ever do. No one yells there. Not ever. So you don't have to be alone unless you want to. sometimes I just want to, so I can think things out. Know what I mean?"

I nodded, believing then that I had really chosen the right person in which to confide. He had accepted the fact that I had a problem and offered a place of retreat. No false sympathy, no solutions, no attempt at topping my tale of woe with one of his, although I supposed he could easily have done so.

As the summer wore on, we spent more and more time together and, in the process, became quite close.

We met midpoint at the ditch one day, as we so often did, and tried to decide how to spend the next few hours.

"Let's play marbles," I suggested. "We haven't for ages. But I didn't bring them. Ride with me back to my house and we'll get them."

"Can we play there?" he asked eagerly.

Jackson Lee never insisted on playing at my house because he knew I was touchy about it, but he was always glad when we did. I allowed it only when one of my parents was out of the house. Even though I knew Jack would be understanding, I did not want him to listen to one of their quarrels.

"Sure," I said. Dad was at the office. "I told Mother I'd be at your house, but she won't mind if we're there instead."

I think Jack liked it at my house because things were shiny new there while he lived amid antiques. The cookstove in the Fraser kitchen was even a wood-burning one. The only bend to modern living the ladies had made was the black and white TV in the front room, through which they took much delight in soaps and game shows.

Back at my house, I ran up the stairs, Jack close behind me, and took my sack of marbles from the top drawer in my bureau. Not seeing Mother anywhere, I went on a search. Both my parents had always insisted I keep them informed of my whereabouts.

In my hurry to be about my play, I did not knock or hesitate, just pushed open the door to their bedroom. And, as always, Jack was right behind me.

Mother was on the bed, long fair hair spread across her pillow. A man was across her body, his body providing all the covering she had, for the rest of the bedding had been kicked out of their way. I did not see his face, but I knew he was not my father.

She saw me then and the cunning, pleased look on her face changed to alarm.

"Katie," she called out.

"I'm going back to Jack's house," I managed to say. "Come on, Jack. I think you have a better place to play marbles anyway."

When I reached the bottom of the stairs, he was not with me. I called back up, "Jackson Lee, you coming or not?"

"I'm coming, Katie."

Without a word, I jumped on my bike and rode like the wind in the direction of his house. Never had my short, chubby legs pedaled as furiously.

In his backyard, we parked the bikes. With chalk, I marked the boundaries for our game while he went in the house and brought out plastic tumblers of hand-squeezed lemonade. It tasted so good, both tart and sweet, after the furiously pedaled ride.

"Katie, what was he doing with your mother? I thought only..."

My face turned as hot as fire. "Jackson Lee Fraser, don't you ever, not ever, talk to me about that again. If you want us to keep on being friends, just act like it didn't happen, okay?"

"Okay. Who shoots first, you or me?"

When I went very reluctantly home, hours later, Mother was truly alone. Fully dressed, very pale and distraught looking. Every golden hair in place, she sat in the family room embroidering the edges of a pillowcase. The perfect southern lady... the most charming and beautiful doctor's wife. This was not the same person I had seen in the bedroom, limbs wrapped around a stranger.

"Katie, I need to talk to you." Her voice was not much above a whisper, a curiously jarring sound in the summer afternoon.

"I don't feel so good. My stomach hurts. I think I got too hot. Can we talk later?"

"I have to make you understand, honey. I know you're too young to really understand, but... well, I'll tell your father myself. I really will. Would you please not tell him? Katie?"

I stared at her for the longest while. My pretty, pretty mother.

"I don't understand. I don't know what you're talking about. I don't have anything to tell Daddy."

The scent in the room was heavy of roses. She always wore the floral colognes.

"Dr. Hollister? Dr. Hollister, are you okay?"

Blinking, I opened my eyes. As they adjusted to the dim light and to my present surroundings, I realized how deep into the past I must have gone. Not sleep, just a trip it is hard to explain. The tears were running down my face, tears I had held back for sixteen years.

"I'm okay, Mike. And call me Devin, please. I guess I just had a bad dream. I didn't think I'd fall asleep, but I guess I must have. I'll try not to let it happen again."

"Oh, that's okay. I'm not in the least sleepy, so I'll keep watch. But you cried out, so I got worried."

"I'm okay. Really."

In a weird way, I was. Or, in any event, on the road to being that way.

Funny how the human mind works. I had lived to be twenty-six without letting a man get close to me. I had lied to myself about the reasons for that. But now I somehow knew that the image of my mother in bed with that man had always been with me, always warping my view of how it should be, making love seem wrong and somehow ugly. I hadn't remembered it . . . and yet I had never let it go.

The man. Who had the man been? Jack had been behind me and had been late coming down the stairs with me. Perhaps he had seen the face. How I wished I could ask him! I glanced at the clock. At this hour, I should not disturb him outside of an emergency. He was badly hurt and needed his rest. What had waited for this many years could wait until I knew he was awake. And maybe it really did not matter that much.

What had killed me inside was the betrayal by my mother. The name and face of her lover were only incidental after all.

Chapter Nineteen

It was as if a passageway to my subconscious had been opened up and, once opened, was not going to allow itself to be resealed.

A lot of things, once I had let that memory escape, suddenly became clear to me. My parents had argued less in front of me after that. Never again did I see any indication that my mother let a lover into our house. Because she feared, I think, my mother tried harder. She was less shrewish with my father, less demanding. With me, she did not try as hard to make me into another version of herself . . . that tactic did not start up again until we moved to Boston. *Now* I knew the main reason why I had cut Jack out of my life . . . not that I hadn't been a little bit of a snob. Still, the main reason was that he *knew*, he too had seen "the act," and I could always read that scene in his eyes. To cut him out of my life had been to cut out the reality of what had been. With my surface friends, I could once more pretend things were perfect with the Clarks . . . when, indeed, they were not and may never have been.

As a grown-up, I had now, albeit somewhat unwillingly, faced the adultery of my mother. That still left me wondering what good the memory did me. I felt pain and hurt. Not that, realistically, I expected my parents to be saints. But in truth, realistic or not, I had been too idealistic of them. My mother had feet of clay. Perhaps *his* feet had been cast in the same mold. Even if now I

238

knew that, what had I gained?

I could *not* believe Mother had killed him. Well, she *hadn't*. She had taken me to the mall. I had returned before her. My father had been alive when we left. Whatever else she had done, she had not staged that murder to look like suicide. Her shock had been real. As if it had happened yesterday, I could remember that pale, drawn look. It had been so very easy to "forget" she had once taken a lover, to believe she had loved my father so very much. To me, her grief had been a palpable thing . . . so palpable that I had forgiven her finding Charles Hollister and remarrying so quickly. No one could pretend that much . . . not even her.

That put me back at square one.

My reverie was abruptly halted when the door to the room began, quite noiselessly, to open. A strip of light widened, telling me that a world still went on out there. Mike Faulkner sat bolt upright in bed. I could tell by motions beneath the sheet that he had reached for his gun.

"Lie back down," I hissed at him. "Jack isn't strong enough to sit up like that."

Quite obediently, he lay down. I took comfort in his presence, his alertness.

I did not realize how much I was holding in until I heard the soft voice say, "Devin? Someone told me you were still in here."

Whispering so as not to awaken the patient, I said, "Come on in, Ms. Goldstein. I thought you'd gone home long ago."

She sat down across from me. "I did. I found I couldn't remain there. Devin . . . or do you prefer to be called Katie?"

"Devin, I suppose. I've grown more used to it."

"I found my conscience would not let me stay at home. First, let me say I don't know who killed your father. If I did, I'd be tempted to go after that person myself. Maybe you'll hate me for this. Or maybe you're grown-up enough now that you'll understand. I loved him. I was some years older than he was. I was already here, assistant administrator then, when he came back to open up a practice after his residency. He was already married. You were already here. Such a beautiful family. I was envious. More than envious. I was as jealous as hell. Not just because I was alone in the world, but because it was *him*. I had, you see, wanted him from the moment we first met. I did not, even in my fantasies, expect him to ever return my feelings. Time went on. My feelings did not diminish. When Becker, the previous administrator, died suddenly of a heart attack. I took on the job until they could find someone else. The search went on long enough that I felt I proved my competence and asked that my position be made permanent. Your father backed me for that, and against a good deal of opposition. Although the words were never spoken, several board members *and* members of the medical staff felt a woman could not do the job properly, present the right image. His kindness only made me more fond of him. And then . . ."

"Yes?" I asked softly. "It's okay, Ms. Goldstein. I think I've already guessed what you're going to tell me."

"Perhaps. You have a brilliant mind, just as he did.

"As I said before, I had no one. My choice, I suppose, but there were times the loneliness was excruciating. Your father was unhappy. Unfortunately, I guess most marriages end up like that. The people change, want different things. He spent long hours here. And so did I. It happened at first by accident, not by design. I know it was just sex with him in the beginning . . . sex and escape. I did not ever ask, ever pressure, but he said he wanted to be with me, that he had come to love me. He said they had agreed on a divorce, but couldn't agree on custody of *you*. He said he wanted to marry me when it was all over, that he wanted it to be the three of us, but that he wasn't giving you up to her, that you were part of him. Maybe he didn't mean what he said to me. I like to believe he did. All of the women he could have had, who would have gone to bed with him even knowing there was no question of love or marriage, and he was saying he wanted to be with me. It wasn't like a fairy tale. It *was* a fairy tale. Can you understand? Understand and, perhaps, forgive?"

In the dim light, I searched her face. I tried to see her as my father had. Not beautiful like my mother, so few people are, but certainly not ugly, serviceable and plain—trim, neat, and meticulous as he had been. Perhaps her relative plainness had been a welcome change to him, a change from my mother who had, perhaps exacted too great a price for her beauty. I did not hate her. If anything, I felt pity. I knew how embarrassed she would be to know that her tale had fallen on the ears of a very awake local policeman instead of on the ears of a comatose patient, but I had not felt I could warn her of that.

"There is nothing to forgive," I found myself saying. "It was long ago and had nothing to do with me. If he said he loved you, I am sure he meant it. Whatever else he was, I do not believe he was ever a liar. Look, this is very important. Since you knew him better than anyone suspected, and better than you let on when you first knew who I was, do you still think he could not have committed suicide?"

"Devin, I *know* he didn't. In my heart. But they all said it was so, and he was most definitely dead, never to hold me again. But I didn't know then where to start probing. I still don't."

Very slowly, I said, "My mother had a lover, too. For years, I blocked that out. I didn't remember because I didn't want to remember. I wanted to believe, seemed truly to believe, my memories were so clear. Now I have to face the fact they're flawed memories. Ms. Goldstein, how much did my father confide in you? Earlier, you had told me he kept personal things to himself. Obviously, if you were lovers, that was not entirely true. I'm sure he must have communicated some of his unhappiness to you. Tell me, did he ever tell you who my mother's lover was? In my memory, I can't see enough of him to know. His face was away from me and the room was dark, and I did run away very quickly after discovering them. Or I think it was that way. If I could block out what I did, maybe I blocked out his face, too. I'm not asking in an effort to hurt anyone or to track anyone down."

"No," she said softly, "but that may well be what happens, Devin. You surely know that. When the guilty are punished, the innocent often suffer along with them."

"I know that. But it can't be helped, really, can it? In order to put my mind at rest, I have to know. Maybe the knowing will be enough. Maybe that part isn't connected to my father's death."

"Even as you say that, you don't believe it."

I tried to study her face, but the light in the room was, for more than one purpose, very bad, and I found I could not read her well. Something here was not ringing true. I just wasn't quite sure what it was.

"I didn't start this thing with the aim of catching and punishing someone. Yet, if someone killed my father or actively contributed to his death, then why should that person be free from punishment? If you don't want to tell me, fine. I'll find out another way. Just be square with me. That's all I ask."

"I am being square. I do not know any of the details. Your father's words to me were that the marriage was dead and he did not see how it could be resurrected. He did not seem inclined to give further details. I did not interrogate him. I was never, it seemed, the kind of woman men were drawn to. To be blunt, I was willing to settle for crumbs. His reasons did not matter to me, or at least I pretended they did not at the time. I don't know if what I have told you helped, but it is all I have to offer. Now, if you'll excuse me, I'd better get home. Not that I expect to sleep. Is Mr. Fraser getting better?"

"Somewhat, I believe. He rallied and spoke some earlier in the evening, even spoke with the police. But I'm afraid it must have tired him out, for he's slept so soundly ever since."

"Such a nice young man. I *do* hope he recovers fully."

"So do I."

When she was gone, I looked down at the form beneath the covers.

"Get an earful, Michael Faulkner?" I asked.

"You bet!" he said, laughing. "Knowing that one, it's hard for me to imagine . . . but, oh, well, that's what she said. She'd have no reason to make it up, would she?"

He and I stared at each other in the near-darkness. As so happens in Medicine and, I suppose, in police work, one so often works in such close contact with people who were strangers up until that moment. Our jobs were very different, but in a way we were working on the same "case."

"I don't know," I said slowly. "Before you said that, I was thinking something about her story didn't ring true. But, heaven help me, I have no idea *why* I think so. You heard what was said. I've faced the fact that my parents' marriage wasn't perfect. For sixteen years I've shut away the memory of finding my mother with another man. I adored my father, but I'm grown-up now, not a little girl. I no longer reject the possibility that he may have had an affair. Who knows? Maybe even more than one. If this turned out to be the truth, considering everything, I could accept that without it crushing me completely. But . . ."

"But Jane Goldstein?"

"I don't mean to be cruel, but . . . yes, exactly."

"I told you I knew your father. Not well. I was something of a shy kid, and a kid from the wrong side of the tracks. I was intimidated enough that I didn't talk to him a lot. But I remember him as youngish, as good-looking as the doctors on the soaps, and quite nice."

"He was all of that. He was only in his midthirties when he died. Only about ten years older than I am now. But he was special, both quiet and approachable. Most people did think he was special, or so I'm told."

Mike nodded. "From my experience, women of all sorts throw themselves, almost literally, at professional men, doctors especially."

"Oh, believe me, I've observed that. And it's not so hard to believe that, in a moment caught off-guard, Jane revealed her feelings for him. But I *know* how he talked about her. As she said, he may have had some respect for her as an adversary and as a hospital administrator, but I can't believe he wanted to *marry* her. If I can believe that, I can almost believe he killed himself. He would have had to be warped. Still, why would she lie?"

He shrugged. "People are strange. If she worshipped him from afar, so to speak, she probably was terribly jealous of anyone he did care about, your mother and possibly even you included. Maybe, if she is lying, it's a way of 'winning,' to make you believe your dad was in love with her. I know it doesn't make sense."

"I don't know about that. In a cockeyed sort of way, maybe it does make sense . . . at least as much sense as a lot of other stuff I've encountered. For instance, when I've told you what my father was, *why* would my mother seek out someone else?"

Even not seeing him well, I sensed his sympathy, and his words echoed that. He obviously chose them carefully, not wanting to further injure the hurt child that he sensed in me.

"I'm no philosopher, Dr. Hollister. But I've been a policeman long enough to see some ugly domestic disputes and to get pretty well acquainted with human nature. Infidelity has lots of reasons, and most of them don't make a hell of a lot of sense. Some do it for the thrill. Some do it to get even. Some do it because the sex is lousy to nonexistent on the home front. Some do it because they're lonely. Some because they're jealous . . . and not always jealous of another lover, but of a job, a hobby, or anything that takes the spouse away from them, or so they think. I've seen men play around with women who couldn't hold a candle to the one they're cheating on. I'm sure the same is true in reverse. It's just that I know more men than I do women, I guess."

I heaved a deep sigh. All of what he said was undeniably true. I could no longer be unrealistic enough to believe my parents were exempt from the emotions that haunt all other mortals.

The policeman and I fell into silence. Despite my determination not to sleep, I did. I awakened with a start when Mike reached through the bed railing to poke me.

He placed a finger across his lips to warn me into silence. The door was, once again, opening. For a moment, I felt in a near-panic. It came to me we had not discussed strategy. Do I let the person know I am awake, or do I feign sleep until we see what is going on?

Heavy footsteps approached across the carpeted floor. Even before I could see clearly, I knew somehow this was no nurse making his or her appointed rounds. The steps were too stealthy, too hesitant. Besides, the others had pushed the door open widely, announced themselves in quiet voices. No announcement here. Just a slow, hesitant approach. A shadow cast against the wall showed me this person did not seem to be carrying a clipboard or a chart.

I held my breath, pulse pounding rapidly, both from fear and uncertainty. I drew comfort from the fact that Mike was awake and armed. Funny, a few days ago, I would have denied I could find comfort in a man with a gun. But things have a way of changing, the events of life spin us around, make us do and feel in ways we did not believe possible.

He stepped toward the bed and bent over it. I knew then who it was, although his face was still away from the light. He reached in his pocket and withdrew an object. From where I sat, I could not ascertain what it was. Through narrowed eyes, I saw that Mike had his eyes closed. Possibly he felt it important to be an unconscious patient until we knew what was coming off, but I did not know what the object was, nor its holder's intent, and I was relatively sure Mike had been unable to see the action of that hand.

"Don't you need a better light for examination, Paul?" I asked, reaching out to pull the chain that brought the light over the head of the bed to full brightness. He blinked as if stunned and I was quickly at his side. Giving a strange laugh, he looked down at the bed. There was no use pretending. The two men were not enough alike that the wattage I had unleashed could cause Mike to be mistaken for Jack, especially when Paul apparently was well-acquainted with Jack. The object in Paul's hand was an ophthalmoscope, a small instrument with a mirror. I flushed uncomfortably at the sight of it. Not exactly a lethal weapon.

Obviously bewildered, the handsome surgeon looked from the face on the pillow to my face. "I don't understand. Why the switch? And, Devin, why the hostility? Surely you don't think . . . forget it, obviously you *do* think."

"Sargent Faulkner," Mike said lamely.

Looking straight at Mike, avoiding eye contact with me completely, Paul Linden said, "I couldn't sleep. I have that problem a lot since my wife was killed, Sargeant. I don't pretend Jack Fraser and I were close friends, but I have eaten at his place regularly and have come to like him. It was on my mind how he had become so involved in this. First, being taken in for questioning because he had seen Dru home the night she was killed. Now this, nearly being killed himself. I guess I just wanted to see that he was all right. As you can see, I'm obviously unarmed. I have the reputation of being somewhat of a perfectionist, I'm afraid. It wasn't enough to look on the chart. I wanted to check him out myself. Can you understand that?"

"Certainly, Dr. Linden. No problem. You work at this hospital. You have certain rights and privileges here. But we're just trying to do a job, too. We felt, or my superiors did, that it's very possible someone might try to finish Mr. Fraser off. We have to take every precaution against that."

"I understand. In your place, I'd undoubtedly do something similar. Just out of professional curiosity, not that I'd try to see him under such circumstances, but where *is* the patient? I'm quite concerned. Jack sustained a rather significant head injury. He really shouldn't be shuttled around here and there."

I shot Mike a warning glance. I hadn't meant for Paul to see it, but he did. I immediately felt bad about that, bad and very little. Mike was intelligent and competent. He did not need a warning from me on how to conduct his business. What I had done was hurt Paul for no good purpose.

I heard Mike saying, "I'm afraid I can't tell you that, sir. Nothing personal. I was just told to tell no one, and that does include you. Again, nothing personal."

"Fine, you're just doing your job. I appreciate that. But precautions were taken, considering his condition?"

"Most definitely, sir."

As they talked, both carefully *not* looking at me, I was filed with abject misery. Paul had suffered a lot lately. For some reason, the story he had told me about the red-haired nurse who had jilted him came to mind. He looked so proud and invincible; however, like the rest of us, he was vulnerable to pain. I deeply regretted that I had, in a moment of carelessness, added to that pain.

"I'll say goodnight, then. Devin, could I see you in the corridor for just a moment?"

Since my eyes were accustomed to the darker room, I blinked at contact with the more direct light. It hurt my eyes. Or so that is what I told myself when I found I could not look Paul Linden full in the face.

"I won't pretend I'm not hurt by what went on in there, Devin, because I am . . . deeply hurt. More so than I thought I could be. I was attracted to you from the beginning. I liked to think there was a special rapport between us. God help me, not that I needed the complication, but I was even beginning to fall in love with you. It's quite a blow to find 'sweet Devin' is so suspicious of me. Do you think I killed my wife also? Is that what you think?"

"Please, Paul, don't take it that way. I have no reason to suspect you. And I, too, wanted to think there was a special feeling between us, that I wasn't just one of many you flirt with so easily. But I had been so warned not to tell anyone that I guess that was on my mind and I wasn't thinking. I'm tired. I'm scared. I'm under a good deal of strain. Forgive me, please?"

There was no avoiding his face. I felt compelled to look straight into those eyes of ice blue . . . truly ice now, cold and hard, registering his hurt and his contempt for me.

"If I am so trusted now, sweet Devin, then I suppose you're going to tell me where Jack Fraser is hidden?"

I bit my lower lip. He was not, I felt, wanting to know where Jack was at this point. He was testing me, tormenting me, and possibly even trying to get even with me. I wanted to confide in him. I wanted to trust him completely. Never had I met a man so perfect. In so many ways, he was my ideal man. As a child, I had almost idolized him. Those feelings do not fade quickly. Still, I could not. I had been warned. Falteringly, I said, "Surely you know I cannot tell you that, Paul. It isn't a matter of not trusting you. It's a matter of obeying orders. If I told you, and you let it slip to someone you trusted, well . . . you can see where it might lead. And it would be my responsibility. I just cannot do that. Not even for you. I hope you can understand that, for I do value your friendship. The last thing I want, whether you can believe it or not, is to hurt you."

His eyebrows raised mockingly. "The last thing you want? Obviously not, my dear. Obviously not."

He turned and left me standing there alone. For a long while, I stared after him, even when he had completely disappeared, his white coat and proud stride just memories, around the corner.

Furious at myself, I blinked back tears and reentered "Jack's room," sure that I would get a tongue lashing, even if tactfully phrased, for the way I had handled things. It did not matter. It truly did not. Compared to the other hurts I had sustained, I doubted this one would smart very deeply.

Not for the first time, I wished I had never started all this. I had told Paul I was under a good deal of strain. What an understatement! At a time when I need to be at my best, my sharpest, when my whole being needed to be focused on my internship and what was to come after, I was being pulled in so many ways. This nighttime vigil shouldn't have been on the agenda, yet here I was with no one to blame but myself. Still, how could I have changed it? I had a feeling the answers were right around the corner. Armed with the truth, however unpleasant it might be, I could then face the future, give my all to being the very best intern I could be.

Chapter Twenty

Thirty-seven hours later, I was in my own apartment finishing up some laundry and other odds and ends I had been neglecting. The rest of that night had passed at the hospital without event, as did the next day. I had been right about adrenalin and determination seeing me through. My thirty-two hours on duty had brought no crisis situations and had even afforded me the opportunity for a couple of short naps—an opportunity I had gladly seized.

Jack's condition was improving by leaps and bounds. Tests had revealed a nondisplaced linear skull fracture and the CAT scan had demonstrated a minimal amount of damage. The electroencephalogram had been completely normal. In layman's terms, his head had been slightly cracked and slightly bruised, but not seriously injured. He still did not remember what had happened to him. Anthony and I had jokingly threatened to hit him on the head again to see if the second blow, as it so often did in the movies, would return his memory.

Dr. Robinson and Dr. Gentry both said Jack was ready for discharge. He should take it easy, they said, for a week or so and not over exert himself, but there was little else hospitalization could do for him. He was still under twenty-four hour guard at the hospital. Once discharged, no one was sure what would happen, least of all the authorities. Neither the city police department nor the county sheriff's department was a large, well-manned operation. They were not prepared for things like providing around-the-clock protection. Even I could see the dilemma. It was unrealistic to expect them to provide such coverage indefinitely, and I'm sure the constant companionship would wear on the nerves of a private person like Jack. However, the fact remained that the danger did still exist. Nothing had happened yet, but we all knew it could.

It was a weight on my mind, very heavily so because I felt responsible. If I had heeded all the advice and let sleeping dogs lie, well. . . . But I hadn't. And, deep inside myself, I knew I would not have done anything differently if I had the choice to make over again. Jane Goldstein had warned me at least twice about the hurting of the innocent. She was right. I ached for the innocent. Once, I had been among them.

With a sigh born of discontent, I looked around the apartment. It was tidier now than it had been since I first moved in. In me, frustration leads to a flurry of activity. My housekeeper's eye spotted the one thing out of place, a heart-shaped sachet bag I had found in the spare room during my cleaning spree. It was Mother's, of course. As far back as I could remember, she had used similar little sachets, soaking them in a floral essence and always carrying one in her handbag, another in a pocket if she had one. I picked it up from where I had tossed it and tried not to think of my feelings about Mother. I knew I had a choice, to be adult and forgiving or to hate her for the past, resent her for falling off her pedestal. I knew the right choice. I just wasn't sure I could manage it yet.

The telephone rang. It was Jack informing me that he was to be released at 11:00 A.M.

"I'm not sure," he said lightly, "why you wanted to know that, but I did promise I'd call."

"I'll be there well before eleven, so hang tight."

"But . . ."

"Forget it. Whatever it is, forget it. I'll be there. Uh, Jack, I don't suppose you've remembered anything yet?"

"No, dammit, not a thing."

"I was afraid you'd say that. See you later."

Afraid of that? True, but only part of the truth. When he had said his memory wasn't back, I had been aware of a lightness within me, a sense of reprieve. I had come back to Dalton in search of the truth. Most likely, the truth was just around the corner, and I found that I feared it.

I glanced at my watch. 9:30 A.M. Too early to go to the hospital, not really enough time to do anything else. Something clicked in my brain as I called up the image of Lucinda Platt and the way she had tried to help me. I had not yet gotten around to talking about Dalton "History" to any of the people she had suggested. Perhaps an hour would be long enough to locate one of them and have a small chat. I decided my first choice would be Mathilda Clairmont. I felt Lucien Stuart and Virginia McVeigh might feel the need to "protect" me from any ugly truths they knew ... Mr. Stuart because he was a southern gentleman and a virtual stranger to me, Miss McVeigh because she would still think of me as her student, and thus a child.

No need to look anything up. I knew exactly where the Clairmont home was. Grabbing my handbag, I ran for the door. In the hall, I jiggled the doorknob to make certain I had locked the door to the apartment. That was when I noticed I still had the silly pink and white sachet in my hand. With a shrug, I tossed it carelessly into the handbag, then ran to the Mustang.

Widowed now, Mrs. Clairmont resided on Trinity Street, the street just behind Magnolia where the Fraser house was. On these few streets were clustered a great deal of Dalton history, at least as far as the architecture went ... and, if those walls could have talked, history of another sort would undoubtedly be very interesting indeed. The Clairmont house was redbrick with antebellum style white pillars out front. It was not as large or as beautiful as the Fraser house, but impressive enough and immaculately maintained.

My knock was answered by a slightly built woman who viewed me through eyes narrowed with suspicion.

"Is Mrs. Clairmont in? I'd like to talk to her, please. I

won't take but a few minutes of her time. My name is Devin Hollister."

"Miz Clairmont don't get much company. She ain't real spry. That's why I'm here, to help her out. I think you best go on. She don't cotton to salespeople much."

The door started to close, slowly but definite. I resisted the impulse to put a foot in the door as real "salespeople" have been reputed to do.

"Please," I pleaded. "She knows me. I'm not *selling* anything. I'm a doctor . . . that is, an intern. I'm working over at Albert B. Creighton. Tell her it's Dr. Jim Clark's daughter here to see her . . . and that I have to be at the hospital before eleven, so I truly won't stay long."

The sniff was highly audible, but the crack did not narrow. After a long pause, she conceded enough to say, "I'll ask. Dr. Jim Clark's daughter?"

"That's right. When I was little, people called me Katie."

She returned very shortly to say, as I had felt almost certain she would, that Mrs. Clairmont would be glad to see me.

Convinced I was "okay," the housekeeper/companion even offered tea and cookies. Unashamedly, I accepted. In my flurry of busyness, I had forgotten to eat anything for breakfast and my stomach was feeling hollow indeed.

Mathilda Clairmont was seated in a wing-back chair near the wide front window of the parlor. I noted that the wine velvet chair faced the lace-curtained window. Some things did not change. Despite her advanced years and obvious frailty, I suspected Mrs. Clairmont still had a taste for knowing the affairs of others.

Her silvery white hair was piled high on her head and she peered at me intently through wire-framed spectacles.

"Little Katie Clark? Jim Clark's little girl?"

With a smile, I agreed to that. "Do you remember me at all?"

"Remember you? Of course, I do. Such a busy and skittish child. Never time to have a proper chat, always on the go, the way I recall."

Not with everyone, I recalled. I just had always been in a hurry to get away from *her* because she liked to pump me, and none to subtly, about my parents . . . even knowing what they paid for the last automobile or where they were going on vacation was of interest to her in those days.

"What brings you to see me, girl? Not that I'm not delighted, just surprised. The young have a way of forgetting the old, it would seem."

Opting for flattery, I began, between bites of crisp sugar cookies, to explain my purpose, "Someone told me that you knew more about Dalton history than just about anyone." She made a small sound in her throat and stirred slightly in her chair. I think that meant she was pleased at having her "knowledge" recognized.

"I don't know how much you've heard. Your companion says that you don't receive visitors much. But what I need to know—and it's very important . . ."

She listened intently while I talked. I made my story very brief, aware that the clock was ticking away and that she very possibly might ramble in her answers.

"Is it history you're wanting, girl, or is it dirt?"

Beneath her piercing gaze, I, as always, flushed. However, my voice was firm and steady as I replied, "Call it what you will. People are being hurt, even killed. It has to be stopped. If the 'dirt' of the past can provide a clue to help us out, then I'm not too good to ask to hear it. Can you understand that?"

She nodded. "Quite well. We southerners, especially of our gender, tend to want to pretend the dirt does not exist. It does. My beloved late husband used to kid me about my 'gossip.' I pretended I didn't mind, though sometimes his teasing took on a tone that hurt me. Do you know the definition of 'gossip,' Katie Clark?"

"The dictionary definition? I doubt that I ever looked it up. Why?"

"I did once. It says, 'mischievous or idle talk, usually about the affairs of others.' Doesn't make it sound nice, does it? I've always wondered when gossip quits being 'gossip' and starts being history."

"Maybe when it's established as the truth or, if the truth is still in doubt, then when the rumor has persevered long enough to be regarded as legend."

She cackled at that. "A sharp one, you are. Best I can recall, you always were smart as a whip."

"Sometimes I have real reason to doubt that. Anyway, Mrs. Clairmont, can you help me?"

Very carefully, she placed her cup on the saucer, then put the china pieces down on the table. Her eyes took on a dreamy look. For a moment, I feared that she was going senile on me. "Yes, girl, I think I can. If you're sure you can bear to hear what I have to say."

"I asked for it. But, tell me, is what you're going to tell me history, or is it merely legend?"

"That will be for you to decide. I'll tell you what I remember. What you make of it is strictly up to you."

Senile, my eye. If I was smart as a whip, I was in good company.

As she had as good as promised, she did not spare my feelings. She told me what the rumors had been fifteen or so years ago. She told me things she had observed that put her tales beyond the realm of rumors. It is sad that so often "mischievous and idle talk" are based in truth. I felt sick at heart at what she told me. I would have given anything to tell myself she was wrong, but I could not lie to myself to that extent. When she wound down at last, I rose from my chair. She looked very disappointed at that.

"You have to leave so soon?"

The antique parlor clock chimed, telling us it was half-past ten.

"I really do have to get to the hospital," I said apologetically, determined not to let my pain show." But I'll be back in touch. I do appreciate your help."

She was flattered. She believed me. I had asked, I had received, and I suppose I was, in a way, grateful. With another part of me, I hated her, despised all she stood for. Some things don't change, and one that hadn't was that I was still Katie Clark, still skittish when it came to gossip.

In the car alone, it was not so easy to pretend. Knowing she was probably watching me from behind that spotless lace, I resisted the impulse to press my head against the steering wheel and bawl like a baby. That might come, but it would have to be later.

I drove to the hospital and, emotions still in check, went straight to Jack's room. In jeans and shirt, glasses in place, he looked more back to normal. Pale and bruises, yes, but no longer so obviously damaged. We stared at each other.

"Troubled?" he queried.

I fell into the way of the game. "Deeply."

"Help?"

"No."

"Sorry."

"Thanks."

"What is this?" Anthony asked from the doorway. "What's with the monosyllables? You two mad at each other?"

Laughing, I held up my hand as a greeting. "No, of course not. Just a remnant of our childhoods."

"I've just come from the administrator's office, Devin. We, you and I, that is, are excused from all duties for the next three days. They think ABC just might just hold together that long without the pair of us, but not much longer."

"Anthony, you're a miracle worker!"

"I know. And for my next act, I walk on water. That is, as soon as I can find some. Know anyone with an indoor pool?"

"Come off it . . . how did you manage?"

He shrugged. "The powers-that-be know we're heavily involved in this. Believe it or not, they understand. All we need now is a plan."

I felt all sorts of twinges at Anthony's news: relief, guilt, irritation, worry, and enough other emotions to make me feel like a basket case. It was, of course, good to have the time off to see this thing through, but was it really *right*? My first duty was to ABC, right?

Anthony looked into my scowling face and read me correctly—something he was getting too good at doing. "You'll pay it back, Devin. Don't think you won't. Look at it this way, this is for the hospital, too, right?"

What could I say? In a cockeyed sort of way, he was right. Besides, right or wrong, we were too far in to back out now.

"As I was saying," he continued, "we need a plan."

We stood there, the four of us: Jack, Anthony, Mike Faulkner (who was back on duty again), and me. "What now?" was the silent question we asked of each other.

"I'll check out," Jack suggested, "then we'll go to my house. The three of you can settle me on the couch with a frilly afghan over my knees to ward off the drafts and we'll talk."

It wasn't much of a plan, more of a delaying tactic, but no one had a better suggestion, so we all trooped along like ill-matched soldiers, willing and ready to do battle even if more than a bit unsure of the strategy. We were further handicapped by not knowing our enemy.

At the Fraser place, we were welcomed by the inn employees. Suddenly, Jack turned talkative. He seemed to have so much to say, thanking them for carrying on so well while he was gone, instructions as to what they should do until he was able to return to work fully, and asking questions about how this had gone, what had happened there, and what to do about that.

"Enough, guy," Anthony said at last. "You're under orders to lie down, remember? Give it a week or so and you'll be back in the saddle."

Inside, we settled Jack on the couch. Anthony's stomach rumbled loudly and a survey led to the conclusion no one had really lunched. While Mike called the station for instructions, Anthony and I raided Jack's small private kitchen for edibles.

"I don't have much," he called. "Don't embarrass me by discovering my deficiencies. Just let me call the inn and have them bring something over."

"No need," I called. "We're too hungry to wait while something fancy is prepared and catered."

In ten minutes or so, we were seated around the living room with microwaved hot dogs and soft drinks.

"I've never eaten in the living room here before," I

said. "Your aunts fed us well, Jack, but it was always in the kitchen or picnic-style outside."

Laughing, he said, "When I first moved back in, I felt all this guilt at eating here and there, breaking the rules imposed by Aunt Em and Aunt Dorrie. I've almost gotten over that now . . . *almost*. The remodeling helped. Only a few rooms are 'mine.' The rest belong to the inn. I tell myself they'd be glad I've done what I've done, that they'd say it was a kind of sharing."

"The way I remember them, I'd say that's exactly the way they'd feel. This house is quite a hunk of Dalton history." My gaze swept the room, then returned to where Jack was. "Speaking of history, before I went to the hospital this morning, I went to see Mrs. Clairmont. Remember her, Jack, Mathilda Clairmont?"

"Remember her? How could I forget? When I was very small, I thought she was a witch. I remember hiding behind Aunt Dorrie whenever we ran into her . . . always Aunt Dorrie because she had more to hide behind, poor thing! She hated being heavy, and especially so since she and Aunt Em were always together and were such a contrast. I don't think Aunt Em ever weighed over a hundred pounds. Anyway, why did you go see Mrs. Clairmont?"

"She was never a witch, but if you vary the spelling just a little, you'd have the right term. In her own way, she is the biggest 'historian' this town has. She always made it her business to know other people's business. Someone had told me she was still alive and that she might know something that would be helpful to me."

"I see. And did she?"

A sob caught in my throat.

"Devin," he said quickly. Anthony, too, was on the alert, looking at me, his dark eyes filled with concern.

Angry at myself for once more giving way to emotion, I reached for my handbag and began searching for a tissue . . . just in case I'd need to dab at my eyes or blow my nose. I would, if I could at all, control the errant tears, but I wanted to be prepared if they had their way. The sachet heart that I had tossed carelessly into the handbag fell out on the floor during my search.

"Pretty doodad," Mike commented, picking it up for me. As it was fanned around, the room was filled with the fragrance of roses.

"Let me see that," Jack said, his voice strange. Mike tossed the sachet bag to him and he turned it over and over in his hands.

"Devin, where did this come from? Is it yours?"

When I explained how it had come to be in my purse, he nodded and, with a weary sigh, tossed the piece of frivilousness over onto the table.

"What is it? Please, tell us."

"Devin . . ."

My voice was firm. "It doesn't matter. Whatever it is will have to come out. You know that as well as I do."

"Nothing, really. Probably just a coincidence. But the scent . . . it's just like the one I told you about. The only damned thing I remember about my injury, that smell. I couldn't have said what it was until I smelled it again, then it came back. Roses. That was what I smelled, a whole arbor of roses. But I'm sure your mother isn't the only woman in the world to have that or a similar perfume. And, after all, she was gone."

Still bordering on tears, I said, "I'm not so sure about that," and I found myself telling them about calling home and finding she wasn't there. "She told me she was going back to Boston. She told Charlie she was going to New York City before returning home. Maybe she changed her mind after she left me. I don't know. But my mother isn't . . . wasn't . . ."

Seeing how difficult it was for me, Anthony said, "Take it easy, Devin. Tell it in your own way. Give yourself time. We all see it's hard for you."

"Hard? You might say that. I thought the truth would set me free. Perhaps it will. But it certainly isn't making me happier."

"You know what happened to your father?"

"No. But I think we're getting closer. Jack, did you see the man we found with my mother that day so long ago, see him well enough to know who it was?"

He nodded. "But you would never talk about it. You ran off before you could see. I didn't. But you didn't want me to tell you. You wanted to pretend it never happened. Early that fall, you cut me out of your life. I always supposed that my knowing the truth played a part in it. You wanted to pretend the incident hadn't happened and it was easier to pretend if you were around people who didn't know. I take it you know now?"

With a grimace, I agreed that I did. "Not for certain of course. After all, Mrs. Clairmont wasn't *there*, and I didn't tell her about that day. But I did ask her to tell me about my parents 'affairs.' Funny how I thought I knew my mother and suddenly I'm finding out she was a different person than I believed all along. I don't know if *he* was the last. He wasn't, according to Mathilda, the first. Local talk had it that, by the time I was in kindergarten, my mother had faced the fact she'd never have other children. It was a disappointment to both my parents, more to her perhaps because he had his work. And he spent a lot of time at his work. She was jealous, demanding, and thoroughly unhappy. So she took lovers. That's why people in Dalton believed my father killed himself, over her affairs."

"You still don't believe that?" Anthony asked.

"No. Because I know how he was then. He was at peace and he was planning for the future."

"Do you think *she* killed him?" Mike asked.

"I've been over and over it. I don't see how. Even if she had sneaked back ahead of me . . . but she didn't. It would have been physically impossible for her to be back there more than five minutes ahead of me. Not enough time to kill him, cover it up, and get away again. And I remember her at the time . . . she was in shock. Whatever happened was not something she had expected. As long ago as it was, I'd still swear to that. I'm finding out so much, most of it unsavory, and yet I don't know what I set out to determine."

"What about your father?" Mike asked. "Did this old busybody know if he'd had an affair with Jane Goldstein?"

Before I could answer, Anthony let out a whoop of laughter, reminding me that he and Jack had missed out on that tidbit. Poor Jane. How they both laughed!

When they had calmed down, I resumed my tale. "Mrs. Clairmont said word had it that my parents were divorcing, that he'd finally had enough of her. He was keeping both me and the house and she was not to fight over that or he'd make public her indiscretions."

"But did he have indiscretions of his own?"

"If he did, he was discreet about it. I did not tell Mrs. Clairmont about Ms. Goldstein's 'confession,' but I did say I'd heard he had a lover also. She seemed offended, as if she most certainly would have been the first to know of such a thing. Maybe he was walking the straight and narrow for my sake, so she wouldn't have any ammunition to fight him with. I don't know. Mike, do we have permission from your superiors to take part in this investigation?"

He laughed nervously. "Depends on what you mean by 'take part.' Frankly, I don't think they know what to do at this point. But I'm sure they can't officially give their blessing to private citizens taking risks. What did you have in mind?"

"Just a second," I said.

I made another raid on the kitchen and supplied us with more soft drinks and a bag of Oreos. Sitting down, I faced the three of them.

"I do not *know* who killed my father. There is nothing I can prove. But I have a strong suspicion, strong enough that I think we need to take precautions. And perhaps we should plan a trap."

As I talked, they listened.

How I wish they had told me I was insane. But they did not. And by their acceptance, I had to accept the possible truth of my hypothesis. It was not an easy thing to face.

Chapter Twenty-One

"Memory is a funny thing," Jack said into the receiver. "I've told no one else of what I just remembered. I think for, oh, say, $50,000 . . . yes, I believe $50,000 would do it nicely . . . it could be arranged that my memory loss is permanent."

There was a pause as he listened to the reply. He then countered with, "Oh, it really isn't a lot of money. Not to someone with your resources. But it would make a real difference to me. My business is new. A little extra revenue can make a difference in whether it succeeds or fails. I want to build a reputation for being the best. That's hard to do on a shoestring budget. It's really up to you. I don't think you'll dare try to kill me again. So we can just forget the first incident and let bygones be bygones . . . that is, *if* you come through with the $50,000. Otherwise, I'll tell everyone I can think of about the return of my memory: the police, the sheriff, the medical staff and board of directors of ABC, the local newspaper . . . actually, a hot story like this will undoubtedly spark off more than local interest, and, of course, I'll tell Devin. Funny how she couldn't seem to guess. But when Devin trusts someone, she leads strictly with the heart. Not very smart, really. What do you say?"

Mike sat on his chair and shook his head. "I really can't be a party to this," he kept muttering. "I'd be better off to go and act like I know nothing about this."

Probably he was right, he would be better off. But I noted that he stayed with us. Jack continued with the phone conversation. From what we would hear him say, it was pretty easy to guess what sort of comments the other person was making.

With insulting slowness, Jack gave instructions for delivery of the $50,000. He turned back to face us and said softly, "You guessed right, Devin. He bit."

All eyes were on me, all trying to gauge my reaction. I felt sick all over. The anger and hurt would come later. Right now, I was shaky and weak, not really able to put a label on what I was feeling.

Anthony was the first to speak. "Devin, I'm so sorry..."

"So am I, group. So am I. But this is one time I let logic prevail over emotion."

"How did you know?" Jack asked. "Just because he and your mother... well, a lot more people have affairs than commit murder. At least, I think they do. The one doesn't necessarily lead to the other, does it?"

"No. No, of course not. And he wasn't the first, the only, or maybe even the last. I still don't know *why* either. But his name kept cropping up and there weren't any other good possibilities. Then there was that white coat."

"White coat?"

"Jack, if Mike hadn't been in that hospital room instead of you, we wouldn't be talking to you right now. He made me feel like such a heel! But that's his way. He said he came from home just to check you and was going right back home to try to sleep. So why bother with putting on a white coat? I panicked when he reached into his pocket. It threw me when he was holding only an ophthalmoscope. Later, it occurred to me that was just the first thing he withdrew from his pocket, not necessarily the last. I'll bet there was a syringe in that pocket filled with a lethal dose of something. With the coat on, anyone seeing him drawing up a syringe of anything would not suspect him, just think he was seeing patients. Those big patch pockets hold a lot."

The three men all looked at me without saying a word, and I felt myself go red all over.

"Not scientific enough for you, gentlemen? I'll be the first to admit that. I had no proof. Just like I didn't *know* Jack was in the ditch. It was just a place I knew about that seemed possible to me. I'm not in the least psychic. That is, if I am, it's news to me. What is important is that Paul Linden bit. I wish he hadn't, but he did. So, Jack, what's the plan? Midnight out by the water tower?"

"You know better than that, idiot. You heard my part of the conversation. In front of the hospital seemed appropriate . . . and relatively safe. The place is well-lit. At 9:00 P.M., it won't be exactly deserted. No one seeing us there will be suspicious since he works there and since I was recently a patient."

"The catch is that you aren't supposed to be up and about."

"It will only take a few minutes. I can't see that it would be overly strenuous."

"We can't have it," Mike said. He wore a stern and forbidding face and was trying to get his voice to match. "It's too dangerous, even leaving your medical condition out of it. Look, Fraser, that guy isn't going to hand you $50,000 in cash. If there's a way to waste you, he's going to try."

"That's the idea, get him out in the open. If he tries anything, there'll be witnesses."

"Will that comfort you much at your funeral?" was Mike's dry return.

"Maybe there'd be a better plan," Anthony said, "but we pretty much have to go through with this. We set it up and we all know Linden is reacting. He'll be around close. You can bet on that. Jack, I'll go in your place."

Pale Jack eyed swarthy Anthony with understandable skepticism. "Guy, I appreciate the offer. You've been great through all this. We're both male and about the same age . . . and that's where all similarities end. No one would ever mistake us for each other, not even at a distance. And the front of ABC is always well-lighted. No, this is something I have to do myself."

"Absolutely not," Mike put in. "Look, let me call the chief."

And so it went for several minutes, a lot of talk that got us nowhere.

Mike Faulkner did call the station, but he bowed to our wishes and did not tell of our plans. It had been, he told us, decided to discontinue the twenty-four protection of Jack. He would be kept under close surveillance, however.

"I'm leaving," he said unhappily. "And if anyone asks, I know nothing about this. I'm against it. If anything happens, it'll be on my conscience the rest of my life that I didn't report this hare-brained scheme. Take my advice and forget meeting Linden there at the hospital at nine. Sooner or later, contact or not, he'll surface. You've put him on guard, Fraser."

"Sure, Mike. Thanks for your help."

"And?"

Jack shrugged. "I'll think about it. You're probably right. On the other hand, a guy has to do what a guy has to do. From this point on, we have to play it by ear, okay?"

The next few hours were emotionally wearing. I had never seen the hands on a clock move so slowly. It was as if time knew and was trying to hold itself back. The three of us did not talk to each other a lot. No conversation seemed to catch on. We made a few attempts at card games, but no one was in the mood. Nerves frayed, Anthony and Jack even got into a mild skirmish over what type of music to put on the stereo. As a result, we had no music at all.

"I can't believe you're letting him do this," Anthony said to me when, at 8:00 P.M., Jack got up off the couch to ready himself for his departure.

"He's a grown man, Anthony Toretta. What do you expect me to do? Paul tried to kill him. He has a stake in this. I doubt he's going to listen to me, or to anyone, at this point."

"Why are you talking about me like I'm not in the room or something?" Jack asked plaintively.

More talk, more snapping. All it did was delay us, give the hands on the clock a little more time to move. To my surprise, and dismay, Jack came up with handguns for all.

"Are they legal?" I asked, standing well away from the things, much as I would have from snakes coiled to strike.

"All registered to me. Actually, I have quite a gun collection. Remind me to show you sometime. It all got started when the aunts gave me a rifle that had belonged to a relative a few greats back, a rifle that had supposedly been used in the Civil War. I kept building the collection and now have quite a little arsenal."

I stared at the weapons in continued distaste. "But these don't look historic. They look like Saturday night specials."

"Close, Devin. Very astute of you. But they *are* registered. As owner of a business where the receipts are sometimes heavy with cash, the authorities understand why protection is necessary . . . regrettable that it is, but necessary all the same. I doubt I like to carry a gun much more than you do. But we're facing a person who has proven himself to be without scruples. How do you suggest we defend ourselves if he gets one or all of us in a bind?"

With a deep sigh, I picked up the offered gun and transferred it quickly to my handbag. Anthony pocketed one also. Right after that, we left together. In case the house was watched, we turned the corner away from ABC, went several blocks out of the way, and then circled back around. While we were doing that, Jack, concussion or no concussion, was going ahead with his plan of driving alone to the hospital. Anthony and I were to stand behind the hedge for protection. It sounded corny and staged, but my stomach felt as if it had rocks in it because, no matter how it sounded, it was real.

Jack sat on a bench in front of the hospital, directly under a light pole. Anthony and I were only a few feet away, but we hoped out of sight to anyone who came near Jack.

Nine o'clock came and went. As did 9:05, 9:10, and 9:15. At that point, the sky opened up and the rain began to fall. My mind had been so occupied that I hadn't even realized rain had been a threat. Even as the rain gathered both speed and volume, Jack continued to sit. We hissed at him through the hedge. Since we were getting soaked to the skin, I was sure Jack was too, not exactly good for a person on a chilly night, especially one in precarious physical condition anyway. "Just a little more time," he hissed back. At 9:30, his posture telling of reluctance even then, Jack arose from the bench. Even through the hedge, he appeared pale and distraught.

"Let's go in and dry off," Anthony suggested. "Get something hot to drink."

In the cafeteria, we opted for hot tea. Grandmothers always claimed it was therapeutic and we didn't feel we had anything to lose. Jack was clearly both despondent and scared, obviously feeling as if we were groping in the darkness. While we talked, the intercom paged Anthony, not by name but by page number.

"I'm off-duty."

"Apparently someone doesn't know that. Or happened to see you and decided to bother you. Go call and check it out."

Seconds later, he was back at the booth. "It's Rick Sinclair. He wants me in ER. He promises it'll just be a couple of minutes, no big deal. Just wants my opinion more than anything else. Can you beat that?"

Smiling, knowing how proud he must feel to be consulted by one of the "real" doctors, I said, "Go on. I'll stick with Jack. We'll wait right here for you. Don't hurry. We don't know what we're doing anyway."

Jack and I looked into each other's eyes across the steaming mugs.

"Ever think," he said slowly, "what you're going to do if . . . *when*, that is . . . this thing is resolved?"

"That's a question that can't be answered in one word, you know."

"It couldn't even be asked in one word, and I'm sure you noticed that. You're trying to avoid the issue. I didn't ask it in one word for another reason. It isn't a game."

A shudder went through my body so violently I felt myself convulse. As I saw no reaction on Jack's face, I assumed the reaction was more mental than physical.

"I know some people think I've made things worse. Maybe I have. When I was only a little girl, I lost my father. There is no way I can ever get him back. I know that. So I can't have him back and in some ways I've lost my mother also. I suppose that's what you meant: how am I going to feel about her, what is our relationship going to be like from now on? I can't answer that yet. I don't *know* what I feel, let alone what I'll feel when it's over. You see, we still lack so many facts. We don't know the extent of her involvement, either then or now. We don't even know that Paul killed Dad. We're just assuming that because he tried to kill you. And technically, we don't know that either because you can't remember. We're, again, just assuming because of my suspicions and the way he reacted to your attempt at blackmail. It's all so . . . well, it's a nightmare turned to truth. That's exactly what it is. It's hard to believe the treachery. My mother . . . that hurts the worst. But when I lived here before, I saw Paul Linden as a near-god. When I encountered him again, I have to admit I was more than ready to fall in love with him, perhaps even willing myself to do so. And look what *he* is. But sorry I started it? I don't think so. I'm sorry it's the way it is, but I'd do it over again. I've been like Alice in Wonderland, revering a past that didn't exist. I have to grow up, to face what is, not what I wish it to be."

"And I think that includes me."

"Pardon?"

He smiled slightly, the same grave smile I remembered on the child of so long ago.

"I don't know if you're also willing yourself to fall in love with me, Devin. Only you know that. But I know that it's what Anthony Toretta believes . . . and it's ripping his heart out."

"Did he tell you that?"

"Of course not. He didn't have to. I have eyes and ears and a certain amount of mental acumen. Maybe, when you have a chance, you should ask yourself how you really feel, rather than what you want to feel or how you think you should feel."

Rather dryly, I answered, "I'll do just that. Just as soon as I get around to it. Right now, we have a murderer to catch. I wonder what's happened to Anthony. He said it would just be a few minutes."

"That's all it has been. I suppose he'll be back right away."

Time ticked by and Anthony did not resurface. Our mugs were emptied, filled again, then well on their way to being emptied again.

"Something's wrong," I said, my voice almost a whisper.

"I think you're right. Call the ER, see if he's still there."

Going to the wall phone, I called the ER and talked to an EMT I knew slightly. Anthony was not there, nor had he been. What's more, Rick Sinclair had just then come on duty and had *not* paged Anthony. As far as they knew, no one there had. The EMT did not even remember noticing the page. A quick conference with those in the background revealed that one person had heard the page, but didn't know who made it.

"Was Dr. Linden in there at all in the last thirty minutes or so?"

"Linden? Gee, I don't think so ... let me ask the others."

Every fiber in my body tensed, I waited for the answer. When it came, I was not surprised, just scared. "Yeah," the EMT said, "a couple of people saw him, but no one seems to know why he was here. He didn't see any patients. That much I'm sure of."

Back at the table, I said, "Jack, Anthony is in trouble. We have to find him. Do we split up or stay together?"

"We split up," he said grimly. "If he has a gun, he can get us both if we're together. If we go in separate directions, one if not both of us can avoid him. Where do we start looking?"

"First, I'm calling the police."

"Sure, but don't count on a lot, as slow as they seem to react. He's only been gone thirty minutes."

"Still, in the face of everything else . . ."

"I agree. Make your call. Then we'll try to cover a few bases ourselves."

After calling both the police station and the sheriff's office and receiving soothing, if somewhat vague promises, Jack and I discussed a plan of action.

We divided up the areas of the hospital in which we were to check and see if anyone had seen Anthony in the last few minutes . . . Anthony and/or Paul Linden. Since we felt I would be more listened to, it was agreed I would check with the security personnel and try to enlist them in the search. We agreed to meet back in the coffee shop in an hour to assure ourselves that we were okay and to report what we had found out. If anything transpired before then, we were to get in touch with each over the intercom.

My first stop was at the wall phone, which I used to call Jane Goldstein. When I explained my fear that something had gone amiss with Anthony, she agreed to make any hospital personnel I needed available with her blessing. I did not use Paul's name to her, merely referring to "the same person who nearly killed Jack Fraser, probably the same person who killed Dru Linden." She did not ask the identity of the murderer, probably assuming we did not know. Briefly, I wondered about the unlikely story she had told me of her affair wth my father. Could it possibly, despite all of our denials, be true? And, if not, why on earth had she made up such a tale? But there was really no time for such ruminations now. My head was in a whirl as it was, and I willfully pushed those thoughts to a back shelf in my mind.

As I saw Jack go out the door of the coffee shop, I gave him a timid wave. I tried not to think I might never see him again. Setting out to check my assigned areas, I reached into the pocket of my light jacket and felt the hard metal of the handgun. I had never thought I would take comfort in having a lethal weapon on me, but I did. There was even, God help me, comfort in thinking of using that gun to put a bullet through Dr. Paul Linden's head, especially if I were to find out for certain that he had, indeed, killed my father.

Since I had been locked in there before, I thought of the medical records storage room and had Security check there first. Nothing, nor was there any sign of life of disturbance in the even more far-reaching storage area that had been mentioned to me that day.

"There's always the morgue," a guard suggested. "It's a dead place this time of night . . . if you'll pardon the pun."

"I'll pardon it. Since it wasn't much of a pun."

But it was a good idea. Grateful for his presence, I advanced to that area. He unlocked the door and we stepped into a room where the temperature was at least forty degrees less than it had been in the corridor. Since there was no way it could be made a pleasant place, no one had tried. The walls were a stained and peeling lime green. The tiles over the concrete floor were ancient and cracking. The air was heavy with the smell of chemicals, their odors well-preserved in the refrigeration.

Only one body was in the room. Probably par for the course. ABC being a small hospital in a relatively small town, there weren't many Jane or John Does and not many autopsies. Most patients who were brought in DOA, or who died on the premises, were taken directly to the funeral home of their family's choice. Occasionally, there were cases when the hospital did not know the wishes of the patient or family and the body was stored until that information could be ascertained.

"Nothing here either," the guard said. "Jeez, this place gives me the creeps!"

"Me, too, Stanley. Let's get out of here. And thanks for everything. But keep looking, will you?"

"Sure thing. Ms. Goldstein left word to do whatever you asked and she's the main boss, after all. Sure hope you find your friend."

"Yeah, so do I."

So eager was he to be out of the morgue that he broke into a run as soon as he was outside the door. I was half-amused, half-sympathetic. Logically, I knew the dead could not harm us. Illogically, I knew why he felt like he had to escape.

I was at the door when something caused me to turn back and stare at the one occupied cart. One arm dangled down off the cart. Surely that was unusual? Surely whoever brought them in had enough respect to tuck all the limbs nicely onto the cart. But I suppose it does not really matter. Whoever the poor soul was could receive no physical comfort now. I said a small prayer for him, whoever he was. And when I opened my eyes, I saw those fingers twitch.

I let out a scream . . . and the fingers twitched again. Hysteria mounting within me, I moved toward the cart. All of my instincts said to run, but rationality won and I kept moving, albeit slowly, forward.

Reaching down, I touched that arm about the wrist and felt the slow beat of a pulse. I jumped back and looked at the arm as if it could tell me something more. It did. That arm, now that I was staring directly at it, was distinctly familiar. I threw back the drape and looked into Anthony's face, his mouth covered by tape. He stared at me mutely, dark eyes filled with appeal.

Tears of anger stung my eyes as I peeled the tape away and removed the wad of gauze from inside his mouth. He began talking immediately, a string of words that were almost unintelligible because they were heavily peppered with Italian phrases. At his direction, I quickly undid the strap that had held him fast against the cart's hard bottom.

He jumped from the table, then asked, "Where's Jack Fraser?"

"Looking for you. Anthony, what on earth . . ."

"Later. Let's get out of this place. I am, more literally than I want to think, about frozen to death."

We moved swiftly into the corridor. I hunted up the nearest phone and used it to page Jack to call the extension number listed on its face. My eyes then turned back to Anthony. He hadn't been kidding. His skin had a decidedly bluish hue to it.

"Paul?" I asked, already knowing the answer.

He nodded grimly. "He was outside the ER door waiting for me. He pulled a gun on me and ushered me here through back stairways and hallways I'd never even seen before. He strapped me to the damned cart, then took a syringe out of his pocket. He started plunging it into my arm, but I was able to fight back enough with my arms to keep it from going in all the way. It fell to the floor and most of it spilled out. It really seemed to upset him. I guess because it was the only one he had with him. I don't know what it was he was going to give me, but I don't think any significant amount got in me, if any. I kept trying to land blows on his head. He took the gun back out and hit me on the skull with it. That was the last I knew. I guess he taped my mouth after that. He definitely wasn't concerned by the possibility of killing me. I think he was just afraid the noise would bring people. He knew no one would look for me there and that I'd be dead from cold by morning anyway. Or so he thought."

As he talked, I moved toward him. I reached up and moved my fingers through his hair.

"What on earth are you doing, not that I'm really complaining?"

"Seeing if there's a bump where he hit you."

"And?"

"There is. A sizable one. At least it didn't cause you to lose your memory the way Jack did." I stared at him a moment, then added, "Anthony, we're back to square one. I found you, but Jack is out there on his own. So we're back to looking for him, you and I. He hasn't answered the page. Something tells me he can't."

Only when he bent slightly to kiss my cheek did I realize I hadn't moved away from him once I had found the bump on his head.

"We'll find him, Devin. We did it before, we'll do it again. By the way, have I thanked you for saving my life? Puny thing though it is, I'm most grateful. Through the years, I've grown rather attached to myself."

I stifled a giggle, since laughter didn't seem particularly appropriate.

The giggle gave up and died on its own when I heard a familiar voice say, "I still have the gun. Don't either of you move. The first one to move, the other one gets it. Now, walk forward. No sudden moves, please. I'm in a bit of a hurry. I have to take care of you two, then go find your friend Jack Fraser. I've no time for foolish acts of heroism."

He was convincing enough that we both moved forward without hesitation. The smell of his musk cologne floated up to me. Once I had gloried in the scent of him. Now that same scent was nauseating me.

Chapter Twenty-Two

Paul shoved open the door of the morgue again and forced us back inside. The smell of musk joined the other smells.

"Too bad I didn't succeed the first time, Toretta," he said. "I won't make that mistake a second time. I was following Devin when she and the guard came in here. When she didn't follow him out, I suspected she had stayed behind, nosing around, and found you. So now I have to do what I started, then hunt up Fraser."

"You'll never get away with it, Linden," Anthony said. "It's gone too far."

"Maybe. But the three of you will never keep your mouths shut if I let you go. With all of you dead, I might stand a chance. What do I have to lose at this point? I do regret this. I wish you hadn't gotten involved, Toretta. It wasn't your fight. Still, the choice was yours. You've left me with no alternatives."

He sounded almost pleased as he talked, and I recalled how much he had seemed to like praise. If he felt he had been clever, pulled off a coup, then his ego would like being massaged. At any rate, we could try to stall him.

"Paul, tell me, did you kill my father? And Dru, what about her? Did you kill your own wife?"

"So many questions, sweet Devin." Still holding the gun on us, he moved slightly closer to us, close enough that I had a clear view of his face. Once again, I was struck by the sheer perfection of that face. He was an Adonis. A maturing one, perhaps, but Adonis all the same. With his free hand, he reached out and stroked my cheek. "Such a waste. I do wish you hadn't made this necessary. I was trying to find a way to spare you. Now, like Toretta, you've made that impossible. Why couldn't you have left things well enough alone and stayed far, far away from Dalton?"

"Please, can't you answer my questions? If you're going to kill us anyway, it can't hurt if we know, can it? It would mean so much to me. You can't imagine how it's hurt all these years to believe my father left me by choice . . . I had to prove it wrong. And now I have done that, haven't I? Please, don't deny me that. Tell me the truth, then I can die at peace. Not that I want to die. Still, I'd rather die knowing than still in such confusion."

It worked. A cunning, pleased expression took over his face and he began to talk. I was buying time, stalling for precious minutes. Maybe someone would think to look here again if I did not reappear. It was a slim hope, but a hope all the same.

"Jim thought he was so important. He had them all snowed. Young as I was, I was as good as he was, but no one seemed to notice that. It was always 'Dr. Clark this and Dr. Clark that,' and I would only do if he wasn't available. I wanted to be where he was in life. But that was a decade down the road for me. The bitterness grew, the resentment grew. He was oh-so-nice to me, but I felt he was patronizing me. 'Nice' would have stopped if I had stepped into his territory. Professionally, I deferred to him. On a personal basis, I seduced his wife. It wasn't hard. She, too, was fed up with always being in his shadow. She hated what he was doing to you, Katie. Turning you against her, making you so serious about being a doctor when you were still so little. She liked what her sister said about the east. She wanted to go there. He wouldn't hear of it. The arguments grew. She was a flirt. A woman accustomed to being admired, being wanted. But she hadn't dealt with me before. I know how to play a woman. Not that I didn't want her. . . . God, she was a beautiful thing! But I saw to it that she wanted me back. That day when you kids found us, she tried to call it quits. She never let me back in the house again. But I would threaten to tell Jim if she didn't keep seeing me. So she would. I hadn't meant it to happen, but I grew to where I needed her. I had others, but only with her did I feel like I had made love."

"Then she didn't have many lovers?"

"Elaine? God, no! Almost the chaste maiden . . . but only almost. Sometimes she cried in my arms after we had made love because she knew what she was doing wasn't right. A few times while making love she called me Jimmy. I didn't mind. In fact, truth is, I loved it. I had taken his place to that extent anyway.

"But it got complicated. I was still meeting Laney every chance I got when George started inviting me over to the house. It would seem his daughter wanted me. She was pretty, rich, well-connected. But I didn't want her. Not as a wife. She was used to having her way, you see. Not able to deprive herself, she slept with anyone who took her fancy. I'm like that myself, so I can understand it. Which isn't the same thing as wanting it in a wife. But McCracken wanted it. And if he knew what Drusilla really was, he wouldn't admit it to himself or others. 'You two behave and save it for the wedding night,' he'd say when we went out . . . said it jokingly, but meant it, I think. Needless to say, we did not obey. First time we were out, she had borrowed a key to a friend's apartment. We went there. She was wild. In a way, it was great. But I didn't want to marry someone like that. And I was in love with Elaine. Maybe more than that, I just wanted to take her away from Jim."

"She wouldn't leave my father?"

"She said she couldn't bear to hurt him. I suspect she really didn't want to leave him, liked being Mrs. James Clark. I suspect also that she still loved him and was just using me to get back at him for neglecting her, for doing things she didn't like.

"I called her one night and demanded that she meet

me. She begged to get out of it but, again, I said I'd tell Jim.

"When I took her to bed, she cried the whole time. She was dressed, ready to go home, when Dru came in unannounced. Dru didn't really see anything, but she guessed. She called your mother names and threatened to tell Jim. When Elaine tried to leave, Dru physically blocked her. I pulled her out of the way and let Elaine go.

"Dru was furious with me. She said now I *had* to give up Elaine and marry her or, not only would she tell Jim Clark, she'd tell her parents that I had seduced her with promises and used her while carrying on with a married woman behind her back.

"It grew into a bigger and bigger mess. I begged for time. She wouldn't give it to me. She did tell her parents. But before that, Elaine had called me. She told me it was finally all over. She had told your father herself, said she was sorry, that she had started it because she was angry and hurt, and had kept it up out of fear. Not only did he forgive her, he agreed to move to Boston, set up practice there, give the whole family a fresh start. She said they were even going to see about adopting other children. Women don't do that to me, they don't walk out on me. *I* do the walking. But, of course, it was his fault. He couldn't stand losing to me. He always had to triumph over me. You know what she said to me?"

I watched and listened, nausea rising, as he mimicked her voice, "'Paul, it isn't that I don't love you at all. I could never have been tempted by you if I didn't care for you. But *Jim* is my life, can't you understand that? It has nothing to do with his position or his money. It's been that way since we were children. We were always somehow tied.'

"It was then that I decided he had taken enough away from me. I drove to his house, hoping to catch him alone. I was in luck. I saw your mother's car pulling out as I rounded the corner. I had a needle and syringe filled with potassium chloride in my pocket.

"He didn't want to talk to me. He hated me. I could see it in his eyes, the golden boy who was in good with everyone hated me. Instead of telling him what I really thought of him, I played the weakling. To let him gain confidence, I cried and sniveled and told him how sorry I was to have betrayed his trust, but that I loved Elaine so much I just couldn't help myself.

"He softened. He was just that sort and I had known he would. When he leaned forward to put his hand on my arm, I grabbed hold and threw him down. I'm no black belt, but I have studied karate. It took him so by surprise that I was able to hold him down, inject the potassium. In seconds, he was gone. Then I hunted up his revolver, did what I had to do, then got the hell out of there.

"It worked. No one doubted that he committed suicide. I saw to it that there were rumors about Elaine. People heard. Even those who didn't want to believe did because, after all, he was so very dead. Why else, indeed, would he have killed himself?"

"But you married Dru anyway. Why did you do that, Paul?"

He glanced down at the gun he held in his hand, almost until then seeming to have forgotten its presence.

"I told you that it was a mess. I don't know if Elaine suspected what I'd done. She's a hider. She didn't *want* to know. But she said we could never again be together. She'd have too much guilt.

"In time, I think I might have won her over. But we didn't have time. Dru had been following me. I didn't know that. But she had followed me around for days without my knowledge, trying to catch me with Elaine again, I guess. She saw me go in and come out. She knew I'd done it. To buy her silence, and to appease George and Helene for the way I had 'used' her, I married her. We had the biggest and most elaborate wedding the town has ever seen up to the present time. But I continued to take up with other women. And she took up drinking. You see, she'd gotten her prize. But she knew I hadn't married her by choice. I think she was trying to forget that."

A tone came into his voice that sounded close to real regret.

"I know why you tried to scare me away. But how did

you know who I was? And why did you feel you had to kill Dru?"

"We were breaking up. Oddly enough, the divorce was more her idea than mine. I found I liked marriage. I could have my way with women and they'd understand I could never commit to them. To get the settlement she wanted, she was threatening to tell what I had done. I don't think she would have because of what it would have done to the boys. But I couldn't take that chance. She was, after all, a lush. No telling what she'd do when she had a tank full. That night she'd been to see you, Jack took her home. She called me, said she'd figured it out. Seems you look more like Elaine than you think you do. Her father had mentioned at home that 'that new female intern looks like someone I know.' It came to her who that someone was. Suddenly, she was on your side. She had an attack of conscience. She had to tell you, she said. She seemed determined. So I had to do what I had to do. I hoped to make it look like a robbery and mugging, but got frightened and dumped the body out without taking her purse.

"How did I know it was you? I like to think I would have known in any event. But I made it my business to know where Elaine went, when she married, and who she married. I'm not saying I was obsessed with her, but I came closer to it than I ever have with anyone else. I allowed her to hurt me. That hadn't happened before, or since."

"What about Stephanie, the red-haired nurse," I blurted out.

He smiled slightly. "There was no such person. I was wanting to cry on your shoulder. No better way to make a woman fall for you. And it worked, didn't it? At least for a while. I'm good at storytelling. Now, I do think I've answered all your questions."

"But I have just one more."

"One and only one. And?"

"Why did you want me to 'fall' for you? Why did you make a play for me? I don't understand."

"Don't you? Then look into a mirror sometime, sweet

Devin. How could I resist? Perhaps you spend too much time with your nose in the medical texts. You came into my life, looking so much like my Elaine. If I had managed to bed you, it would have been the ultimate revenge on James Clark. To have gotten both his wife and his daughter to make love to me . . . ah, yes, the ultimate revenge."

Suddenly I could stand it no longer, this playing cat and mouse games with the man who had taken my father's life, ruined my childhood.

"What did he ever do to you that was so bad?" I literally screamed.

Realizing I had lost my cool, Anthony reached out and put a restraining hand on my shoulder. "Take it easy," he said quietly.

"Yes, Devin, take it easy. And, you, Toretta, get your hand off her. Keep both hands where I can see them at all times. You got lucky the last time. You won't be so lucky this time."

The gun waved menacingly and I swallowed, realizing I had purchased about all the extra time I could and that it was not enough. The men on white horses had not arrived for us. Each minute that ticked by might be the last for us.

"You aren't going to answer that last question?"

"Actually, I already have. You just weren't paying attention. I have to be first, the best. Can't you understand that? He was the same way. There wasn't room for two such large egos under the same roof. I was determined to stay, to be known as the master surgeon of Albert B. Creighton. He did things for me, yes, opened professional doors, introduced me to the right people, referred his overflow my way. But he wanted to keep *teaching* me, patronizing me, and I was better than that. He couldn't see I was already a peer, not a student. He liked having the students and interns around, looking up to him. When he was around, they had no eyes for me. I could see that easily enough. Oh, yes, we were alike. Which is why he didn't want to move to Boston. *There* he might be one of many, not *the* master surgeon."

Wearily, I said, "When he agreed to move, why didn't you just let them go? You could have been *the* surgeon then. Why did you have to kill him?"

"I told you that, too. Because he had won, he was taking her away from me. He knew about Elaine and me. Dru knew, her parents knew. McCracken had been so irate he went to Goldstein and tried to get me kicked off staff. Before he left, Jim was going to join forces with McCracken and get the job done."

"Jane Goldstein knew?" I felt my voice was barely audible, yet he heard me.

Smiling, he nodded. "Of the affair? Of course she knew. But I had my ways of dealing with her. I had no difficulty at all in persuading her to be on my side."

It clicked then, the whole sordid mess straightening itself out in my mind. My father hadn't been Jane Goldstein's lover, but Paul had. Probably still was. Quite young enough to be her son, he plied her with promises, undoubtedly taking her to bed now and then, making her feel as no other man ever had.

The stress had gotten to Paul and it was obvious his psychotic side was taking over. He was no longer able to pretend to be affable and kind. That mask had dropped from his face and he looked what he was: evil and twisted.

He began to tell us then, in detail, things he had done to his lovers. I tried to shut my ears, but the words flooded past anyway. Then, that particular flow of thought shut off inside his brain and he started in on Jack. "I remember turning and looking at that creepy little kid. He recognized me. I could see that. His aunts used to drag him along to my office when they would come to see me. When he came back to town, I mentioned it to him, asked him if he remembered. That was how I knew you didn't know, that you hadn't seen me well enough to know and wouldn't let him talk about it. It backed up what Elaine had told me at the time, that you had shut the whole incident away and wouldn't talk about it. That worried her that you were 'repressing.' I figured repression was better than spreading it all over town. But now I know how she felt. I worry about my

281

kids, too. That's why you and lover boy there have to go, Devin. I regret it, but we can't have my children knowing all of this. Jack was ready to tell you, I know. I had to protect my kids."

"You killed their mother, you son-of-a-bitch," Anthony said.

"Don't call me that, young man," Paul said, the very authoritative surgeon used to commanding respect surfacing. Anger made him wheel in Anthony's direction. There was just enough time for me to reach into my pocket and pull out the handgun.

There was no time to be sporting and issue a warning. That might only allow him to pull the trigger of his own gun and shoot Anthony.

For the first time in my life, I knew what it felt like to pull the trigger of a real gun. I was shaking so I knew my aim could not be good. Instead of his shoulder, which I was aiming at, I hit his elbow. I heard the report of the gun, then a sound that may have been metal against bone.

Wheeling around to face me, disbelief in his clear blue eyes, Paul let his gun clatter to the floor. Anthony moved to pick it up. But instantly comprehending Paul had his foot on the gun, then bent to retrieve it with his other hand. "For that," he said, "you get to see your lover boy die first . . . with a bullet right in the head."

"I wouldn't be so sure of that," Anthony said, springing forth with all his weight against Paul's injured side.

It worked. The surprise took Paul completely off guard. He toppled and fell to the floor, the gun falling to his side. Taking no chances this time, Anthony kicked it clear out of the way and we watched it go sliding across the worn but spotless tile surface. That done, Anthony withdrew his own borrowed handgun from his pocket.

"Citizen's arrest," he said wryly. "Linden, want me to read you your rights?"

I almost laughed out loud. Even under this kind of stress, Anthony kept that wacky sense of humor.

At that point, the door burst open and Mike Faulkner entered, gun in hand. Jack was right behind him, also armed. Behind them was the same security guard who had first seen me into the hospital morgue.

"Fine time to show up," I said.

Mike took over, officially arresting Paul and reading him his rights.

"Reinforcement is on the way," he said to us, that done. "But let's move on out of here. God, it's so cold in here I can see my breath when I talk."

"Tell me about it," Anthony cracked. "How would you like to be strapped on a metal table and left to freeze to death in here?"

"Speaking for myself, I wouldn't be too partial to it," Mike said in that slow southern drawl that was still a delight to me even though I was growing more used to it.

Within a few minutes, Paul was taken away. First to be treated for the minor gunshot wound, and then on to jail.

"I find myself almost wishing I'd killed him," I told Jack and Anthony. "Not only for what he did to my parents and the harm he did to my life, but for what he's done to his own sons. I think it would be better if he had died than for them to know what he did and know he'll be in a prison for the rest of his life."

"You survived, Devin," Jack said softly. "So will they, I suspect. It can't have been easy for them thus far, living in a home where their parents didn't love each other, didn't take, at least in Paul's case, their marriage vows seriously, and then there was the way Dru was drinking. The McCrackens will take them now. They'll give them the stability they need. It'll be the best for them all. They're in pain, having lost their only child. The boys will keep them busy, give them a reason to go on."

"Then you think it'll be okay?"

"If it isn't, there's nothing you can do about it, right?"

"Right," I said, giving a shrug. "Now, let's get you and your concussion back to bed. The doctor in me shudders to think what this has done to you. You look all pale and woebegone."

"That's what I do best," he quipped.

Because we feared Jack had overexerted himself, I took

him home in his car. Anthony drove behind in mine.

"Go on home," he told us at the door. "I'm showering and going straight to bed. Honest. Truth is, I don't feel like anything else."

"I could spend the night," Anthony offered.

"No need," he said firmly. "I'll call if there's a problem. Thanks again, you two, for everything. There are no words." He turned and looked deeply into my eyes. "I'm glad you're back in my life, Katie-Devin. For a few months, I had a sister. That was a special time. After that, I always missed you. Now I have my sister back again. In some ways, we're so much alike on the inside it's almost scary. I guess it's that way with real brothers and sisters."

"I don't know. I guess so. I never had any. So I'll accept the offer. Sleep well, brother."

Anthony and I were largely silent on the way to his place. I think it was really beginning to hit us just how close to death we had all been. It was only luck, and the man upstairs, who had seen us through alive. For most certainly, our brilliant strategies had not saved us.

"You really should let me take you back to the hospital," I said, "and get that bump looked at and your head X-rayed."

"I'm okay. At the end, I wasn't even cold. In fact, I was sweating. Which shows you how nervous I was, sweating in below-freezing temperatures. What now, Devin?"

I pulled up in front of his apartment house and parked.

"While Jack and I waited for you in the coffee shop, he asked me close to the same thing. I didn't know then how this was going to turn out. Now that it's more or less over, I'm still not sure. Anthony, why do you think Jane Goldstein told me my father was in love with her?"

"I imagine she'll be clearing that up with you herself. My guess is that she was trying to protect Paul. Part of what she told you may have been the truth—that is, that she never could believe your father killed himself. She knew of Paul's affair with your mother, so she probably suspected him all along. But she didn't want to know it, didn't want to act on it. I think what she was doing was

284

trying to throw you off the track. If you thought about that, then maybe you wouldn't think about Paul. She wouldn't be the first woman to protect a man who didn't deserve it."

"I suppose not. And I suspect you're right. You asked me what next. I don't know. I guess I'll stick my internship out here. I may even stay. But there's still time to decide that."

"You'd have to go away for a surgical residency."

A surgical residency? Something inside me suddenly clicked into place. I now knew as much of the truth about my father's death as I would ever know. Although I had faced things that were not pretty, at least I wasn't living a lie, living behind a veil. Now it was time to put away the past, to get on with what the future held for me. As a child, I had wanted to be a surgeon to emulate my father. After his death, I had felt duty bound in that direction. But my head was clearer now, my heart freer. Never had a girl had a better father than James Clark. So what if he hadn't been perfect? That last day he had lived he had told me he would always love me and support me no matter what I did with my life. The choice was mine. I could be a surgeon, but I didn't have to be.

"Devin, you still there?" Anthony asked with a laugh.

I hadn't known the answer until it was on my lips, but once it was I knew it was the right answer.

"I don't think I'm going to be a surgeon. I think I want to do what Rick Sinclair does in ER. He needs help and I'm good at it. And as wrong as Paul Linden was about so many things, I think he was right about my ability to deal with people. I can soothe them down from a panic. Look at the way I kept *him* talking? And it isn't as if I'd *never* get to do surgery. I'm sure there are plenty of emergency repair jobs. What about you, still think you'd like a small town?"

"It's sounding better all the time."

I smiled at him. "One of the first things I have to do is talk to my mother. Not on the phone. In person. We cracked this case sooner than expected and still have a day or two. Maybe I'll make a flying run there and back.

Deliver her sachet bag."

"You were afraid she was in on trying to kill Jack, weren't you?"

"You read me too well. When he said that the smell was the same, I was crying on the inside. But when we were shut up in the morgue with Paul, the smell of his cologne was so strong. He overdid it, just as Mother always did. When he didn't ever say Mother had been with him, I figured what Jack had was the memory of strong cologne used too heavily rather than the memory of a particular brand. He's probably not that good at telling them apart. Most men aren't. Roses, musk, all the same to them."

"Do you hate her?"

"No. I did at first. Now I can understand how she fell prey to him. And there weren't others in her life. That was a falsehood deliberately started by Paul, and eagerly spread by people like Mathilda Clairmont. I almost fell prey to him myself. So gorgeous, so charming, so impressive in every way."

"But he turned out to be the bad guy."

"Yes. Yes, he did, didn't he?"

"However, Jack is still a good guy."

"Very good. One of the best."

"What was that little speech about, back at his house? I didn't know you two thought of each other as brother and sister."

Smiling, I said, "I think I knew, I just wasn't smart enough to define it. I believe Mr. Jackson Lee Fraser was telling me not to be a fool."

"Huh? How's that?"

"I know a man who is handsome and smart and who shares my love of the medical profession, a man who has a great sense of humor and who has the courage to follow his convictions, a man who has the kind of loyalty that doesn't come along very often . . . and a man whose kisses weaken my knees, so much so that it frightened me and made me want to run in the other direction."

He looked at me, as he always did, with his heart in those dark brown eyes. "And now that you know such a man, what are you going to do about it? Run?"

I shook my head. "I'm through running. I'm ready to face life head-on. But I do have to deal with my mother first. Understand?"

"Oh, yes."

There was a long silence.

I looked at this young man who had stuck by me, helping all he could, even when he thought I loved someone else.

"You ever been to Boston?"

"Nope."

"Like to go? You could sightsee or something while I straighten things out with my folks. They'll be glad to have you. I think Mother worries awfully that I'll be a spinster."

He roared out loud. "No one uses that word anymore."

"They do in some circles. In Boston anyway. Interested in these plans?"

"Enough that I'm ready to go in and start packing."

"Great. On the way home from Boston, we can talk about other things."

"Can't happen soon enough for me. But there's just one problem . . ."

"Yes?"

"I'll have to borrow the airfare until my next paycheck. I may even have to make installments, depending on how much this is going to cost me."

"Don't worry about it. Things work out, we'll be into community property one of these days anyway. That is, if you still want someone who is such a mess."

"I want," he said with conviction. "Didn't I tell you your eyes were like fine sherry?"

"You or some other guy. I get it all mixed-up. Before I go, kiss me. I'll see if I remembered that correctly."

He did as he was asked and I found I hadn't forgotten a thing.

The pain was still there, but in a peculiar way I was quite happy. I loved a good man and he loved me back. I think somewhere, on some plane, Dad knows that and is glad for me. He hadn't left me by choice. All along I had known that, just as I now knew Anthony Toretta would never leave me by choice either.

As Jack and I had each proven in different ways, what the mind remembers can be erased, but what the heart knows cannot be as easily put aside.

I'm going to be a doctor, just as I have planned for as long as I can remember. My shingle won't say Dr. Clark, but that's okay. It's the *doctor* part that counts, isn't it?